D0170454

Ultimate Kill

Kristine Mason

ISBN: 1499108613
ISBN-13: 978-1499108613

For Jamie Denton —

Seven books ago…I wrote, you read and then ripped it to shreds. I rewrote, you read, then shredded it some more. You put me through hell during that first book, to the point I was plotting my revenge (insert maniacal laugh). Thank God you believed in me, and that I didn't go through with my revenge plot. You've made me a better writer and a better person. You taught me to take risks with my writing and career, and to believe in myself. Thank you for years of patience and encouragement, and for being one of my dearest friends.

ACKNOWLEDGMENTS

Special thanks to my husband, Mark, and our four kids, for pushing, supporting and staying out of my way so that I could finish this book. Thank you, Nikki Erickson, for taking care of Baby Girl so that I could keep the words flowing. As always, a big thanks to my brainstorming partner, Christy Carlson...we had a lot of fun with this one! Thank you, Tessa Shapcott for your editing skills. I'd also like to thank my fabulous cover designer, Kari Ayasha of Cover to Cover Designs.

PROLOGUE

How many narcissists does it take to change a light bulb?
One.
He holds the bulb while the world revolves around him.

"DID YOU FIND her?" He glared at the man he'd overpaid to find the one thing that belonged to him. Rage simmered in the depths of what most men might consider a soul. Not him. Essence, the nonphysical aspect of a person, that which survived after death and all of the other metaphysical, intangible drivel of poets and priests...that kind of shit was for pussies. He had one life to live and he'd live it to the fullest.

With her.

Carl Blackborne, the former CIA agent and the investigator he'd forced into his employment, shifted his gaze to the desk. "I'm sorry, sir, but...no. That's not to say that I didn't discover any new leads," he quickly added.

He followed Blackborne's gaze and looked at the handcrafted replica of the first ship ever built by his great-

great-grandfather. Made of gold, and worth over three hundred grand, the piece had been in the family for five generations. "It's lovely, no?" he asked the investigator and touched the ship's golden mast.

Blackborne blinked. "Yes. Truly one of a kind, sir."

"If you break down what's in your savings and life insurance, it's worth more than you are."

"I...I don't know how to respond to that."

He ran a manicured finger along the golden stern and wondered if the ship would become damaged if he slammed it against Blackborne's over-sized head. "Of course you don't."

"Sir, if I may, I've exhausted—"

"Do you know how old my great-great-grandfather was when he built his first ship?" he asked and touched the life-like sailor standing at the helm of the golden ship. From what he'd been told, his forefather had been a ruthless son of a bitch. He didn't emulate the man, nor did he worship him. He didn't have to. Not when he was better than him. More powerful. More coldblooded. More merciless.

"No, sir, I—"

"He was twenty. *Twenty*," he repeated, sliding his gaze to Blackborne. "By the time he was twenty-five, he was worth over one million dollars. That was in the mid-1800s. By today's standards, he would have been worth over twenty-five million. Amazing, no?" He waved a hand, and leaned into his chamois-soft leather office chair. "Over the past one hundred and fifty years, his company has endured many ups and downs. Right now, under *my* rule, it's up. I've had the foresight to take this company to new places. Literally. My planes, ships and trucks are worldwide. I've made this company a household name. Now *that's* amazing shit."

Blackborne rubbed the back of his neck. "Truly amazing, sir. But if you'll let me explain my new leads."

He folded his hands and rested them on the luxurious, handcrafted desk. Made of six different kinds of exotic woods, like ebony and Carpathian elm, it too was worth more than Blackborne. "By all means. It's not like I don't have anything better to do with my time. Right, Ric?"

Ricco Mancini, his aide-de-camp and most loyal confidant, sat stone faced, his focus on the investigator. "All the time in the world. I see no reason why Blackborne shouldn't waste yours."

Clearing his throat, Blackborne nodded. "Understood. Sorry, sir. I'll make this quick. When I was investigating her past, I came across family lineage that might be of interest. I thought that maybe—"

"How is this a new lead?" Blackborne wasn't the first investigator he'd hired, and based on the others, he could rattle off the woman's family tree by heart. Hell, he'd stripped that tree of its leaves and snapped the branches until she no longer *had* a family.

"Well, it's not exactly a lead, just a new avenue."

"My trucks travel down avenues all the time," he said, finished with Blackborne and their conversation. He'd had high hopes for the investigator. During his previous employment with the CIA, Blackborne had been known to successfully track terrorists and international criminals. Diabolically brilliant men who had the means to hide and, if they'd wanted, never be found. And yet Blackborne couldn't find a simple woman? Fucking useless idiot.

"I'm not interested in hearing about avenues—at all," he said. "I paid you a lot of money to bring me—"

"I told you I wasn't sure if I could find her," Blackborne countered, his voice rising.

His rage went from simmering to boiling.

No one interrupted him.

No one dared to shout at him.

He slid his gaze to the two men flanking the office's double doors. Santiago Ramirez, the Columbian he'd taken under his wing over fifteen years ago glared at Blackborne's back. So did Santiago's counterpart, former Russian heavyweight boxer, Vlad Aristov. He looked to Ric, whose mouth tilted in the subtlest of smiles. Knowing that the chance of this conversation ending well was slim to none, the sadist *would* enjoy Blackborne's faux pas.

"She's obviously changed her name," Blackborne continued without apology. "Covered up paper trails. She has no immediate family, her friends and associates have no idea where she moved to...I've bribed several IRS officials and even they couldn't help me. That's why I thought if I could—"

"Pull up her family tree?" he asked with an easy smile that in no way matched the raw fury constricting his chest. "It's a brilliant plan. I wish my other investigators had the foresight to come up with such a unique idea."

"Thank you, sir." Blackborne relaxed and grinned, obviously not understanding sarcasm. "I appreciate the compliment."

He looked to Ric and caught the laughter in his eyes. "What would you need for this brilliant plan of yours?" he asked, transferring his attention to the investigator.

"More money and, of course, more time."

His last four investigators had given him the same request. They'd eventually come to him empty handed and wound up dead.

"I suggest we expand the scope and not just focus on her family," Blackborne said, his tone enthusiastic. "The friends and associates I checked with...these were people who knew her, or rather knew *of* her, when she was in her early twenties. As you know, she went off the grid around the time she turned twenty. I think if I go back further, say into her childhood, and find people she was close to, then maybe—"

He raised a hand. "No."

Blackborne's face contorted with confusion. "Sir, we might be able to find a link from her childhood that could lead us to her current whereabouts."

"Might...could." He rested an elbow against the leather armrest and cradled his chin between his index finger and thumb. "If a broke redneck plays the Lotto enough times, he *might* eventually win. If you give a seasoned whore the money to go to college and educate herself, she *could* go on to run a Fortune 500 company. Mr. Blackborne, what are the chances of a broke redneck winning the Lotto and a seasoned whore going on to run a Fortune 500 company?"

Blackborne looked to the desk again. "Let me rephrase then, digging into her past may…I mean, it's probable…" He scratched his head. "Sir, I can't guarantee anything, I can only *try* this route."

He straightened and opened the desk drawer. "Not interested." His fingers stroked the AAC Evolution-45 silencer, a weapon ironically used by U.S. Military Anti-Terrorist units. He grasped the handle of the gun. "I know everything about her past. Her preschool teachers, her fourth grade Girl Scout troop leader, who she lost her virginity to during her senior year of high school." His stomach tightened with anticipation as he pulled the lightweight gun from the drawer and aimed it at Blackborne's head. "I know *everything* about her, except where she is now."

Blackborne staggered back, holding his hands in front of his body. "Please, sir. This investigation—"

"Is over." He tensed for the slight recoil and pulled the trigger. As if the man had sneezed, a puffy mist of blood burst from Blackborne's face before he crumpled to the ground. He slipped the weapon back into the drawer, then pulled out a file from the hidden center console. "Well, that was a disappointment." He glanced to Ric who, in turn, looked to Santiago and Vlad.

"Get him out of here, then kill his wife and kids," Ric told the men.

Without a word, Santiago and Vlad picked up Blackborne and took him from the office. When the door closed behind them, Ric rose from his chair. "And the woman?" he asked. "Should I find another investigator?"

"No." He opened the file and stared at the eight by ten glossy of her. Although not beautiful in the classical sense, she'd caught his attention the moment he'd seen her. While she'd been bustling through the club where she used to work, taking drink orders, he'd pictured her naked, curvy body on his bed, her long, straight brown hair fanning out along his silk sheets as she spread her legs and welcomed him. He had eventually made what he'd imagined into a reality. And after having her once, he'd wanted her again.

Only she hadn't.

That was her first mistake.

When she ran from him…that was her second.

After he'd found her, he'd tried to be reasonable. He'd tried to give her everything she would ever need, and she'd rejected him.

That was her last mistake.

He always got what he wanted. *Always*. Growing up with enough money to run a small country, the world and its contents were his for the taking.

She was his to take.

Ric pressed his hands against the desk and leaned forward. "You've spent eight years looking for her. Are you giving up?"

He looked up from the photograph and met Ric's eyes. *Eight years*. A lot had happened during that time, and over the years he'd assumed he would eventually grow tired of searching for her. But he hadn't. She was the one object his money couldn't buy. The only woman who had walked away from him without a second glance. He never understood why. Quite frankly, he didn't care whether she wanted him or not. She was a lost possession he wanted found. "Have you ever known me to quit anything?"

"Never." Ric smiled. "Now what?"

He closed the file, then returned it to the drawer. "Now we do things my way." He rose from the chair and walked to the windows. As he looked around the spacious backyard, he found his wife and two children sitting on the lawn having a picnic lunch. "Hiring another investigator isn't going to cut it. We've been down that road one too many times," he said, and watched grape jelly drop onto his four-year-old son's pristine white shirt as the boy waved to him.

"And your plan is…?"

"Simple." He gave his boy a two-finger salute. "If I can't find her, I'll make it so she has no choice but to come to me.

When I'm finished, she'll beg me to take her back."

"Interesting," Ric said, his voice laced with amusement. "And *why* would she come to you?"

He smiled, as his wife frowned and worked on their son's jelly stain. "Because if she doesn't, I'm going to kill a lot of people."

PART I

The past is never where you think you left it.

— Katherine Anne Porter

CHAPTER 1

Four months later...

JAKE TYLER COUNTED the sixth dead armadillo he'd seen lying on the side of the road since exiting onto Georgia's US 17. They were ugly creatures, and when he'd spotted the first two he'd thought they were turtles. The owner of the one pump gas station he'd stopped at thirty minutes ago had informed him otherwise, in a friendly yet condescending way. Armadillos, turtles...he could give a shit.

A big-ass bug splattered against his dusty windshield. As for palmetto bugs? He sprayed the windshield with fluid and turned on the wipers. Yeah, he could do without large flying cockroaches. As the wipers smeared the disgusting bug across the window until it finally fell off, his cell phone rang.

"Do you need me to schedule you a flight?" Rachel Malcolm, CORE's computer forensic analyst, asked when he answered.

"No. I'm good."

"Are you still in Florida?"

He swerved around a copperhead snake sunning itself on the road. He could do without venomous snakes, as well. "Not exactly."

"Then where are you?"

"It's Friday. I already emailed Ian and told him I delivered the package. Now I'm taking the weekend for myself. Is that a problem, or does he have another *errand* for me to run?"

"Bitter, much?"

Hell, yeah, he was bitter. Because of Ian Scott, his new boss and founder of CORE (Criminal Observance Resolution and Evidence), he'd lost his job as sheriff and had to uproot from Bola, Michigan, to move to the investigative agency's Chicago headquarters. Ian was a manipulative son of a bitch who oozed bullshit from his pores. After Ian had screwed with his career and coincidentally had an opening at CORE, the former FBI profiler had lured him with promises of a high salary, excellent benefits, travel and intriguing cases to investigate. While he'd been tired of living in a small town where he had to deal with Bigfoot sightings, hunters and ridiculous townie disputes, what he was doing for CORE had proven to be even less exciting. As a former Marine and sheriff, he'd take a Bigfoot sighting over being Ian's errand boy any day.

"I'm fine," he lied.

"Then why don't you just tell me where you are? I promise not to tell Ian."

At this point, he didn't owe Ian anything. If the man didn't like how he planned to spend his weekend, he could kiss his ass. "I don't care whether he knows or not. Last I heard, he didn't have a new assignment for me."

"Not true. He told me he wanted you to work on a cold case for him."

Boring. He'd spent the past six months training with CORE agent, Dante Russo. He'd tagged along with the man during his assignments and, in the end, Dante had assured both him and Ian that Jake was ready to handle his own investigations. Instead, Ian had sent him on errands. First to Tulsa, where he'd had to personally return a stolen brooch, worth seventy-five thousand dollars, to an old woman who had been fleeced by a con artist. And most recently, to Merritt Island, Florida, where he'd hand delivered supposedly super-secret documents to a wealthy businessman.

While a cold case wasn't exactly an errand, he had no desire to sift through old documents and files. With the Marines, he'd seen action. As sheriff, except for the Hell Week case Jake had worked on with Rachel and her husband, Owen, he'd mostly sat around with his thumb up his rear. Even then he'd been restless and had the itch to move on and do something that would actually stimulate his brain. A cold case might give him *some* stimulation and he understood there was always paperwork involved with any case. Still, if he wanted to spend his days sitting behind a desk, he would have become an accountant.

"If the case has been cold, it can wait a few more days."

"Wow, are you in a mood. Okay, Oscar the Grouch. If you don't want to tell me where you are, I'll just check your phone records and find out myself. Thanks for making more work for me."

He cracked a smile. He loved Rachel, and loved working with her, but she could be relentless when she decided she needed to know something. He supposed it wouldn't matter if she knew or not. Actually, it was because of her he was driving through rural Georgia. "Fine. I'm on Georgia's US 17 counting dead armadillos."

"Gross. I've never seen an armadillo."

He could hear her tapping away at her computer keyboard. "Not even in a zoo?"

"I don't do zoos. They make me sad." More tapping. "And if you're on US 17, then that means… Oh. My. God. You're going after her."

Naomi. He rubbed the tension at the base of his neck. He hadn't seen or spoken to his former fiancée in nearly five years. She'd never been far from his thoughts, and a part of him still loved her and what they'd had together, but bitterness had kept him from bothering to try and find her until now.

After he began working at CORE, started hanging out with Rachel and Owen, something inside of him kept nagging and urging him to look for Naomi. To put the past to rest and move forward. Since she'd left him, he'd dated, but nothing regular. He hadn't wanted to become involved in a relationship that could end as badly as the one he'd had with Naomi. But

Rachel and Owen, the way they looked at each other, their body language toward each other and their occasional PDA, had him thinking about the past, about Naomi and how good it used to be between them.

Now he wanted answers. Naomi had told him she needed to leave Bola because she couldn't handle small town life, even though she was the one who'd talked him into moving there. When she'd brought up leaving, he'd been a year into his first term as sheriff and hadn't been able to walk off the job. Instead, he'd suggested a long distance relationship. She said she'd think about it. When he'd returned home that night, she was gone. Her clothes, her books, whatever she could pack in her car. Gone.

Anger and betrayal caused the tension in his neck to intensify. "I'm not sure what I'm going to do," he said. "I might drive into town and keep on going."

"Well, according to the map I'm looking at, unless you make a few turns you'll drive right into a river." She released a sigh. "Jake, I'm not going to tell you your business, but have you thought this through?"

He'd done nothing but think about Naomi since Rachel discovered where she'd been living the past four and a half years. Was she dating? Married? Did she have any kids? Jealousy stabbed him in the chest. Even though her betrayal still cut him deep, he wanted her happy. Only he wanted her happy with him. Or, he used to.

"I'll play it by ear," he answered, and added another dead armadillo to his count.

"Brilliant plan," she said with heavy sarcasm. "Look, I'm going to be blunt."

Great. Here we go. "Shocking. I can't wait."

"I'm being serious, Jake. There's a reason why she ran, and you know damn well that's what she did."

"I don't know *anything*." He gripped the steering wheel tight. "Hell, I don't even know her real name." When Rachel had used Naomi's social security number to track her whereabouts, the computer hacker had discovered that Naomi

McCall hadn't existed until eight years ago.

"Shit. I'm sorry. I know this has to be hard. You obviously loved her and she…well, she had another agenda."

One that hadn't included him. If Naomi was on the run, if she was part of the Witness Protection Program—which sounded like a ridiculous theme from a Hollywood movie—he could understand her secrecy. But they'd been together for three years before she'd disappeared. They'd planned to marry, start a family, a future. For her to not trust him enough to tell him the truth…that frickin' sucked. And hurt.

He slowed the rented Lincoln Navigator and eyed the remains of the Georgia Girl Drive-In to his left. Weeds and small saplings filled what used to be a parking lot. Like so many of the old, abandoned buildings and cars he'd seen during the drive, nature was doing its best to reclaim the land. Then he saw a road sign.

Five miles to Woodbine.

Five miles to Naomi.

His stomach knotted with both anticipation and dread. Maybe Rachel was right. Maybe he should leave Naomi alone. If she was running from the past, who was he to stop her?

Her fiancé, damn it. Her lover. Her best friend. The man who had promised to love her and cherish her. Maybe not in front of a minister or judge, but he'd made that pledge to her. And he'd meant every word.

"This is simply a recon mission," he said. "Like I told you, I might keep on driving through." Another lie. He'd come this far and he never did anything by half.

"Like Owen, you couldn't lie your way out of a paper bag."

"What the hell does that even mean?"

"You're full of it. You're going to go there and meet with her and possibly mess with her life. On top of that, if this goes as bad as I think it will, you're going to come back to Chicago surlier than when you left."

"Surly, huh?"

He heard more tapping from the keyboard. "Yes, gruff, brusque, curt, boorish—"

17

Chuckling, he shook his head. "Are you reading from a thesaurus?"

"Yes, I am. And while this entry wasn't in there, I'd like to add crab-ass to the list."

"I haven't been that bad." Or had he?

"That's what you think. You know, maybe you should meet with Naomi. Get her out of your system once and for all, then come back to Chicago. I already started a profile for you on one of those online dating sites. You need to get laid. And with the picture of you I have up there, I have no doubt you'll find someone new in no time."

His cheeks burned. While used to Rachel's bluntness, her 'you need to get laid' comment was too straightforward, even for her. "First, worry about your own sex life. Second, don't you dare put me on some dating site."

"I said I have it ready to go. I would never do that to you." She let out another sigh. "I care about you, Jake. I just want to see you happy."

The Lincoln approached a sign.

Welcome to Woodbine. Established in 1893. Home of Georgia's Official Crawfish Festival.

The anticipation and dread strengthened as the overgrown terrain he'd been driving past morphed into mowed lawns and well-kept houses. Minutes from now, he'd pull up to the school where Naomi worked at as a nurse. If Rachel wanted to see him happy, this could be her chance. Unless…

Needing fresh air, he rolled down the window.

Unless Naomi blew off his ass.

"Thanks, Rachel. I'll call you when I'm heading out of here. It's a fifteen hour drive from Woodbine to Chicago. I might want to catch that plane, after all. Either way, I'll be home by Monday to work on Ian's cold case."

"I'll let him know. And, Jake…I know this sounds pessimistic, but prepare yourself for the worst."

Right. If he didn't expect too much, he might not be let down. "Got it," he said, then after saying good-bye, he ended the call. The well-kept houses disappeared into marshland as he took the bridge into Woodbine. When the marsh disappeared and the houses returned, he slowed the Lincoln and turned into the parking lot of the Rainbow Lodge, an old single story motel. While he wasn't sure if he'd stay in Woodbine, he planned to secure a room just in case.

Screw it. He pulled back out of the parking lot and followed the Lincoln's GPS to the local elementary school. Rachel was right. He should prepare for the worst. The nearest major airport was in Jacksonville, Florida, and only a forty minute drive. He'd check on Naomi, try and catch her as she was leaving work and invite her to dinner. If she flat out wanted nothing to do with him, he'd head right back the way he came.

Unacceptable.

He had a lot of questions that needed answering. Namely, who was the real Naomi McCall?

"All better, Joey?" Naomi asked the adorable and klutzy second grader who had been a frequent visitor to the nurses office since kindergarten.

The boy nodded and handed her the ice pack. "Better."

"Good. I hope this means you won't be running through the library anymore."

"And have to flip my star? Uh-uh. If I flip my star, I don't get to pick anything from the candy box."

She took his hand and led him out of her office. "Oh, my. That would be bad."

"Yeah, and if my mom found out I flipped my star, she might make me stay home instead of going to Disney World."

"You're going to Disney World for spring break? Wow, you're a lucky guy. But I can't imagine your mom leaving you behind."

"I dunno. My dad is always calling her a tease. So maybe she was just teasing me when she said if I'm not good at school I can't go on vacation."

"A tease," she echoed and hid a smile. "Yes, I bet that's exactly what she was doing. Teasing you." She gave his little shoulder a gentle squeeze. "Have fun and tell Mickey Mouse and Goofy I said hi."

Joey grew serious. "You know those are just people in costumes, right?"

"Yes, I'm fully aware. Thank you. Now scoot. The principal is going to be calling for buses soon."

As Joey dashed down the hall, Claire Brundle, one of the school's special ed teachers and her close friend, came around the corner. "Geez, Nurse Naomi, don't you know anything? Mickey Mouse and Goofy aren't real."

She laughed. "Thank God Joey clued me in, huh? That kid is a riot. You should have heard what he said his dad calls his mom."

"I don't even want to know. Olivia's preschool teacher told me that she'll believe half of what my daughter says happens at home, if I believe half of what happens at school."

"Good advice. So, are you ready for your vacation?"

"Yep. It's scary how ahead of the game I am. Everything is packed, and all my darling husband has to do is load the car and we're outta here. You know we still have room for one more."

Over the past few months, Claire had asked her a dozen times to join her and her family to spend spring break with them at the house they'd rented in Siesta Key, Florida. While she'd appreciated the offer, spending the week with Claire, her husband and daughter, her mother and father in-law, not to mention her brother and sister in-law and their three kids sounded not only like a recipe for disaster but a vacation from hell. Besides, she had her garden to tend to and some serious spring cleaning to do.

She wrapped an arm around Claire's shoulder. "Thank you. But I'll let you have all the fun."

"Please?" Claire batted her lashes. "I promise you won't have to pay for a thing."

"I am so on to you. You just want me there as a buffer from a houseful of in-laws."

"No. I need a drinking partner. If you're there, my mother-in-law won't give me the 'Claire, do you really think you need that glass of wine' crap."

She laughed. "Okay, so you want me there as an excuse to get drunk. For shame."

"That's me. The town drunk."

Their principal chose that very moment to round the corner. Claire's cheeks grew beet red when he raised his eyebrows. After he went into the office, Naomi nudged Claire with her shoulder. "Smooth."

"No kidding. On that note, I'm leaving." Claire started down the hall, then glanced over her shoulder. "If you change your mind, the minivan leaves at thirteen hundred this evening."

"You realize that's one o'clock, right?"

Claire gave her a wave. "Whatever. I'll send you a postcard."

Shaking her head and grinning, Naomi went into her office. As she shut off her computer and locked down her supplies, she thought about the next ten days. No bloody noses, no bumps on the head, no pink eye or chances of lice. While she loved working with kids, being a school nurse wasn't exactly dull but it also wasn't the most exciting job, either. Back in the day, she'd worked in busy ERs and had dealt with all sorts of crazy cases.

Those days were long gone.

Rather than dwell on the past she looked to the week ahead. To the gardening, the spring cleaning. Maybe she'd even paint her spare bedroom or catch up on some reading or the shows clogging her DVR.

Alone.

"Have a great week," Donna, one of the school's secretaries called from the main office.

"You too," she said and couldn't help envying Donna. She and her husband were leaving for an all-inclusive resort in the Dominican Republic for the next five days. They had no kids, but were trying. And Donna was hoping they'd come back from the resort with *extra* baggage.

She finished closing up her office, then locked the door. As she left the school, she waved to a group of kids waiting to climb into the idling bus and headed toward the main parking lot. While she walked, she dug into her purse for her keys. Once they were in her hand she looked at her Toyota 4Runner, which was probably about forty feet away, and clicked the button on her key chain to unlock the car doors.

A large, dark grey SUV drove down one of the parking lot aisles, then turned and slowly moved in her direction. Although she assumed the driver was a parent coming to pick up their kid, and she refused to allow old insecurities to fester, she still quickened her pace. While she hadn't heard a word from the murdering bastard in eight years, and the chances that he was still even looking for her were—damn it.

Don't think about him. He's not worth the time or energy.

She reached the Toyota, opened the driver's side door and tossed her purse onto the passenger seat. The dark grey vehicle slowed, then pulled into a parking spot two away from hers. With no other cars between the SUV and her Toyota she could see the dark silhouette of a man. And it looked as if he was staring. At her.

Those insecurities took root anyway. Always aware of her surroundings, always on alert, she quickly slipped into the driver's seat, closed then locked the door. Sliding the key into the ignition, she glanced out the window, then froze.

Her heart raced. Her mouth went dry. An uncontrollable shiver ran through her body.

The past five years suddenly disintegrated. As if she'd just woken from a disjointed nightmare, the months of running, of searching for the perfect place to hide in plain sight, the lonely days and even lonelier nights faded into a blur.

Jake.

Tears welled in her eyes. For the lost years, the lost love, for the future they could never have. She quickly blinked them away and opened the car door. Her legs weak, her stomach somersaulting with embarrassment, excitement and regret, she placed a shaky hand on the door for support. A small part of her wanted to climb back into the car, drive off and pretend Jake had never come to Woodbine. But a large part of her, the part that had never stopped loving him, that had never allowed the memories of what they'd had together die, wanted to run to him. Throw her arms around his neck and kiss him.

"Jake," she whispered, then cleared her throat. He looked so damned good. Tan, lean, muscular, his big toned arms showing from beneath his short sleeve golf shirt, his dark hair no longer in his trademark military crew cut.

Chin trembling, hand still clinging to the opened car door, she took a small, tentative step forward. "Jake," she said louder, firmer.

He pushed off the SUV and slowly approached, his gaze never wavering from hers. Lightheaded, she stayed put, kept her hand on the door for fear she might crumble to the asphalt. She'd dreamed of seeing him again, had imagined what she might say, the excuses she could give him. But anything she'd ever come up with had sounded terrible, selfish and ridiculous. Even if what she'd tell him was the truth.

Now that he was less than five feet away from her, she had no idea what to say or do. A million questions buzzed through her mind. Was he married? Did he have children? Fresh tears filled her eyes. God, she really was a selfish bitch. She wanted him happy, had always prayed he'd find someone to love, but deep down she'd hated the thought of him loving someone else. Making love to another woman. Creating a child. A future that hadn't included her.

"You look beautiful," he said, his voice rough, raw. He blinked, looked to the ground and took a couple of more steps until he stood within arm's reach. When he met her gaze, she expected anger and resentment, instead she found anguish, longing and heat in his dark eyes.

She pressed her lips together to stop her chin from trembling and swiped at an errant tear. She'd hurt him. Because she'd loved him so much, she had no choice but to leave. With too many deaths on her conscience, she'd refused to add Jake to that ugly list.

Her mom, dad and brother's dead bodies chased through her mind.

"School nurse?" he asked and tilted his head toward the building.

Unable to speak, afraid she'd burst into tears in the parking lot where buses, kids and faculty were only a short distance away, she nodded.

"That's probably a nice change for you. Better hours, less stress."

She gave him another nod, while her mind and heart continued to race. Why now? Why was he here? She broke eye contact and glanced at his left hand. No ring.

A surge of relief swept through her, but when she met his gaze again, it quickly dissipated. While the heat remained, his eyes no longer held a trace of hurt, but definitely anger.

"Are you happy here?"

I've never been truly happy since I left you. The words were there, but she couldn't say them. Still too stunned to speak, too afraid she'd turn into a puddle of mush in the school parking lot, and worried people might be watching them, she gave him another lame nod.

"I know this is a shock," he said, his voice holding resentment. "Coming here was a mistake. I'm sorry." He turned his broad shoulders and moved toward the SUV.

Don't go. Don't go. "Don't," she said and choked back a sob.

He stopped and turned his head slightly. Not enough to face her, but enough where she could see the hardening of his strong jaw.

"Don't what?" he asked, his tone bitter.

"Don't leave. Nothing with you was ever a mistake." *Except when I was forced to leave you.*

He looked over his shoulder. The doubt in his eyes had her letting go of the car door and moving a few steps. Although not prepared to cope with the past, to cope with everything she'd given up, she wasn't ready to let him go. Again.

"You came here for a reason," she said. "I'd like to…catch up and see how you've been. Just not in the school parking lot."

Nodding, he faced her. "I saw a diner on the way in. Can I buy you a cup of coffee?"

"No." She refused to deal with their reunion in a diner. There were too many issues left unsaid. "I—"

Andy Webber, the school's gym teacher, strolled by and waved. After he walked past them, Jake took a step back.

"You don't want me to leave, but you don't want to—"

"That's not it." She looked to see if anyone else was coming by and turned to him. "Follow me back to my house. It'll be more comfortable than the diner."

His handsome face relaxed, but his eyes probed and questioned. She suspected his being here wasn't a 'just passing through the area' visit but something more calculated. Jake had always been a balls-to-the-wall type of guy. Now that the initial shock of seeing him had abated slightly, she went into self-preservation mode. Next to the loss of her family, leaving Jake had been the lowest point in her life. Whatever his reasons for being here, she'd need to keep her shields up and her heart guarded.

Lately, years of running, of looking over her shoulder, the lonely days and nights and not having someone to share them with, had been catching up with her. Although it had been years since they'd been together, she could easily see herself falling into his strong arms. Picture them making love, imagine them going back to the way things used to be between them.

But they couldn't. She'd run from him for a reason. Until the bastard who'd murdered her family and forced her into this self-imposed exile was rotting in Hell, she'd keep running. Otherwise, Jake would end up like everyone else she'd loved.

Dead.

Harrison Fairclough's eyes burned and watered as he stared at the laptop screen. Thanks to the damned Russian's chain smoking, a hazy fog hung in the small, shitty motel room and made the place smell like a dirty ashtray.

He rubbed his eyes and drew in a breath. Damn, even his mouth tasted like an ashtray and he didn't smoke. "Vlad," he said to the Russian. "Do you mind?"

Vlad leveled his ice blue eyes on him, his dark blond brows forming a V as he took a long drag of his cigarette and blew smoke rings. "Do I mind what?" he asked, his thick accent reminding Harrison of Boris Badenov from the old *Rocky and Bullwinkle* cartoons.

The Russian could probably rearrange Harrison's face and cause his internal organs to bleed with one blow of his meaty fists. Growing up in the one of Norfolk's most undesirable areas, he'd spent his entire life surrounded by men like Vlad. Between his mom's numerous, abusive live-in boyfriends, the notorious cutthroat neighborhood street gangs, and his short stints in juvie and then later in prison, he knew Vlad's type. Brawn with no brain. While Harrison would prefer to keep his nose, jaw and internal organs intact, he refused to allow Vlad to intimidate and bully him. Besides, the way he saw it, Vlad and his counterpart, Santiago, needed him.

For now.

"Your smoking is hell on the laptop," Harrison said, reaching across the table to snatch up Vlad's vibrating cell phone.

"Harry, you hurt Vlad's feelings so," the Russian replied and took another drag. "Here I thought you tell me it bad for my lungs." He shook his blond head. "No concern for Vlad, only your machine."

"How insensitive of me," Harrison said and read the text from the Columbian, Santiago. *On way. Prepare to go live.* He set the phone on the table and shoved it toward the Russian. "They should be back soon."

Vlad snuffed his cigarette into the over flowing ashtray and grabbed his phone. After he viewed the message, he moved to the window. "Good." He pushed the nicotine-stained curtain slightly and pocketed his phone. "Vlad hate it here. I hate all the places we go. Well, except Las Vegas. Vlad want to go back." He let go of the curtain and turned. "Pretty women, booze, gambling," he said, smiling. "Vlad loves tits and ass."

Vlad loved to refer to himself in third person. "You guys are the ones with the plan, not me." A plan he no longer wanted to be part of if his suspicions were correct. And they usually were. Still, he couldn't help agreeing with Vlad. Leavenworth, Kansas, was definitely a far cry from the Vegas strip.

"True." The Russian nodded. "Vlad wonders…does Harry love tits and ass?"

Harrison ignored Vlad and pretended to review the program file on the laptop screen. A file he wished he could find the chance to mess with and add his own firewalls and viruses to. But Vlad and his partner, Santiago, never left him alone. Not once during the past week had he been able to go into the laptop they'd given him to use for this job and infiltrate the system files. He needed to before they reached the East Coast. For what he suspected Vlad and Santiago were up to, if he didn't, the two years he'd spent in prison would be more like a walk in the park compared to Death Row.

"No answer?" Vlad drew another cigarette from the pack and shrugged. "A man's sexual preference is own business. Know this, Harry, Vlad no care if you like men. Vlad's very…" The Russian snapped his fingers several times and looked to the ceiling. "Progressive. Right word, no?"

"Right word, wrong assumption," Harrison said. While he enjoyed women, he didn't enjoy paying for them. Vlad, Santiago and Mickey had hired prostitutes the night they were in Vegas. Not tempted to sink his body into a woman who had had countless dicks in her vagina, and not permitted to leave the room, Harrison had spent the night in the claustrophobic bathroom without his phone or computer. That night had been the longest and most boring night of his life. Even in prison he'd have found something to do to amuse himself. Instead, he had to listen to the three other men's grunting and their women's exaggerated moans.

"Ah, so Harry *do* like women," Vlad said and lit his cigarette. "Good. Vlad will buy Harry a woman when job is kaput. Tell Vlad. Blonde, brunette or redhead?" The Russian laughed and slapped him on the back. "Maybe Harry want all three, eh?"

Vlad was either fucking with him or the man was clueless. When the job was *kaput*, Harrison worried he and his brother would be, too. Whoever Vlad and Santiago worked for wasn't going to allow him and Mickey to go back to their neighborhood, to their crappy jobs at the restaurant, to their crappy lives. And he'd prefer crappy over dead.

"I couldn't handle three women," Harrison said, deciding to play along. He couldn't let the Russian or Santiago know about his doubts and needed to maintain the charade. "But if I had to choose, a redhead would be nice."

"Ah, Harry like them fiery." Squinting as smoke drifted in his face, Vlad took a long drag on the cigarette. "Me? Vlad prefer your California girls. Blonde, tan, big titties," he said and grabbed his own big pecs. "But we no talk about Vlad. Yes, Monday night Vlad give Harry fiery redhead to keep dick warm."

"Monday night?" Harrison rubbed his itchy eyes. That gave him only three days to either disable the devices he'd been syncing to the laptop, or immobilize the laptop itself. He'd rather deactivate the devices, which, according to Santiago, were high tech security cameras. But he didn't buy Santiago's bullshit. Why in the hell would someone plant and sync security cameras across the country?

During their first two stops, other than worrying about being busted for violating probation, he hadn't given the job they were on much thought. Actually, he'd been enjoying himself. The fancy private plane that had flown them from Norfolk to San Francisco, then later to Las Vegas where they'd spent the night at the Bellagio. Granted he'd spent the majority of that night confined to the bathroom, but prior to that, they'd eaten, drunk and gambled like high rollers. After being locked in a bathroom in Vegas, things became even stranger. The cities and towns they were delivering the cameras to appeared random. One morning they were in Pocatello, Idaho, and by that evening Ford, Wyoming. The next day Denver, the day after that, Amarillo, Texas. Where the supposed security equipment had been placed was also equally unsystematic. A bar, convention center, funeral home, shopping mall, airstrip, school…

His pulse quickened with anxiety. Yeah, something wasn't adding up—at all. Because Vlad and Santiago showed no sign of knowing anything about computers, he could, given the chance, easily take care of those *cameras*. As for the computer, until they reached the East Coast, he'd rather not destroy the laptop.

"Is this the last city?" he asked, part of him hopeful while the other part was concerned. He needed to create a virus, or at the very least leave a trail of breadcrumbs. Should the shit go down the way he suspected, Vlad and Santiago's boss would need to be stopped.

"Nah." Vlad shook his head and waved the cigarette. "And miss out on fun? We like Griswolds, no?" He pretended to drive a car. "We travel cross country in search of fun. And we have fun, no?"

No. He was not having fun. He was fucking freaking out. This was supposed to be an easy job. Sync security devices to the laptop he'd been given, make sure they could be activated remotely. Simple. Easy. Only it wasn't that simple. If the devices Santiago and Mickey had been planting were for security reasons, then why wouldn't Vlad and Santiago let him and Mickey out of their sight? The guns and concealed knives they carried, those he understood. The two men supposedly ran security detail for a powerful individual. Still. Something wasn't ringing true.

Or maybe he was paranoid.

If only he could talk to Mickey alone. Find out exactly what he'd been syncing to the laptop. Mickey didn't do tech stuff and probably wouldn't know what he'd been dealing with, but if his brother could describe the devices Harrison might be able to either dismiss his paranoia or confirm it. And he wanted confirmation.

The motel door bounced open sending in a stream of sunlight. Mickey entered first, wearing a smile that didn't reach his eyes. "Hey, bro. How's it hanging?"

"Low and long," he replied, studying his brother and catching the wariness in his eyes. "You?"

"Large and in charge." Mickey glanced to Vlad and nodded. "What's up?"

"Is this where Vlad say penis?" Vlad asked with a shake of his head. "You American men have strange obsession with your anatomy."

Santiago entered the room. "Harry, you ready to go live?" he asked, his accent slight in comparison to Vlad's. He checked his watch. "*Mierda*, I wanted to leave thirty minutes ago. We need to be in St. Louis by nine."

"Sure," Harrison said, and moved his fingers across the keyboard. While he typed, Santiago pulled Vlad aside and spoke to the Russian in hushed whispers. Vlad's expression hardened and he shifted his ice blue gaze on Mickey. After nodding, he folded his arms across his chest, his focus remaining on Mickey.

Damn it, Mick, what did you do? He looked to his brother. Mickey's hand shook as he raised his fingers to his temples. When Mickey met his eyes, and Harrison caught the panic, the horror, the depths of despair, his stomach rolled with nausea while fear tightened his throat.

Swallowing hard, he looked away from his brother and concentrated on the laptop screen. "We're live," he said to Santiago and Vlad.

Santiago nodded. "*Bien*. Pack up," he ordered and headed into the bathroom.

Wearing a threatening scowl, Vlad walked over to the table and leaned next to Mickey. "What wrong, Mickey Mouse? You look like you see ghost."

Mickey kept his gaze on Harrison's. "Not a ghost," his brother said, his voice low, shaky and dripping with terror. "More like The Angel of Death."

CHAPTER 2

THE FRAGRANT, CITRUSY scent wafting from the blooming magnolia trees did little to calm Naomi's nerves. With her stomach performing a continuous somersault, she led Jake along the walkway leading to her modest, ranch-style home's wraparound front porch. Normally she'd relish the way the gorgeous, vibrant fuchsia azaleas, the purple, red and yellow tulips, the hearty boxwoods and hostas filled her flowerbeds. But with Jake by her side, she had a difficult time thinking about anything but him.

His familiar scent, his dark knowing eyes, how he hadn't once smiled since showing up in the school parking lot. She'd missed his smile. The press of his body. His kisses. The way he made love to her.

But she'd missed more than the sex. The comfort, the security of his strong arms, knowing he understood her, accepted her, shared her dreams, wanted to create a future…

She drew in a quick breath and came to an abrupt halt.

"What's wrong?" he asked, his eyes alert as he glanced at the front porch.

Everything. "Nothing," she managed, when deep in her soul she wanted to shout the truth. She'd wanted that future with Jake. She always had, always would. Seeing him now was a cruel reminder of what she'd given up the day she'd left him. A lifetime of happiness filled with love and friendship.

"Look," he said, and took her arm. When his big, warm

31

hand touched her bare skin, memories surfaced. How many times had he touched her, caressed here, held her close late into the night or pulled her into his arms for a quick hug? When they'd been together, she'd taken those moments for granted. After being separated from him, after years of living with bittersweet memories, she realized she should have soaked up every second. Cherished those moments as they'd happened. Memories alone couldn't fill her lonely days and nights.

He looked down to where he touched her arm and rubbed the pad of his thumb along her skin. "We never had an issue with talking," he said and met her gaze. "No reason to start now. So let's just get a few things out of the way."

"Like?"

He reached for her left hand. "No ring. Boyfriend?"

She could lie and tell him there was someone and instantly create a safe barrier between them. The hope and longing in his dark eyes, and the way simply being near him tugged at her heart forced her to be honest. "No boyfriend. And you?"

His face softened as a playful smile tugged at his lips. "No boyfriend for me. I'm still straight."

Grinning, she squeezed his hand. "You know exactly what I meant."

"I know." His smile fell as his gaze drifted to her lips. "And no, I'm not married, engaged or with someone."

"So now what?" she asked, freeing her hand from his. Knowing there wasn't anyone else in his life scared her. She could easily see herself falling back into his arms, falling back into their old routine, only to face the constant worry and fear of losing him. Permanently. And death, she knew too well, was permanent.

He let out a low chuckle and rubbed the back of his neck. "Hell, I don't know. When I was driving here I tried to come up with what I'd say when I saw you and even then I didn't know. I figured I'd wing it, but now that I'm standing on your front porch barely able to spit out a few words, I feel like a jackass. I'm sorry, Naomi, I didn't come here to make you uncomfortable."

"You're not," she lied. "Actually, I'm the one who should be apologizing. I invite you to my house, make you stand on the porch…made *you* uncomfortable. Come inside." She unlocked the front door. "Hungry?"

"I'm good, but something cold to drink would work."

She led him from the foyer down the hall and into her kitchen. Sunlight streamed in through the opened windows, bringing with it the aroma of lilac and lavender. "Iced tea, beer, water, soda…?"

"Iced tea would be great, thanks." He glanced from the updated kitchen into the small family room. "This is a great place." He moved to the sliding patio door and looked out into the backyard. "That's a lot of yard to maintain. How big's the lot?"

Holding two glasses of tea, she stared at his rigid back. She didn't want this reunion to be painfully awkward and from what he'd said on the front porch she knew he didn't want that either. Yet neither one of them could relax or let their guard down long enough to move past inane small talk. Born and raised in Virginia by a mother who had strong roots in the South, she'd been schooled with proper Southern etiquette and had been taught to never let a guest feel uncomfortable. Then again, she'd never had a former fiancé in her home.

Deciding to embrace the short time she would have with him and anxious to hear how he'd been, she handed him the glass of tea. "Three quarters of an acre. But it's not too bad. When I moved in I bought a riding mower." She opened the patio door. "Let's sit outside."

He took the seat next to hers, probably because it offered the best shade from beneath the umbrella. Still, the close proximity was more than she could handle. The last man who'd touched her, held her, loved her body, sat less than a foot away. Time and distance might have separated them, *she* might have separated them, but she still couldn't help longing for his touch. She'd never loved any man the way she'd loved

Jake.

When she'd met him, the attraction had been instantaneous. She'd been sitting at a beach café in Pensacola, Florida, chatting and sipping daiquiris with friends and watching a wedding taking place along the shore. Jake had been part of the wedding. Wearing his Marine-issued dress blue uniform, he'd looked badass and sexy. Even in that uniform she could tell he had a powerful body and although never one to throw herself at a man or become involved in a one-night stand the daiquiris had suggested otherwise. So had her meddling friends.

But the moment Jake turned those dark brown eyes on her she knew in her heart he wouldn't be a one-night stand.

"You're smiling," he said, setting his iced tea on the table and sweeping her away from Pensacola and back to her patio. "Not to sound clichéd, but what are you thinking about?"

"The day we met."

He grinned. "That was a great day. I'll never forget the white sundress you wore. You outshined the bride."

Her cheeks warmed. "Did not. She was beautiful."

"So were you. I never told you this, but I almost beat the hell out of one of my buddies because he wanted to make a bet to see which one of us could sleep with you that night."

She chuckled. "Nice."

"You know I'd never take a bet like that."

"Of course. Even if you had, you would have lost."

"I didn't, though."

"If memory serves me." She tapped a finger to her temple. "And I have a very good memory, you didn't get to first base until our fourth date."

He glanced at her mouth. "But you let me kiss you."

When his firm lips had brushed along hers, coaxed and teased, he'd stolen her breath and her heart. The kiss had been electrifying and soul tugging. As if her body and heart knew Jake was the missing link, her other half, the man who would make her world right. Even then she knew she was taking a risk. The bastard who had been hunting her had already taken her parents from her, but her brother had given her a new identity, a new lease on life. In the end though, he'd given her false hope. She didn't blame Thomas, he'd been trying to protect her. She blamed herself. For loving Jake, for assuming the past wouldn't catch up to her.

Not wanting to ruin the mood or their tentative conversation, she nodded and smiled. "What can I say? I'm a sucker for a man in uniform."

He half-laughed. "Then why couldn't you wait to get me out of it?"

Her cheeks burned as she remembered the way she'd practically torn his clothes off his body. "On date seven," she reminded him.

"A technicality."

"Says you." Needing to change the subject before her mind continued to drift to sex and how good it used to be with him, she asked, "So, how are your mom and dad doing?"

He held her eyes for a moment, the teasing glint fading. "They're good. Healthy. My dad finally retired and my mom plans to this year. Two years ago they sold the family home and moved into a townhouse. Now my dad doesn't have to worry about the yard or shoveling the driveway."

"Or your mom nagging him to hire someone to do it for him," she said, remembering how Jake's mom used to harp at his dad about those things, which she was right to do. Jake's dad had suffered a heart attack a year after she and Jake were engaged. Between his age and potential health risks, his dad shouldn't have been out shoveling snow, especially when the temperatures in Pittsburgh dropped into the teens and twenties.

"True," he said with a smile.

"And your brothers? How are they?"

"Also good. They're all still in the Pittsburgh area. Billy and Susan have two kids now, Jimmy and Michelle are up to three."

Regret twisted her insides. How many kids would she and Jake have had?

Shoving the thought aside, she picked up her glass. "And

things in Bola? Still kicking butt as sheriff?"

Six months after they'd started dating, they'd become engaged and were living in Pittsburgh. While she'd preferred Florida's gulf coast, she knew how important family was to him. Before he'd left for Iraq, they'd moved to Pittsburgh, found a condo and planned to remain in the area once he returned home. Although she loved his tightknit family and they'd generously welcomed her into their clan with open arms, living in a bigger city, especially one closer to Virginia, had been hell on her nerves. Even though she could be surrounded by thousands of people in Pittsburgh, she'd have preferred a smaller community. In a small town people knew who lived there, if visitors were traveling through, if a stranger was in their midst.

A few months after Jake had come home, injured and needing physical therapy, she hadn't told him right away about her need to leave Pittsburgh. But, as always, he'd sensed a change in her and had questioned her needs and wants. When she'd told him she wanted to move to a small town he hadn't objected, but he hadn't done any cartwheels over the idea, either. He'd gone along with her desire to move anyway, and a few weeks later she'd discovered Bola, a speck on the map in northwest Michigan. She'd moved first, found them a cute bungalow to rent, taken a job as a nurse at the local county hospital and had put Jake's name in the running for an opening at the Dixon County Sheriff's office. Less than a year after he'd arrived in Bola, she'd campaigned for him and he was elected sheriff.

They'd had the perfect situation in the perfect setting. Until her brother's death turned her perfect world upside down.

"I'm no longer sheriff and moved to Chicago about ten months ago."

"But your second term as sheriff won't be up until the end..." Damn it. She'd said too much, let him know she'd periodically checked up on him.

"How'd you know I ran for a second term?" he asked, his eyes holding a hint of hopefulness.

"Just because I left doesn't mean I don't care. I checked out the county website and saw you were reelected."

"Yeah, well, something came up and forced me to leave," he said, his tone laced with resentment.

"Why Chicago?"

"I got a job there. I'm working for a private investigation firm called CORE. I'm still low on the totem pole, but in the end I think it'll end up being a good move for me."

Private investigation firm. Since moving to Woodbine, she'd kept her information unlisted. Now she had an idea of how he'd found her.

"Regardless of where you're at within the firm, I bet it's more exciting than boring Bola."

"It's been okay so far. For a little while Bola wasn't so boring. We had a serial killer preying on college kids."

"Oh, my God. You're kidding me."

"I wish I was. A couple of investigators from CORE came to help with the situation and that's how I ended up joining their agency."

Although curious about the particulars of the investigation that had resulted in his new career, she'd seen enough death and murder in her life. She didn't think she could stomach listening to the gory details. Instead, she continued to question him. About the people she'd come to know in Bola, more about his family, the condo he'd bought in Chicago.

As the sun's rays waned and shadows from the pines began to creep along the patio, her stomach rumbled. "How about some dinner? Obviously I wasn't expecting company, but I have some burgers we can throw on the grill and salad stuff in the fridge."

"I don't want to intrude," he said, but made no move to jump up and leave.

"You're not. Come into the kitchen and keep me company while I get dinner ready."

Once inside, he sat on the bar stool in front of the small kitchen island and set his empty glass on the counter.

"More iced tea?" she asked, taking the salad fixings from

the fridge.

"I'll have a beer, if you don't mind."

"Not at all. I'll join you." After grabbing a couple of beers and popping the tops, she handed one to him. Several times during the afternoon she'd wanted to ask him why he'd decided to find her now. While the question nagged at her, she'd also been enjoying herself too much to let reality sneak in and ruin the moment. Instead she asked, "How long do you plan on staying in Woodbine?"

"I have to be back in Chicago by Monday." He kept his gaze focused on hers, then took a drink of his beer.

"So, you're staying the weekend?" she asked, part of her hoping he would. She'd missed him so damned much, had spent years missing him and daydreaming about the day they could be together again. Reality chose that moment to punch a hole in her dreams. They couldn't be together, not if she wanted him to remain alive and well.

He rose from the stool and edged around the island. Picking up a knife from the counter, he placed a carrot on the cutting board she'd set out earlier and began slicing. "That depends on you."

Frustrated by his short, cryptic answer and the way he'd kept himself guarded, she touched his forearm. "Stop."

"Don't you like how I'm cutting the carrots?"

"I don't like that our entire conversation seems forced and..." She stepped away and reached for her beer. "You've never had a problem telling me what's on your mind. I know it's been a while—"

"Five years."

She ignored the painful reminder. "I wish you'd just—"

"Open myself up? Lay it all out there?" He set the knife down and stared at her with wariness, cynicism and, God help her, hunger. "I didn't think any part of our conversation seemed forced." He let out a sigh and went back to the carrots. "Honestly, I haven't had a day as good as this in a long time."

"Then answer my question," she said, watching his hands, remembering what it felt like to have them touch her bare skin.

"Do you plan to stay the weekend?"

"Do you want me to?"

She realized he wasn't going to blurt out his intentions, but understood why. She'd walked away from him and he'd taken a risk by finding her. He had no idea how she'd react, if she wanted to see him or spend time with him. She'd hurt him once and she doubted he'd allow that to happen again. If anything, she had a feeling the only one who would suffer from this unexpected visit was her. The good memories and happy times they'd had together mocked her, showed her how things could have been. The bad memories, the reasons she had to leave him taunted her, as well. Did she want him to remain in Woodbine for the weekend? Spend more time with him and create new memories that would later leave her empty and alone?

"Yes," she admitted. "A few hours of conversation isn't enough to make up for five years."

"Good," he said, stopped cutting and looked over his shoulder. While his eyes still held a hint of wariness, they also showed relief and, yes, hunger. She loved the heat in his eyes, but hated the wariness and knowing that she was the one who'd caused it.

For years she'd craved his touch, his kisses, his comfort. Walking away from Jake had been the hardest choice she'd ever made. She wanted to admit that to him, but wouldn't. The truth would only lead to questions she wasn't ready to answer. Still, she wasn't ready for him to leave. How the weekend would play out, she couldn't be sure. Deep in her heart, in the depths of her soul, her love for him was still alive. She'd spent years fantasizing about being with him, making love, making a future, but knew her fantasies could never come to fruition. Because in the end, she wouldn't risk his life to satisfy her selfish needs.

She eyed his broad shoulders, pictured him without his shirt. Remembered the way his muscles bunched as she'd clung to his back while he drove himself deep inside her. And she wanted him deep inside her again. If he couldn't be a permanent fixture in her life, she'd love to make new memories this weekend. Except the physical satisfaction would only cause her more emotional discontentment.

What was she thinking? Reconnecting with Jake, hell, just seeing him again already had her emotions running haywire. Guilt and regret ate at her soul, along with anger and hatred for the man who had forced a rift between her and Jake. At the same time the love and desire she'd kept hidden and controlled was more predominant than ever.

Why did he have to come here? Why now? Her life was fine, not what she'd pictured, but she liked Woodbine, the few friends she'd made here, her house and her job at the school. Most days she was content. With the past now colliding with the present, she realized that contentment had been a lie. She hadn't been truly happy since the day she'd left Jake.

Moving next to him, she set her beer on the counter, picked up a knife and grabbed a green pepper. When she caught his scent—earthy, male and pure Jake—her stomach tingled with sensual awareness. She wanted to greedily take the time she could have with him and utilize it to the fullest. Wrap her arms around him, soak up his strength, erase the years of loneliness, of regret. She wanted to know how much his feelings for her had changed. If he still loved her and found her desirable. Damn, she really was being selfish. What right did she have to his heart? Hadn't she already hurt him enough?

As she sliced into the pepper, she tried to come up with something else to say. She'd originally figured he'd shown up in Woodbine with an agenda. But after learning about the private investigation firm he now worked for, she'd dismissed that idea. Working for CORE, not having to shoulder the responsibilities as a county sheriff, had given him the opportunity to find her. But again, why now? What had motivated him to come here today? Why hadn't he married and started a family like his brothers?

The knife caught the tip of her finger. Wincing, she quickly grabbed a paper towel and applied pressure to the small cut.

He took her hand. "Are you okay?"

"I'm fine." She ignored her throbbing finger and stared at him. "Why did you come here?"

"I wanted to see you," he said, his dark eyes on hers.

"Why now?" she asked even though she'd told herself she wouldn't. The warring emotions, the longing, the regret were too much to bear. Before she allowed herself to let him back into her life, even for just the weekend, she needed answers. Leaving Jake the first time had been the hardest thing she'd ever done. Missing him, wishing their lives could have taken a different course, second-guessing her choices, she'd cried herself to sleep for months. She couldn't go back to those dark days. Not again.

Keeping the paper towel around her finger, he curled his big hand into hers. "I needed to know you were happy," he said, his eyes earnest, honest. "Are you?"

No. "I am," she lied and mustered a smile.

"Good." He cupped her cheek. "I also missed seeing your face."

Tears clouded her eyes and slipped down her cheeks. She touched his strong jaw. "I've missed seeing you, too."

"Don't," he said, and brushed her tears away with his thumb. "I hate it when you cry, especially if I'm the one causing it."

She let go of his hand and hugged him tight. In an instant he cocooned her in his embrace. Their bodies molded together with familiarity and comfort, as if time and distance had never separated them. She didn't want to let him go and worried if she did, she'd find herself alone in the kitchen grasping at the misty veils of another dream.

And she was tired of dreaming, of living in the past, of wishing for a different present and future. She'd suffered a burden she hadn't deserved and wanted happiness, even if it lasted for only a weekend.

Pulling back, but not letting go of him, she met his questioning gaze. Her body immediately responded to the heat and intensity in his eyes. Desire swept through her and settled in her core. "Since you're staying the weekend, you'll need a place to stay."

"I saw the Rainbow Lodge on my way into town," he said, the hunger in his eyes nearly taking her breath away.

"It's a decent place, but why not stay here." Her dormant sex came alive and a throb built between her thighs. "I have a spare bedroom."

Jake shifted his gaze to Naomi's lips. The urge to kiss her, strip her naked and bury himself in her heat made him hard, tense. He slid his hand from her lower back and gripped her hips. "I don't think that's a good idea."

A small smile curved her mouth. He glanced away and met her gaze. Damn, he'd missed looking into her bright blue eyes.

"Why not?" she asked.

Why not? Because he wanted them skin to skin, chest to breast. He wanted to pretend he didn't know about her lies. That she was simply Naomi McCall, his lover, best friend and future. Not a mystery woman who hadn't existed until eight years ago.

He'd come here with the intent to put the past to rest. Instead he'd discovered his love for her hadn't died. He knew in his gut he couldn't sleep in the same house without wanting to be with her. He didn't trust himself where she was concerned. From the moment they'd met he'd wanted her. She'd allured him, drawn him in with her smile, those beautiful blue eyes and sexy curves. But what had attracted him the most was her personality. The night he'd met her, he'd just come off a short tour in Iraq. Within minutes of talking with her, the fighting, the fear, the anxiety that came with war and conflict had been replaced with a quiet peace. And as their relationship had developed, he'd craved not only her touch, but her soothing words and her nurturing yet pragmatic way.

He'd missed her so damned much. Although he could survive without her and had for the past five years, he didn't know if he could handle being under the same roof as her. Despite the time they'd been apart, despite the lies, he still wanted her.

Holding her hips, he pressed her against his erection. "This is why I'm better off staying at the Lodge."

Her eyes darkened and she slid her gaze to his mouth. "I think that's exactly why you should stay here," she said, meeting his eyes again.

Wrong. Maybe a weekend of hot sex wasn't a big deal to her. She'd had no problem walking away from him before and he doubted she'd have a problem doing it again. For him, though…

Despite his body's reaction to her, he hadn't come here for sex and knew it would only complicate their already complicated relationship. How could he be with her again and walk away? How could he taste her, touch her, feel her heat wrapped around him and not want more? He'd spent years pushing her from his mind. He'd tried to find a woman who could replace Naomi and what they'd had together. On both ends he'd had no success. She'd never been far from his thoughts and no woman could compare to her.

With reluctance, he let go of her hips and took a step back. "Maybe you're right," he said even though he had no intention of staying. While he wouldn't take her up on the offer to use the spare bedroom, he also wasn't ready to leave yet. He wanted to continue hanging out at her house, have dinner, pretend they were still a couple.

God, he was pathetic. Naomi was a walking, talking lie. He should hate her, confront her about her past, shout out his resentments. But he couldn't. Until he'd seen her in the school parking lot, he hadn't realized how empty his life had been without her. He hadn't realized how much he still loved her.

Fucking pathetic.

Rather than dwell on his idiocy, he moved back to the counter and resumed helping with the salad. "Tell me about your job at the school," he said deciding a change of subject was the best plan. While he wouldn't stay at her place, he knew in his gut he could be easily swayed. Naomi had a way of seducing and coaxing him into just about anything. He'd have to keep reminding himself why he'd come here in the first place, that their relationship was nothing but one lie after another.

That she'd left him.

"I love working with the kids," she said, pulling burger patties from the freezer.

As they finished the salad and later grilled the burgers, she talked about her job and told him some damned funny stories about the kids. While they ate, he asked her more about the area she'd chosen to live in and kept the conversation light and focused on her. Not them. Not the past. Tomorrow he'd hit her with all the unanswered questions that had been taunting him. Her bullshit excuses for leaving him, if she was really an only child, born and raised in Pittsburgh like him and, damn it, her real name and why she'd kept her identity secret from him.

When they'd finished eating and had cleaned the kitchen, she suggested they move into the living room. As he followed behind her, he tried to keep his eyes off the sexy sway of her hips and the tempting curve of her rear. But couldn't. He also tried to stop his mind from wandering to the past, to those unanswered questions. But couldn't. He also couldn't stop thinking about her offer to stay the night at her house.

Seriously fucking pathetic.

What the hell was wrong with him? He'd been a badass Marine, a kick-ass sheriff and planned to be both as an investigator for CORE. All of these confusing thoughts and emotions were pissing him off. Instead of dwelling, he should be acting. Demanding answers.

He took a seat at the end of the couch. She settled next to him. Close. Too close. He caught the swell of her breasts as she shifted her arm over the back of the couch. Remembered how they'd felt in his hands, how her nipples had responded to his touch. Shit. So many memories. Spreading her legs, dipping his head, tasting her, making her come alive.

His dick throbbed. His head ached from thinking too damned much. He wanted to stay and lose himself in her body. He wanted to run before he did something stupid.

Scrubbing a hand down his face, he quickly stood.

"What's wrong?" she asked, her brow furrowing, her eyes

questioning and uncertain.

"It's getting late," he said.

She glanced at the clock on the mantle. "It's only eight-thirty."

"Yeah, but I've been up since dawn."

Understanding softened her face. "Well, in that case, let me make up the bed for you. There're towels in the bathroom linen closet, shampoo—"

"Thanks, but I'm going to head out. I think it's best if I stay at the Lodge."

She looked away. "I see."

"Do you?"

Standing, she moved toward the door. "Yep."

In a few strides he caught up with her. "You sure about that?" he asked, snagging her arm and turning her until she faced him.

"Didn't I just say—"

"Yep."

She pulled away but he kept her near him. "Whatever, Jake. I'm not going to play this game. You don't want to stay here, then don't."

"Oh, I want to stay," he said, crowding her until she backed against the closed door. Sliding his hand from her arm, he cupped her breast. "But I don't want to stay in the spare room."

She grabbed a fistful of his shirt. "So don't," she said, her voice low, breathy and sexy as hell.

His erection swelled. He had to leave. Now. "And then what?"

A slow, sexy smile tilted her lips. "Has it been that long?" She let go of his shirt and ran her hand down his chest until she reached his belt buckle. "I'm sure there're a few things I can do to refresh your memory."

When her palm grazed his erection straining against his jeans, he grabbed her hand, then the other and pinned her against the door. "I've been living on memories for five years," he said, his voice rougher than he'd intended. Damn, he wanted her. But not like this. Not a quick fuck for old times' sake.

"Funny, earlier I was thinking about making new ones," she said, her eyes matching her seductive tone. She pulled against his grip, causing her breasts to thrust forward. "I've missed—"

He crushed his mouth against hers. He didn't want to hear what she'd missed. Him? Them? Sex? It didn't matter. At this point he wasn't sure what to believe, he couldn't be sure if the words coming out of her pretty mouth were lies, the truth or a variation of both. He'd kiss her hard and fast and walk away. Tomorrow they'd discuss the past and put it to rest. As for tonight, he had no plans on making any new memories that would only—

She opened her mouth and slid her tongue along his. His body switched into overdrive. Need rushed through his veins.

Screw it.

Releasing her hands, he tangled his fingers through her hair and grabbed a fistful. He held her head still and assaulted her lips. His conscience warned him to back off, that he was being rough. That he was doing the exact opposite of what he'd planned. But he couldn't stop. He'd missed the taste of her, the feel of her body against his. She cupped his jaw with one hand and palmed his erection with the other. He'd missed *her*, damn it. Needing more, needing his conscience to shut the hell up, he pressed her against the door, ran his free hand down her sexy curves and lifted her leg.

Moving her hand from between their bodies, she held onto his ass, pushing him closer and settling her heat on his thigh. She rotated her pelvis and sighed against his mouth. He should make her come, he *could* make her come, remind her what they used to have together and leave her wanting more.

He tore his mouth away. Breathing hard, he stared into her eyes. They glittered with desire, with the same need pulsing through his body. With trust.

Damn, he was an asshole and a selfish bastard for wanting to make her want him, when all he craved was her and the love they used to have. Knowing now was the moment to end a kiss that could go further than he'd intended, he ignored the rational side of his brain, gripped her hips and moved her along his thigh.

Her breath hitched as she kept her eyes on his. Aware of what she liked, he slid a hand under her shirt and pushed the material up her torso. Hot pink lace covered her breasts. Aching to taste her, he gave the lace a tug and exposed one taut nipple. With his eyes still on hers, he dipped his head and took what he wanted. Ran his tongue along her nipple and kept her heat pinned against his thigh.

She shoved her hands through his hair, gripped his head and forced his mouth away only to kiss him again. Scorching hot, deep and demanding, *she* was the one who took and tempted him. She ground her pelvis against his thigh, untucked his shirt and ran her hands underneath along his bare skin. He wanted to be skin to skin but knew that wasn't an option. If he allowed this so-called kiss to go that far, it might cloud his judgment and make the questions he'd demand answers to that much harder to ask. But he could leave them both satisfied and not in a way that would make him out to be a total jackass.

He moved his hand between their bodies and unbuttoned and unzipped the front of her capris. When she slid her hands down his bare back and gripped his ass, he fought to keep his own desires in check, raised her up slightly and worked his hand beneath her panties. Swollen, soft and wet, he sank his fingers into her heat.

With a low moan, she released his lips and rested her forehead against his. Her warm breath mingled with his and came in short quick puffs. As he drove his fingers deeper into her, over and over, she sagged against the door. He kept her upright, kept her pinned and dipped his head again for another taste of her nipple. He tugged and sucked on the hard peak while she hugged him close and clung to his back.

His stomach clenched with desire. He wanted her to come. He wanted to come. But now wasn't about him. Everything he'd done from the moment he'd met and fallen hard for Naomi had always been for her. The pleasure he could give her, the life she deserved, her wants and desires. He'd loved her more than life itself. He still did, and still wanted to please her in every way possible.

Her inner muscles clenched around his fingers. Her breathing grew labored. The leg she stood on trembled. Knowing she was close, wishing he could taste her orgasm, he quickly moved away from her breast and sought her lips. He captured her mouth as her body went rigid. Her groan vibrated against lips as she kissed him back, this time unhurried and with so much damned tenderness it made his heart ache.

With reluctance, he let go of her leg, slipped his fingers from her heat and tugged her shirt back down. She drew away slightly, a small smile tilting her lips as she kept her arms twined around his neck. "Still thinking about that room at the Lodge?" she asked.

"I'm having a hard time thinking about anything right now," he admitted with a half-smile.

"Then don't think. Stay."

The day she'd told him she needed to leave Bola and what they'd just begun to build there, he'd asked her to stay. To give their new life a chance or to at least try to maintain a long distance relationship until his term as sheriff had ended. But she'd refused.

He wouldn't stay now out of spite or childish recourse. He'd leave to keep the small amount of restraint he possessed intact, and to give himself time to come to terms with the confusing emotions unraveling inside him.

"Not tonight," he said, tucking a lock of her silky hair behind her ear. "Can I see you tomorrow?"

He swore he caught regret in her eyes before she hugged him. "Yes," she said against his chest, then quickly took a step back. "Be here at nine for breakfast."

"Good night, bossy," he said and touched her cheek, then opened the door and left before his willpower completely dissolved.

As he drove away from her quiet street and headed for the Lodge, his body and mind waged a vicious battle. Spending the day and evening with Naomi hadn't brought him any closer to putting the past to rest. Instead, being with her was not only a bitter reminder of what they could have had if she'd never walked away, but that he was still in love with a liar.

CHAPTER 3

HE STARED ACROSS the table at his wife of six years, wishing she would do them both a favor and die. Liliana had once been a means to an end, a way to gain her father's trust, confidence and the share holdings of a failing shipping company. A vessel to implant his seed in and create two children. Now, he no longer needed her. He'd wiped that long-standing shipping company, which had once been an American icon and his competition, from existence. In the process, he'd ruined her father and forced him into an early grave.

Yes, he wished she'd slit her wrists or swallow a bottle of pills. Or maybe drive into a telephone pole at eighty miles per hour. He could and should simply do as Ric had suggested and have her throat slit in a staged robbery. But then he'd have to deal with the press and the police, not to mention his children who would likely need therapy and coddling.

The pretty young kitchen maid he'd been meaning to fuck entered the dining room with a serving cart. Shy and no more than twenty-two, he could easily picture her coming to his office, dropping to her knees and taking him into his mouth. Maybe after he was through with the maid he'd let Ric have her. He eyed her pert tits as she leaned over and set a plate in front of Liliana. Yes, Ric had been working hard lately and deserved a little fun. He'd just have to make sure Ric didn't take the fun to a level that required disposing of the young maid's corpse.

"Thank you, Alison," Liliana said to the maid. "Have the children had their breakfast?"

Alison. Yes, now he recalled the hot little maid's name.

"Yes, ma'am," Alison responded, filling his wife's Rogaska crystal glass with orange juice. "Waffles, eggs and sausage. Their nanny took them to the music room for their lessons after they finished breakfast."

"Very good. I'll have to stop by and see them. Charlotte has really taken to the piano, don't you think, dear?"

He shifted his gaze from Alison's breasts to his wife's shit-brown eyes. "Yes, she's doing well," he said. "Mary Had a Little Lamb has never sounded better."

Alison giggled as she set his plate in front of him. After she poured him a cup of coffee, she asked, "Do you need anything else?"

My wife dead and you sucking my dick. "Nothing, thank you."

With a smile first to him, then to his wife, Alison left the dining room through the servants' entrance. Once the French doors were closed he looked across the table again. "Liliana, do you *really* plan to eat all of that?" he asked and nodded to the sparse breakfast morsels on his wife's plate.

She blinked and looked to the six small chunks of grapefruit, half of a hard-boiled egg and half of a slice of dry toast. "I worked out for sixty minutes this morning and burned over five hundred calories."

"So?" he asked, and raised a forkful of scrambled eggs to his mouth.

"This food is less than one hundred calories." She pointed to her plate. "I think I can afford to eat it."

He set the fork on the plate and picked up his coffee cup. "Are you sure? The charity ball is in two weeks and I refuse to go out in public with a fat ass."

Her eyes widened and filled with contempt and insult. She glanced to her plate with longing, then picked up her glass of juice.

"That's also high in calories," he reminded her. "But you do what you think is right."

After setting the juice back on the table, she folded her hands in her lap and stared at her plate of food. The dumb bitch had no backbone. She obviously needed glasses, as well. There wasn't an ounce of fat on her scrawny body. If anything she should eat everything on her plate and his before her body shut down from malnutrition. Then again, death by starvation *would* save him from having to find a way to rid himself of his useless wife.

"Why do you hate me so much?" she asked, a tear slipping down her boney cheek.

"I don't hate you," he said and sliced into a sausage link. "I feel nothing for you." He took a bite of the sausage and savored not only the delicious flavor, but the shock in Liliana's eyes. She'd never been welcomed in his home. He'd never wanted her, but what she could give his empire. Lying with her, having to force himself to have sex with her, had been about as hot and satisfying as a root canal. But he'd wanted the children. Everything he'd worked for would not be inherited by distant relatives, but by his blood.

She wiped her cheek with her napkin and stared at him with hurt and hatred. "Then why not divorce me? The prenup you made me sign lets you keep your fortune. If you feel nothing for me, then let me go." Her chin trembled. "Please," she begged, her voice raw and ragged.

"Divorce?" He leaned back in his chair and shook his head. "And ruin my image? The press would have a field day. And I can't allow that to happen. Until death do us part," he said with a smile and raised his mug in a mock toast.

Tossing her napkin on her plate, she stood. "Then maybe I should have an affair," she said, her voice shaking. "Maybe I should take a page from your book and have an affair. The pool boy is very attractive."

Lack of sustenance must have warped her brain. Rage momentarily blurred his vision and he had to grip the armrests of the dining room chair to keep from climbing across the table and choking the life from her.

No one threatened him.

"Do that, and I'll cut his dick off and stuff it down your throat."

She gasped and held a hand to her neck.

"Do you doubt me?" he asked, narrowing his gaze.

"I wouldn't," Ric said as he entered the dining room through the main entrance. "Actually, I'll probably end up being the one to cut off said dick and do the stuffing. And quite frankly, the thought of touching another man's junk just doesn't settle well with me. So do us all a favor, Liliana, keep your legs closed and your mouth shut."

He grinned at his right hand man. "Well said." He glanced at his wife with disgust. "Now get the fuck out of my dining room and go listen to my daughter play the piano."

The fear and defeat contorting his wife's face made him chuckle. When she didn't move, he rose from the chair. "And by the way, *dear*, just for being a whiny bitch, the next time I bring a woman to my bed I'm going to make you watch."

Ric burst into laughter as Liliana rushed from the room. "You wouldn't, would you?" he asked, wiping tears from his eyes.

He pictured Liliana bound to a chair and watching as he bent the sexy little maid over the bed and pounded into her body. Aroused, he decided he most definitely would make good on his threats.

"What do you think?" he asked Ric.

The sadist grinned. "Forget I asked," he said and poured a cup of coffee from the serving cart Alison had left behind. "I heard from Santiago."

He resumed eating breakfast. "Are we on schedule?"

"They reached St. Louis last night around ten. Took care of business and then flew to Peoria, Illinois. Today they'll take care of the stops in Indiana and Ohio. Tomorrow, Tennessee and Virginia. We'll be set to go Monday morning."

"Excellent. And the hired help?"

Ric shrugged and took a seat. "Bright enough to do the job, but too dumb to know what they've gotten themselves in to."

The men Ric had hired were brothers who lived in the area.

The one brother had tried to find a job with his company and after he'd been quickly dismissed due to his prison record, he'd gone to a local bar where many of his crew would hang out and drink. While there, he'd proceeded to become inebriated and had spouted off about how he and his brainy brother had pulled off a bank robbery without even entering a bank. Santiago had been there. Knowing what he and Ric needed to flush out the bitch who had evaded him for eight years, the Columbian had called Ric. After looking into the brothers' background, he and Ric had decided they would not only be useful for this particular *job*, but easily dispensable.

"Very good." He pushed his plate aside. "And my speeches, are they ready?"

"Already on your desk. Of course I'm biased, but I think they're probably my best work to date. You'll look like a hero and leave the country longing to have a man like you in the White House."

He smiled. *President of the United States of America.* Now wouldn't that be some wild shit?

"Let's not get ahead of ourselves. Besides, could you imagine Liliana as my First Lady?"

Ric chuckled and shook his head. "You know my opinion of your wife."

He did. Which was why he wouldn't give Ric free reign over her. Yet. If she didn't die of malnourishment or suicide within the next year, then he'd let Ric do as he pleased. He couldn't imagine having to be married to the scrawny shrew for any longer than that.

"Speaking of which," Ric said and set his cup on the table. "If she is stupid enough to have an affair, please let me just kill her and her lover. I really don't want to cut another man's dick off. Aside from being a bloody mess, I wasn't bullshitting Liliana. The homophobe in me really couldn't stomach touching a man."

He laughed and pushed his chair back. "Ric, if you're going to eventually follow me to the White House, you're going to have to learn to become politically correct, as well as more accepting of our fellow Americans."

"Like you?" Ric asked.

"I'm very accepting," he said and feigned insult. Race, sexual preference, age, religion...he didn't care who he killed to obtain what he wanted. "And by Monday afternoon this country will be in chaos."

"They'll be looking for answers."

"No. They'll be looking for a savior."

"Amen," Ric said with a chuckle and made the sign of the cross. "If only they knew their lives depended on one woman."

He grinned. "True. But *she* will know and that's all that matters."

"And what will you do with her once she comes to you?"

"Everything and anything I want." She belonged to him and once he possessed her, he'd never let her free.

Naomi pressed a hand against her nervous stomach and looked around the kitchen. She'd sliced fruit, made blueberry muffins and had Jake's favorite egg casserole warming in the oven. The table was set and the coffee brewing. The only thing missing was Jake.

Nothing new there.

She'd been missing him from her life for too long. After last night and the way he'd held her and kissed her, she didn't want to force him to leave. Eventually she'd have no choice. For now she would, as she'd told herself last night, enjoy the moment. Savor his touch, his smile and the familiar comfort his presence gave her. God, and his rock hard body and all the wonderful things he could do with it.

Awareness settled in her core and brought her sex drive back to life again. Making love would be fulfilling and sensually satisfying. It would also be the best mistake she could make at this point in her life. In her heart she knew she'd have to deal with the aftermath of Jake's absence all over again. But she could refill the well with the love she'd suppressed for five years and in the process feel whole again. At least for a little while. Because once he left and the past was shoved back where it belonged, she'd be left with a loveless, lonely future.

A future that couldn't include Jake.

If she was going to enjoy the moment and the weekend they could have together, she needed to stop feeling sorry for herself and deal with the present. After the way he'd kissed her and made her body come alive, she had no doubt they'd finish what they had started last night. Only she'd seen the determination in his eyes before he'd left and she had to prepare herself for whatever questions he might ask her.

As she'd lain in bed last night, completely turned on and frustrated he'd chosen to leave, her mind had begun to spin. In between fantasizing about how the evening should have ended, it occurred to her that if Jake had run a background check using her social security number, he might have discovered that Naomi McCall didn't exist until eight years ago. Then again, knowing Jake, if that were the case he would have brought up her false identity right away. She couldn't imagine he'd have kissed her the way he had—hot, passionate— knowing she'd lied to him about her past.

Or would he?

"Damn it," she muttered and stared out the kitchen window. She had to prepare herself. If he wanted answers, she owed it to him to be as honest as possible without placing him in danger. But how?

With more lies.

The doorbell rang. Her stomach tightened with eagerness and trepidation. She had two more days with him and wanted to spend today and tomorrow in his arms. Not fighting or dredging up the past. As she left the kitchen and headed for the front door she decided to wing it. If he asked about her fake name, she'd give him enough information to satisfy his curiosity. If he asked why they couldn't try and make things work between them again...

She opened the door and drank in the sight of him. Every reason why they shouldn't be together fled from her mind, along with the lies she'd tell to protect them both. Instead, last night came back in a rush. The heat and hunger in his eyes. His hot open-mouthed kisses. The way he'd pressed her against the door and filled her with his fingers.

"Good morning," she managed, and motioned for him to come inside.

He closed the door behind him. With the same heat and hunger that had darkened his eyes last night, he cupped the back of her head and crushed his mouth against hers. Her heart raced and her body melted against his as she kissed him back. When she slid her hands over his tight ass, he quickly tore his lips away. "Morning," he said and holding her hand, took a step back. "You smell delicious."

"I smell like sausage."

"My favorite kind of perfume."

She chuckled and led him into the kitchen. "I wish I'd known that a long time ago. Instead of spending money on expensive perfume, I could have rubbed sausage all over my body."

"Eau de sausage. Now there's a sexy image."

Laughing at the ridiculousness, she let go of his hand and poured him a cup of coffee. "We can start a whole new perfume line. Eau de bacon or maybe eau de steak."

"Eau de Budweiser," he suggested, a grin playing across his kissable mouth. "I think we might be on to something."

"Maybe, but I'm not going to quit my day job yet. Hungry?"

His gaze raked over her bare legs, short shorts and tight tank top. She'd dressed with purpose this morning and, based on the desire in his eyes, it had worked. "Starved."

"Good. Take a seat. I made your favorite."

After she set the fruit and muffins on the table, she dished him a large slice of the casserole. "How'd you like your room at the Rainbow Lodge?" she asked and sat across from him.

He shrugged and picked up his fork. "The bed was lumpy and the room smelled like nicotine. The hot water lasted all of two minutes before I just about went into hypothermia."

"I'm sorry to hear," she said, a part of her satisfied. Maybe tonight he'd decide to forgo the Rainbow Lodge and crash at her place.

"You sound all broken up about it," he said with a smile.

Busted. "Hey, you're the one who insisted on leaving. My bed has no lumps, my room smells like lavender and I have a large hot water tank. You could take a twenty-minute shower without freezing." She picked up a muffin and eyed him. "Imagine the possibilities."

His smile fell and the look in his eyes turned carnal. "I did. All night long."

"So maybe you should consider your options tonight."

He looked down at his plate and dug into the casserole. "That depends."

"On?"

He set his fork down and wiped his mouth with his napkin. "You."

Oh, shit. He knows.

"Me?" she asked and played dumb. Maybe what he was hinting at had nothing to do with her false identity.

"Yeah. What's your real name?"

She froze. The muffin she'd just bitten into tasted like sawdust. So much for hinting at anything. Although she'd suspected he might question her about her identity, she hadn't expected him to be so blunt. With her mind quickly racing, along with her heart, she held his gaze. "Lisa Monroe," she lied. If he knew her real name, he could find out about her parents and brother, and about the circumstances surrounding their deaths. Knowing Jake, he'd go after the bastard who'd ruined her life and murdered her family. And Jake couldn't go after him. If he did, he'd die and she'd rather have lying on her conscience than his death.

"Lisa," he echoed, and she inwardly cringed at the distaste rolling off his tongue.

"But no one has called me that in eight years," she said. "And I'd like to keep it that way."

He picked up his fork again and pierced a chuck of the casserole. "Why the name change?" he asked as if they were discussing the weather.

She stared at him. Stunned. And worried. While he ate his eggs, his posture had gone from relaxed to rigid, his shoulders were now tensed and his biceps flexed from beneath his short sleeve shirt as if he were ready to pounce.

"I had issues with a stalker," she answered, giving him the skeletal version of the truth. "His threats had become so bad, I was forced to change my identity."

"Changing your name is one thing, but getting a new social security number? That's not easy to do." He plopped a grape in his mouth. "How'd you manage to keep your nursing license and college transcripts?"

Deep sorrow meshed with the anxiety churning in her stomach. Her brother, Thomas, had taken care of her identity change when she was twenty. But she'd lied to Jake when they'd first met and told him she was an only child. Thomas's career with the FBI was not something she would or could share with Jake. Her brother had insisted that if she were to go into hiding, she had to cut all ties. That included him.

"When I changed my name, I'd already spent a couple of years earning my nursing degree. So, I started from scratch as Naomi McCall, switched colleges and breezed through the program." Before she'd become Naomi McCall, she'd also claimed the life insurance benefits and inheritance her parents had left for her and Thomas. With a half a million dollars and a new name, she'd been lulled into thinking she'd escaped her stalker, met Jake and thought she could have it all. Love, family, career. Until Thomas had been brutally murdered because of her.

"You're right though," she said. "It wasn't easy to do, but it was something that needed to be done. I was tired of spending my life looking over my shoulder." She still was, but left that to herself. She'd answer Jake's questions, would likely compound the lies, but refused to tell him who had driven her off the grid. Jake had no problem with confrontation and sometimes lived in a fantasy world where justice always prevailed. In her world, justice would not come to the man who had destroyed her family and her life. His power stretched too far. His wealth was limitless. Bottom line, Jake, as much as she hated to admit it, couldn't stand up to him. Well, he could, but she knew firsthand how that would go. Thomas's crooked smile and laughing eyes filtered through her mind, along with his headstone.

"Where's this stalker now?" Jake asked and helped himself to a muffin.

"How can you keep eating while asking me questions I guarantee most people do *not* ask over breakfast?"

He shrugged. "I'm hungry and I miss your cooking. Where's the stalker?"

"You just asked me that," she said, growing irritated. Her insides were a mess. She was damned tired of the way the past continued to haunt her. And it pissed her off that Jake could continue to eat when all she wanted to do was vomit.

"So answer."

"Last I heard, Virginia." Another truth.

"He lives there?"

"As far as I know."

"What did he do to you?" he asked, his voice nonchalant but his eyes hard and probing. She was so onto him. He was trying to keep her at ease, but he had no idea how this conversation tore her apart. He had no idea how much she'd lost, and she'd make sure he never did. She remembered a quote that went something like, "There is no wealth like knowledge." In this case, knowledge would bring Jake death.

"Like I told you, he stalked me." She crumpled the napkin in her fist as disturbing memories punched her from the inside out. "He harassed me at my apartment, at my parents' house, at work and school. He called and emailed me constantly. I couldn't tell you how many times I've changed my number and email address." She shook her head. "But then the threats started."

Jake set his fork on the table and clenched his jaw. "And?" he asked, the single word harsh, demanding.

Her hand moved to her neck and her mouth went dry. That

night had been one of the scariest of her life and one she didn't want to relive. But there were some things she could tell Jake without really telling him anything. This was one of them. "One night I was cocktailing at a club and had just gotten back to my apartment. It was late, about three in the morning. I hung up my coat, got myself a glass of water…everything was normal, fine. When I went into my bedroom to change, he attacked me." She swallowed past the lump in her throat. "He wasn't alone." The man who left death in his wake always had an entourage with him. The Columbian man who had been with him that night at her apartment had always been a staple and at one time she'd thought he was his bodyguard. Although he probably was, she'd suspected Santiago also handled the dirty work. Like holding a knife against her throat. "The man he was with held the knife, while my stalker tore my shirt from my body and told me that if he couldn't have me, then no one could."

Because he'd robbed her of her family, she'd become numb to what had happened that night. She no longer experienced nausea when she thought about it, no longer cried. She saved her tears for those who mattered—her parents, brother and Jake.

"I was terrified, not because he'd kill me but because no one would know for sure it was him who did it. I kept thinking about my family, about what they'd go through. Pictured them standing in the morgue viewing my dead body." She drew in a deep breath. "I couldn't let that happen. So I screamed, loud and long, even when he and his *friend* tried to silence me with their fists. Thank God the walls to my apartment were paper-thin. My neighbor came banging on my door yelling that he'd called the police. The two men left through the window." She shrugged. "It was only a ten-foot drop."

"Did you report the attack?" he asked, his tone low and menacing, as if he had murder on his mind.

She shook her head. "You have to understand, he came from money and his family had a lot of influence. No one was going to believe me, a nineteen-year-old cocktail waitress, over

KRISTINE MASON

him. Besides, he was very careful and covered his tracks. Even though I could've had him arrested for attacking me at my apartment, he probably would've gotten out on bail and then…finished the job."

His forearms and biceps remained flexed, tense. His eyes narrowed and filled with hatred. "Who is he?"

She'd already told him too much. "It's in the past and I want to keep it there. I haven't been Lisa Monroe for eight years."

He leaned back in the chair and looked to his half empty plate. "Who is he?" he repeated.

"Someone you can't touch."

His eyes quickly captured hers. "Why?"

"Let it go, Jake." She stood, grabbed her plate and moved toward the sink. "I have."

His chair scraped against the tile. In seconds, he gripped her arm and spun her away from the sink. "Bullshit."

"Think what you want. I don't care."

"That's the problem. I do care," he said, his voice still harsh, but his eyes softening. "And I can't believe that you'd willing allow yourself to be bullied into being someone else, instead of fighting. Honestly, I can't believe your parents went along with it." He tightened his hold. "Are your parents really deceased? Did they know your plans?"

Tears filled her eyes as her mom and dad's faces swept through her mind. If only Jake knew the half of it. After she'd been attacked at her apartment, both she and Thomas had tried to talk their parents into changing their identities, too. Her mom and dad wouldn't hear of it. They were both in their late fifties, were zeroing in on retirement, had a ton of friends and refused to give up their lives. Although they were terrified on her behalf and wanted her safe, they'd wanted to go through the legal channels to end the stalking. Only her mom wound up dead in a car accident and her dad passed away two weeks later of a heart attack. But their deaths hadn't been accidental or natural. They'd been murdered. *He* had contacted her, showed up at both funerals and had made it crystal clear

62

that if she didn't come to him, everyone she loved would end up like her parents. Dead.

"Yes," she said on a sob, resenting Jake for reopening old wounds, the past, her mistakes, her regrets and guilt. "They knew, but died before I went through the process. Satisfied?"

Jake tried to reign in his hatred and rage for the asshole who had forced Naomi to change her identity and life. He pulled her closer and caught one of her tears with his thumb. "No." God, he was a dick. He hated himself for making her cry, but he'd come here to put the past to rest and had needed answers. He'd spent three years loving a woman who had been nothing but a lie, and then the next five years pining over her.

She jerked her head away and her arm free. "Too bad. If you're looking for an apology, then I'm sorry I lied to you about my name. I'm sorry for a lot of things. But enough. I've answered your questions, hopefully soothed your ego and—"

He crowded her against the counter, her earthy, flowery scent invading his senses and bringing back memories of last night, of the many nights he'd spent loving her body. "I'm not gonna lie. I was pissed you didn't trust me enough to tell me the truth about your past. But my ego has nothing to do with it."

"Now who's throwing out a line of bullshit?"

"Damn it, Naomi, I loved you. I wanted to marry you, grow old together and make a bunch of kids. And *that's* no bullshit." When more tears spilled down her cheek, he pushed away and turned his back on her. He didn't want to see her cry, didn't want to be the cause, but she had to understand. "Turn it around. How would you feel in my position? Wouldn't you want to know?"

He flinched when her hand touched his shoulder. "Yes," she said, her voice raw, pained. "I would. But now that you do, what's next?"

Running a hand through his hair, he shook his head while trying to come up with an answer. "Is this stalker the reason you left me?" he asked instead, hoping that was the case. Leaving him out of fear, he could handle. But if she'd left because of him, because she'd no longer loved or wanted to be with him…yeah, that would definitely be a blow to his ego.

"Please look at me," she said.

When he turned and caught the pain, misery and love in her eyes, he wanted to forget the entire conversation and haul her against his chest. Hold her, kiss her, give her comfort. "You don't have to answer me." He touched her tearstained cheek. "I'm sorry I put you through this. I'll leave if that's what you want."

Her lush lips tilted in a small smile. "I don't want you to go. And you're right. If our circumstances were turned around, I would want to know, too." She stepped closer, her breasts brushing his chest. "Leaving you was the hardest thing I've ever had to do. But I had no choice. *He* didn't give me any. I worried about him coming after me and you, so—"

"You left," he said, the wasted years suddenly weighing heavily on his shoulders. All because of one man, and Naomi's fear of him, they'd lost five years…their future.

"I'm sorry, Jake." Her chin trembled and her eyes watered. "I loved you so much, I couldn't bear to let anything happen to you. I worried if I told you about him, you'd get all macho and badass on me and go after him."

He cupped her face. "I'm a big boy."

Her grin filled his palms. "I remember how big you are."

Half chuckling, he shook his head. She always had a way of trying to lighten the tension. And he was wound tight, filled with anger and bloodlust. He wanted her stalker dead and he'd find a way to make it happen. Fuck Ian's cold case. He'd just given himself a new assignment. "Tell me who he is and I'll put a stop—"

She kissed him hard and quick. Resting her forehead against his chest, she let out a sigh. "No. Please, let it go." She raised her head. "Promise me."

"I don't like it, but…I promise." Hell, she'd been lying to him the entire time they'd known each other, what was another lie? He smoothed her thick hair away from her face and held her head. "Five years is a long time. Maybe it's time to stop running."

Her eyes searched his. "I don't know how."

"You could start by not going at it alone."

"The risk—"

"Is something I'm willing to take."

She twined her arms around him and hugged him tight. Running his hands through her hair, he slid them down and held her against him. She'd carried this burden for a long time. Alone. But she didn't have to deal with this on her own anymore. Given the chance, he would do anything to have her back in his life. When they'd been together, he'd loved her so damned much. During the years they'd been separated, he'd told himself he was over her, that the love he'd harbored for her hadn't been as real as he'd once thought. Now that he held her again, he knew in his gut he'd been lying to himself. Naomi or Lisa, her name didn't matter, had and always would be the only woman he'd love.

Although they'd squared away the past, they hadn't settled the future. He'd pushed her enough today, and once he tracked down her stalker and took care of him, he'd push her again. Hopefully back into his life. For now...

"I have to be back in Chicago on Monday," he said and tightened his hold on her. "Unless you've changed your mind, I want to spend the weekend with you."

She let go of him and swiped at her face. "Does this mean you won't be sleeping on the Rainbow Lodge's lumpy bed?"

"That's what I'm hoping."

"Me too." She grinned. "Um, I came up with some things we could do today."

The stalker momentarily forgotten, his mind slid into the gutter. After tasting her lips last night, feeling her come around his fingers, he had a few ideas as to what they could do today, too. "Yeah? What are you thinking?" he asked and drifted his hands to her rear.

"I have fishing gear in the garage. I thought we'd head over to Harriett's Bluff. We could rent canoes or kayaks, or fish from the floating dock. It's also a good spot for shrimping or crabbing." She ran her hands over his chest. "We can catch our dinner. Unless, of course, you have something else in mind."

He loved fishing and hadn't had the chance since moving to Chicago. Although he'd rather strip Naomi naked, spending the day with her, talking and catching up was almost just as appealing. Almost.

"I had a few things in mind," he said and squeezed her ass for emphasis. "But I like your idea. Fresh fish for dinner sounds good to me."

She grinned and relaxed in his arms. "Excellent. Maybe later this evening you could show me what you had in mind."

He tilted her chin, grazed his lips against hers, then sank in and gave her a long, leisurely kiss. Although aroused and wanting more, he released her mouth, and pressed her against his erection. "We have five years to catch up on. I plan on showing you all night long."

CHAPTER 4

HARRISON'S SKIN PRICKLED with dread. At the same time, his stomach balled with a potent mixture of excitement and anxiety. He sprang from the chair and moved the motel curtain a fraction of an inch. Then watched as Vlad looked both ways, before crossing the busy intersection toward the convenience store.

Now or never.

He rushed back to the small table and opened the laptop. He quickly glanced at the alarm clock setting on the nightstand and noted the time. Vlad would only be gone for five, maybe seven minutes. For what he had to accomplish, he needed every single second.

Heart racing, he moved his fingers across the keyboard and opened the system file that controlled the security devices the Columbian and Mickey had been planting across the country. He quickly logged on to the Internet, used a code he'd created to make his actions untraceable, should his employer do a little exploring into the system, and accessed his Cloud service.

Drumming his fingers on the table, his leg jerking in time as he glanced at the clock again, he waited for the files he'd placed within his Cloud to appear on the screen. "Hell, yeah," he whispered when several programs emerged. He quickly accessed the one he knew he'd have time to install. After entering his encrypted password, and the program showed up, he attached it to the laptop's system files.

Eyes on the clock, then again on the screen, he waited. And

waited.

He'd gone to prison for hacking into a bank and shifting money from customer accounts to the one he'd set up for him and Mickey. While the Norfolk PD had confiscated his computer and all of his files, they hadn't been able to find the Cloud he'd set up prior to his arrest. His Cloud account held programs he'd created. Some were quite brilliant and would likely benefit any company looking for a strong deterrent from hackers, malware and viruses. Others were exactly what those companies would fear. The program he was currently downloading wouldn't give the laptop a virus—he just didn't have the time to upload it and still cover his tracks—but it would serve as insurance. The program, which he called Martha, after the pet hamster in his fifth grade class, would create a digital footprint that would identify domain names and networks associated to the company he'd been hired by, and access the company's network. While he hadn't looked at the program in years, and he'd likely need to make a couple of quick adjustments, once finished, the program should be able to scan the company's operating system and extract valid user accounts. From there, the data filtered should show encrypted passwords, erase his current activities and create backdoors. Although Harrison doubted he'd have another opportunity like the one he had right now, should he find himself alone with the laptop again, he *could* easily gain privileged access and return to the compromised system.

He looked to the clock again. Three minutes had passed. He glanced at the screen. Eighty percent complete. Jaw clenched, he rushed to the window. With no sign of Vlad, he went back to the table.

Eighty-five percent.

If everything went to plan, anyone who found the devices Santiago and Mickey had been planting, could, if they knew what they were doing, link back to the company's main network. He'd ensure that the data transferred from the laptop to the devices was traceable. If the security devices were what he thought they were, his employer was going to go down. Big time.

Ninety percent.

"Come on, come on, come on," he said with frustration and fear, then looked to the clock. Four minutes.

He still needed to run a quick check to ensure the program worked properly.

Ninety-eight percent.

He glared at the clock. Five minutes. "Fuck me," he muttered and ran a hand through his hair, then looked to the screen.

One hundred percent.

"Yes," he hissed, quickly moved to the window and froze. Vlad exited the convenience store holding two Styrofoam cups. He set them on the ledge in front of the store's window and drew out a pack of cigarettes. As Vlad tapped the pack against his palm, Harrison knew he only had a matter of seconds before he needed to shut down the laptop.

He dashed across the room. Not bothering to sit down, he hovered over the laptop, quickly scanned the program and made a few minor adjustments, then exited the system. After making sure he wiped away his Internet activity, he logged off and closed the laptop.

Mouth dry and a sheen of nervous sweat coating his face and neck, he headed into the bathroom just as the motel door opened. After splashing water on his face, he took a towel off the rack and left the bathroom, drying himself. "Did they have any donuts?" he asked and kept his eyes off the laptop. When Vlad had left to buy a pack of cigarettes, the laptop had been closed and setting on the center of the table. Just like it was now.

No need to panic. No need to worry. When the Columbian and Mickey returned, Harrison would be the only one using the laptop. If there was an issue, he could kill the program he'd implanted with a few strokes to the keyboard.

Vlad nodded to the Styrofoam cup near the outdated TV. "No donuts, but Vlad brought Harry coffee. No cream, right?"

He sent the Russian a half smile. "With as much time as

we've spent together, I think you're starting to know me better than my last girlfriend."

Vlad released a loud bark of laughter and wagged a finger. "No go there, Harry." Vlad withdrew a cylinder package from his coat pocket and tossed it to him. "No *fresh* donuts."

Harrison stared at the package of Hostess Donettes mini donuts. Powder sugar, his favorite. "Thanks, man. For the coffee, too. These weird hours are screwing with me."

"It good for Harry. Vlad? He can stay wake for thirty hours without shuteye."

"No shit?" Harrison asked and opened the cellophane wrapping. "The most I've managed was twenty-two. That was my first night in prison. I was too frickin' scared to close my eyes."

The Russian laughed again. "Vlad understand." He grew serious, his expression almost thoughtful. "Vlad no can picture Harry in prison. Harry too...ah, the word, Vlad no remember."

"Nerdy?" Harrison offered.

Vlad snapped his fingers, then took out his cigarettes and lighter. "Yes. Your brother, the mouse? He no good for Harry. Vlad believe Mickey Mouse get Harry in trouble."

He already has. More times than he cared to count.

"Mickey's a good guy. He just needs direction."

The Russian frowned and took a long drag off the cigarette. "Maybe. Or maybe Harry need to grow яйца яички," he said, finishing in Russian and grabbing his crotch. "Who planned bank robbery that put Harry in prison?"

Harrison wiped powdered sugar on the towel. "It was Mickey's idea, but it's not like I told him no."

"Before that? Who put Harry in the kiddie jail?"

Chuckling, Harrison picked up the Styrofoam cup. "It's call juvenile detention or just juvie, not kiddie jail. And even though what had landed us there was Mickey's idea, again, I went along with it."

"Vlad curious. I like Harry, but not the Mouse. Harry smart. A computer wizard, no?"

"That's why I'm here, right?"

The Russian smiled and snuffed out his cigarette. "Why not go to university, get nerdy job? Why follow the mouse when Harry could be big cheese?" he asked and laughed. "Get it? Mouse, cheese."

Harrison smiled, but inwardly cringed. He'd been asking himself those same questions for years. When he'd been released from juvie, his parole officer had told him to break away from Mickey. That he'd go nowhere but prison if he continued to follow his brother's lead. But he'd ignored the advice and a few years later had wound up in the Virginia Department of Corrections.

"I get it," Harrison said, popping the last donut in his mouth.

"Do you? Take Vlad's advice. Cut tie with the mouse." He reached into his pocket and took out his cell phone. "Ah, text from Santiago. They'll be here in ten. Hurry. Drink coffee. Vlad no want Santiago to know I went to store."

"Got it," he said, even though he really didn't. Was Vlad afraid of Santiago? The Columbian scared the shit out of him, but he couldn't imagine Vlad being afraid of anything. The Russian's size alone could intimidate anyone.

Draining his coffee, he handed the cup and the donut wrapper to Vlad, who stepped out of the motel room and disposed of the trash in a nearby garbage can. When he returned, he gave Harrison a pointed look. "Remember what Vlad told Harry. Cut ties. When we arrive in Norfolk and job is kaput, you listen to Vlad. Finish job. Take money and run to university."

"Got any brothers or sisters?" Harrison asked, unsure why the Russian decided to have this little heart to heart conversation.

Vlad gave him a big grin. "Ten of them."

"Any of them your twin?"

The Russian frowned. "Mickey Mouse is twin brother?" He shook his head. "Vlad never guess. You no look like twins."

"Trust me, we are. And I hear where you're coming from. But this job is legit, so I think Mickey and me will be okay." He kept his focus on Vlad, looking for any indication that the job they were on was *not* on the up and up. Instead, he received another grin.

"Harry right. You be okay, but Vlad still think university where Harry belong. Maybe you meet sexy co-ed, eh?" he asked and wagged his blond brows.

The motel door opened and Vlad immediately tensed. "Job done?" he asked Santiago.

The Columbian nodded as Mickey came inside and closed the door behind him. "*Sí, es completo.*" He looked to Harrison. "Sync it and we leave."

Harrison glanced at Mickey, who wore a blank expression. Mickey had drastically changed since they'd been with Vlad and Santiago. He no longer smiled or joked around, but instead had become quiet, brooding…fearful.

"Will do," Harrison said and, praying to God that everything had closed properly on the computer, he opened the laptop. It booted up without issue, the program he'd installed earlier nowhere in sight. With relief slowing his racing heart, he took a seat and went through the task of syncing the laptop to the device. Ten minutes later, they were ready to leave Bloomington, Indiana.

"If you have to use the head, do it now," Santiago said. "It's three and a half hours to Columbus, Ohio. I want to push through, install the device and *tomar la carretera.*"

"говорят по-английски, Колумба," Vlad said in Russian.

Santiago's forehead scrunched. "What the hell did you say?"

"Speak English, Columbian," Vlad said with a smile.

Laughing, Santiago slapped Vlad on the back. "Sorry, *amigo*. Bad habit. What I said is that I want to hit the road and leave Ohio this evening. It's almost five hours to Knoxville from Columbus."

"See if Honey Badger will give us plane," Vlad suggested.

"Good plan," Santiago responded and pulled his cell phone from his pocket. "I don't mind driving to Columbus, but Knoxville?"

As Santiago placed the call, Harrison looked to his brother. Mickey kept his head down and his eyes on the floor. Whatever Santiago had him doing, it was messing with Mickey's head. If only he could find a moment to talk to his brother, but Vlad and Santiago had made that impossible from the start. And who in the hell is Honey Badger? He'd heard the two men mention the name before, and assumed that was the code name they were using for their employer.

Whoever Honey Badger was, he was in for a big surprise. Although the *security* devices would still work, thanks to the program Harrison had installed while Vlad was at the store, those same devices would link straight back to the bastard once used.

Harrison hoped like hell the authorities knew what to look for when they finally found the devices. If they didn't...people would die.

He rose from the chamois-soft leather office chair and approached the large windows overlooking the vast acreage surrounding his estate. The labyrinth in the center of the backyard had been created over eighty years ago. Made of tall manicured hedges and covering three quarters of an acre, the maze had fascinated him as a child. Especially because, according to his father and grandfather, at the center of the labyrinth buried treasure had been left behind by his great-grandfather, who had commissioned the structure.

His great-grandfather, who he was named after, had been a crazy son of a bitch. Under his rule the family business had lost speed. More money had been spent on extravagant and useless things, like the labyrinth, than the company had earned. When the old bastard had died, his grandfather had not only turned the company around, but had been prepared to tear down the maze. Fortunately his namesake had left a clause in his will protecting the intricate cluster of hedges. To his grandfather, the labyrinth had embodied failure. To him, it symbolized challenge and disappointment.

A knock came at the door. The same eagerness that had run through him as a child, when he'd fantasize about the labyrinth's treasure, ran through him now. "Enter," he said and glanced over his shoulder as the door opened.

The pretty maid, Alison, pushed a serving cart into the office and gave him a shy smile. "The lunch you requested, sir. Shall I set the table for you?"

He looked to the large table in the corner of the office. "No, just leave the cart by the table. I'll serve myself."

As Alison did as he asked, he stared at her curvy hips and ass. If he recalled, she'd only been employed for about six months. Yet there was something about her that reminded him of someone else he knew. Not that he cared. But for what he had planned it might be in his best interest to know a little more about the woman. As he'd told his pathetic wife, he did have a reputation to maintain.

"Will there be anything else?" she asked.

He motioned her to him. "I'm sure your duties don't give you the luxury to stop and take in the beauty of my estate. Come. I'd like to show you something."

Wariness and curiosity shown in her green eyes. She placed a hand to her flat stomach and the other to the bun holding back her dark blonde hair. "I don't want to disturb—"

"Think nothing of it. I could use a little company." He could use a good fucking. "Please, come look."

She moved across the room, her steps light and tentative, until she stood a few feet away from him. When she glanced out the window, her eyes widened. "I've never seen the maze from this view," she said.

Considering she worked in the kitchen and Mrs. Burrows, his head housekeeper, ran a tight ship, he'd figured as much. "What do you think of it?"

"It's beautiful." She smiled. "And a little on the scary side."

"Scary? Interesting. Why do you say that?"

She looked at him hesitantly.

"Please, speak freely."

"Well," she began and glanced out the window. "When I

first began working here, Mrs. Burrows showed me part of the grounds. She took me to the entrance of the maze and told me all the pathways combined equaled nearly a mile, and that the shrubbery stood about six feet. She led me inside and I couldn't help feeling claustrophobic. The hedges are so immense, I swear I felt like they blocked out the sun."

"Or maybe you're just short," he said with a smile and eyed her petite body.

She grinned. "True. I don't know. I guess maybe I don't like not knowing which direction to go or, more importantly, if I can find my way back."

"You sound like my mother. She hated the maze and hated when I'd disappear inside of it." He took a step closer to the maid and leaned against the window ledge. "When I was nine, I would sneak away from my tutors and nannies and lose myself in the complex paths. You're right, the pyramidal cedars that make up the maze are six feet tall and I could see how they'd intimidate you."

"They didn't bother you?" she asked, her posture relaxing. "Even at nine?"

"Did Mrs. Burrows tell you how there's supposed to be buried treasure within the maze?"

Alison raised her dark blonde brows. "Buried treasure?" she asked, her tone skeptical.

"Yes, that's right. Supposedly my great-grandfather had buried riches near the center of the maze once it had been complete. Even though I was only nine, you better believe I was determined to find the buried treasure and, because I'd been told about my great-grandfather's elaborate and expensive eccentricities, I imagined discovering a treasure chest filled with gold coins, diamonds, rubies and ancient Egyptian artifacts. After all, my great-grandfather had traveled the world and visited exotic locations. What kid wouldn't have fantasized about treasure?"

"And? Did you find it?" she asked, her tone a combination of excitement and skepticism.

"It took me almost an entire summer to reach the center.

I'd carry strips of different colors of ribbon in a backpack and tie the ribbon around branches so I could map out where I've been and where I needed to go. The day I found the center I swear was one of the best days of my life. I'd proven to myself that I could accomplish what I'd considered impossible. Of course, I was a kid, and kids do tend to be melodramatic."

She chuckled. "Yes, they do. But I imagine you had to have been so proud of yourself."

He moved closer. "I was. Using the colored ribbons, I ran back to the house, collected a shovel and pick from the caretaker's garage, then ran back to the center of the maze. I worked throughout the day and evening, digging holes. Then did the same thing every day for several weeks. But I didn't find the treasure." What he had found had made him realize his great-grandfather truly was a crazy son of a bitch. Instead of gold coins, diamonds, rubies and ancient Egyptian artifacts, he'd found bones. Human bones.

Her eyes softened and she nodded. "That had to have been disappointing, especially after you worked so hard and had such high hopes."

"It was," he said and moved behind her, pointing toward the labyrinth. "See the center?" He rested one hand on her shoulder.

"Barely. All I can see is the top of a magnolia tree."

"Yes, but that magnolia tree and the ground surrounding it taught me something that day." It had taught him that the maze was a perfect place to keep secrets. "I can act like a mouse in a maze, darting from one path to another, hitting walls until I find a piece of cheese. Or, I could take a bulldozer to those same walls, knock every obstacle out of my way and reach the prize without breaking a sweat."

"But there wasn't a prize at the center. You said—"

"The prize was knowledge. I didn't find a treasure chest, but I accomplished what I'd set out to do. What I learned was that I can do *anything* I want."

Her shoulder tensed beneath his palm. "No one can do anything they want."

"How old are you?"

"Twenty-two."

He inhaled her youth and light, flowery scent. "Have you run into any obstacles in your life?" he asked, not caring but proving a point. "A proverbial maze that had you running into walls and keeping you from the prize?"

"Yes. Money has always been tight. I wanted to go to college, but couldn't afford it. My mom was a housekeeper and I swore I wouldn't do the same thing as her, only…I'm a single mom. I have a two-year-old and when there are bills to pay, you do what you have to do."

She had a child? Well, at least the kid would be too young to remember its mother. Lust, the excitement of finding his lost possession and the bullshit he'd been forced to listen to from his pitiful wife had him craving more than sex. He required dominance. He needed to confirm his power and control.

"I understand," he said to keep her at ease.

Scoffing, she looked at him. "Not to sound disrespectful, but you can't possibly know what it's like to live check to check, to worry about the lights being shut off or whether you'll be able to feed your kid." She glanced down. "I'm sorry. That was out of line. I should go. Your lunch will end up cold if I keep you any longer."

He unzipped the back of her uniform. She quickly jerked away and spun, her hands gripping the window ledge. "Sir, this is inappropriate. Mrs. Burrows will be expecting—"

"Get on your knees," he ordered. If the girl were smart, she'd do as she was told. He hadn't been lying. He could do anything he wanted and get away with it. He had the money, the power, the name and over a dozen of dead men and women buried in the labyrinth to prove it.

When she didn't move, didn't look at him, he crowded her against the window. "Do it. Now."

"No." She glared at him. "I quit. This is one obstacle I don't need," she said, her voice shaking as she pushed passed him.

He hated when they fought him. What a pain in the ass. He grabbed her arm. Standing taller than the pyramidal cedars in the labyrinth and probably outweighing the maid by nearly one hundred pounds, he shoved her to the floor with ease. "I refuse to accept your resignation. Now do as you're told. Trust me. It's in your best interest."

Tears streamed down her cheeks and hatred darkened her eyes. "You have everything in the world. Money, a beautiful house, cars, yachts, planes. I had so much respect for you," she said with disgust and contorted her pretty face. "But you're nothing but a piece-of-shit rapist."

He thought about what she said for a moment, then shook his head. "No, I'm not. I've never forced myself on a woman."

"Then what do you call this?"

"Coercion."

"Same thing."

He glanced at his watch. His lunch would indeed be ice cold by the time he finished with the maid. Plus he had a conference call in an hour. But he wanted the maid and now that he'd gone this far, he really had no choice but to finish what he'd started. So much for her being shy and timid like he'd thought. She apparently had the backbone his wife lacked and would have to be dealt with before she blabbed about this to anyone who would listen. Like the press. The police he could handle. He had enough cops on his payroll to make this go away. But the press? The fucking bloodsuckers would love to knock him off his pedestal.

"Actually, it's not the same thing. Here's the deal, Alison. I'm going to coerce you into doing what I want, not by force, but by threat. In my mind, there's a difference. The two-year-old you mentioned. Do you love it? Would you do anything to make sure it had a happy life?"

Her eyes widened with fear as more tears streamed down her cheeks. Chin trembling, she unzipped the front of his Brioni suit pants. "My son is not an *it*. I'll do what you want. But please leave him out of this."

He sighed when she touch him, her silky soft hands

bringing him so much pleasure. "You have my word. No harm will come to your son. Now suck."

As she obeyed, he stared out the window, at the labyrinth that had taught him to embrace disappointment and, as the saying went, make lemonade out of lemons. When he'd discovered the human bones in the maze, he'd initially been pissed for having wasted his entire summer searching for treasure. But then he'd realized he'd stumbled upon something. Something rare and true.

He'd never told his father or grandfather or anyone else for that matter about the bones, but had barraged them with questions about his great-grandfather. He'd also done quite a bit of his own research. In the end, he had learned that his namesake wasn't necessarily a crazy son of a bitch, but Machiavellian. He'd been a deceitful opportunist who'd schemed and connived. He'd rid himself of those who had threatened his ways. And while his father and grandfather had been convinced his great-grandfather had squandered the company's money, they'd been wrong. He'd found that money. He'd found the buried treasure—millions of dollars in cash and jewelry—hidden throughout the estate. He'd also found information. Enough evidence to extort and destroy his family's enemies. By the time he'd made his discoveries, his grandfather had already been six feet under for several years. But his father had remained in his way. The treasure he'd discovered had allowed him to usurp the man who had fathered him, take his life and take control of the company.

He looked away from the maze and stared at Allison. "Suck harder," he told the maid and gripped her head. His cell phone rang. He released a frustrated groan and withdrew the phone from his pants pocket.

"Don't stop," he said to the girl, then answered the call. "What is it?"

"I just heard from Santiago," Ric replied. "They're getting ready to head to Columbus now."

He gritted his teeth as his orgasm approached. "Good. Anything else. I'm in the middle of something."

"Yeah, Santiago wants to know if there's any way they can charter a plane from Columbus to Knoxville and avoid the five and a half hour drive."

He slid his eyes closed at the pleasure the maid gave him. "No. I don't want them drawing any attention to themselves. They need to stay on the road."

"Understood. I'll let him know."

"How long will that take?"

"Ah, minutes. I just need to call him back."

"Good. Come to my office when you're done," he said, then disconnected the call. Once the maid finished servicing him, he'd turn her over to Ric. For once, he'd let his right hand man have more fun than usual.

He looked down at the girl. He'd had high hopes for her. Had pictured tormenting his wife, forcing the pathetic, scrawny bitch to watch as he had his way with the maid.

Such a shame. Ric would eventually kill her, once the fun was over.

And she'd end up with the others…buried in the labyrinth.

Santiago pocketed his cell phone and climbed into the SUV's driver's seat. Based on the scowl the Columbian wore, Harrison assumed the news wasn't good.

"Well?" Vlad asked. He'd been sitting next to Harrison in the back seat.

Shifting gears, Santiago hit the gas. "We drive. Honey Badger wants us to stay on the road. It's less conspicuous."

Vlad looked to him. "Define conspicuous, nerd Harry. Vlad know not this word."

"Noticeable," Harrison responded. "Your Honey Badger wants us to maintain a low profile."

The Russian nodded as if he understood the reasons behind the inconspicuous use of the SUV versus the plane, then leaned his head against the headrest. "Good. Planes scare Vlad. Especially small ones."

Honey badger scared Harrison. Especially because he

couldn't be one hundred percent sure what the man was up to. When Santiago turned on the satellite radio to a Latin station, Harrison turned to Vlad. "Is Honey Badger your boss?"

"Yes." Vlad rolled his head to the side. "Do not ask real name," he said in a hushed tone.

Harrison shook his head. "I won't, but..."

"Go ahead, Harry. Trust Vlad."

"Why do you call him Honey Badger?"

The Russian glanced toward Santiago, then back to him. "Because Honey Badger don't give a shit, he do what he want and get what he want. If you go after him, he attack. Keep Vlad words in mind when Harry meet him," Vlad said quietly. "I work seven years for Honey Badger. Trust Vlad. Harry no want to mess with Honey Badger."

He do what he want and get what he want.

And he'd kill a lot of people in the process.

Stomach nauseated with guilt, head aching with regret and anger, Harrison leaned into the seat and closed his eyes. His program *had* to work. If this Honey Badger was up to what Harrison believed, the man needed to be stopped. Unless he found another opportunity to be alone with the computer and add the virus he'd created before going to prison, his program was all he had to combat his employer. He couldn't talk to Mickey about any of this. Hell, he couldn't find a moment alone with his brother. As much as Vlad kept telling him to trust him, Harrison wasn't convinced. Vlad had worked for Honey Badger for seven years. His loyalties would be to his boss, not him.

Damn it, Mickey. What the hell did you get us into?

The better question... How in the hell could he disable the devices before it was too late?

81

CHAPTER 5

JAKE WIPED SWEAT from his brow and finished hanging the fishing poles and nets in the garage. He turned, then rushed back to his rented SUV. "I've got that." He took the cooler from Naomi.

"It's not heavy," she said, her toned biceps shaking from the strain.

He understood her independence and need to take care of herself. In this instance, hell, from the moment she'd told him about her identity change and stalker, she no longer needed to prove her strength or rely on only herself.

Now that he knew the truth, he wanted her to unburden the weight she'd been carrying and lean on him. His boss might piss him off, but Ian ran a private investigation agency that had a nearly impeccable track record for solving cases. CORE could give him what he needed to solve the mystery behind Naomi's stalker. As they'd sat on the floating dock at Harriett's Bluff, fishing and shrimping, he'd been tempted to discuss this with her several times throughout the day. Try to turn her on to the idea of allowing him to investigate and ultimately stop her stalker from ever threatening her again.

Yet each time he'd prepared himself to bring up the topic, she would flash him a smile and make him forget about everything but her. Or, she'd start talking and joking around like they used to do, as if being apart hadn't mattered. Only it did matter. The hatred he harbored for the man who had caused their separation consumed him with resentment and the need for revenge. He wanted to rip the son of a bitch's beating heart from his chest. Of course, he'd beat the piece of shit to a bloody pulp first and that would be after he'd destroyed—

"Where are you?"

Holding the cooler filled with their leftover lunch, along with a big bag of ice and the fish and shrimp they'd caught, he looked at her. "Sorry," he said, tamping down his plans of vengeance and sending·her a reassuring smile. "Where do you want the cooler? Back patio or kitchen?"

She reached into the back end of the SUV and pulled out the wet towel that had been beneath the cooler. "Patio. That thing leaks," she said, nodding to the cooler.

Using the garage entrance, he followed her inside, wound his way through the house, then out onto the patio. Sweat trickled down his back and he swore he could still taste the salt that had been in the air around the tidal marsh.

He turned when Naomi stepped onto the patio, then grinned when he noticed the beer bottles she carried. "Thanks," he said when she offered him one. "I can't believe how hot it is here."

She pressed the beer bottle against the skin exposed above her tight tank top, drawing his attention to her breasts. "In April it's normally in the mid-seventies, but the temperatures have been crazy hot the past week. Be prepared, it'll drop into the fifties tonight."

She took a drink of her beer. He did the same, his focus still on her breasts. Hell, throughout the day, he'd been looking at them and her ass whenever he had the chance. He loved her body, had loved feeling her against him last night and ached to strip her naked and have a proper reunion.

"I need a shower," she said, turning toward the sliding door. "Since the fish are already cleaned and filleted, it won't take long to cook them. We can eat in an hour or so. Unless you're hungry now."

He *was* hungry. Not for dinner, but for her. Picturing her naked and standing beneath the shower spray, water sliding down her breasts, her flat stomach and curvy hips had him hard and ready.

"I can wait," he said, then chugged half his beer, telling himself not to rush anything. They'd had a great day. Caught a bunch of seafood, caught up on each other's lives, created new memories. He needed to exercise patience. Since he had no intention of returning to the Rainbow Lodge, he had all night to spend with Naomi. Whether he'd spend it in her bed, he wasn't one hundred percent sure. But based on the small touches she'd given him while they'd been fishing and shrimping and the quick glimpses of desire in her eyes, he considered the odds were in his favor.

She paused at the door and glanced over her shoulder. "If you plan to stay the night, feel free to bring in your luggage. You can either use the guest bathroom shower or mine. There are fresh towels in either linen closet."

"Thanks," he said, his mind working quickly. Did she just invite him to take a shower with her? Maybe. Back when they had been living together, he'd never considered needing permission to join her in the shower. Naomi had always been a highly sexual woman and always welcomed his advances. In the shower, in the bed, against the kitchen counter—it didn't matter where.

He drained his beer and headed outside to his rental. After retrieving his small suitcase, he went back inside the house. When he stepped into the hallway, he noticed Naomi's bedroom door stood open and he could hear her shower running. As he walked down the hall, he considered his options. Strip out of his clothes and join her in the shower or use the guest bath. The former sounded better than the latter, considering it had been a while since he'd had sex.

Still.

After dropping his suitcase in the guest room, he opened it and grabbed his leather travel kit. Instead of heading for her shower, he stepped into the guest bathroom and turned on the shower. As the water warmed and he pulled his toiletries from the travel kit, he kept picturing Naomi. Sudsy water covering her nipples, dripping down her stomach and between her legs, leaving a tempting trail…

"Damn," he muttered and stripped out of his t-shirt and shorts. After dinner, after more conversation, he'd make his move. They hadn't made love since the night before she'd left Bola. He'd rather bite the bullet now, bank his lust and take his time with her later. Taste her, touch every inch of her body, sink into her heat. If he went to her now, he knew in his gut how things would play out between them. Turned on, his dick hard and aching, there'd be no finesse, no time to savor the taste of her, no time for slowly making love.

He shoved the shower curtain aside and stepped under the hot spray, then immediately turned the faucet to cold. He'd bitched about the freezing shower he'd been forced to take this morning at the Rainbow Lodge, but needed to do something to cool off his body and his lust.

Because he hated standing under the cold water, he finished his shower in record time. Towel around his waist, he stood in front of the mirror, applied deodorant, then finger combed his hair. Although the shower didn't do much to tame his arousal, he knew he'd done the right thing. Yesterday, they had relived and joked about how they'd met and the beginning of their relationship. Eight years ago, he'd been eager to sleep with her, not because of the bet he'd refused to make with his buddy, but because he'd fallen for her sweet smile and even sweeter personality. He hadn't minded waiting, though. If anything, the wait had only built up the anticipation and made their first time together that much hotter, sexier…hell, emotional.

You fell in love with a stranger.

He refused to think about that right now.

You didn't even know her real name.

So she'd lied about her name. She'd had good reason. So she had carried on the ruse even after they were engaged and living together. Did it really matter? Naomi could change her name a dozen times and she'd still be the same person on the inside. The same person he'd fallen in love with on the beach eight years ago. The same person he still loved.

All of this thinking about emotions and love, and why he

shouldn't have raced into her shower and taken her against the wall, messed with his head. Had him getting way too in touch with—*shit*—his feminine side.

Screw that.

He needed to do something manly. Chop wood, skin a deer, change a flat tire.

As he dressed, he couldn't help chuckling. There wouldn't be any wood chopping, deer skinning or tire changing going on at Naomi's. Instead, she'd probably have him peeling and deveining shrimp or dicing up salad fixings. So much for doing something manly. Then again, maybe he'd have a chance to show his man skills and smash one of those flying cockroaches he'd seen earlier in her backyard.

Dressed, looking presentable and now relaxed after amusing himself with a mental manly pep talk, he left the bathroom. He dropped his dirty clothes and travel kit with his suitcase in the guest room, then went into the hall again.

The door to Naomi's room was still wide open, but the shower was no longer running. Figuring she might be in the kitchen, he went in search of her. When he didn't find her there or on the patio, he headed toward her bedroom again. "Naomi?" he called and rapped on the opened door.

Wearing a towel wrapped around her body and brushing her long hair, she hovered at the bathroom doorway. "What's up?"

If only you knew. He eyed the towel and pictured it on the floor. "Nothing. Want me to fix you a drink or bring you a glass of wine?"

"Sure," she said with a slight shrug.

"Sure to which one? A drink or wine?"

"Whatever."

She stepped back into the bathroom, but he caught her reflection in the large mirror. He wasn't sure what had happened from the time she'd left the patio to now. Regardless, her mood had changed, and not in a good way.

Edging closer to the bathroom doorway, he made eye contact with her in the mirror. "Something wrong?"

She glanced at his damp head. "Nope. Find everything you needed in the *guest* bathroom?"

Holy hell. She was ticked he hadn't showered with her. Damn it. Instead of tormenting himself with ice cold water and all of those reasons why he shouldn't have come to her, he could have had a hot shower and, better yet, hot sex. "Not everything," he said and stepped inside her bathroom. Standing behind her, he looked to the mirror and kept his eyes on hers.

She ran the brush through her hair. "Oh? What did you need?"

He tugged at her towel, letting it slowly reveal her naked curves. "You," he said and ran his hands along her stomach, then up until he cupped her breasts.

Her lips parted when he caressed his thumbs along her nipples. She dropped the brush and leaned against his chest. "Why didn't you—" She slid her eyes closed and her breath caught when he tugged at her taut peaks. "Why didn't you join me in my shower?" she asked, her voice breathless.

Sliding one hand up her neck, he caught her chin and angled his head so that they were almost face-to-face. "Why didn't you just come right out and invite me?"

She reached behind and ran her hand along his erection. "Since when did you need an invite?"

Since you left me.

"Are you inviting me now?" he asked, massaging her breast.

Through his khaki shorts, she cupped his testicles, then palmed his length. "We both already showered. Besides, I need to make dinner."

"Dinner can wait." Moving his hand from her breast, he worked his way down her torso until he reached the apex of her thighs. "This can't." He dipped a finger into her heat, pulled out, then did it again. This time with two fingers. Her warm breath fanned against his mouth. Aching for a kiss, he leaned forward to graze his lips along hers, then tilted her chin until she faced the mirror again.

Her eyes, bright with desire, immediately dropped to where his fingers sank into her. With her arm still behind her, she continued to grip and stroke his length. "Are you sure?" she asked, her tone embodying sex.

Moving his hand from her chin, he cupped her breast. At the same time he withdrew his fingers from her heat and brought them to his mouth. As he tasted her, he kept his eyes on hers, loved how her gaze darkened with a hunger that matched his own.

He pressed his erection against her palm. "Positive," he said, settled his hands on her hips, swiveled her around and lifted her onto the counter. Needing to taste more of her, he lowered to the bath mat and spread her legs.

The instant his tongue made contact with her sex, she gripped his head and raised one heel to the counter and the other on his shoulder. Open and exposed for him, he pushed his hands between the countertop and her bottom, cupped her sweet ass and raised her to his mouth. He ran his tongue along her labia, then in between her folds. He kissed her sex as if he were kissing her mouth. Swept his tongue inside her and used his thumbs to spread her lips.

Her breath quickened and she released a soft moan as she grasped his hair. Damn, how he'd missed her. Her taste, her scent, her smile and her touch.

Mouth still locked on her, he watched as her beautiful face contorted in ecstasy. Wanting to give her more, aching to taste her orgasm before he stripped naked and buried himself in pleasure, he lashed his tongue along her clit.

Over and over.

Her silky soft legs began to tremble. Her breasts rose and fell, her nipples hard and begging for his attention. But that would have to wait. Even after five years, he remembered the signs. Knew when she was close. As much as he'd love to drag out this moment, afraid it wouldn't happen again or that he'd wake up and realize it was nothing but a dream, he was wound tight and needed her to come. He needed to be inside of her. To remind her of how they used to be together. Of how they still could be, if she gave them a second chance.

Knowing what she liked and how to please her, he flicked

his tongue hard and fast until she arched her back and pressed his head against her heat. As she held his head steady, moaning her pleasure, he latched onto her clit, tugging and sucking, tasting her orgasm.

Drawing in a deep breath, she pulled his head back, looked down and gave him a sexy smile. The last time he'd seen a smile that sexy had been the last time they'd been together. No other woman had been able to match Naomi. Not sexually and certainly not emotionally. He still loved her. Still wanted to be with her. He wanted to tell that to her now, but knew it wasn't the right time. They were on a road of rediscovery. And he worried if he said too much, too soon, he'd wind up having to make a U-turn, sending him back to being alone and without her.

Determined to give her multiple reasons to keep him in her life, he stood and scooped her off the counter. Capturing her lips, he poured his passion and emotions into the kiss and carried her to the bed.

The moment Jake set her on the mattress, Naomi reached for the waistband of his khaki shorts. She'd been disappointed when he hadn't joined her in the shower. They'd had such a great day, and after their conversation this morning, he'd acted as if he held nothing against her for lying about her name change. Yet when he hadn't bothered to show up in her bathroom, insecurity had set in and she'd begun to think that maybe he'd lost interest in being physical with her, or that maybe he really was upset after all. His skillful mouth and fingers had knocked all of those thoughts right out the door. As she shoved his shorts and boxer briefs over his lean hips, and he ran his big rough hands over her back and shoulders, the only thing she wanted to think about, the only thing she *could* think about was removing his clothes. It had been so long since they'd been together, she needed him. His hard, naked body on top of her. Filling her. Reuniting in the most hot and intimate way.

Once his shorts and boxers hit the floor, she scrambled to her knees, bent and took his length into her mouth. She looked up at him. Caught the satisfaction and hunger in his dark eyes just before he pulled his t-shirt over his head and dropped it on the bed. Like she'd done to him, he held her head, taking a fistful of hair and moved it away from her face.

Moving her mouth over his erection, she stroked him with one hand and cupped his testicles with the other. They'd been together for three years before she'd been forced to leave him. During the time they'd been apart, she'd fantasized about him, would lie in bed wishing he was beside her. Loving her. Kissing her. Making her body come alive.

Knowing he would leave, that she'd make him leave, she focused on now. He was here and she wanted to take advantage of every moment she could spend with him. Memories of kisses and touches that had once been so familiar and an everyday occurrence had mocked and taunted her for years. The memories they would make this weekend would follow suit. Loving the possessive way he tugged at her hair, his rough, rapid breathing, the way he pulsed in her mouth, she didn't care. Maybe she was selfish or maybe she was a glutton for punishment, either way she wanted what he could give her. After being away from him, being alone and carrying so many unwanted evils, she needed him to remind her she wasn't dead inside.

He blew out a deep breath. Still holding her hair back with one hand, he touched her cheek with the other. Running her tongue up his length, she met his gaze. His lips tilted in a small smile. "You're so damned sexy," he said, his voice husky. "Come here."

The bed dipped as he rested his knees on the mattress. When he brought their bodies together, she twined her arms around his neck and kissed him. Skin to skin, chest to breast. The warmth of his body radiated where they were connected. As he swept his tongue into her mouth, tangling it with her own, he used both hands and caressed her back, her rear, her thighs. He pressed against her inner thigh, forcing her leg to widen, then slipped his fingers into her sex. As much as she loved having his skilled fingers on her, she wanted more and moved slightly to grasp his length.

"I need you inside me," she said, stroking him.

He pressed himself into her hand. "Are you still on the pill?"

"No. Don't you have a condom on you?"

Sinking his fingers deep, he tugged at her long hair. "I haven't carried a condom around since I met you," he said a wry smile curving his lips.

"Improvise. I need you inside me," she repeated, and pumped his erection harder for emphasis. "Now."

His smile fell. The look in his eyes became animalistic, carnal and so damned sensual it made her heart race with desire and anticipation. "Bossy," he murmured before capturing her lips. He removed his fingers from her heat, cupped her rear and eased her onto the mattress. Widening her legs, he settled himself between her outstretched thighs and kissed her sex with his erection.

Tearing his mouth away, he brushed a strand of hair from her face. Keeping his eyes on hers, he leaned forward. Inch by agonizingly slow inch, he filled her. Then stopped. Her inner muscles clenched, drawing him deeper. Her over-sensitized nerve endings ached and screamed for more. For him to stop teasing her and take her the way she loved. Hard, fast, dominating.

Wrapping her legs around his back, she reached up, sifted her hands through his hair and gripped his head. She drew his lips back to hers. "Jake," she whispered. "Please. I need you."

He moved his hips, drawing out his length, then slammed back into her. "It's been so long, I thought you'd want me to go slow," he said, his voice rough as he pulled back out and thrust again.

She moved her hands from his head to his ass and gripped him. "Don't you remember what I like?"

The erotic look filling his eyes sent goose bumps across her skin. She loved when he looked at her like that, as if she was the only woman for him.

He thrust again. "Yeah."

"Then what are you waiting for?"

In an instant, her legs were on his shoulders. He leaned back, rested his palms on her thighs and rocked his hips. Hard, fast. Slid a hand to where they were joined and rubbed her clit. Smoothed his other hand over her stomach, then up until he palmed her breast. He massaged her, plucked and tugged at her nipple. Giving her pain, giving her pleasure.

His muscular chest rising and falling, his flat, tight abs flexing, she reached up and touched him. Sifted her hands through the dark dusting of hair along his chest and clung to his pecs. God, she loved his body. Loved what he was doing to her.

One thing she hadn't lied about, she did need him. Not just for pleasure. Sex had always been great between them, but, to her, it had also been an extension of their love and commitment to each other. She hadn't held up her end of the bargain when it had come to commitment and wished her circumstances could be different. Having had Jake in her life, only to lose him, had left her empty and hollow. Until he'd showed up yesterday she hadn't realized just how unfulfilling and meaningless her life had become. Without him, she'd been going through the motions, surviving and enduring the self-imposed loneliness and isolation.

She gripped his strong biceps, fed off his strength and welcomed each thrust of his hips. Seared this moment to her memory while wishing it could last a lifetime.

As he looked down at her with lust and love in his eyes, guilt niggled at her heart. She was nothing but a selfish hypocrite. She'd never stopped loving him, and yet had lied to him again this morning. She would never take him back, and yet she'd pouted like a bitch when he hadn't made a move to have sex earlier.

"You're thinking too much." He slowed his pace and smoothed his thumb along her forehead. "I must be rusty if you can't stay in the moment."

She touched his strong jaw and smiled. "You're not rusty at all," she said. "I was just wondering if I could get away with chaining you to my bed."

"Were you now?" He quickly rolled her, positioning her on top of him. "Show me what you'd do to me," he coaxed and, gripping her rear, gently bucked.

Grinding her pelvis, she pressed her palms against his chest and rode his length. Each time she dropped down, he pressed up, driving deeper, heightening and stimulating, sweeping the amazing and euphoric sensations through her body. Keeping his hands under her rear, he helped take the pressure off her burning legs, glided her along his erection, driving her closer and closer to the edge.

Just as she thought her body might implode, he quickly rolled her again. Holding her legs wide, he thrust hard, his tempo quick and determined. His pure male scent, the feel of his hard body, the sight of him coated in a light sheen of sweat, had her inner muscles clenching, her belly tightening, her breasts swelling.

"Come for me, baby," he grunted, rocking faster. "Let me see you."

His words, the passion and love in his dark eyes, the hot friction from his thrusts drove straight to her womb and her heart. Her core burst. Her orgasm splintered and shattered throughout her body. She gasped as the delicious sensation went on and on, then groaned when he rubbed her clit and gave her one hard final thrust.

He quickly pulled out and gripped his length, releasing his passion along her stomach. Her inner walls and muscles continued to compress and tighten, her body protesting the loss of him.

Breathing hard, he let go of her legs, braced a chiseled arm next to her shoulder, leaned down and gave her a hot open-mouthed kiss. Greedy for his kiss, she arched her neck to maintain contact. When he tore his mouth away, he pushed up and climbed out of the bed. Resting her arm on her forehead, she tried to slow her racing heart, but it did little good when she caught sight of his sexy bare ass. When he disappeared into the bathroom, she realized she really was greedy and selfish.

She wanted more. She needed him in her life to feel whole again. Her stalker hadn't contacted her in years. Maybe he'd lost interest and was no longer obsessed with the need to own her. Maybe she should throw caution to the wind and take what she knew her heart and life deserved—Jake and a long, happy future with him.

When he came out of the bathroom carrying a washcloth, he sat on the edge of the bed and cleaned off her stomach. The tenderness in his eyes and gentle touch had uninvited guilt crashing into the perfect moment.

No matter what her heart deserved, no matter that she knew to the depths of her soul that she belonged with Jake, she wouldn't play with his life. She refused to risk his safety.

After tossing the washcloth to the floor, he moved next to her, pulled the comforter around them and cocooned her with his body.

She needed to distance herself from him. At least emotionally. Making love to him had been a beautiful, bitter reminder of what could never be.

"I should go start dinner," she said and, with reluctance, moved.

He held her still and forced her even closer. "Dinner can wait."

Damn it. If only he understood.

Tell him the whole truth.

Too risky. What he didn't know couldn't kill him.

With that thought in mind, she shoved at his arm. "I'm starving," she said and, finally free of his safe, protective arm, she scooted off the bed. She caught his gaze in the dresser mirror as she grabbed clothes from the drawer. "Go ahead and take a nap while I make us something to eat."

Clothes in hand, she headed into the bathroom and quickly dressed. Still not prepared to deal with the guilt and the cold way she'd treated him, especially after they'd just made love, she rushed from the bathroom to the bedroom door.

"Naomi," he said, stopping her.

Hovering at the threshold, she kept her back to him.

"Yeah?"

"Aren't you tired of running?"

Her throat tightened and her vision blurred with unshed tears. "Take a nap, Jake. I'll call you when it's time for dinner."

She closed the door behind her and let the tears fall. Yes, she was tired of running, tired of living a lie, of living in fear and mourning. But the fight had been knocked out of her. Too many people had already died because of her. Although she had no idea if her stalker still searched for her, she wasn't about to take a risk now. As much as she wanted to take a chance on Jake again, she would not chance his life.

Jake leaned his head against the pillow and stared at the rotating ceiling fan. In a matter of seconds, things between him and Naomi had gone from scorching hot to icy cold. Maybe he shouldn't have made the 'aren't you tired of running' comment. But he knew her, knew how her brain worked. He'd guarantee that between her orgasm and the time it took for him to grab a washcloth, her mind had spun in all kinds of directions. Where would this lead them? Would he expect more now that they'd made love? Would he want to start where they'd left off? Would he pressure her, make her tell him about her stalker so he could put an end to it?

Or maybe he was questioning himself.

He still loved her, could picture them putting the past to rest and moving on with their future. Together. If only she trusted in him enough to let him finally find a way to put her fears to rest. If only she'd stop allowing her stalker to dictate her life.

The bed felt empty without her in it, just like his world had since she'd left him. He climbed out, then headed into the bathroom. While he took another quick shower, he considered how to approach her. Shaking sense into her wasn't an option, but giving her the illusion that he was willing to take things at her pace or that he was okay with looking at this weekend as something fun and just for old times' sake might work. Even if none of those things worked for him.

Dressed and prepared to hash it out with Naomi, he walked into the kitchen. Wearing running shorts and a t-shirt, she stood at the counter peeling the shrimp they'd caught. "Need any help?" he asked and hoped she'd give him a job that didn't include deveining the shrimp. He loved eating the stuff, but those black veins were just gross.

"I already started the grill and have the fish seasoned. Mind spearing the shrimp onto these?" she asked and pointed to the wooden skewers on the counter.

"Sure." He grabbed a beer from the fridge, before approaching the counter. "Need a refill?" He motioned toward her almost empty wine glass.

"Nope," she said without glancing at him. "I'm good. I'll wait until we eat."

"Naomi, look at me."

With a sigh, as if he was bothering her, she dropped the shrimp into the colander and looked at him. Her eyes held hints of sadness and wariness, the total opposite from when they'd been making love.

"I'm sorry about what I said earlier, but can you blame me?"

She shook her head. "No. It's just...never mind." She turned back to the sink.

Moving next to her, he forced her to face him. "It's just what?"

"Being with you again has been wonderful. But I know it's going to come to an end tomorrow."

"We have another day." He settled his hands on her hips. "I'm making arrangements for my flight to leave Monday morning. But that doesn't mean we can't continue to see each other."

She sent him a rueful smile. "Sure, if one of us makes the fifteen hour drive or catches a flight."

"I didn't ask you this earlier, but I'm asking now. And I want an honest answer." Did he really, though? If she'd left him out of fear for both his and her safety, that was one thing.

He didn't like it, but he could handle the excuse. If she'd left him because she had no longer been happy being with him, then that would be a blow to his ego. His stomach tightened. "Did you leave me because you were afraid of the stalker?"

Holding his gaze, her chin trembling slightly, she nodded. "I should have told you."

"Yeah, you should have. But now that I know—"

"It's still too risky."

"Why? You said yourself he hasn't contacted you." He let go of her and stepped back. Realizing he was being way too presumptuous and moving way too fast, he leaned against the counter and ran a hand through his hair. "Sorry. I have no right to push you. You've got a life here. I can't expect—"

"I want to be with you," she said, standing in front of him and wrapping her arms around his waist. "It's all I've ever wanted."

"But?" he asked, his heart racing. He'd come here for answers, received a few and ended up realizing his feelings for Naomi hadn't changed. He still wanted her in his life.

"I can't help worrying he'll come back and try and hurt me through you. I couldn't let that happen five years ago and I can't let that happen now."

Let the bastard try.

He cupped her cheek. "Did you ever consider letting it be *my* choice?"

"I knew what your answer would be," she said, a tear slipping down her soft skin. "I couldn't let—"

"Stop. I was with Marine Division Recon—1st Reconnaissance Battalion. I've been shot at, blown up and did quite a bit of my own ass kicking. I'm not afraid of this bastard. Give me his name and I'll end this."

"No."

"Fine." He clenched his jaw and tamped down his frustration. "Look. No pressure. But I'm going to want to see you again after this weekend."

"What if he surfaces?" she asked, the terror and worry in her eyes infuriating him.

When he was back in Chicago, he would make it his mission to find the pathetic prick who'd kept her living in fear. "I'm willing to take the risk." He gently squeezed her shoulder. "Just as I would have been five years ago."

She swiped at a tear and drew in a shaky breath. "Long distance relationships never work."

"We did just fine when I was stationed in Iraq."

"That was different."

"No. At least now I can hop in a plane and be here in a few hours."

Although some of the fear had left her eyes, the worry lingered. "We'll take baby steps, right?"

"Baby steps work," he said. Considering what had just happened in her bed, he'd say they were beyond taking baby steps. He wasn't going to mince words though. He planned to enjoy the rest of the weekend with her, go back to Chicago on Monday and begin his search for her stalker. While he was at it, he planned to call her daily and ease his way back into her life. Now that they'd put the past to rest, he planned to remind her they deserved a shot at a future.

CHAPTER 6

HARRISON EASED OUT of Santiago's SUV and stretched. While the Columbian pumped gas and Vlad smoked a cigarette on a grassy patch away from the gas station, Harrison looked toward the front passenger door. When his brother remained seated, he rapped on the closed window. Mickey waved him off, then folded his arms across his chest. Although worried about his brother and how this job was affecting him, Harrison had bigger worries. As of tonight, the laptop would no longer be in his possession unless Honey Badger allowed it.

After they'd left Bloomington yesterday, they drove to Columbus, did the job, then quickly left for Knoxville. They'd been in and out of Columbus so quickly that Santiago had decided to forego the motel room. Which was fine by Harrison. Over the past week, he'd seen enough shitty motel rooms to last him a lifetime. Plus, that meant he didn't have to be subjected to Vlad's chain smoking. Also a nice break. His lungs were happy. Santiago wouldn't allow Vlad to smoke in the SUV, which meant Harrison had been free of secondhand smoke for almost the entire day. Not much of a silver lining, but considering what he suspected him and Mickey were up against, especially once they reached Norfolk, he'd take it.

Knoxville had been a different story. Santiago had found them another shitty motel room, then the Columbian and Mickey planted the device. Harrison had then done his part, syncing the device to the laptop.

They'd left first thing this morning to make the eight hour

drive back to Norfolk and were now halfway there. His stomach clenched. According to Vlad, they had one more device to plant before they were finished. Once done, Vlad promised that tonight they'd stay at Norfolk's downtown Marriott. Not exactly the Ritz-Carlton, but the Marriott beat the hell out of staying in places that had reminded him of the Bates Motel. Vlad also said he'd make good on his word and treat Harrison to dinner, drinks and a sexy redhead. With how nauseous and anxious his stomach had been, he didn't think he could eat. As much as he'd love to drown his worries in a bottle of gin, his queasy gut told him not to bother, and his mind agreed. He didn't want to be hung over tomorrow when he finally met Honey Badger. Given the chance to be alone with the laptop, he wanted to have his wits about him and install the virus he hadn't had time to program into the laptop when they'd been in Bloomington.

Vlad dropped the cigarette, crushed it under his boot heel, then made his way toward the SUV. "Vlad needs to visit little boy room," he said to Santiago, but kept his ice blue eyes on Harrison. "You come, Harry?"

Harrison had come to realize Vlad might be his only way out of the mess Mickey had placed them in with this Honey Badger. He and the Russian had spent the majority of the trip together. During that time, Vlad had kept offering him advice, giving him pep talks on what Harrison should do with his life. At one point, Harrison had joked that Vlad could quit his day job and become a life coach. The Russian, with his good sense of humor, had laughed and agreed. But Harrison had also noticed the longing in Vlad's eyes. As if the man might really harbor the desire to leave the line of work he was in and explore other options.

"Yeah, I gotta go, too," Harrison said, then rapped on the passenger window again. "Mick, you want anything from the store?"

His brother shook his head and kept his arms folded. Mickey hadn't eaten a thing since yesterday morning. Now that Harrison thought about it, he didn't remember seeing his brother drink anything either. He'd buy Mickey something anyway. If things ended up going bad later today or tomorrow, his brother needed to be ready. Not dehydrated or weak from lack of sustenance.

Harrison fell into step with Vlad and headed toward the gas station bathrooms, which were located inside the store. "Good," Vlad said when he opened the bathroom door. "Two urinals. We can моча together."

Harrison chuckled and unzipped his jeans. "You're starting to freak me out, Vlad."

The Russian grinned as he used the urinal. "No worry, Harry. Vlad told you. I like—"

"Big titties," Harrison said and finished his business. "Just messing with you, man. I know you and Santiago don't like to leave me and Mickey alone."

Vlad zipped his fly and looked at him. "Vlad only following orders."

"Is Santiago your boss?"

"нет." The Russian shook his head. "Vlad listen to Honey Badger only. But…Santiago and Honey Badger go way back. Remember, Harry, we are all throwaway."

Throwaway? Vlad's broken English, at times, made communication difficult. "I'm not sure I'm following," he said and washed his hands.

"одноразовый," Vlad said in Russian. "Like dirty diaper."

"Do you mean *disposable*?"

"да." He nodded and pumped soap into his large hands. "Vlad with Honey Badger long time, but can go bye-bye like that," he said with a snap of his soapy fingers. "Harry and Mickey Mouse…"

Harrison's nauseous stomach knotted. "What about us?" His mind raced, all of his suspicions clicking into place. "Are you saying when the job is over, Honey Badger is going to dispose of us?"

The Russian put a wet hand on Harrison's shoulder. "Tomorrow night you must go. With or without the mouse. Understand?"

"No. Explain."

"Harry, Vlad fears for your life. Honey Badger makes **русская мафия** look like saints."

"English, damn it."

"Russian mafia." Vlad dropped his hand and reached for a paper towel. "Trust Vlad. Many years the **русская мафия** owned me. They brutal killers. Honey Badger worse. Much worse. Once Harry sees Honey Badger's face…" He shook his head. "Vlad fears for Harry and the mouse."

"What if we sneak away tonight?" Harrison asked, thinking of how he and Mickey could leave Norfolk, leave the frickin' state and go into hiding. If they could do that, he could go to the authorities and warn them.

"No, Harry." He shrugged. "Vlad not ready to die."

"But can you help—"

A man and young boy entered the bathroom. Vlad ushered Harrison out the door and toward the coolers. "Pick something and we go. Santiago waits for us."

"Vlad. I need to know—"

"Enough," the Russian said, his voice low, intimidating. "Keep silent. Vlad will find a way." He handed him a bag of Doritos. "Eat snack, no worry."

Easy for him to say. Harrison was beyond worried and scared. Mickey might've had no clue what he'd gotten them in to, but based on the way he'd been acting, his brother knew now. Even though Harrison didn't know the truth behind the job they were working, Vlad had confirmed his suspicions and fears. Mickey had involved them in a deadly game that would result in the deaths of hundreds, maybe thousands of innocent people. With Vlad's cryptic warning in mind, Harrison could group his brother and himself with those people, even if he and Mickey weren't so innocent.

As he stood next to Vlad, who paid for their drinks and food, Harrison knew in his gut Honey Badger wasn't going to let them walk away from this. He and Mickey knew too much and by tomorrow night, if they didn't find a way to escape, they'd be dead.

***

Jake rested a hand on his full stomach and smiled at Naomi. "You're going to make me fat." He eyed the half eaten cookie left on his plate, tempted to gorge himself with another bite. "I forgot what a great cook you are."

She pushed her plate aside. "Please. You haven't put a pound on in years. I think you can afford to eat my cooking."

"How do you know?"

"I have eyes." Her lips tilted in a sexy smile. "And I've seen you naked."

"Only a couple of times. I think you'd have to see me naked at least a dozen times before you can come to any conclusion."

"Oh, really? Hmm. You might be on to something." She tapped her chin and eyed him. "Okay, strip."

He laughed and held up a hand. "Not sure if your neighbors would appreciate the experiment."

"The widow next door might," she said with a chuckle. "But you're right. Help me take the dishes inside, then strip."

He'd always been ready to ditch his and her clothes. Anytime. Anywhere. Their sexual chemistry had never been a problem. He'd never not wanted her, had never left their bed dissatisfied. And he was more than ready to take her to bed again right now.

Rising, he reached for his plate. "You really have gotten bossy over the years."

"Have I?" she asked, her eyes innocent and teasing. "Sorry. But I know what I want. At this moment, it's you. Naked."

Now fully aroused, if she didn't stop with the naked talk, he'd strip her and take her against the kitchen island. Actually, that's exactly what he'd do. Bend her over and—

His cell phone rang. Releasing a sigh, he grabbed the phone off the patio table and checked the caller ID. *Rachel.*

"I'm sorry. I have to take this call. The gal I work with is arranging my flight for tomorrow."

Although Naomi smiled at him, she caught a hint of

disappointment at the mention of his leaving tomorrow. "Go ahead. I've got the dishes. But when you're through, prepare for me to get all kinds of bossy on you."

Smiling at the prospect, he answered the call and entered the house. "Hey, Rachel. How are you?"

"Wow," Rachel began, "I'm sorry, I must have the wrong number. The guy who I'm looking for is a total crab-ass, not...perky."

Perky? "I don't think anyone has ever called me perky. Quite frankly, I'm good with that."

"You're right," she said, the keyboard clicking away in the background. "Perky isn't a very manly word. How about sprightly, bouncy, buoyant or—"

"How about closing out of the thesaurus and sticking with happy."

"Jake Tyler is happy? Wow. Stop the presses, this is big news."

Grinning, he shook his head and headed into the guest room where he'd stowed his suitcase and laptop. "I don't know how Owen puts up with you," he said, and pulled a pen and notepad from his briefcase.

"He loves me so much he tells me all the time that I'm a work of art."

"No. He tells you you're a piece of work. Meaning, you're a pain in the ass."

"Why do you hurt me?" she asked, her tone teasing. "Especially after I just took time out of my Sunday—my day off by the way—to help take care of your travel arrangements."

"You're right. I'm sorry. You're not a pain in the ass. At least not all the time."

She chuckled. "Okay, I'll take that. As for getting out of there tomorrow, the earliest nonstop flight I could find out of Jacksonville leaves at twelve-thirty. I've emailed you your e-ticket."

The drive from Woodbine to Jacksonville was about forty minutes. Calculating the time it would take to drop off the rental and check in at the gate, he'd need to leave around ten-thirty. He wished he could stay longer, but at least he'd have tonight and tomorrow morning with Naomi.

"Great. Thanks for taking care of this for me. I owe you a couple of spools of yarn." Since Rachel gave up chewing pencils, a bad habit she'd started to help her stop smoking, she'd taken up crocheting. Thanks to Rachel and her new hobby, everyone at CORE owned an uneven, unraveling afghan.

"I'm holding you to it. So...are you going to tell me *why* you're happy, or are you going to make me wait? Considering how our conversation went on Friday, I assumed the worst."

He set the paper and pen on the briefcase, then popped his head out the door. Water ran from the kitchen faucet and dishes clanked. "I'm not going to get into it right now, but let's just say that Naomi admitted she changed her name and we've hashed through a lot of issues."

"*She* changed her name *and* her social security number?" Rachel asked, her voice holding disbelief.

"Yeah, why?"

The keyboard clicked away in the background. "What's her real name?"

"Lisa Monroe," he said and looked out into the hall again. "Why? What are you doing?"

"Unfortunately, I'm about to dump a big bucket of ice cold reality onto your head."

He tightened his grip on the phone and closed the guest room door behind him. "What'd you find?" he asked, taking a seat on the bed. A large part of him didn't want to know. He'd just rediscovered Naomi, had rediscovered his feelings for her and they'd made tentative plans for the future. The other part of him wanted the truth. And not the sugarcoated version which, based on Rachel's bucket of ice cold reality remark, was what he was about to receive.

"As you know, anyone can change their name. But their social security number? That's not easy."

He did know that and Naomi had backed all of this up yesterday morning. "Right, Naomi told me."

"Sorry, Jake. She's still lying."

"Bullshit," he said with resentment. Rachel hadn't been here. She hadn't listened to what Naomi had to say, or what she'd had to deal with for the past eight years.

"Look," Rachel began, "I'm sorry, I shouldn't have said anything. We can talk about it—if you want—when you're back in Chicago. Enjoy your time with Naomi."

"Nope." He had to know. If what Naomi had told him was nothing but a lie…he wasn't going to go there. Not yet. "You started this, now I need you to finish it. How is she lying?"

She let out a sigh. "If *she* changed her social security number, there would be a paper trail. Guaranteed. There isn't one leading back to Lisa Monroe or anyone else linked to Naomi McCall. The *only* way you can have your social security number changed and *not* have a paper trail is with a government agency."

"Witness Protection? She said her reason for the name change was because she had a stalker."

"The Witness Protection Program is for *witnesses*. Not stalking victims. They wouldn't be involved with this."

He ran a hand through his hair and looked out the window. There had to be an explanation. Maybe there wasn't a stalker and that was the cover she was giving him to keep him…happy.

"Can you run a search on Lisa Monroe? Check the Pittsburgh area, that's where she said she was from."

"Jake, I can check, but it'll take a while. You can't be sure of her exact birthday and who knows, maybe she's lying about being from Pittsburgh. Then again, maybe not. Maybe she's using the stalker as a cover up for something bigger and she really is in Witness Protection."

"Those were my thoughts."

"Jake?" Naomi called and knocked on the guest room door.

"I have to go," he said to Rachel.

"Gotcha," Rachel replied and blew out another sigh. "I'm really sorry I dumped this on you. We'll sort it out when you're back here."

"Don't be. I'd rather know the truth." After saying good-bye, he disconnected the call. He needed to think. He needed to swallow his disappointment and give Naomi the benefit of the doubt. So she couldn't have changed her social security number on her own and not leave a paper trail. So she might have lied about the stalker and was actually in Witness Protection. If that were the case, he didn't like it, but he understood. She wouldn't have been allowed to tell him the truth.

Still. They'd been together for three years. Lived together, had been engaged to marry. While he hadn't known then that she'd been lying about her past, he'd found out her *version* of the truth yesterday morning. He'd accepted her answers. They'd made sense and…he'd wanted to believe her. He wanted to be with her so damned bad. Forget about the past and start fresh. He'd missed her, had grown tired of coming home to an empty place.

Rachel had punched a huge hole into Naomi's story. Before he began demanding more answers from Naomi and caused a potential rift between them, he needed to figure out what to do with the information Rachel had given him. He could confront Naomi, but would rather wait until he had all the facts first. Last night, they'd decided to continue to see each other even after he went back to Chicago. What if Rachel was wrong? The bigger question, what if Naomi was in Witness Protection? Did he care?

Yes and no. No, because her safety came first. Yes, because she obviously didn't trust him. She didn't have to hide from him and could bare her secrets. He would never judge her and never do anything to hurt her. Although he had nothing to hide from her, he understood the past could be painful. Even now, seven years after his final tour in Iraq, he didn't like to talk about the Humvee explosion that had killed, injured and deformed the men he'd been with, and that had ultimately landed him in the hospital for two months. The memories were too painful, the guilt that he'd come out better than the rest still too raw.

He glanced to the closed door. Before the call from Rachel, he'd planned to spend the afternoon naked and making love to Naomi. He'd been aroused and ready to bend her over the kitchen island and take her. The problem was, he still wanted to spend the afternoon naked and making love. What the hell did that say about him?

Without any answers, he shoved off the bed and opened the door. When he didn't see Naomi in the hallway, he called for her.

"I'm in here," she answered from the bedroom.

His body responded. He'd spent all night in her bed, making love and holding her. Last night had been heaven. He'd lived out dreams and fantasies that had been tormenting him for years. Despite his conversation with Rachel, he wanted to continue to live out those dreams and fantasies. Because deep down, the pathetic, foolish side of him didn't care that he was in love with a liar.

Fucking pathetic.

He headed into her room, then froze. Naomi was lying on the center of the bed. Completely naked, her long brown hair spread across a small stack of pillows.

"Did you get everything squared away?" she asked, running a hand along her stomach. When she reached her breast, she gave her nipple a tug.

He swallowed and nodded. "Yeah, all set."

She moved her other hand over her stomach, then to the small patch of dark curls above her sex. "Good," she said, spread her legs and dug her heels into the mattress. "Any other business calls you need to attend to?"

His erection throbbed as she rubbed her fingers along her heat. "No."

Keeping her gaze on his, she slipped a finger between her thighs and parted her lips. "Very good," she said, her voice breathless, sexy. "If I recall correctly, you suggested I should see you naked at least a dozen times before coming up with a conclusion about your weight."

Unable to resist, he stood riveted, staring at her sex, at the way she eased her fingers in and out of her body. His conscience, heart and body warred with one another. His conscience told him to walk away and find out the truth before things between he and Naomi became deeper. His heart, although betrayed because she wouldn't be honest with him, didn't want to miss out on any chance of being with her. His body had a mind of its own. Fully aroused, his stomach quickening with need, he tore off his shirt and quickly shed the rest of his clothes.

His eyes on where she pleasured herself, he moved across the room and settled his body between her outstretched thighs. Dipped his head and kissed, nipped and licked her fingers and her heat. When she groaned and spread her lips for his taking, he knew, despite the war going on inside of him, he'd always want her.

Liar or not, Naomi would always hold a piece of his heart.

"Santiago just called," Ric said, as he entered the luxurious custom built bar and game room. "They're back in Norfolk."

Not looking up, he eyed the black eight ball left on the pool table, lined up his shot and then sank in it in the corner pocket. He picked up his empty glass and made his way behind the bar. "Very good," he said, pulling out the bottle of fifty-year-old Glenfiddich he'd been saving. "I think this calls for a celebratory toast, don't you?"

"Didn't Liliana give you that bottle for your birthday last year?" Ric asked.

He poured three fingers worth of the whiskey into a glass and handed it to Ric. "She did. And I think it's rather fitting that we drink the whiskey my pathetic wife had bought and celebrate the woman I will soon possess." He filled his glass, then raised it. "Cheers."

"Damn, that's good," Ric said, setting the glass on the bar and taking a seat on the high back bar stool.

"For twenty grand, it'd better be." He topped Ric's glass with another shot. "I'm assuming Santiago knows to continue to keep the brothers on a short leash."

"He does. He and Vlad took them to the Marriott for the night. They're going to ply them with food, alcohol and women." Ric rolled his eyes and picked up the glass of whiskey. "Vlad insisted. He's looking at tonight as something akin to a prisoner's last meal before execution."

"Vlad's something else," he said with a chuckle. "I actually like the idea. Keeps those boys happy and unaware. Just make sure Santiago and Vlad don't allow the brothers to have too much fun. We have a schedule to meet and I need the smart one focused, not hung over."

"Already warned Santiago." After taking another sip of the whiskey, Ric leaned back. "He and Vlad will bring the brothers to the warehouse at six-thirty in the morning."

The old warehouse, a combination of cinder blocks, steel and wood, had been in his family for generations. Due to the undesirable, high crime location and the cost it would take to have kept the building up to code, it hadn't been in use for the past ten years. At least that was what most people would assume. The broken windows had been boarded. The doors locked and chained. But inside, he had created a perfect hideout for his somewhat…illicit affairs.

While he hadn't been willing to drop a dime into bringing the warehouse up to code, he was accustomed to certain luxuries. Several years ago, he'd spent quite a lot of money making sure one of the building's floors had been renovated into an apartment to fit his standards. He'd paid handsomely for a custom kitchen, office/TV room, several bedrooms and bathrooms, all properly wired, all elegant and completely secure.

"You and I will be there at six," he said and poured whiskey into his tumbler. "I want everything ready for the big show."

Ric grinned and raised his glass. "It's going to be one hell of a show, too." As if it was some no-name shitty swill, rather than worth twenty thousand dollars a bottle, he finished his whiskey in one swallow. "Yeah, I'm really looking forward to tomorrow. Only…never mind."

He leaned against the bar. "Only what if my plan doesn't work?"

"I have confidence it will, don't get me wrong." Ric ran a finger around the rim of the crystal tumbler. "One thing I'm worried about though is what if she doesn't take the bait and instead goes to the cops?"

He'd thought of that, too. For a millisecond. "She won't."

"How can you be sure?"

He shrugged. "Because I remember what her brother looked like after you finished with him. I'm sure she does, as well. More?" he asked, holding the bottle of Glenfiddich.

"Not if we have to be at the warehouse at six." Ric said with a shake of his head, his expression turning thoughtful. "What if she's out for revenge? If she comes to you, you'll never be able to turn your back on her."

Smiling, he placed a hand over his heart. "I'm touched by your concern," he said with sarcasm. "Never fear, Ric. Once I have her, once she learns the rules, she'll be a good girl."

"How can you be sure?" Ric countered.

"Because I have you. And what you did with the maid will set a good example." After the maid had pleasured him with her mouth, he'd turned her over to Ric and had given him the rest of the day off to play. His right hand man lived in the three thousand square foot guest cottage located five hundred yards from the sprawling estate house he'd lived in his entire life.

A tunnel, once used during the Civil War to hide Confederate soldiers from the Yankees, ran from the cottage to the house. Ric had transferred the maid from his office to his cottage via the tunnel, taking her belongings with him. Because Alison took the bus or caught a ride to the estate, there'd been no need to worry about disposing of a vehicle. The body was another story, but Ric had taken care of that. He also hadn't needed to worry about his housekeeper, Mrs. Burrows. Alison hadn't been in his employment for long and Mrs. Burrows assumed the girl had simply walked off the job.

But she hadn't. Ric, the perverse sadist, had kept her in his cottage and played with her until the wee hours of the night. One thing he liked about Ric, he never hid secrets and was always eager to share gory details. The ones Ric had shared with him this morning were definitely gory. The pictures Ric had showed him, the proof.

He smiled. "It's a shame the labyrinth was too full. Alison admired the magnolia tree at its center and it would have been quite fitting as her final resting place." After Ric had choked the life out of her, he'd buried her broken body behind his cottage. Considering the center of the maze held dozens of skeletal remains—many courtesy of his great-grandfather—they would have to start using many other parts of his property to bury their secrets.

Excitement brightened Ric's eyes. "Yes, it would have been quite fitting. And you're right. I'm sure once you've drawn her out from wherever she's been hiding, if she gives you trouble, I can convince her that she belongs with you."

"You'll convince her she belongs *to* me," he corrected. And she did belong to him. From the moment he'd seen her working at that shitty club, he'd wanted to possess her. Her body was the type a man could enjoy for hours on end. Her smile had transported him to another time, to when he'd been a naïve child seeking adventure and treasures. To before he'd found the center of the labyrinth and his great-grandfather's boney surprises. More than that, the light in her eyes carried hope, dreams and innocence.

He hadn't hoped for anything in more than twenty years. Hope was for those who were afraid to risk, dreams were for the ignorant who would rather fantasize than act, and innocence…. He'd lost his innocence in the maze that hot, sunny day when he was nine. The dead had spoken to him that afternoon, along with his great-grandfather. If he planned to make something of himself, be stronger and more powerful than his enemies, he would need to shed his naivety, be ruthless, be a conqueror.

The night he'd taken her to his bed and made her his, she hadn't realized she'd given him more than her body. The moment he'd entered her, she'd unknowingly turned her life over to him. The pleasure he'd found with her had been more than physical. She was his opposite, but unlike his stupid wife whose cowardice sickened him, at least she had gumption. She challenged him. Her spirit and strength matched his own and he wanted to drain it from her. Soak up her very essence and show her who held the power.

He stowed the Glenfiddich on the shelf behind him, planning to finish the whiskey tomorrow evening when the real celebration would begin. "Many men want to be me. They want what I have. My money, my company, my possession...my power." He lifted his tumbler. "Many men also fear me."

"As they should," Ric said, narrowing his eyes and giving him a single nod.

After sipping his whiskey, he smiled. "Yes, and even though they're afraid of what I can do to them and know that I could destroy them, they still do what I ask despite the consequences. She fears me, too. But she's resourceful. I don't know how she's managed to hide from me, and although I hate to admit it, I admire her. For now." He set the empty glass into the sink. "I've spent too many years and too much money hunting her. Now she's forced me to kill. The people who will die tomorrow, their blood will stain her hands. Then again, their blood will also help propel me into a political position that will make my power limitless. For that alone, I might have you go easy on her."

Ric cracked a grin. "In the beginning."

Amused, he chuckled. "And probably not for long. Our time together will likely be short. Speaking of which, have you upgraded the locks in the cellar?" After he'd had Ric put his plan into motion, he'd also had him make sure his prey's accommodations met his standards. The secret room in the cellar was only known to him, Ric, Santiago and Vlad, and had once been used by his great-grandfather. He'd discovered the room while still searching for his great-grandfather's treasures. Hidden off the tunnel to Ric's cottage, beneath the ground and built within bedrock, the room, although outdated, had plenty of indulgences and would prove a comfortable place when he chose to use her body. The servants knew nothing of the tunnel. Discovery would not occur. And she would remain in the room until Ric buried her.

"Yes, everything is set. I've also stocked the mini fridge and added extra lighting. Using a generator was a great idea."

Of course it was. After all, it was *his* idea. He glanced at his Patek Philippe watch. "It's getting late. Go home and rest. I'll meet you in the garage at five-thirty."

As Ric stood, a knock came at the door. Seconds later, Liliana entered the room and his mood soured. He hated the woman. Despised being saddled to her and couldn't wait for her funeral.

"What do you want?" he asked as Ric left the room. *Lucky bastard.*

She glanced around the bar and game room, a part of the estate she rarely visited thanks to his strict rules. "I'm sorry to bother you, but I want to go to bed and needed to talk to you about something first."

Exiting from behind the bar, he shut off a few lights and made his way toward the door. "So talk," he said, ushering her out of the room.

She kept up with him as he walked. "Do you have plans for tomorrow?"

Big plans. "My schedule is none of your business."

"Of course it's not," she said, her tone curt and disrespectful.

He turned and shoved her against the wall. "I'm glad you understand that. Watch how you talk to me. I won't tolerate your insolence. Do you understand?"

Eyes wide and filled with fear, she nodded. "I wanted to see if it was okay for me to fly to New York tomorrow. I thought I'd take the private jet in the morning. I haven't been able to find anything to wear to the charity ball, but when I spoke with my stylist, she suggested I meet her in New York and—"

"How long do you plan to ramble?" He pulled away from

her, disgusted after touching her skinny, boney body. "Don't waste my time and get to the point. You want to know if I care whether or not you go to New York and spend my money on a dress that will, most likely, not do anything to make you less ugly, correct?"

Her shit-brown eyes filled with tears as she nodded.

"Go. Stay the week for all I care. It'll be nice not having to see your face around the house." With Liliana gone, he could bring his prize to his bedroom, rather than having to fuck her in the cellar. "Actually, I insist. I also want you to take the kids and their nannies, too. I could use a break from all of you." The kids didn't really bother him. Fortunately, they favored him in looks and personality.

"A week?" she asked, her tone hopeful. "You don't mind?"

He rolled his eyes and shook his head. The woman was the epitome of stupid. "I told you to leave," he said, and began making his way up the ornate staircase to where his bedroom was located in the east wing of the house.

Although he'd forced himself to remain blasé in front of Liliana, excitement infused his body. His wife and children would be gone for the week, leaving only a few servants. Tomorrow would set off a chain of events that would not only lead the woman he'd sought for eight years back to him, but turn the country upside down with fear and terror.

When he reached his room, he stood in front of the dresser mirror and imagined standing at a podium. Cameras and reporters would surround the stage, clamoring to hear how he planned to bring the country together and offer refuge to those decimated by tragedy.

He smiled at his reflection.

Tragedy that *he* would unleash tomorrow.

CHAPTER 7

WITH FEAR AND LOATHING, Harrison eyed the tall, barbed wire fence surrounding the boarded-up warehouse. Nervous, anxious, he looked past where Vlad sat next to him in Santiago's SUV. Across from the warehouse, morning rays from the rising sun fissured through the rundown buildings marred with graffiti. A handful of older, rusty dented cars lined the street. Along the cracked sidewalks litter rustled on the light breeze.

The Columbian stopped the vehicle. Vlad immediately climbed out, pulled a set of keys from his pocket and unlocked the metal gate. Santiago didn't wait for Vlad to return and drove through the gate, while Vlad hefted the metal garage door leading into the darkened warehouse.

As Santiago parked the Yukon and Vlad closed the garage door with a hard thump, panic and claustrophobia seized Harrison by the throat. He'd grown up in a bad neighborhood, but not as bad as the one they were in now. Crime had ended up so out of hand here that businesses had shut down or moved to another location. Low income housing and apartments weren't far from the warehouse, along with several gang hangouts. Last he'd heard, one gang ran a prostitution ring, while another dealt in drugs. If he and Mickey were to find a way to escape, and they ran into some people on the streets, he doubted they'd find any help. He understood the mentality of most of these people. They took care of themselves, took care of their own and, unless they saw opportunity to make a profit, shit on everyone else.

"Out," Santiago ordered and killed the ignition.

Harrison stepped out of the SUV and followed Santiago and Mickey. As they made their way through the garage toward a metal staircase, he noticed a black Bentley in the far corner of the garage.

"Beautiful, eh?" Vlad asked as he caught up with them.

"For almost a quarter mil, it better be more than pretty," Harrison responded, and stared at the bolted door next to where the car was parked. Although too far away to tell, he wondered if he could break the lock by simply smashing something large and heavy against it.

"Trust Vlad. Bentley go zero to sixty in four point three seconds. The car worth all pennies."

Harrison stepped onto the metal stair. "You mean the car is worth every penny."

"Harry needs to give Vlad break. You Americans have no idea how hard your sayings are to remember."

When they reached the second floor of the four story building and approached a dented, corroded metal door, his stomach knotted. But then Santiago kept going up the staircase. Although Harrison didn't relax, he looked at each step as a reprieve. A postponement to the inevitable. Eventually they'd wind up on one of the floors. Until they did, he tried to pretend none of this was happening. He wasn't in an old warehouse, about to meet a man named after a vicious, savage animal.

He wasn't about to aid in murder.

His skin crawled. His head grew light. He reached out and touched the wall, steadied himself from the vertigo.

"Vlad told Harry to eat," the Russian said, his voice loud and echoing through the stairwell. He grabbed his arm. "You are weak as kitten."

He shrugged Vlad off. "I'm fine."

Vlad took him by the arm again and leaned toward him, his ice blue eyes imploring and understanding. "Show no fear, Harry," the Russian whispered. "Honey Badger loves seeing fear in man's eyes. Keep cool like ice cream. Trust Vlad."

Although Vlad's words didn't help put him at ease or stop the anxiety coiling through his body, he did trust Vlad. The Russian had shown no indication that he planned to harm him. Instead, he'd given him numerous warnings. He'd take the other man's advice and force himself to be strong in front of Honey Badger. In the process, he'd do his damnedest to find a way for Mickey and him to escape.

"I'm good now," he said and started walking up the stairs again. "And it's cool as a cucumber, not ice cream."

Vlad frowned. "Ice cream colder than cucumber." He shook his head. "Vlad will figure out these saying one day."

When they reached the third flight, Santiago stood with Mickey in front of a door that, in comparison to the rest of the building, appeared brand new. The Columbian glanced to Vlad. "Once we're in, take Mickey into the back room." He then looked to Harrison and Mickey. "I'm going to give you two some advice. Do as you're told and when you meet our boss, don't call him Honey Badger. *Comprende?*"

Harrison nodded and looked to his brother. Mickey's eyes held contempt, while his ashen face twisted in anger.

"Understand?" Santiago repeated in English.

Mickey finally gave the Columbian a curt nod.

"*Bueno,*" the Columbian said and then banged his fist against the door.

Seconds later, the door opened. A man Harrison placed in his mid-thirties greeted Santiago with a rueful smile. "He's been impatiently waiting for you," he said, his hazel eyes holding hints of amusement.

Santiago angled his head around the door. "Maybe he needs to upgrade his two hundred thousand dollar watch," he said in a quiet voice. "We're early."

The man chuckled and tugged at the sleeves of his suit coat. "Why don't you tell him that and see what happens?"

"No thanks," Santiago replied. "I like my head and balls just like they are. On my body."

As both men laughed, Vlad ushered him and Mickey inside.

The man turned to the Russian. "Vlad, good to see you. Mickey, I trust my Columbian and Russian friends made sure you and your brother had everything you needed during the assignment."

Harrison held his breath as Mickey stared at the man, willing his brother to keep as cool as ice cream and not cause any problems. Based on what Santiago had said, it looked as if he and Mickey were going to be separated. But if Mickey behaved, maybe they wouldn't remain in different rooms. If there was any chance of fleeing, he couldn't leave his brother behind. Mickey might be a loose cannon, he might make bad choices, but deep down, he was a good guy.

He was his only family.

"This must be your brother," the man said and offered his hand to Harrison.

"Harrison," he introduced himself and shook his large hand. The guy wasn't as tall and bulky as Vlad, but stood a good four inches taller than Harrison's six foot frame.

"Ricco Mancini. Please call me Ric."

Shit. He didn't want to know the man's name, or Honey Badger's, and looked at each introduction as another nail in his coffin.

Ric checked his watch. "Almost show time. We have a long day ahead of us, so let's get everyone settled," he said with an easy smile and led them into a huge room. "Come on in and make yourself at home. Coffee?"

"No thanks," Harrison said, glancing around the open concept floor plan, and imagining it in some rich guy's giant house. Not an old, dilapidated warehouse. He was no home expert, but knew the hardwood floors, the kitchen cabinetry, granite countertops, along with the kitchen table and leather furnishings, likely cost a small fortune.

"How about you, Mickey? Need anything?" Ric asked, pouring himself a cup of coffee. When Mickey didn't say anything, Ric looked to Santiago.

As if the Columbian had read Ric's mind, Santiago turned to Vlad and jerked his head toward an open door off of the great room. Vlad nodded and took Mickey by the elbow, leading him out of the room and closing the door behind them.

With Vlad and Mickey no longer in the room, claustrophobia returned with a fury. He didn't trust Santiago. Even Vlad had made it clear the Columbian's loyalties lay with Honey Badger. He didn't know anything about the other man, but sensed that behind the business suit, the bright white friendly smile and perfectly combed dark hair, Ric was a snake poised to strike at any given moment.

"Where's the boss?" Santiago asked and helped himself to coffee.

"Right here," a deep voice called from behind him.

Panic cinched his stomach and made his limbs weak.

Show no fear... Honey Badger loves seeing fear in man's eyes.

Harrison dug deep. Brought back memories of when he'd been in prison. Many inmates had tried to intimidate him, had tried to put the fear of God into him. When he'd first been incarcerated, he realized he had two choices. Man up and make sure no one fucked with him, or end up being another man's bitch. After he'd given a few of his fellow inmates broken noses, no one had bothered him during the rest of his prison sentence.

Unfortunately, right now he was Honey Badger's bitch. Knowing he couldn't go toe to toe with Santiago or Ric, he'd play the part until he found a way to escape. Until then, he'd make sure he took Vlad's advice. Show no fear and stay cool like ice cream.

He turned to meet Honey Badger, then froze.

Fuck. He was a dead man.

"Do you know who I am?" Honey Badger asked as he straightened his tie.

Harrison nodded, staring at the man who had graced the covers of numerous financial and political magazines. At twenty-three he'd taken over the family business. By the age of twenty-eight, he'd turned his business into a household name, earning him billions and, at the time, making him one of the youngest and wealthiest men in the United States.

"Of course you do," Honey Badger said and looked around the room. "Where's Vlad?"

"With the brother," Santiago answered and motioned toward the closed door.

Honey Badger clapped his hands together. "Good. Then let's get started. Ric, where's the laptop?"

"In your office."

"This might be an all-day process." Honey Badger grimaced. "I'd rather work out here where it's more comfortable."

"Of course," Ric said and left the room. Moments later, he returned with the laptop Harrison had been using over the past week.

"Smart brother, what's your name?" Honey Badger asked him.

"Harrison."

"Well, Harrison, Santiago assured me that you'll be able to send signals from the laptop to the devices, and that the result would be almost instantaneous, correct?"

"Yes. I can send the signal to all of them at the same time, or—"

"I want them done separately. Starting with the device in San Francisco."

"That's easy enough to do. Actually, you don't even need me here." He mustered a grin. "Once I show you the program, all you have to do is—"

Honey Badger pierced Harrison with his dark blue eyes. "You'll do it."

Scared, his conscience and morals tearing him in two, Harrison rubbed his sweaty palms along his jeans. He didn't want to send the signal. He didn't want to be the triggerman responsible for killing innocent people. "Sir, I'd be happy to show—"

"Vlad," the Billionaire Badger shouted, but kept his cold gaze on Harrison.

The Russian opened the door. "Sir?"

"Bring me the dumb brother."

Vlad quickly entered the room with Mickey. Honey Badger gave Mickey a quick once over, then rolled his eyes and let out a sigh. He turned to Santiago. "Get a garbage bag and make him stand on it."

Santiago quickly did as he was told, forcing Mickey to stand on the bag. Harrison's heart raced with unease. He darted his gaze from the garbage bag, to his brother, then back to Honey Badger, every worst case scenario clicking into place. "I'll do it," Harrison blurted. He didn't want to be Honey Badger's triggerman, but he couldn't let his brother die.

As if he hadn't heard Harrison, Honey Badger turned to Ric. "Give me your gun." After Ric handed the weapon over to him, Honey Badger smiled and pointed it at Mickey.

Harrison made to move, but Santiago gripped his shoulder. "I said I'll do it," he shouted, staring at his brother. Mickey's pale face had grown freakishly white. His body shook and swayed as he gaped, wide eyed, at the gun directed at him.

"I never doubted for a second you wouldn't. But here's a little incentive anyway," Honey Badger said and squeezed the trigger.

Harrison's knees gave out when his brother fell to the floor. Santiago kept him upright, giving him a hard shake. Harrison's throat tightened, tears threatened to fall, but he quickly tamped down the urge. Mickey lay on the garbage bag, howling in pain and clutching his leg. Relieved his brother had been shot in the leg rather than the head, Harrison let the fear go and replaced it with anger. He was on to Honey Badger. The man planned to kill a lot of people, he planned to make Harrison be the one to do it and, in the process, would use Mickey for motivation.

They were so fucked.

"Get him out of here and shut him up," Honey Badger ordered Vlad.

The Russian's jaw ticked as he hauled Mickey to his feet and helped him from the room. Once they were out of sight, the twisted billionaire handed the gun back to Ric, then took a seat in a chair reminding Harrison of a king's throne. "Where were we?" he asked, glancing at his watch. "Ah, yes. You were going to get on the laptop and signal the device planted in San Francisco. Correct?"

Other than bugs, Harrison had never killed anything. Right now, he had murder on his mind and could easily picture doing the world a favor and putting a bullet in Honey Badger's head. He masked his hatred and anger. "Yes, sir."

"Good." He sent him a mocking grin. "I want the device activated at seven, which is in less than ten minutes. I suggest you get to work. I abhor mistakes and won't tolerate a missed deadline."

Harrison sat on the sofa in front of the coffee table and opened the laptop. "I understand."

"Do you? Have you ever played Hangman?"

"Yes," he said, booting up the laptop.

"Then consider your brother the man in the noose. For every mistake you make, he'll either be shot or cut. He's already taken a bullet to his leg, next time you make a mistake, it'll be his other leg. Then his arm, then the other… You're a smart man, Harrison. I think you understand where I'm going."

Loud and clear. He opened up the system files and found the code he'd written for the device Mickey and Santiago had planted in San Francisco. "The program is up and running. Just say the word and I'll send the signal to the device."

His stomach twisting with fear and hatred, Harrison waited while Honey Badger kept focused on his wristwatch. Seconds ticked by, then minutes. Despite the room's comfortable temperature, sweat beaded along his upper lip and brow.

Still focused on his watch, Honey Badger raised a finger. "Now."

Harrison's chest tightened as his finger hovered over the key that would activate the device. *Please forgive me*, he silently prayed to God and the Universe, then he pressed ENTER. He slid his eyes closed, not sure what exactly he'd just activated, but knowing in his gut it wasn't good.

"It's done?" Honey Badger asked.

Harrison opened his eyes, kept his gaze on the laptop and nodded.

"Good. Santiago, turn on the TV," Honey Badger said with a smile and rubbed his hands together. "I'm in the mood to be entertained."

Holding Naomi tight, Jake rolled onto his back and pulled her against his chest. Making love to Naomi, being with her this weekend, had been surreal. He'd spent so many years thinking about what it would be like to hold her again. Now that he had, now that she was in his arms, he didn't want to let her go. He wanted to stay locked in her bedroom, in her bed, and forget about everything else. Unfortunately, he had to leave. He might still be in love with her, he might still harbor fantasies about the kind of future they could have, but reality had a funny way of creeping in and stealing those fantasies. If Rachel was right, Naomi was still lying to him.

As he stroked Naomi's bare back and his heart rate and breathing returned to normal, he pushed those thoughts aside. He'd be heading for Jacksonville in an hour and didn't want to leave on a bad note. Regardless of whether Naomi had lied to him or not, she was a good person. If she'd lied, she had good reason. At least that's what he'd been telling himself since ending his conversation with Rachel. Otherwise, what kind of man did that make him if he'd knowingly stayed and made love to a woman who was lying to him?

Fucking Pathetic.

She ran her hand along his chest, her warm breath caressing him as she sighed. "I wish you could stay another day," she said and kissed his shoulder.

"Me too." He moved them so they were face to face. "I meant what I said. I…" Damn, she was beautiful. He could look into those eyes of hers forever. He'd never seen judgment in them, only love and pride. She was the one person who knew him best, even over his family. There were things he'd told her that he had never told another soul. No matter how dark those secrets had been, she'd accepted him. Hell, she got him. Understood him like no one else. "I'll call you tonight," he said.

"And the next day?" she asked, the uncertainty in her voice bringing out the primal side of him. How could she show any insecurities after what they'd just done in her bed?

"And the day after that," he assured her. "Before I leave, let's look at our calendars. I think I need to come back for Woodbine's Crawfish Festival."

She grinned. "It's a good time."

"It's always good with you."

Her grin turned into a full smile. "I have my moments."

"And if I didn't have to catch a plane, we'd have more moments," he said, and grazed his hand along her breasts.

"Don't start something you can't finish." She gave his chest hair a gentle yank. "Go get ready. I'll make some breakfast."

On cue, his stomach grumbled. They both laughed, and he rolled on top of her for one more kiss. Just when that kiss started to turn carnal, she tore her mouth away.

"Seriously, if you don't stop you'll miss your flight." After giving him another quick kiss, she climbed out of bed. "How do you want your eggs?"

He stared at her breasts, wondering how she could go into chef mode when his mind was still on sex. Again. "Whatever's easiest."

"Scrambled it is," she said and, to his disappointment, put on a tank top and shorts.

After she left the room, he climbed out of bed and headed for the shower. Once finished, he repacked his suitcase, then stowed it into the back of the rental. As he made his way into the house and toward the kitchen, the rancid odor of burnt eggs hit him hard and fast. He entered the kitchen, grabbed the pan filled with dark brown, overcooked eggs and removed it from the burner. The toaster had already popped up the charred toast Naomi had made. The butter dish sat on the counter, along with plates, silverware and glasses, as if she'd started breakfast and had to make a sudden break for it.

Concerned, he stepped back into the living room. When he didn't find her in there, he checked both bedrooms and bathrooms.

Where the hell was she?

No longer just concerned, but downright worried, he reentered the kitchen, checked for her in the backyard, then stopped and listened. The faint sound of a TV came from the short hallway off the kitchen. He hadn't been down this hallway and had assumed it was where her laundry room was located.

"Naomi," he called as he rushed into the hall and discovered two doors. He opened one, saw the washer, dryer and utility sink, then left the room and opened the other door.

A small flat screen sat on a stand in the corner of the room airing what appeared to be a newscast. He let out a sigh of relief when he found Naomi hunched over a small desk and typing furiously at the computer keyboard. "Naomi?" he asked as he approached her. "Everything okay?"

When she didn't answer him, he moved to the edge of the desk and touched her wrist. She stopped typing and kept her head down.

He dropped to a knee and nudged her chin, forcing her to look at him. When she did, and he caught the horror in her eyes, he immediately gripped her shoulders. Alarmed, he stared at her flushed, tear-soaked face and gave her a slight shake. "What happened?"

She drew in a ragged breath. Her face crumpled and more tears sprang from her eyes.

"Please, baby," he said, trying to keep his tone calm and soothing. "Talk to me."

Her watery gaze shifted to the TV. He turned and looked at the small screen. Disgust, grief and fury swept through him as he started at the news footage. "Oh, my God," he murmured as the camera panned out, revealing what was left of the entrance of a school.

Flames engulfed a large portion of the building. Firefighters aimed their hoses at the blaze. Black smoke spewed from a gaping hole filled with debris. The camera switched scenes. Adults and older children ran through the parking lot peppered with police cruisers, ambulances and fire trucks. Injured, frightened kids, their faces streaked with tears and smoke, sobbed and wailed, their wide terrified eyes searching frantically. Men and women—parents he assumed—ran through the chaotic scene, checking one kid and then the next, likely looking for their child. Unable to stomach the fear and sadness on the parents' and kids' faces, Jake looked to the caption below the footage.

"Bombing at Idaho middle school. Five dead, dozens injured."

He rubbed Naomi's arms. "That's horrible, hon. I hope to God it was accidental and not—"

"This was no accident," she said, her tone flat, bleak. "Look."

He glanced to the computer screen. At the top of the page she had typed in a search for Rose Wood. Below that were pictures of a restaurant that looked as if it had also been bombed. A yawning cavern had replaced the roof, revealing charred singed rubble. The front of the restaurant was covered in soot and ashes, the glass from the large front windows broken and scattered along the sidewalk patio. Part of the sign, which must have once hung along the front of the building, had broken in half. One part remained suspended and barely clinging to the brick, while the rest lay in pieces on the concrete front walkway. He read the caption beneath the images, *"The Rosewood Bar & Grill, an iconic San Francisco restaurant known for its good food, atmosphere and celebrity appearances, exploded this morning (4:00 AM PDT). Fortunately no one was injured. The cause for the explosion is currently under investigation."*

He glanced away from the screen and met her red-rimmed eyes. "What does this restaurant have to do with the school?" he asked, looking back to the TV. When he caught a fireman carry a woman's limp, soot covered body from the building, he quickly turned away. He'd been in the Marines, had witnessed and personally experienced bombings and explosions in Iraq. To see this kind of destruction—at a school—brought back haunting memories he'd thought had been put to rest.

Instead of answering, she scrolled down the search page, then stopped at another set of photographs. Shocked, he stared at pictures of flames shooting out of what looked like a high-rise hotel, at the billowing black smoke streaming from the shattered windows, at the bloodied and injured people running from the building. Before he read the caption below the photos, the news anchor reporting the school bombing said, "We're going to do a split screen to help keep you up to date on the other devastating explosion that took place a little over an hour ago in Henderson, Nevada."

Jake met Naomi's gaze, caught the sadness and, strangely, guilt in her eyes before focusing on the TV. "At five o'clock this morning, Pacific Daylight Saving Time, an explosion ripped through the Sun Valley Hotel and Convention Center," the reporter said, motioning to the decimated building behind him. "The hotel was at full capacity due to the large IT conference scheduled this week. Fortunately it was early in the morning when the explosion happened." The reporter shook his head. "With the amount of people expected, one hour later and the devastation would have been significant, killing hundreds. As it stands, we've been told seven have been confirmed dead and at least forty people have been injured. The cause of the explosion is yet to be determined. Firefighters are still working on putting out the blaze and making sure everyone has been evacuated from the building."

The news anchor thanked the reporter, then the screen was dedicated solely to the middle school. "Just like with the Sun Valley Hotel and Convention Center, the explosion at Coolridge Middle School could have resulted in more deaths and injuries. During the night, a water main break had knocked out power, delaying the opening of schools and many local business by an hour throughout Rosewood County, Idaho."

Goose bumps crept along Jake's skin. He quickly looked back to the computer screen, at the search Naomi had typed. He took over the computer mouse and scrolled down further, read through the article about the convention center explosion, then sucked in a breath. "7854 Rosewood Court," he said, staring at the convention center's address.

"I have to go," Naomi said, her voice shaky. "*You* have to leave." When she tried to rise, he pressed on her shoulders, forcing her to remain in the office chair.

"What the hell is going on?" he demanded. The Rosewood connection definitely knocked him off guard. While the coincidence was uncanny, he couldn't understand why or how she would have even tried to make a link between the three explosions in the first place.

With more strength than he expected, she shoved him away. Knocking the chair back, she stood and hugged herself, tears streaming down her face. "Leave, Jake. Just go and don't call me again."

Confused and angry, he grabbed her by the upper arms. "Fuck that. I let you walk away once without an explanation, I'm not about to let it happen again. You owe me—"

"Stop," she shouted. "You don't understand. This is *my* fault." She pointed to the TV and computer screen, her breath hitching with a sob. "All of those people, their deaths, their injuries…it's my fault."

"You're not making any sense. How could explosions in California, Nevada and Idaho have anything to do with you?"

She hugged herself tighter and stared at the TV with so much pain in her eyes it made him ache. He loved her and hated that whatever she thought, whatever ridiculous conclusion she'd come up with and firmly believed, left her frightened and ready to run. Ready to push him out of her life again.

"Please, just trust me. You have to go."

"No, damn it. You're scared shitless and I want to know why."

She dropped her hands and paced the small office. Her breathing grew labored as she ran her hands through her hair and pulled on the strands. When she let go of her hair, she swept her arm along the bookshelf near the TV, knocking everything to the floor. She moved to the next shelf below, upending its contents, then did the same to the shelf beneath until finally dropping to her knees. Hands covering her face, she wept.

He rushed to her side and pulled her in his arms. Running his hand down her back, he cradled her. "Please, baby. Tell me what's happening. Don't shut me out, let me help you."

She shook her head against his chest and fisted his shirt. "You can't. No one can. No one can stop him but me."

He forced her to look him. "Who? Your stalker?"

Nodding, she swiped at her eyes. "He's sending me a message and I don't think he'll stop hurting people until I go to him."

Trying to reign in his patience, he cupped the back of her head with a gentleness that belied the anger and turmoil coursing through him. "How can you be sure he's sending you a message?"

Chin trembling, her eyes filled with immense anguish, she gripped his shoulders. "Because my real name is Rose Wood."

PART II

It's being here now that's important. There's no past and there's no future. Time is a very misleading thing. All there is ever, is the now. We can gain experience from the past, but we can't relive it; and we can hope for the future, but we don't know if there is one.

— George Harrison

CHAPTER 8

Bloomington, Indiana
8:40 a.m. Central Daylight Saving Time

VINCENT D'MATTO POURED Fruit Loops into his four-year-old son's cereal bowl.

"Don't forget the milk, Daddy."

He glanced down at his son, Gustavo, focused on his chubby cheeks before looking into his big brown eyes. His mother's eyes. "Never, little dude. How 'bout some worms and spiders with that milk?"

Gus's eyes grew big and round, before he looked down at the Spider-Man costume he wore—the same costume he'd been wearing regularly since Halloween. "Do you think it'll help?"

"Help what?" Vince asked, topping the cereal off with two percent milk.

"Fight bad guys." Gus hopped off the chair and flexed the foamy, built-in muscles of the Spider-Man costume. "Sandman is going down," he said, his expression fierce and determined.

Vince rubbed his son's short brown hair before kissing his head, then looked up when his wife, Anna, entered the kitchen carrying their youngest son. "Morning." After giving Gus's head a final pat, he held out his hands to take the eighteen-month-old from his mother's arms. "How do you feel today?" he asked Anna, his gaze drifting from her tired eyes to her swollen belly.

The baby, Benito, grabbed Vince's cheeks to keep the attention on him. "Loop," Benny said, staring at him as if they were negotiating a million dollar deal rather than cereal.

Anna poured the Fruit Loops into a small bowl and set it on the baby's highchair tray. "She kicked up a storm last night." His wife placed a hand on her stomach. "Sorry if I kept you up."

Vince set Benny in the highchair and secured him. "You didn't," he replied, opened the fridge and pulled out his lunchbox. Anna's tossing and turning hadn't kept him awake, worry had. If the cysts the doctors had found on the baby's brain remained, and she was born with—he shut the refrigerator door. He couldn't go there. They'd deal with whatever came their way and make it through.

Somehow.

He flinched when Anna ran a hand over his tense shoulder. "You'll make it to the ultrasound?" she asked, her voice laced with uncertainty.

Glancing at her, catching the concern in her eyes and wishing he could absorb every one of her fears, he set the lunchbox on the counter and quickly pulled her into his arms. He hugged her as tight as her protruding belly would allow and drew in a deep breath through his nose. Despite the severity of their situation, he grinned. When he'd first met Anna, her perfume had reminded him of sunshine and wildflowers. Now she smelled like baby lotion and diaper rash cream. And he loved it. Loved that she'd given him two beautiful, healthy sons, that she'd sacrificed her own career to raise their children. That she'd been cutting corners and coupons to help make sure every extra penny from his paycheck went toward paying for his degree.

He loved her.

One day, in the not so distant future, he'd give Anna the bigger, newer house she deserved. For now they'd make do. And if the ultrasound showed that the baby girl Anna carried was—

He hugged her tighter, smoothing his hand down her back

and tangling it in her long, thick, silky soft black hair. "Nothing could keep me from missing it. I'll meet you at the hospital at three." He kissed her lips. "Who's watching the boys?"

"My sister." She glanced at their sons, who, completely oblivious to his and Anna's anxiety over the new baby and pregnancy, continued to stuff their faces with Fruit Loops. "She said if we needed to...if things don't go well and we need..." Tears filled her eyes. She blinked several times and pulled away.

He held her tighter. "Don't go there. We'll deal with whatever God gives us. Okay?"

"Come on, Vin," she said, gripping his arms. "We're scraping by as it is. Your insurance is okay, but it won't be enough to cover—"

"Don't go there," he repeated, the guilt weighing heavy on his heart. He made forty-five grand a year and the government took a shit-ton of it. His schooling was costing them, but he had only one more year to go and he'd have his degree. They'd have a better life. He'd do whatever it took to make sure of it.

Drawing back, he settled his palms on his wife's hard stomach. "It'll be okay. No matter what happens, it'll be okay. And we'll love this one just as much as those two monkeys."

"Hey, I heard that, Daddy," Gus said, waving his spoon at them and grinning.

Benny giggled, then shouted, "Loop."

Anna smiled at their sons. "That explains why you two love bananas so much," she teased their boys, then widened her eyes. "Vince, holy crap, look at what time it is. You're going to be late."

"Crap," Benny echoed, shoving a fistful of cereal into his mouth.

"Potty mouth," Vince said and kissed the top of Benny's head. He pulled his black company-issued coat off the back of Gus's chair and kissed him, too. "I'll be fine. Traffic is always lighter when the kids are off school."

"What are you talking about?" She handed him his lunchbox and thermos of coffee. "Spring break doesn't start until next week."

"Holy crap," he yelled and jumped around as if freaked by the time. When his sons laughed, he did to, then he grabbed his bride of seven years. "I'm teasing you. I don't have to pick up Troy today, so I had a few extra minutes this morning. Just enough time to give my beautiful wife an extra kiss and my two stinky monkeys a couple of tickles."

Anna relaxed, while the boys giggled. "You're still making me nervous. Go before you really *are* late." She ushered him toward the back door leading to the detached garage. "Remember. Three o'clock. Second floor of—"

"Honey, stop. Between this pregnancy and the last two, I've been to how many ultrasounds? I *will* be there."

She crossed her arms. "Maybe I should cancel and try to get a later appointment."

Three o'clock *was* the latest appointment. "Anna, please stop worrying." Damn, she was a ball of nerves. Normally *she* was the cool one, the calm voice of reason. "Don't you remember me telling you I asked Lance Stevens to switch routes with me today?"

Frowning, she tucked a lock of hair behind her ear. "You know I have pregnancy brain. Refresh my memory."

"Even if I'm not finished with all of my deliveries, with Lance's route I'll still be close enough to the hospital that I can park my truck and run in for the ultrasound." He grabbed his car keys off the hook hanging by the door. "But if that happens I'll be late and won't be able to take Gus to his soccer practice. You'll be on soccer duty."

"What's Lance's route again?"

He turned the knob and opened the storm door, noticed it could use a coat of paint and added that to his mental chore list for next weekend. "He handles the small businesses and housing developments in Beachmore and Wilshire Park. I've done this route before, so it shouldn't be too bad."

"Wait, isn't that fancy neighborhood I like over in Wilshire Park?"

Vince grinned as he recalled Anna showing him a house

she'd found online. Her dream house, she'd told him, and only worth seven hundred thousand dollars. He knew Anna had been joking around with him and would never expect to live in a ten thousand square foot home. Still, he wished he could give her that dream house. For now, a dishwasher would have to do.

"Yeah, Rosewood Estates is in Wilshire Park," he confirmed. "Unless things have changed, it should be the second last stop on the route." He checked the Timex Anna had given him for his last birthday. "If I don't get out of here I really *will* be late."

He leaned forward for one more kiss, this one longer and meant to show her how much he loved and adored her. That no matter what happened, he'd be there for her.

"Eww. Kissy-kissy," Gus called from the kitchen table.

"Crap," Benny added with a big smile.

Vince laughed. "On that note, I'm outta here. Love you."

"Love you, too," his wife replied.

"See you soon you two big baboons," he yelled to his boys.

Gus broke into a fit of giggles, while Benny kept saying "crap."

Smiling, Vince closed and locked the door behind him. His smile fell as a cool spring breeze blew in from the east. In order to keep Anna's spirits high and the worry off her shoulders, for weeks he'd been trying his damnedest to pretend the pressure and stress hadn't been affecting him. But it had. The bills, the concern over how they would outgrow their small bungalow once the baby was born...the baby's health.

He climbed into his 1998 Chevy pickup and started the truck. His mom was a fan of saying, 'God never gives you more than you can handle'. Anna's obstetrician had also assured them that the choroid plexus cysts, found on the baby's brain during the last ultrasound, would likely go away on their own and not have any side effects. The research they'd done on the Internet had told them otherwise and had scared the hell of them.

Vince glanced at the clock on the dash as he backed out of

the driveway. Six hours from now, the weeks of waiting, wondering and worrying would come to an end. He just hoped to God the news was good. In the meantime, he was grateful to have to go into work. Delivering packages all day would keep his mind off the baby and on his job.

Yeah, today was definitely one of those days he could use a major distraction.

Woodbine, Georgia
9:50 a.m. Eastern Daylight Saving Time

Jake let go of Naomi, leaned back on his heels and stared at her bloodshot, tear filled eyes. Disappointment, resentment, anger and overwhelming grief collided together and sank deep into his bones. He'd loved her and she was nothing but one enormous lie.

"Who's Lisa Monroe?" he asked, fisting his hands on his thighs. Damn it. He'd been so sure of himself, so sure that he knew her. Her name change and the reasons behind it were important, and he'd had every intention of going after the son of a bitch who'd forced her into hiding. But he'd decided not to dwell on any of that. Blinded by love and lust, he'd given her the benefit of the doubt and had enjoyed his time with her. Only she'd taken her lies to another level. Hell, she'd stripped away his trust in her. And it fucking hurt.

She rose from the chair, but he quickly grabbed her arm and forced her to remain seated. "Answer me, damn it," he demanded, through with her bullshit.

"Is that all you care about?" she sobbed and pointed to the TV. "People are dying because of me." She shoved at his hand and fought against his grip. "Let me go. I have to go to him. I have to stop him."

Guilt crept in, but he didn't release her. "Stop fighting me. You're not going anywhere until you tell me the truth."

She swiped the tears from her face with her free hand. "Fine. I made up Lisa Monroe to get you to stop questioning me."

"And the stalker?"

"He's real." She glanced away. "What I told you about him wasn't a lie."

"Bullshit. You're still lying to me." Disgusted with her and with himself for believing in her and in them, he released her and stood. "CORE's computer forensic analyst has assured me that there's no way in hell you can change your name and social security number without leaving a paper trail. The only way that's possible is through a government agency like Witness Protection. Are you part of that program?"

Rubbing her wrist she shook her head.

"Then who gave you the new identity?" When she didn't answer him, he knelt in front of her, gripped her shoulders and gave her a slight shake. "Who? Damn it, *Rose*, answer me."

Her eyes narrowed with outrage and bitterness. "Don't *ever* call me that again," she said, her tone seething and threatening. "Rose Wood is dead and has been for eight years." Her chin trembled and more tears filled her eyes. "*He* murdered her and her entire family."

A chill washed over him. Naomi had claimed that she was an only child. Her mom had died in a car accident and her dad of a heart attack. "How? Did you lie to me about how your parents died, too?"

She shook her head again. "No. Only..." After drawing in a shaky breath, she reached out and touched his jaw. "I knew the truth. He showed up at both of my parents' funerals and made sure I understood that he'd stop at nothing until he *owned* me." She pressed the heel of her palm against her temple. "*Owned* me," she repeated. "When he showed up at my mom's funeral and made his threats clear, I tried to warn my dad. But he was so grief stricken, he refused to listen to me. When I told my brother, he agreed that—"

"You have a brother?" Damn, did he ever really know her?

Nodding, she dropped her hand to his shoulder. "His name was Thomas."

"Was?"

"He's dead too." Another tear trickled down her cheek. "Because of me."

"Oh, my God," the news anchor gasped and Naomi looked over his shoulder at the TV. "We just learned that there's been *another* explosion."

Jake glanced away from the horror in Naomi's eyes, turned and also focused on the report.

"Minutes ago, there was an explosion in Smithfield, Wyoming. We're live with local reporter, Scott Maddox, who just arrived on the scene. Scott, I know you don't have video yet, but can you tell us what you see and what you know?"

"It's pure chaos here," Scott informed the anchor. "An explosion ripped through Saint Dorothy of the Roses Nursing Home at nine o'clock Mountain Daylight Saving Time. The Wood County fire department is on the scene trying to contain the blaze and ambulances are standing by."

Stunned, Jake leaned against the desk.

Saint Dorothy of the Roses…

Wood County…

Rose Wood.

Even after all of Naomi's lies, he could not discount the four explosions as coincidence. Not with the Rose Wood connection. Not with Rose herself sitting in the room looking terrified, her face ashen, her eyes bleak.

"I have to go," Naomi said and stood. Instead of rushing from the room, she edged closer to the TV. "He has to be stopped."

"Go where?" he asked, snapping out of his shock.

She hugged herself. "Please, Jake. Not being able to tell you the truth has been killing me. But if I tell you everything now, I could risk getting *you* killed. I already have enough death on my conscience."

"No." He pushed away from the desk and shut off the TV. "We go together."

"Leave. This doesn't concern you," she said and headed for the door.

He caught up with her. "The hell it doesn't," he countered

and followed her into her bedroom. "You're my first concern."

After dragging a small suitcase from the bedroom closet, she tossed it on the bed. "What if I don't want to be?"

"Too bad," he said and pulled out his cell phone.

She rushed to his side and reached for the phone. "Who are you calling? You can't tell anyone what's happening. If he finds—"

"Finish packing and make sure you bring warm clothes," he said and waited for Rachel to answer his call.

"Why? Where are we going?"

"Chicago. You'll be safe there," he replied, and hoped to God he was right. Naomi was a liar he no longer trusted. He resented her for deceiving him and making him look like a fool. But the fear in her eyes, the catastrophic explosions taking place out west and the thought of losing her to a murdering lunatic trumped his anger and pride.

Despite everything, he still loved her.

Damn. He really was fucking pathetic.

Norfolk, Virginia
10:15 a.m. Eastern Daylight Saving Time

He gripped the massive growling lion heads that had been hand-carved into the armrests of the mahogany, medieval replica throne chair. Although satisfied with the news reports that had taken over today's regularly scheduled programming, his stomach demanded a mid-morning snack. He looked to Ric, who sat next to the smart brother on the sofa. "How about some refreshments?"

Nodding, Ric rose and headed into the kitchen where Santiago remained at attention. While Ric attended to his request, he studied the smart brother. Ric had told him the brothers were twins, but he couldn't find any resemblance. The dumb brother was thicker, stockier and had blond hair and blue eyes. The smart brother was the opposite, tall and trim, he had a darker complexion, along with brown hair and eyes.

Maybe one of them had been switched at birth and there were two other men roaming the streets who were the exact duplication of the men being held in his warehouse apartment. He smiled at the ludicrous idea, then grinned when the smart brother glared at him with disgust.

Good. The man didn't show fear, not yet. But he would. In the end, they always did. And the fun he'd have proving who held the power...

"A man who wants to make it in this world needs to be dressed for success," he said to the smart brother and eyed his faded, worn jeans, scuffed sneakers along with the graphic t-shirt he wore beneath an unbuttoned flannel. "That includes making it to the barber on a regular basis."

The smart brother knocked his scruffy bangs from his forehead with a defiant jerk of his head. "Thanks for the advice. Maybe you can give me the name of your tailor and when I have a billion dollars I'll give him a call."

Chuckling, he ran his finger along the mahogany lion's mane. "Money is definitely a good thing. But do you know what's even better? Power. When the renovation was completed on the third floor of this warehouse and the rooms were fully furnished, I decided I needed something in this great room that screamed *power*. I paid a furniture maker twenty-five thousand dollars to create this." He rapped his knuckle on the throne chair's armrest. He was, after all, king of his castle, owner of a shipping company worth billions and had needed to make sure that anyone who visited him was fully aware of who was in charge. Right now, the impertinent shithead sitting across from him was in need of clarification.

"Next to blowing up innocent people, it's definitely a conversation piece," the smart brother said, his tone filled with contempt.

He laughed and touched his chest. "Ouch. That little barb stung." Ric approached carrying a tray filled with water bottles, fruits and a variety of Danishes. "Maybe a snack will help change your attitude and make you less passive aggressive."

"I wasn't being passive aggressive," the smart brother said, reaching for a cheese Danish. "I was being aggressive."

Laughing again, he shook his head and looked to Ric. "It appears that me and the smart brother have something in common."

"Yes." Ric grinned. "You're always aggressive."

"Harrison," the smart brother said, and took the cap off of the water bottle.

He turned to Ric. "What do you suppose he wants me to do with that information?"

Ric shrugged. "I think the smart brother would prefer if you called him Harrison."

"Is that true?" he asked Harrison.

The other man nodded. "Yes, sir. I might be smart, but my brother isn't dumb. You can also call him Mickey."

While he knew their names, he'd become quite fond of calling them either dumb or smart. Giving them nicknames gave him power over them. He'd concede though. Not because he needed Harrison to send the signal from the laptop to the devices—he'd already had the man show Ric how to perform this task. He'd call Harrison by his given name…for a price. He would pay dearly for his impertinence.

"Ric," he began, "have Vlad bring Mickey into the room. I'm sure Harrison's brother would like to see what's become of the devices he helped plant."

Harrison's eyes widened a fraction and he set the water bottle on the table. Hands on his knees, his body tensed, Harrison looked as if he were preparing to jump up and run. He'd love to see him try. The hour between setting off the signal from one device to the next had become boring. He'd already sat through three full hours, listening to the bleeding heart news anchors and reporters, viewing the destruction, watching the body bags being lined up outside of each establishment he'd bombed. He didn't give a shit about the dead and injured, or the millions of dollars in damage he'd caused. They were a means to an end.

They would give him Rose.

Grunts of pain caught his attention. He turned just as Vlad escorted a limping Mickey into the room. Eerily pale, the dumb brother looked as if he was already knocking on Death's door. Maybe he'd lost too much blood. He focused on where he'd shot Mickey. Whatever Vlad had used as a tourniquet for Mickey's leg looked as if it had been dipped in blood red paint. What a fucking mess. Maybe Ric was right. Maybe he should just kill the brothers and finish the job without them.

The droning voice of the news anchor he'd been listening to buzzed in the background. No. He wouldn't kill them yet. After all, he needed something to do to occupy his time. Besides, if they ran into a computer glitch, he'd need Harrison's expertise.

"Santiago," he said to the Columbian. "Bring me a pair of scissors and a garbage bag."

Harrison jumped from the couch. "I don't know what—"

Ric shoved him back onto the sofa. "Sit. You're not to get up unless you've been given permission. Understood?"

Harrison didn't answer and kept his gaze riveted on Mickey, who didn't move, didn't even flinch. Considering the end result the last time he'd asked for a garbage bag, he thought for sure Mickey would have reacted. Then again, maybe he really was dumb.

When Santiago entered the room carrying the scissors and a garbage bag, he rose from his throne chair. "Vlad, bring Mickey over here," he said, motioning to a spot on the hardwood floor that was near the TV, but far enough away from the area rug and furniture. "Santiago, have Mickey stand on the garbage bag and hand Vlad the scissors."

"Look at the TV," he ordered Mickey and used the remote to raise the volume. "Look at what you've done."

When Mickey didn't obey and kept his head down, he nodded to Santiago. The Columbian grabbed the dumb brother by his hair and yanked, forcing Mickey to watch the TV.

"Much better," he said and turned to Harrison. "Why don't you fill your brother in on all the excitement?"

Harrison's jaw clenched. He drew in a deep breath and stared at Mickey. "We, ah…" He cleared his throat and blinked several times. "The devices you and Santiago planted are explosives. At seven o'clock our time, the first device exploded and blew up the Rosewood Bar & Grill in San Francisco. No one was hurt." Harrison ran a shaky hand along his forehead, shoving his bangs aside. "The second explosion went off at eight and took out a large part of the Sun Valley Hotel and Convention Center in Henderson, Nevada. Last we heard, fourteen people are dead."

The depths of grief, clearly written all over Harrison's face, both fascinated and disgusted him. He hadn't mourned his parents' deaths, or his grandparents' for that matter. In his defense, it was rather hard to grieve for his father, considering he'd been the one to kill him. His mother had been a decent woman, but he certainly wasn't heartbroken when she died. Her inheritance belonged to him. Still. How could Harrison feel an ounce of pity for people he didn't know? The dead, the injured, were mere casualties in his cause.

"In Idaho," Harrison continued. "We blew up a middle school. So far nine are dead." His Adam's apple worked along his throat as he hardened his jaw. "One was a twelve-year-old kid."

Mickey had yet to move, but a tear slipped down his pale cheek.

"And," he prompted Harrison to continue torturing Mickey with the deadly results.

"And about fifteen minutes ago another explosion destroyed a nursing home. We haven't heard how many people are dead or injured yet, but I...it doesn't look good."

More tears streamed down Mickey's cheeks as he stared at the carnage showing on the TV.

"Nothing to cry about," he told Mickey. "Those people were old and in a nursing home for a reason. If anything, I did Americans a favor. Now we have less people feeding off of Medicare and Social Security." He pointed to the tray of refreshments Ric had brought out earlier. "Care for a Danish?"

His face twisting with hatred, Mickey slid his gaze to him. "Fuck you."

144

Vlad and Santiago gripped Mickey by the arms and jerked him. He held up a hand and motioned for them to stand down. "Fuck *me*? Is that anyway to treat the man who gave you a good paying job, who brought you into his home and offered you shelter, food and drink? Your manners are atrocious. Both you and your brother need to understand that I do not tolerate belligerence from anyone. You—"

"You're a fucking murderer," Mickey shouted. "A monster. I didn't sign us up for any of this. Because of you, *we* killed innocent people."

The wave of rage coursing through him momentarily blurred his vision. He backhanded Mickey in the face, then grabbed the man's chin. "How dare you interrupt me when I'm speaking," he said, pressing his thumb and index finger, forcing Mickey's mouth to contort and open slightly.

The dumb brother lived up to his name and spoke. With the way he held Mickey's face, he couldn't decipher what the man had said. Letting go, he took a step back and reached for a napkin setting on the refreshment tray. "Didn't quite get that," he said, wiping his hand. "Dare to repeat it."

Although Mickey started at him with defiance and hatred, he kept his mouth shut.

He turned and dropped the used napkin on the tray. "I didn't think so. You and your brother are both a couple of puss—"

"Fucking crazy son of a bitch," Mickey shouted.

He froze. Time to show the piece of white trash just how crazy he could be. Straightening his tie, he faced the dumb brother. "Open your mouth." When Mickey didn't comply, he nodded to Santiago. The Columbian threw his fist into Mickey's stomach, causing him to double over. "Other than blowing up another eight places, I have nothing on my schedule. We can end this quickly or I can drag it out all day. Your choice."

"Do it," Harrison encouraged. "Please, Mick. Just do what he tells you."

He jerked his head toward Harrison, but kept his eyes on

Mickey. "See? That's why he's the smart brother. You might want to listen to him."

Mickey shifted his gaze toward Harrison, then opened his mouth.

"Good. Now stick out your tongue." He looked to Santiago. "Hold his tongue in place." Once Santiago complied, he nodded to the scissors Vlad held. "Vlad, cut off his tongue."

"Wait," Harrison cried over Mickey's fearful grunts. "Please, don't do this. You've proved your point. Please. I'm begging you *not* to do this."

Oh, but he really wanted to cut the shithead. Make him understand that no one interrupted with him, that *he* was the one who held the power.

With a shrug, he turned to Ric, who said, "He deserves it."

The sadist *would* say that. But Ric was also right. Without a tongue, the dumb brother could no longer utter a word and the smart brother would likely change his tone, too.

"Agreed, he does deserve it. Vlad, do it."

The Russian used his thumb and index finger to open the scissor. As he rested both blades on either side of Mickey's tongue, the dumb brother jerked his head and struggled against the grip Santiago had on his slippery flesh. As he fought, the sharp blade nicked and scraped Mickey's tongue. If he kept it up, he'd sever the damned thing off himself. Although the irony would amuse him, the process would result in a bloody mess.

"Ric, hold a gun to Harrison's head. Let's see if Mickey feels his tongue is worth his brother's life."

Mickey stopped struggling the moment the barrel of Ric's .38 touched Harrison's temple. "Now there's some brotherly love, eh? Vlad, do it."

"He'll bleed all over the place," Harrison said, his eyes shifting from him to Mickey.

"Not if Santiago duct tapes his mouth shut."

"Then he'll die of asphyxiation. He'll choke on his own blood."

The smart brother had a valid point. And he wasn't ready

for Mickey to die. Yet. Although Harrison had showed Ric how to send the signals to the devices, if he ended up needing Harrison's computer skills, he might also need to use Mickey as motivation and leverage.

Nodding, he held out his hand toward Vlad. "The scissors." Once he had them in hand, he motioned for Ric to drop the gun. "Again, this is why you're the smart brother. You're right, I don't want a mess and I doubt the garbage bag would keep the blood contained. So, why don't we keep it simple?" He stood in front of Mickey, who now had his mouth pressed shut, his tongue safely inside. "You'd like to keep your tongue intact, correct?"

Mickey nodded. While his face regained color, his eyes held a strange combination of hatred and gratitude.

"I don't blame you. But I still need to set an example." He grabbed Mickey's scruffy blond hair and held his head in place. "Just one that's a little less bloody," he said and stabbed the scissors into his left eye.

Mickey gaped, but no sound escaped from his mouth. Thank God. Harrison's screaming and yelling was more than enough noise. He looked away from the blood oozing down Mickey's cheek and turned to Vlad. "Take him back in the room. Remove the scissors and throw duct tape over his eye. I'd like to keep the mess to a minimum."

Dazed, the color drained from his face again, Mickey didn't move and Vlad, with the help of Santiago, had to practically carry the man from the room. Disappointed that ramming scissors into a man's eye socket had ended up being anticlimactic, he took a seat in his throne chair. With a bored sigh, he rested his elbow on the mahogany armrest and his chin in his palm. He eyed Harrison. The man's head hung and he held his hands over his face. His shoulders shook, leading him to believe Harrison wept for his brother. Touching.

"So," he began, "are there any other smartass comments you'd like to make about my chair or the people *you've* blown up?"

Harrison dropped his hands in his lap and raised his head.

His face flushed, his eyes bloodshot from crying like a child, he shook his head. The defeat in Harrison's eyes outweighed his disappointment. He'd proven to the brothers who held the power, but based on their tenacity, he wouldn't be surprised if he'd have to give them a few more reminders throughout the day. He smiled at the prospect.

Torture really wasn't his thing. Sure, he'd killed plenty of men and women, but he'd never *tortured* them, and had always left the messy stuff for Ric. A gunshot to the head was quick and easy, and the way he went about his business. Still, inflicting pain on the dumb brother had been quite…satisfying. He'd always considered holding a gun to a person's head the highest form of power he could have over someone. While he still believed this, he also couldn't deny the rush of adrenaline he'd experienced when he initially struck Mickey with the scissors.

Ric took a seat next to Harrison. "Santiago is finishing helping Vlad duct tape Mickey's eye." He grinned and elbowed Harrison. "Bet Mickey didn't *see* that one coming."

"Bad joke," he said with a chuckle. "Rather insensitive, too."

"Right. I *see* your point." Ric laughed and then looked to the TV. "Once the next device goes off, I'll give it fifteen minutes, then call a press conference. We're only twenty minutes from corporate headquarters, so I figured you can give your speech around eleven-fifty."

"Perfect. By the time I'm finished and reporters have asked their inane questions, the next device will have gone off."

"And you can show America your outrage and support," Ric said with a conspiratorial wink.

He snagged an apple cinnamon Danish from the tray. "Don't look so glum, Harrison. Mickey will be fine. Once the shock wears off he'll be back to his old, potty-mouthed self. In the meantime, have another Danish or some of this fruit. You need to keep yourself hydrated and nourished." He glanced at his watch. "In less than thirty minutes, guess what you're going to blow up?"

Harrison blinked several times before glancing away. "Can I ask you a question?"

"Sure."

"I mean no disrespect."

"Of course," he said with a smile. "You want to keep your eyes and tongue. Please, ask away. If I don't want to answer, you'll be the first to know."

After drawing in a shaky breath, Harrison said, "You have everything. Why are you doing this?"

Gripping the mahogany lion's head, he leaned forward. Since the man would not leave this warehouse alive, he had no problem answering his question. "Some men give women flowers, others give chocolates or diamonds." He plucked a grape off the tray and shrugged. "I blow things up. And guess what? If she hasn't received my message by now, she will after you set off the next device." He grinned. "If you think this is fun, wait until she comes to me. That's when the real entertainment will begin."

CHAPTER 9

Kingsland, Georgia Airport
10:38 a.m. Eastern Daylight Saving Time

NAOMI'S HEART RACED as she buckled the seatbelt. Less than forty minutes ago she was packing her bags, ready to turn herself over to the bastard who had ruined the lives of so many innocent people. But Jake wouldn't hear of it. Instead, he'd made a call to CORE, chartered a private jet out of Kingsland, Georgia, a short fifteen minute drive from her home in Woodbine, and was forcing her to go to Chicago.

"Local time is ten thirty-eight," the pilot announced over the intercom. "We're expected to arrive in Chicago at six minutes after twelve. Please turn off all electronic devices. Once we're airborne, I'll let you know when you can resume using those devices and are able to move about the cabin. Enjoy the flight."

Naomi didn't think she could ever truly enjoy anything after what she'd witnessed today. Goose bumps rose over her skin as the images of the dead and injured flooded her mind. How could he have done this? After all these years, what could have possessed him to go to this level? He'd killed her parents and brother. Their deaths had devastated her and left her wallowing in guilt. But he'd gone beyond murdering her family and was now killing innocent people.

Because of her.

As the plane began to move and pick up speed, her throat and chest tightened. Tears welled in her eyes. All four explosions combined had killed thirty-six people and injured well over one hundred. She brought the photo of the twelve-year-old boy who had been killed at the middle school to mind. Her chin trembled. She fisted her hands as anger and unfathomable sorrow imbedded itself onto her heart and soul. What a waste. What he'd done went beyond criminal. The killings were vicious and wicked.

He was pure evil.

And the only one who could stop him was her.

She jerked when Jake took her fisted hand in his, then fought from crying as he forced her to unclench her fingers and hold his hand. How could he bear to touch her? From the moment they'd met, she'd done nothing but lie to him. She hadn't wanted to and had hated herself a little more each time she gave him another fabrication. Over the years, she'd been able to justify her lies and half-truths, telling herself that keeping Jake in the dark would also keep him alive. She still believed that and now worried about CORE's involvement.

If the bastard was willing to kill innocent people to send her a message, she didn't even want to imagine what he'd do to CORE's agents, should they opt to help her. Actually she wasn't even sure they *could* help her. His wealth was practically limitless. His reach was far and powerful. Worst of all, the man had no conscience and his innate narcissism knew no bounds.

"Are you still afraid of flying?" Jake asked as the plane leveled in the air.

She expected him to add, *or was that a lie too*, but he didn't. Instead, he continued to hold her hand. "Today I learned there are scarier things in life," she said and squeezed his hand. "I'm sorry, Jake. I never wanted you to be involved in this."

His jaw clenched. "Obviously. But I am now. So, no more lies. Are you in Witness Protection?"

"No."

"Then what government agency gave you the new identity?"

"It's complicated."

"Then make it uncomplicated."

"Jake, I—"

"Okay, folks," the pilot's voice came over the speakers. "Feel free to use the restroom and any electronic devices."

She let go of Jake's hand and reached beneath her seat for her purse. After she pulled out her mini-tablet, she turned on the device. The explosions were going off every hour on the hour. Nearly eleven, she prayed he would stop the senseless killing and that another bomb wouldn't be detonated.

"You're not going to answer me, are you?" Jake asked, stretching his long legs into the aisle. "I guess it doesn't really matter who gave you the identity. The only thing that does is the man behind the bombings. Maybe now you'll tell me his name."

She trusted Jake, more than anyone on the planet. But she refused to tell him until she met his counterparts at CORE. For all she knew the private agency dealt with cheating spouses or worked for insurance companies to investigate suspicious claims. If that were the case, CORE would not be an asset, but a hindrance. They would waste her time and, by not allowing her to go to the bastard and put an end to the bombings, could place more innocent victims in danger.

"I'm sorry, but I'm not ready to talk about him," she said and, with guilt and embarrassment weighing heavy on her shoulders, she kept her attention on the tablet.

"Then what are you ready to talk about?"

Nothing. She wanted to crawl into a hole and bury herself underneath her secrets and lies. "Tell me more about CORE and what you do."

The tick in his jaw indicated his frustration, but he gave her a curt nod and said, "CORE stands for Criminal Observance Resolution and Evidence. We handle a variety of cases. From recovering stolen property to helping the authorities solve murder investigations. We also deal with cold cases, too. Remember me mentioning the murders in Bola?"

Had it only been a few days ago that they'd been sitting on her back patio, sipping iced tea and catching up on the lost years? "Yes. You said CORE recruited you after the murders were solved." She'd almost forgotten about that part of their conversation and realized CORE wasn't just an average private investigation agency.

"Right. Trust me. The people I work with will help us come up with a solution. Chances are my boss will want you to go to the FBI. There hasn't been any mention of their involvement on the newscasts, but I wouldn't be surprised if their people weren't already making the Rose Wood connection."

Another chill swept through her at the mention of her former name. Since becoming Naomi McCall, she'd purged many memories of her past life and had made up new ones. She'd submerged herself into her fictional life and had created imaginary friends, teachers and jobs. At first, it had been difficult to keep all of the lies straight, but after a while she'd become so used to fabricating her past, lying had become as easy as breathing.

Until she'd met Jake.

When they'd started dating and she fell in love with him, her heart and mind battled over whether or not to tell him the truth. Her head won. She loved him, trusted him, but feared opening up about her past would cost him his life.

Now that her past had caught up with her, she realized she'd been a fool to think she could wade through life with her head buried in the sand. Pretending she didn't love or miss Jake, that the murdering bastard had given up on her, that she was happy being a school nurse and living in a small Georgia town, hadn't been working for a long time. Even before Jake had blown back into her life and the bastard had blown up buildings and people, the urge to roam had been strong. She'd wanted to pack her bags, hop in her car and drive. She'd fantasized about traveling north and heading straight for Bola, where she'd left Jake behind. She'd even imagined driving to Virginia, buying a gun and putting a bullet into the murderer's head.

Fear had stopped her from doing anything but moving through her mundane life.

Unfortunately, she now had no choice but to face her fears,

along with the man who had instilled them.

"Going to the FBI isn't going to work," she said, scrolling through her tablet while keeping an eye on the time. *Ten fifty-three.* Her stomach twisted. Seven more minutes.

"CORE agents can protect you, but the FBI can—"

"They won't help."

"How do you know? Have you gone to them before?"

She pressed her fingers against her left temple where a throb began to build. Jake was like a damned Pit Bull—smart, brawny and tenacious. If she didn't throw him a bone, he'd keep hounding her. Until they arrived at CORE and she met the people Jake claimed could help her, she'd pick and choose what to tell him to keep him satisfied. "Yes, I've gone to the FBI and they refused to do anything," she said, the half-truth easily rolling off her tongue. Her brother had worked for the FBI, so, technically, she did go to them for help. After Thomas had risked his career to give her a new identity, he'd started to dig into the background of the man who had murdered their parents. When his superiors discovered whom he'd been investigating, they'd threatened to suspend Thomas, which hadn't surprised her. The bastard was well known in Washington and had many friends in powerful positions

"Did they give you a reason why?"

She glanced at the clock on her tablet. *Ten fifty-five.* Her stomach knotted tighter.

Anxious, she tapped her heel against the plane's floor and stared out the window. "I told you he was wealthy, but what I didn't tell you is that he and his family have strong political connections. It would have been my word against his. Even now, with everything that's happened today, the FBI still wouldn't believe me."

"How can you be sure?" He released a frustrated breath. "Damn it, look at me."

"Because I *know*," she said with vehemence and met his gaze. Emotionally drained, exhausted from staying up late into the night making love to Jake, she rubbed her tired, itchy eyes. "God, Jake, this is one thing I'm *not* lying about. This man is rich, popular and well liked. He's given hundreds of thousands of dollars in campaign money to senators and presidents. Politicians consider him a cash cow and because his record is squeaky clean, no one would ever believe that he would risk his reputation and resort to terrorism over a woman." She gripped the tablet tight. "Over a nobody like me."

The earlier anger and resentment in his eyes softened to understanding. "The name change. Whoever did it for you could come forward and—"

She shook her head. "They won't vouch for me." One was dead and the other might as well be. As the guilt compounded, nervous energy took over. She had the urge to jump out of her seat and pace the small cabin and, once they landed, she wanted to hit the ground running. In her heart, she knew she couldn't. Her days of running and hiding had finally come to an end. The bombings, the deaths…he'd forced her from the safe lifestyle she'd created for herself. He'd forced her to face the past and the future.

Jake leaned into the chair and tilted his head back. "Trying to get anything out of you is like pulling teeth."

She hated keeping anything from Jake, but, in time and when she was ready, he'd eventually learn the truth. Until then, she'd keep him in the dark.

She'd keep him alive.

Glancing down at the tablet, she caught the time, then her breath. "It's three minutes after eleven," she whispered, and started a new search for Rose Wood.

He raised his head and leaned toward her seat, his earthy, familiar scent giving her comfort and reminding her of everything they'd shared this past weekend. If only she could turn back the clock. If only—

The co-pilot emerged from the cockpit, his face drawn and his eyes filled with worry. "Folks, we're going to have you shut down any electronic devices."

"Is something wrong?" Jake asked.

While the pilot said something about turbulence and possible rough weather—which she didn't believe based on the clear skies—Naomi quickly scrolled through the tablet.

"Ma'am," the pilot said, just as a new headline appeared from CNN.

Horrified, lightheaded and her stomach nauseous, she held up her hand. "Oh, my God." Two more people were dead because of her. Her vision blurred with tears. Not wanting the pilot to see her cry, she blinked them away and handed the tablet to Jake.

With reluctance, Jake took the device. He knew in his gut there had been another explosion, but didn't want to see or hear about the deaths and destruction. People were dying and Naomi knew who was behind it. If CORE couldn't help them, he firmly believed more innocent people would be killed before the day ended. And if they weren't careful, he worried Naomi could be one of them.

He looked down at the tablet and read the news bulletin. *Nine a.m. Mountain Daylight Saving Time, BH-Xpress Flight 1113, an Airbus A300f4-622R, exploded during takeoff from the Denver International Airport. Firefighters are on the scene and searching for the two pilots, Jerry Rose and Woody Gilmore.* He stopped reading. An eerie sensation caused his skin to pickle with unease. Concerned with how Naomi was handling the news and anxious for their pilot to leave them alone, he turned to the man and said, "If you're worried we're going to become paranoid about flying, don't."

The pilot gave them a slight shrug. "You never know how people are going to react. You're sure you two are okay?"

"Fine," Jake assured him and once the pilot was back in the cockpit, he turned to Naomi. "This is *not* your fault."

She drew in a shaky breath. "Really? If people knew that the bombings were a way to get to me, who do you think they'd blame?"

"The man behind it." He handed her the tablet. "I don't give a shit how powerful this guy is, or who his connections are. I highly doubt the politicians he's backed in the past would want to be associated with a murderer." He leaned toward her, purposefully crowding and intimidating her. "Who the hell is he?"

She shoved his shoulder. "Stop. If I think your agency can help me, then I'll talk. Until then, you need to get out of my face and leave me the hell alone."

Why did she have to be so damned stubborn? Fuck it. He leaned back into his seat, taking the tablet with him.

"Can I please have that back?" she asked.

"No." He didn't care if he was being a dick. Not after all of her lies and secrets. Instead of being a team player and giving him the information he'd need to bring the bombings to an end, she was continuously shitting on him. Feeding him small scraps of the truth. Giving him mismatched pieces to a puzzle he couldn't solve without her help.

Why couldn't she trust him? After everything they'd been through, after this past weekend, after all of the love and support he'd given her when they'd been together, and she couldn't confide in him? Total bullshit.

He'd loved her. He still loved her. Although at this point he was having a hard time remembering why.

Her arm and leg brushed his as she shifted in her seat. He glanced at her and caught her staring at him. The pain and misery in her once laughing eyes made his gut knot. No matter what, no matter her past, Naomi didn't deserve any of this. "Come here." Aching to ease her pain, he moved the armrest out of his way and wrapped an arm around her. "We'll get through this," he said and, when she rested her head against his shoulder, he kissed the top of her head.

He couldn't be sure of how things between them would be in the end, but as long as she was safe and the bombings stopped, nothing else mattered. As the minutes ticked by, her breathing changed and her body became dead weight against his. He glanced down. Naomi had dozed off and was now asleep. Good. She needed her rest. They had a long day ahead of them. Once they reached Chicago, he planned to take her directly to CORE. When he'd spoken to Rachel and had given her what little information he'd had, she'd said she hoped that Ian's contacts at the FBI and Homeland Security would be able to tell them about the devices used in the bombings. He just hoped to God Ian's contacts came through for them. There was no way in hell he'd ever allow Naomi to go to the prick behind this.

As the minutes passed, he kept her close to him and scrolled through the tablet, searching for updates from the different bombings and hoping to find new clues and links other than the Rose Wood connection. Twenty minutes later, he saw that the owner of BH-Xpress, the world's fourth largest shipping and packaging company, was about to give a press conference. He clicked on the link and raised the volume.

Within seconds, a tall, olive-skinned man with black, slicked back hair approached the podium. Beneath his somber image the caption read, *Ric Mancini, BH-Xpress Chief Operating Officer*. The man cleared his throat and leaned toward the microphone. "Thank you for joining us. Mr. Hunnicutt will speak briefly and then answer a few questions." He looked to his left and raised his arm. "Christian Hunnicutt, owner and CEO of Brockheist Hunnicutt Express International."

The CEO replaced Ric at the podium. His expression grave, he turned his solemn gaze on the reporters. "Thank you for coming," he said and shuffled his notecards. "My heart goes out to those tragically affected by today's horrific events. I am deeply saddened, especially for those who had lost loved ones. As you know, less than an hour ago one of my company's planes had exploded during takeoff. The pilots, Jerry Rose and Woody Gilmore, both lost their lives." The pilots' smiling images flashed on the corner of the screen. "Jerry worked for BH-Xpress for seventeen years and Woody, for the past twelve. Both were good men who were dedicated to their families and their jobs. I believe I speak for every employee of BH-Xpress when I say they will be missed."

Hunnicutt took a step back and pressed his thumb and index finger against his brow. After a moment, he drew in a breath and moved to the microphone. "I've spoken with the Vice President and Senator, Ron Bammerlin, who leads a committee against domestic terrorism, as well as the Directors of the FBI and Homeland Security. Each man has assured me that they are doing their best to uncover who is behind the explosions that have affected San Francisco, Henderson, Nevada, Clyde, Idaho, Smithfield, Wyoming and now Denver, Colorado. I am personally donating my company resources to help put an end to the violence. I have also created a fund to aid the victims and their families during their time of need."

He gripped the podium and looked directly into the camera. "The terrorists behind these bombings need to be stopped. Their cowardly acts are despicable and reprehensible. They've gone after the young, the elderly and every age in between. Race, religion and class make no difference to these villains. And while it's unclear what their cause is, what *is* clear—they are trying to terrorize Americans. But we are strong. We have fought as underdogs in the past and have come out on top. Why? We have heart and soul. We have courage and ingenuity. Banding together, helping our fellow Americans hurt by these atrocities, will only strengthen our resolve."

Naomi stirred in his arms. Jake glanced away from the tablet and caught her watching the press conference. When he saw the fresh tears in her eyes, he squeezed her tighter. "You okay?"

She nodded and kept her attention on the tablet. Although not satisfied with her response, he continued to watch the press conference, too.

"As I said," Hunnicutt continued, "I will offer my company's resources and donate my time and money to help stop the madness. I encourage anyone with information regarding who is behind these bombings to come forward. This is America. The land of the free. The home of the brave. We must show a united front and end the terrorism now." He looked at his watch. "I have time for a few questions."

"It's eleven fifty-eight," Naomi said in a quiet, ominous tone. "Please, God. No more."

He tensed. The helplessness and eerie sadness in her voice unnerved him. Naomi might have lied to him about herself and her life, but he'd like to think he knew the woman behind the mask. With each explosion, with each death and injury, she would allow the guilt to fester and control her life. She needed to understand that this was not her fault. Damn it, she needed to stop hiding and trust him.

"Mr. Hunnicutt," a reporter said and stood. "Is it true that you've grounded every BH-Xpress plane?"

"In 1855, my great-great grandfather, Brockheist Hunnicutt, started this company. He'd been a stevedore and worked the docks in London. It has been said that he'd witnessed and helplessly watched as men who worked by his side died or lost limbs, due to poor working conditions. When he'd started his shipping company, he'd sworn that no employee of his would ever suffer on the job. He'd created standards and procedures that are still used by my company today." Hunnicutt scanned the crowd. "Although the Directors of the FBI and Homeland Security do not believe BH-Xpress is being targeted and that these bombings are random, I've ordered every plane to be grounded until they've been thoroughly inspected. I will not put my employees at risk."

"What about your customers?" another reporter asked. "Aren't you concerned about their dissatisfaction over late deliveries?"

"Crass," Naomi muttered.

"Seriously," Jake agreed.

Hunnicutt gave the reporter a condescending half smile. "I would like to think my customers are more concerned about the safety of their fellow Americans. Next question."

Another reporter stood. "Your wife and children are in New York. Are you concerned for their well-being?"

"My wife and children are my *top* priority. I'm always concerned for their well-being. I spoke with Liliana before the press conference. She and my children are safe." Hunnicutt checked his watch again, then scanned the sea of reporters. "One final question."

"Is it true that you plan to run for the U.S. Senate in the fall?" another reporter asked. "Political analysts have suggested that after a couple terms as senator, you could be a possible presidential candidate."

Hunnicutt shook his head. "Now is not the time to discuss politics. Now is the time to reassure Americans that—"

"Oh, my God," someone shouted.

Naomi tensed and leaned forward, as murmurs and whispers ensued from the audience on screen. When voices began to rise, Hunnicutt placed a hand over the microphone and looked to Ric Mancini. BH-Xpress's COO walked across the stage and whispered something to Hunnicutt, who quickly covered his mouth and shook his head. Ric rested a hand on Hunnicutt's shoulder, said something else, then moved back to his earlier position.

Hunnicutt approached the microphone. "Everyone, please. For those of you who haven't heard, there's been another explosion. This time in Amarillo, Texas. I—"

The CNN newsroom filled the tablet's screen. "As BH-Xpress CEO Christian Hunnicutt just stated, there's been another bombing," the news anchor said with disgust. "An explosion just ripped through Palo de Rosa, a shopping mall located in Madera, Texas, a suburb of Amarillo."

Naomi grabbed the tablet from him and began a new search. Within seconds, she slammed her head against the cushioned seat.

"What is it?" he asked.

She slid her eyes closed just as a tear escaped and handed him the tablet. "*Palo de Rosa* is Spanish for rosewood."

Norfolk, Virginia
12:08 p.m. Eastern Daylight Saving Time

Harrison looked away from the big screen TV. He didn't know what sickened him more, viewing the destruction he'd caused at the Palo de Rosa shopping mall, or watching as the billionaire badger snowed the world with his bullshit.

"Honey Badger is going to be *muy cabreado*," Santiago said with a chuckle.

"English," Vlad reminded the Columbian.

"*Oh caramba.*" Santiago rose from the sofa. "Pissed off, Russian. You know Honey Badger don't like it when people interrupt him and that news anchor just dissed his ass."

The Russian grinned. "True." His smile fell as he glanced to Harrison. "Vlad hopes Ric calms Honey Badger down before he come back. Vlad tired of playing nurse to the mouse."

Santiago stretched. "I'll go check on your patient. Hopefully he's not dead."

The knot in Harrison's stomach twisted as Santiago left the room. He hadn't seen his brother since Honey Badger stabbed Mickey in the eye and had no idea how he was doing. But Vlad did. Until the press conference, the Russian hadn't left Mickey's side. "We're not going to make it out of here," Harrison said, keeping his voice low and his eyes on the door.

Vlad shook his blond head. "Vlad will be truthful. Mouse will not live. Honey Badger will use him against Harry, understand?"

He did. As long as Mickey was alive, he'd serve as leverage. Honey Badger had made that painful fact clear from the start. "Your boss has to be stopped."

Vlad shrugged. "Who will stop him? Not Vlad. Vlad likes head on neck."

He considered telling Vlad about the program he'd uploaded in the system, but held back. The Russian was a survivor and worked for the enemy. His trust in Vlad only went so far. He didn't want his brother to be killed and, like Vlad, preferred to keep his head on his neck. But he'd sacrifice Mickey's life, as well as his own, to stop the senseless killing.

Harrison looked to the muted TV and caught the chaos ensuing in the aftermath of the latest bombing. The caption beneath the tragic scene stated that nineteen people had already been confirmed dead.

Sickened that he'd been the triggerman, that he'd been the one to cause those deaths, he turned away. "He's killing innocent people over a woman," he said with disgust.

Vlad frowned. "What Harry talking about? Vlad watch

press conference. Honey Badger does this for political gain."

He could understand the Russian's way of thinking. Honey Badger had gone on TV and made himself out to be sympathetic and torn up over the bombings. Then he remembered the reporter who had asked him about running for Senate and a possible presidential candidacy. A chill moved through him and settled in his chest. If that crazy bastard were to become president—

Harrison leaned forward. "Vlad, listen to me," he said in a hushed tone. "He told me he's doing this to draw out a woman. But I agree. I wouldn't be surprised if his intentions were twofold. Consider this though, would you really want to see him in the White House?"

Vlad rolled his eyes. "The possibility is—"

"Real. Think about it. He has the money, he has political connections, he's making himself out to be a hero fighting alongside the fellow Americans he's killing in order to put an end to the domestic terrorism *he* caused and controls. He's fucking crazy, Vlad. Don't you give a shit about the people he's killed?"

Remorse flickered in Vlad's eyes. "It out of Vlad's control."

"It doesn't have to be. *We* can stop him. *We* can put an end to this."

Santiago came out of the back room, whistling. "Mickey's awake, but he doesn't look good. I'm going to get him something to eat and drink," he said, heading for the kitchen.

"Can you give him something for the pain?" Harrison asked.

The Columbian stopped rummaging through the fridge and looked at him. "Don't tell Honey Badger," he said and pulled a pill bottle from the cabinet.

"Thank you," Harrison replied, and after Santiago went back into the room carrying the pills, water and a banana, he quickly gained Vlad's attention. "Work with me. Please. Help me stop him before more people die."

Vlad shook his head. "No, Harry. Vlad illegal alien, not U.S. citizen. Going back to Russia not an option. Death not an option. Understood?"

Harrison leaned back into the couch and rested his head against the cushion. Thank God he hadn't told Vlad about the program he'd uploaded. The Russian's only concern was for himself. Given the chance, Vlad would likely turn on him in order to save his own Russian ass. Sliding his tired eyes closed, he asked, "If he hadn't stopped you, would you have cut off Mickey's tongue?"

"Yes."

He winced. "If he orders you to cut me or kill me, will you do it?"

The Russian released a deep sigh. "It Vlad's job," he said, his tone weary. "Know this, Vlad wouldn't like hurting Harry."

"And if I find a way to escape?"

"Harry won't, but Vlad hopes."

Harrison opened his eyes and raised his head. "I'm going to die today," he admitted what he'd been denying to himself since first arriving at the warehouse.

Vlad's face and eyes softened with sadness as he slowly nodded.

"If you end up being the one to kill me, no hard feelings. I understand why you're doing what you're doing."

Vlad's sadness turned to anger. "Vlad hate killing," the Russian said with vehemence, his eyes blazing with outrage.

"Then why do it? Why let him—"

"Vlad has no choice."

"There's always a choice," Harrison countered.

"Not for Vlad." The Russian leaned forward and pointed a finger at him. "Understand this, Harry, you pull trigger and blow up buildings to save the mouse. Vlad stay with Honey Badger to keep family alive."

"So you'd rather be his bitch than put an end to his threats."

The Russian's face grew red and his eyes narrowed. "Vlad no one's bitch."

"Are you sure about that?" he taunted, hoping to latch onto Vlad's conscience and reel him over to his side. "From where

I'm sitting, you're in the same position as me and Mickey. Only at least I'll die today and not have to—"

Santiago opened the door of the back room. "Mickey isn't a very good patient," he said with a smile. "He acts like he's the first person to be shot in the leg and stabbed in the eye." The Columbian's face hardened when he looked at Vlad. "What is it?"

"Nothing," Vlad said. "Honey Badger arrives soon. We should have lunch for him and Harry should ready the next device."

"*Convenido*. Especially if he's still upset." Santiago's smile returned. "A pissed off Honey Badger is bad enough, but a hungry, pissed off badger is even worse." He looked to Harrison. "And I'm sure your brother would like to keep his other eye safely in its socket."

As the Columbian laughed and headed into the kitchen, Harrison swore if he had the opportunity, he'd kill the man. Unlike Vlad, Santiago didn't have a sympathetic bone in his body and took pleasure in his and Mickey's pain.

"Careful, Harry," Vlad warned quietly. "The Columbian enjoys slitting throats of enemy."

Harrison knocked his bangs off his forehead. "I'm already a dead man."

"Dead man can't stop Honey Badger." A half smile tilted the Russian's mouth. "Harry has time," he said and followed Santiago into the kitchen.

The tiniest amount of hope crept into Harrison's chest. Vlad was right. There was still time. Although he'd love more than anything to put an end to the bombings now, he knew he couldn't, not with Mickey's life on the line. Plus, he'd uploaded the program that would create a trail of breadcrumbs leading back to Honey Badger's company's operating system when he'd been in Bloomington, Indiana. Considering the devices were being set off in the same order they'd been planted, the Bloomington bomb wouldn't detonate until four—three and a half hours from now.

He wasn't sure how long it would take for the authorities to trace the digital footprint back to Honey Badger, but if he and Mickey could hold out until they did, they just might survive this. And if they survived, what then? He and Mickey would be labeled terrorists and traitors. They wouldn't just go to prison. They'd go directly to Death Row.

Shifting his gaze to the carnage on the TV, he rubbed a hand along his forehead. Not only did they deserve to die, they deserved to burn in hell for what they'd done. Before that happened, he'd do his damnedest to bring down the man who'd brought them into this wicked game.

No matter the cost, Christian Hunnicutt would pay the ultimate price. Harrison had never physically hurt a soul, but thanks to Hunnicutt, he had murder on his mind.

Bloomington, Indiana
11:28 a.m. Central Daylight Saving Time

Vince reached for the ringing cell phone setting in the truck console. Anna. He quickly answered before turning into the parking lot of a small strip mall. "Everything okay?" he asked.

"Oh, my gosh. Did you hear what happened? What's *been* happening?"

Hell, yeah, he'd heard, but hadn't wanted to give his wife any added worry. "It's pretty shocking?"

"*Shocking?* Try horrifying. Did you know Christian Hunnicutt gave a press conference?"

He'd heard about that, too. His supervisor had called him, along with the other drivers on the road, and had said that Hunnicutt had spoken with the FBI, Homeland Security and a bunch of other overpaid blowhards. Before the press conference, the owner of BH-Xpress had issued a companywide statement saying he'd been assured that these acts of terrorism were not solely directed at BH-Xpress, but had been random and made to instill fear into the heart of Americans.

Busy getting ready for work and helping with the kids,

Vince hadn't caught the morning news. He'd also been on the road when the other bombings had occurred.

"My supervisor brought me up to speed. Hunnicutt doesn't think we have anything to be worried about," he said, hoping to ease her concerns.

"Really? Did you know he's grounded every company plane until they've been inspected?"

"It's a precaution," he said and reached for the tablet that held the day's delivery schedule. Three boxes needed to be dropped off at the pet store in the strip mall. "Don't worry about it."

"But I *am* worried. I've been following the news since you left. No, Benny. That's ca-ca," she scolded their son. "Sorry, Ben was trying to eat Gus's crayon."

He smiled and climbed out of his seat. "Have you ever bit into one? Maybe they actually taste good." He moved to the back of the truck in search of the packages he needed to deliver.

"I'll serve you your favorite colors for dinner," she said. "Seriously though, I am worried. Do you realize that the bombings are moving from west to east?"

After finding the packages, he noticed two were large and he'd have to make a couple of trips. Damn. That'd add extra minutes to his schedule that he didn't have if he was to make it to the hospital by three. "No. Sorry, hon. I honestly haven't heard all the details yet."

"Well, let me clue you in. First—"

"Anna, baby, I'm trying my best to make it to the ultrasound on time. Can you tell me about this later?"

"That's fine. I need to work with Gus anyway."

As a former first grade teacher, Anna had decided to teach Gus herself rather than send him to preschool. While keeping Gus at home didn't give her a break in the day, it did save them money. One of these days, when they had extra cash, he was going to sweep her away for a long weekend.

"I'm sorry," he said as guilt filtered in and made him wish he could do more to give her some much needed alone time.

"I don't mean to blow you off, I just—"

"It's okay, Vin. Really. I'll see you at the hospital."

"You bet." He looked at the boxes and decided he'd use the dolly and deliver the packages in one trip. "Hey, I love you."

"Love you, too," she said, just as Benny's cries came over the line. "Oh, boy. Gotta run. Bye."

After he pocketed the phone and loaded the boxes on the dolly, he made his way into the pet store. A middle-aged woman greeted him with a smile. "Hi there. I wasn't sure if you guys were going to come today," she said and led him into the storeroom. "Can you believe what's been happening?"

"Yeah, it's unbelievable," he answered and handed her the tablet. "Can you sign on the pad for me?"

"Makes you wonder where they'll strike next, doesn't it?" she asked as she signed her name. "Damn President should have this county under a state of emergency."

"You think?" he asked while considering *state of emergency* a bit extreme. "I mean, if terrorists are behind this, wouldn't they go after government office buildings or major companies and financial institutions? You know, try to cripple the country."

After he finished stacking the boxes in the corner, she handed him the tablet. "A half hour ago I spoke with a friend who just left the grocery store. She said the place was packed and the shelves were nearly empty. People are scared and I think they're preparing to hole up in their homes." She shook her head. "These terrorist *have* crippled our country...with fear."

On that ominous and melodramatic note, Vince bid the woman a good day and headed for his truck. While he understood the woman's point and it disgusted him that people were dying, he couldn't help worrying more about what was going on in his own little world.

Right now, his sole focus was on arriving to Anna's ultrasound on time. This afternoon could end up being a defining moment and a major impact on his life.

He climbed into the cab and started the truck. He thought

about what the woman had said about people clearing the shelves at the grocery store and shook his head. A bit extreme in his opinion. Terrorists, bombings…yeah, that was scary shit. But this was Bloomington, Indiana. Nothing bad ever happened here.

CHAPTER 10

CORE Offices, Chicago, Illinois
12:42 p.m. Central Daylight Saving Time

"THANK GOD YOU'RE here," a petite, pregnant woman with short red hair said as she motioned for them to follow her. A ball of nerves, Naomi let Jake latch on to her arm and lead the way.

"Ian, Owen and Dante are waiting for us in the evidence and evaluation room," the redhead continued. "Wait until you see what we've come up with." She stopped, swiveled in her flats and held out her hand. "Sorry, I'm Rachel Malcolm, CORE's computer forensic analyst."

Naomi shook the other woman's hand. "Naomi McCall."

"Right," Rachel responded, skepticism clear in her green eyes. "Nice to finally meet you. This way."

Feeling as if she were being led into a hungry lion's den, Naomi reminded herself that she could, at any time, leave. She owed nothing to these people. The only reason she'd even agreed to come to Chicago was because of Jake. She'd kept him in the dark long enough and he deserved an explanation. How much she'd actually explain would depend on his counterparts. If she didn't think they could help her, she'd go back to her original plan and turn herself over to the murdering bastard.

After they walked down a corridor, Rachel opened a door. "Here we are."

Naomi froze and shifted her gaze around the room. One wall was covered with TV screens, another with white boards and corkboards. Several large tables sat in the center of the room and were filled with computers and a variety of other electronic equipment. Three men sat at the table. Her focus wasn't on them, but the TVs. Five of the six screens held a still shot from the bombings, while the sixth screen looked as if it had been synced to a computer. The search engine clear, the subject line unsettling.

Rose Wood.

Jake took her by the elbow. "Let me introduce you. This is Ian Scott, owner of CORE and a former profiler with the FBI."

A man with a thick head of salt and pepper hair rose and shook her hand. His familiar blue eyes studied her and, for a second, she swore she saw recognition in them.

Before she had the chance to shift through her memory bank, Jake nodded to the other men. "This is Owen Malcolm and Dante Russo." As she shook their hands, Jake added, "Owen is former U.S. Secret Service and Dante is a former Navy SEAL."

"Any reason you're giving out our resumes?" Owen asked.

Jake held a chair out for her. "I want Naomi to understand that CORE isn't the average private investigation agency. She knows who's behind the bombings. We need her to trust us and give us his name."

"You don't trust Jake?" Dante asked, his dark eyes held a hint of amusement.

She set her oversized purse on the floor. "I wouldn't be here if I didn't."

"Yet you won't give up the bomber's name." Owen leaned back in the chair and raised his dark blond brows. "It's going to be one o'clock in about ten minutes. Another bomb could go off and another after that at two. Aren't you the least bit concerned for the safety of—?"

"Of course I am," she said louder than she'd meant and fought the tears brimming in her eyes. "How would you feel if you knew you were the reason people were dying?"

"Good Lord." Rachel moved behind Owen and pinched his arm. "Way to break the ice." She looked at Naomi. "Ignore him."

"Actually, Owen has a valid point," Dante said with a shrug of his broad shoulders.

"Agreed." Ian nodded. "Why are you withholding information, *Rose*?"

Her skin prickled with irritation. She should have never come here. These people didn't understand her fears or whom they were up against. She turned to the man who had revealed her identity. "You told them," she said to Jake.

"No, I figured it out." Rachel sat in front of a laptop. "All Jake said was to look for a rosewood connection. After some digging I found this." She tapped at the keyboard. Within seconds Naomi stared at an old driver's license photo taken the year before she'd changed her identity. Then Rachel revealed Naomi's senior yearbook picture, then a copy of her old college ID. "*You* are obviously the connection. I suppose the why doesn't matter, but who behind the bombings does."

"Time's flying by," Owen added and looked at the clock on the wall. "Eight more minutes."

She knew they were right, but couldn't be sure they'd believe her even if she bared the truth.

You'll never know unless you tell them.

Jake took her by the hand and held it under the table. "Make this stop," he said, giving her a gentle squeeze.

"You won't believe me, the FBI, the media…no one will believe me."

"Thomas did," Ian said.

She looked away from Ian's piercing gaze as she finally remembered how she knew the owner of CORE. When Thomas had been in the FBI Academy, she'd gone to see him. At the time of her visit, he'd been taking courses hoping to eventually be part of the FBI's Behavioral Analysis Unit—specifically BAU-1, which, ironically, dealt with counterterrorism and threat assessment. After taking several of Ian's courses, Thomas had ended up requesting assignment in BAU-2, crimes against adults.

"How do you know her brother?" Jake asked Ian.

"This is how." Rachel tapped a few keys, then Thomas's photo and FBI badge emerged on the screen. "I also believe this is how you were able to change your identity without leaving a paper trail. Correct?"

Naomi met Ian's gaze. "My brother is dead."

"I know, and I'm sorry to hear he'd died."

"*He* killed Thomas, and my parents, too." She swiped at an errant tear. "What I say to you about Thomas cannot tarnish the excellent reputation he had with the FBI. Agreed?"

"You have my word."

"After my parents were killed, Thomas and I collected their life insurance and our inheritance. A few days later, he made arrangements to give me a new name and new life. His superiors had no clue what he was up to. The only other person who knew was his girlfriend. She was also FBI, in an administrative capacity. With her help, Thomas was able to ensure that no one would know who I really was."

"Who's the girlfriend?"

"Does it matter?"

Ian crossed his ankles and steepled his fingers. "I suppose not."

"The night my brother was murdered, they'd beaten his girlfriend and left her for dead." Shame heated Naomi's face as she recalled the once beautiful, vibrant and intelligent woman. "Because of me, because of the head injuries she sustained, she has the intellectual capacity and motor skills of a two-year-old."

"Oh, my God." Rachel looked to the ceiling as if searching for words. When she met Naomi's gaze again, she shook her head. "How many other people are you going to let him hurt?"

"Enough," Jake said, loud and firm. "I told Naomi we could help her. All that's happening is a bunch of bullshit finger pointing."

"Come on, Jake." Owen smacked a hand on the table. "In six minutes more people are going to die. She's so damned worried about protecting herself that—"

"Wrong," Dante said, staring at her with patience and understanding. "She's not protecting herself, she's protecting Jake. Right, Naomi?"

She caught Jake looking at her through her peripheral vision, then faced him. "He's killed everyone I've loved. The only reason you're alive is because he doesn't know about you." She didn't bother to fight the tears. These people obviously didn't think highly of her and, at this point, she didn't care if they thought she was weak. The only one she did care about was Jake. "The bombings could have ended hours ago if you'd let me go to him."

Jake clenched his jaw. "Not an option."

"I disagree," Ian said.

The fury in Jake's eyes should have had the other man shrinking back and shutting his mouth. Instead, Ian turned to Rachel. "Tell them what you've found."

Rachel's fingers danced across the keyboard until a map of the United States replaced Thomas's FBI badge. Red markers indicated the locations of the past six bombings. A black line had been drawn from north to south, running from Texas, through the Midwest and ending at the northern border of North Dakota. A rainbow of markers had been placed across the half of the country that hadn't been targeted. Yet.

"First, it's obvious the bombings have been set up to go west to east." Rachel stood and moved toward the screen. "Since the last bombing occurred in the Amarillo area, I've run a line through here under the assumption he's not going to backtrack." She pointed the black line separating the country. "These colored markers represent every variation of rose and wood I could find—cities, streets, counties, businesses, etcetera. Only…the pilots from Denver threw a wrench in my system. He didn't use a place to send you a message. He used the pilots' names. Do you have idea how many people have rose and wood in their names?"

"What I find interesting is that he knew those pilots would be flying that particular plane at a specific time and day." Owen rubbed his chin with the back of his hand. "I also find it interesting that the assistant manager of the Rosewood Bar & Grill in San Francisco remembers getting a delivery a week ago that she'd later learned wasn't authorized by the owner of the restaurant. Because the delivery took place during the lunch rush, she said she had the guy bringing in the produce take it right back to their cooler rather than one of her regular employees."

"Was the bomb detonated in the cooler?" Jake asked.

"No. The storeroom next to it."

"Same goes for the Sun Valley Hotel and Conference Center," Dante added. "Only this time it wasn't produce, but linens. And the company responsible for the delivery is part of the hotel's vendor list. Turns out the regular delivery guy and his truck have been MIA for six days."

"How do you know this?" Naomi asked, shocked they had information that hadn't been aired on the news.

"An FBI agent that's part of the bombing task force has been giving us inside information," Rachel answered. "We've worked with him in the past and he knows what we're capable of doing here. He's looking for an extra set of eyes and it doesn't hurt that CORE is composed of agents with backgrounds in the military, FBI and CIA."

Owen cleared his throat.

"Sorry," Rachel added and rolled her eyes at Owen. "And the U.S. Secret Service."

While Naomi could understand this agent's interest in using CORE's help, at this point she had bigger concerns. "Did you tell him about me?"

"No. Jake asked us to wait." Ian rested his hands on the table. "Naomi, I have friends in very high places. We can't wait any longer. If I give the name of the man behind this, they *will* investigate him."

Ian might know people, but she knew in her gut they

wouldn't back him. Not when the bastard was a personal friend to the Director of the FBI. "You're wrong."

Ian sent her an arrogant smile. "Try me. Who is behind this?"

"Oh, no," Rachel gasped as she stared at her laptop screen.

"What is it?" Ian asked without taking his focus off Naomi.

"There's been another explosion. This time in Leavenworth, Kansas." Rachel looked up from the laptop. "During a funeral at Chapel Woods Presbyterian Church."

Naomi tensed and grabbed onto Jake's hand. "Was anyone...how many people..." Unable to utter the words, she covered her mouth with her free hand. The killing needed to stop.

Rachel blinked several times, then cleared her throat. "Authorities estimate that there was close to one hundred people in the church at the time of the explosion. I...it's too soon to tell how many survived."

"Whose funeral?" Jake asked.

"The woman's name is Rose Michaels."

Dante stood and paced. "How in the hell could he plan *that*? How could he know the funeral would be held there, that her funeral would even take place?"

Rachel looked back to the laptop and began typing. She stopped. "Because Rose Michaels sat on the church board as one of the elders."

Dante quit pacing. "Okay, I'll give you that, but how could he predict...shit. When did the woman die?"

"She was found Friday afternoon." Rachel continued typing, then hovered her fingers over the keys and looked at the laptop screen. "Cause of death...natural causes. She was eighty-eight."

"Natural causes my ass," Owen said and pushed out of the chair. He moved to the map Rachel had created and ran a hand through his hair. "Because these bombings are so frickin' random, we can't predict their next move, only how they managed to plant the devices. How much you want to bet the day Rose Michaels died, she had a delivery or her damned phone line inspected or some other horseshit?" He turned, placed his hands on the back of the chair and leaned forward. "Naomi, you have to stop this."

"Even if I tell you his name, he won't stop until I go to him."

Jake squeezed her hand tighter. "You don't know that."

Actually, she did. She knew the man, knew that he wouldn't quit until he possessed her. He'd made that painful fact clear even before he'd murdered her family.

She drew in a shaky breath, squeezed Jake's hand back and then turned to Ian. "Christian Hunnicutt."

Ian's eyes widened, while Jake tensed. "The owner of BH-Xpress," Ian said with disbelief.

"The very same."

Ian drummed his fingers against the table. "I had lunch with Christian and the Director of the FBI, Martin Fitzgerald, last month. Do you realize—?"

Naomi released Jake's hand and stood. "I tell you his name and you still don't believe me." She looked down at Jake. "Forget it. I'll handle this on my own."

"Wait," Ian called as Jake grasped her wrist. "I believe you. But you're right. No one else will. Hunnicutt is not only a personal friend to the Director of the FBI, he and the Vice President have a long family history. Hunnicutt has also been a big player on the political scene." He glanced to each of his employees. "We're on our own until we have the evidence we need."

"And how are we going to get that in time to stop the next bomb from exploding?" Rachel asked.

Ian turned to Naomi, his eyes filled with regret and concern. "We're going to give him what he wants."

* * *

Norfolk, Virginia
1:09 p.m. Eastern Daylight Saving Time

Christian stormed into the warehouse apartment. Loosening his tie, he entered the great room, glanced around, saw Santiago in the kitchen and told the Columbian to pour him a Scotch. After crumpling up the tie and tossing it on the floor, he slumped into his throne chair.

"That fucking bitch is finished," he said and rubbed his hand along the mahogany lion's head. How dare the news anchor cut him off when he'd been about to reveal to the world that another bombing had occurred. He'd planned for that moment. He'd spent hours practicing his speech and facial expressions in front of the damned mirror.

With fury raging through him, he leaned forward and knocked the tray of refreshments off the table. "Fucking finished."

"I doubt she had a choice," Ric said and took a seat on the sofa next to the smart brother.

Santiago came forward and handed him the drink. "Do I look like a give a shit?" He drank the Scotch in two gulps, then threw the tumbler across the room. "And what the fuck did you just give me?" he shouted as glass and ice splintered against the wall and hardwood floor.

"Johnny Walker Blue," Santiago responded.

"That swill is for the dicks I don't like. Give me the good stuff, then clean up the mess." After Santiago went into the kitchen, he rubbed a hand along his forehead and looked at the TV. He threw his arms in the air. "And, because we couldn't get out of the building—my motherfucking building, I missed the next bombing."

He drew in a deep breath and glanced away from the TV. When he caught Harrison staring at him, he said, "What the hell are you looking at?"

The smart brother quickly focused on the floor.

"Again, that news anchor had no choice," Ric reminded him. "As for missing the bombing...that was unfortunate."

"Unfortunate, he says." Unbuttoning the top two buttons of his shirt, he leaned forward. "What would be unfortunate is if that bitch anchor loses her job or, worse yet, is found beaten to death in a back alley."

Ric grinned. "Indeed."

"After we're through here today, I expect you to make it happen," he said and took the fresh tumbler from Santiago.

"Of course," Ric responded and picked up the TV remote. "Meanwhile, would you like to hear about the latest tragedy that's befallen the country?"

He took a sip of the Scotch and waved a hand. "I heard enough on the drive over here. And, if I do say so myself, the execution was brilliant." He turned to Santiago. "Excellent job, *mi amigo.*"

"*Gracias,*" the Columbian responded and left the room.

"Sixty-eight people died in that church," Harrison said, keeping his focus on the floor.

God, he'd love to kill the insolent prick. "And your point?"

"I'd rather keep my eyes and tongue in my head."

Chuckling, he raised the glass to his lips. "Pussy," he said and took a drink.

The smart brother glared at him. "You're killing people for a woman. What does that make you?"

"That's where you're wrong. I'm not killing people for her. I'm killing people to send her a message." He set the empty tumbler on the table. "Think about it, smart brother. Think about every place that went up in flames so far today. Think about the places that haven't. What do they all have in common? If you can figure that out, I promise you and your brother a special bonus once the job is complete."

"Bonus?" he asked with a mixture of disbelief and pitiful hopefulness. "What kind of bonus?"

He'd like to fuck with Harrison and tell him the truth. That the bonus would be a swift death, but he refrained. If he admitted he would kill them, he'd lose his leverage. "I'd rather it be a surprise."

"Okay," Harrison said. "Then can I have a pen and paper?

I'd like to see if I can come up with the common link and get that bonus for me and Mickey."

"*May* I have a pen and paper?" he corrected Harrison.

The smart brother gave him an *eat shit and die* look before asking, "May I have a pen and paper?"

"Absolutely. Santiago, bring our friend a pen and pad of paper."

"Thank you," Harrison said. "I'm wondering though…this message you're sending, what if she doesn't get it?"

"She will."

"But what if she doesn't?"

He'd never given that option a thought. Although he hadn't seen or spoken with Rose in eight years, he doubted the woman had changed. She had always cared too much and carried too much goodness inside her. Plus, she was smart. She'd make the connection he doubted Harrison would, and she'd want to stop him. During both her mother and father's funerals, he'd taunted her and told her she was to blame for their deaths. When he'd hinted to killing her parents, he'd caught the guilt in her eyes and body language. The people who had died today would weigh heavy on her conscience. Moral and righteous, she'd want to do everything possible to stop him. Now if only the bitch would call.

"She will," he said with confidence. "If she doesn't, I'll just have to turn it up a couple of notches and be sure she does."

Ric laughed.

"You find that funny?" he asked the sadist.

Grinning, Ric said, "You've already outdone yourself. I can't imagine what else you could do."

He half smiled. "Give me some time, I'm sure I could come up with something."

"But you only have six more hours left," Harrison reminded him. "What if she doesn't contact you before the final device is set off?"

He hated to admit it, but Harrison was right. What if she hadn't contacted him by seven o'clock this evening? Would he stop looking for her? Was Ric right? Could he somehow top the bombings and make his message clearer?

When the Columbian brought Harrison the pen and paper, and the smart brother began writing, an idea occurred to him. If the bombings weren't enough to draw her to him, he'd send her another message. Only this time, he wouldn't be cryptic and use different combinations to come up with Rose Wood. This time, his intensions would not be mistaken.

"Santiago, have Vlad bring Mickey to me."

Harrison looked up, the pen he held poised over the paper. "Why do you need Mickey?"

"You'll see. Actually, you can stop trying to come up with the connection. I'm going to give it to you. But don't worry. Because you've given me yet another brilliant idea, I'll still give you and Mickey that bonus."

When Harrison's eyes widened and his forehead wrinkled with concern, he turned. Vlad half carried, half dragged Mickey into the great room. The dumb brother's head rested against Vlad's shoulder. Dried blood coated his face and part of the silver duct tape covering his eye. The tourniquet around Mickey's thigh was no longer bright red. Now that the blood had dried, it had turned a dark, reddish brown. Carmine, his wife had called it when she'd showed him an ugly dress she'd bought in a similar shade.

"Santiago, bring two garbage bags and lay them on the floor."

"Look," Harrison began, "it's okay, we don't need the bonus. I don't need to know the connection."

"I'm fully aware." He cocked his head. "But you were *so* concerned that my...lady friend wouldn't get my message. Ric's right. I don't think I could top what I've done thus far today, at least not without giving it serious thought. What I can do is send a message that'll be more...personal."

After the Columbian placed the garbage bags on the floor, he instructed Vlad to lay Mickey on top of them. "Santiago, I'd like to borrow your knife."

Smiling, the Columbian bent and retrieved the blade hidden within his right boot, then handed it to him.

He eyed the three inch, razor-sharp double edge blade and its blood-groove. He'd given Santiago it as a gift, and had liked this particular knife. When used to stab or slash, the cut was extreme and quite effective. "Excellent. Vlad, expose his torso."

With a nod, the Russian knelt and shoved Mickey's stained t-shirt up to his armpits.

"Really, sir," Harrison said, his voice shaky, nervous. "I'm sure she'll contact you. Give her time. Maybe she doesn't know how to reach you. Or maybe she hasn't heard about what—"

"Unless she's dead, she knows." Since Rose had changed her name, she'd remained completely out of reach and always one step ahead of him. During the first three years she'd dropped from existence, he'd thought she might have died. Suicide, he'd figured. After all, he *had* killed her parents and scarred her for life. But then five years ago he'd considered her brother. Initially, he hadn't gone after him. The saying, 'don't eat where you shit' had been quite applicable at the time.

When Rose had first disappeared, he and the Director of the FBI, Martin Fitzgerald, had just become acquainted and their relationship was still tentative. Three years later, they'd gone from mere acquaintances to friends. During the many luncheons and dinners he shared with Martin, he'd learned quite a bit about the FBI. When he'd heard about a case Thomas Wood had been working on, he'd swooped in and took advantage. Ric had tortured the man and his girlfriend, making it look as if the criminals Thomas had been after had done the job. But neither of them gave up any information on Rose. Well, the girlfriend probably would have, only Ric had taken her beating a little too far. He'd rendered her unconscious to the point they'd all assumed she'd die. She hadn't, but due to the results of the beating, she would have been better off dead.

The day of Thomas's funeral, he'd disguised himself and had made an appearance hoping Rose would show. She hadn't. With no other family, no close friends and no lovers, he no longer had any leverage with her.

He looked down at Mickey and smiled.

He had plenty of leverage now.

"Harrison, come here."

When the man didn't move, Santiago grabbed his arm and forced him to his feet. Harrison's eyes were wild with fear as the Columbian gave him a shove. He stumbled forward, righted himself and stood above his brother.

"How's your handwriting?" he asked the smart brother.

Harrison frowned. "I...it's okay. I'm better at typing."

"Unfortunately you won't be able to type what I'm going to dictate to you. So, I suggest you do your best to make your letters legible. I'd hate for you to have to rewrite the information I'm about to give you."

Nodding, his hair falling into his eyes, Harrison turned slightly toward the table. "I'll grab the pen and paper."

"No need. I have your writing instrument right here," he said and tapped the blade against his palm for emphasis.

Harrison darted his gaze from the blade to his brother's bared chest and stomach. He slid his eyes closed and slowly shook his head. "Please. Don't."

"I haven't even told you what you're to do and you're already begging me to stop?"

Harrison opened his eyes. The grief and hatred in them only made him want to taunt the man even more. The hatred he could accept. Many men hated him for good reasons. The bellyaching, childish sadness he could do without. That was an emotion foreign to him, along with regret and guilt. How could he feel sad or remorseful even if the resulting outcome hadn't been what he'd planned? From a very young age he'd learned that no risk meant no reward. Sometimes those risks had paid off, while other times they hadn't. The risks he'd taken today, planning terrorist acts against his country, against his own business would yield his reward. Rose would come to him. And, yet again, the smart brother would help send her another message.

"Do you believe in fate?" he asked Harrison.

The man nodded.

"I don't. A real man makes his own destiny. There is no God up in the heavens predetermining our lives." He touched Harrison's shoulder and forced him to kneel at his brother's side. "Everything in our lives comes down to choice. Mickey chose to accept this job and you did, too. How you handle the assignment and everything that comes with it, is for you to decide."

He glanced over his shoulder to Ric. "Put a gun to Harrison's head."

"Gladly," the sadist responded and did as he'd been instructed.

Harrison's breathing grew labored. Sweat coated his face, causing his hair to stick to his forehead. Mickey, on the other hand, lay prone and, if not for the slight rise and fall of his chest, appeared dead.

Not yet, but soon.

"Here." He nudged Harrison with his knee. "Take it."

Harrison looked at the knife he offered. When he didn't take it, Ric shoved the barrel of the gun against his temple.

"Do as you're told," Ric prompted him.

Harrison took the knife and, for the briefest moment, he swore he caught calculation in the other man's eyes. He smiled. The smart brother wanted him dead.

Not today.

"You have a knife in your hand and a gun against your head. If you so much as direct that blade at me, Ric will first blow off your ear, then he'll put a bullet in your brother's head. When he's done doing that, Santiago will slice off your other ear and maybe your balls." He shrugged. "We'll have to wait and see just how pissed off I am. Do you understand?"

Harrison nodded. "Yes, sir."

"Good. Now, you don't have to write much, just two short words, so you can start slightly below Mickey's chest."

The smart brother kept the knife at his side and used his other arm to wipe the sweat from his brow. He raised the blade, hovered it over Mickey's stocky midsection, then blew out a deep breath and sat on his heels. "I can't," he said and hung his head. "He's my brother. I can't do this to him."

"Remember *The Little Engine that Could*. Tell yourself, 'I think I can, I think I can.'"

Ric and Santiago both laughed. He did, too, and added a "choo-choo" for the hell of it.

After the laughter died down, Harrison said, "And if I don't do this?"

"I'll have Santiago slice off both of your ears and then I'll force you to watch as he carves a message into your brother's stomach. The choice is yours. Either way, the message will be written and sent. It's up to you to decide if you're willing to man up and keep your ears."

Harrison focused on his brother's torso and mumbled something that sounded like a prayer. He then straddled his brother, and with his hand shaking, raised the blade over Mickey's midsection. "What's the first letter?"

"R."

The smart brother wiped his eyes with his free hand, drew in a deep breath, then smashed his lips together. He placed the tip of the blade against Mickey's flesh and then quickly pulled back. A small drop of blood swelled from the tiny cut.

"I can appreciate why you don't want to do this, but I don't appreciate when people waste my time. The clock is ticking. You have another bomb to set off in forty minutes. So I'm going to be generous and give you ten minutes to write the message. If you don't then we'll go back to slicing and dicing your ears. Got it?" He nodded to Vlad and Santiago. "Vlad, get down on the floor and hold Mickey's arms, Santiago, you take his legs. If Harrison's handwriting isn't good to begin with, it'll be worse if his brother starts moving around."

Once he was confident Mickey was secure, he said, "Proceed."

Harrison sliced into his brother's flesh. Mickey's good eye flew open and he let out a scream. Sucking in his stomach, he raised his head and tried to flail his arms and legs. Vlad and Santiago kept him prone.

"Continue," he ordered Harrison.

The smart brother cried and sniffled as he carved the rounded part of the R. Blood oozed down the side of Mickey's torso and, thankfully, onto the garbage bag. "Not too deep," he warned him. "You don't want to kill the messenger."

Ric chuckled. "No pun intended."

He grinned. "Of course not."

By the time Harrison completed the R, he'd had enough of Mickey's girly screams. He moved toward the corner of the room and grabbed the large metal vase setting on the bookshelf. The thing was heavy and likely weighed about fifteen pounds. It should also do the trick.

Within a few strides, he stood over Mickey. "Let's make this easier on all of us," he said and careful not to hit Vlad, he whacked the dumb brother's head with the vase.

Other than Harrison's crying, the room was now blessedly silent. "Ah, much better. Vlad, Santiago, you can release Mickey. Vlad, get a towel and wipe off some of the blood. Harrison needs to work with a clean area."

After Vlad grabbed a roll of paper towels from the kitchen, he sopped up the blood.

"Very good. Harrison, continue with an O."

As the smart brother sliced into Mickey's flesh, Ric's cell phone rang. Keeping his gun against Harrison's temple, Ric pulled the phone off his belt clip and glanced at the caller ID. The sadist grinned and looked at him. "Could be her."

"Santiago, trade places with Ric and put your gun to Harrison's head," he ordered, then he turned to Ric. "Answer it."

When the sadist did, his smile grew and he gave him a single nod. "Hello, Rose," Ric said. "I'm so glad you got the messages."

Utter satisfaction rushed through Christian's veins. Since he no longer needed to use Mickey as a human billboard, he *should* tell Harrison to stop. Instead, he'd wait until Ric completed the call. "Harrison, the next two letters are an S and an E."

He'd find out what the bitch had to say, first.

CHAPTER 11

CORE Offices, Chicago, Illinois
12:26 Central Daylight Saving Time

NAOMI CLUTCHED THE phone. Ric Mancini. God, she hated the heartless bastard. Just hearing the smugness in his tone brought back the many unwanted memories she'd tried, and failed, to purge over the years. Some wounds never healed and, thanks to what Ric had done to her on Christian's behalf, she had the scars to prove it. "Yes. I got the messages," she managed, the sound of his voice sickening her.

"Good. You had us worried. We were in the process of sending you another one."

"Please, *don't*," she begged. "Enough people have—"

"Where are you calling from? Are you alone?"

"Yes," she lied and looked at Jake, who sat next to her with one headphone resting against his ear. Rachel was doing the same, while Ian, Owen and Dante sat at the edge of their seats. "I'm in Chicago."

"Chicago? That's too bad."

"Why?"

"Because it will take several hours for you to come here. Lots can happen between now and then."

"Please. I'll do whatever you want. Just don't—"

"It's been too long, Rose. How soon can you be in Norfolk?"

"I've already chartered a jet and can leave within the next forty-five minutes. I think I can be there sometime after three," she responded, giving Ric the version of the plan the CORE agents had come up with before she and Jake had even arrived.

"Excellent. It's been a sad day for this country. Seeing you will make it right."

Relief washed over her. "Does this mean there won't be any more messages?"

"I didn't say that. Until you're here, the messages are going to continue."

"But—"

"Where will you be flying into?"

She gave Ric the name of the private airstrip where Ian had arranged for the jet to land.

"Good. Do you remember the Columbian, Santiago?" Ric asked, and she fought a shiver. She most certainly remembered Christian's vicious bodyguard and his fondness for knives. "He'll pick you up. And, Rose, I suggest you come alone."

She swallowed. "I've been alone and on my own for eight years. Thanks to—"

Ric hung up on her. She dropped her cell phone on the table and pulled the wire to the headphone out of the jack.

"Who were you talking to?" Ian asked.

"That was Ric Mancini"

Rachel's eyes widened. "BH-Xpress's COO? Seriously?"

"Yes, and according to him, Christian's going to keep setting off bombs until he *sees* me." The bastard.

"Christian went through all of this trouble to force you to him," Owen said. "I wonder why he didn't speak with you. How do we even know Christian is behind this? Mancini never even mentioned his name."

She caught the skepticism in his tone and tensed. These people didn't know Christian the way she did. If the bastard could have someone wipe his ass, he would. "Because he loves making other people do his dirty work. And don't you dare doubt that Christian isn't behind the bombings. If Ric could have killed me eight years ago, he would have. Trust me on that. The man has no use for me."

Ian shoved his chair back and stood. "We have to move out."

"No." Jake kept a protective hand on Naomi's arm. He hadn't wanted her going to Hunnicutt in the first place, but after seeing the fear in her eyes and hearing the threatening tone in that piece of shit Mancini's voice, there was no way in hell she was going to Norfolk. "I don't like your plan. Come up with a new one."

"It's the most effective," Dante said, his confident tone belying the concern in his eyes.

"Maybe so, but Naomi isn't going in as bait."

"She has no choice," Ian reminded him. "We can't storm in to his offices and demand that he turn himself, and all of the evidence against him, into the authorities."

"Why the hell not?" Jake tightened his hold. "We fly down there, when this Santiago comes to pick up Naomi, we put a gun to his head and tell him to take us to Hunnicutt."

"And do you really think Hunnicutt is going to simply hand over incriminating evidence?" Ian asked and looked to Dante. "Prep Naomi."

Jake stood and forced Naomi to her feet. "No. We need to talk first."

"Jake," Dante warned. "The charter is going to be ready in less than forty-five minutes and we need ten of them to get to the airfield. I'll need time to plant the GPS chip on Naomi."

His skin crawled at the mention of the GPS chip. Dante's brilliant idea didn't work for him and he couldn't believe Naomi would go through with it. "Before you rip a tooth out of her head and replace it with your chip, we need to talk." He looked to Naomi. "Now."

Ian nodded. "Make it quick."

Jake dragged Naomi from the evidence and evaluation room, then down the hall to his small office. Once inside he slammed the door shut and locked it. "You're *not* doing this."

She tossed her hair over her shoulder and straightened. "He's given me no choice."

"Bullshit. There are other ways to handle Hunnicutt."

"You mean like storming off a plane and threatening Santiago? I might've not seen or spoken to Christian in eight years, but I know the man and I know the Columbian. He won't turn on him. If he did, he'd be dead. That's how Christian operates. I'd think after what he's done today, you'd realize that by now."

"Screw that, and screw not going to the Feds or Homeland. No one is that untouchable."

"Okay, so if Ian makes those calls and those agencies contact Christian, he'll know I'm working with CORE. Just imagine what he could do to you and your fellow agents." She cocked her head to the side. "How far along is Rachel? Six months? Christian is sick and twisted. If he knew Rachel and Owen were married, he'd keep Owen alive and make him watch as his pregnant wife was tortured."

Jake's stomach soured with nausea. "Jesus, Naomi," he muttered, and ran a hand through his hair.

She moved forward and latched onto his arms. "He doesn't care about anyone or anything but himself. It's always about him and his objectives. I know what he's capable of, Jake. I've seen him in action, I've experienced…"

He wrapped an arm around her lower back and drew her closer. "Experienced what?"

Her eyes glistened with unshed tears. "I don't want to talk about it."

"There's something new." The anger and resentment he'd been trying to keep at bay resurfaced. "What pisses me off is that you won't talk to me about any of this, but you're willing to tell a bunch of strangers. If the bombings hadn't happened and we started seeing each other again, were you ever going to tell me anything about your past?" he asked, wondering how long she planned to string him along with her lies.

A tear slipped down her cheek. "No."

He looked away and let her go. The last shred of trust he'd been stupidly hanging on to melted away. He had his answer. Time to put an end to the bombings, make sure Naomi survived so she could go on with her life and then move on with his.

Without her.

"Let's go," he said, turning for the door. "You have a plane to catch."

She tightened her grip on his arms. "Stop. Please," she said with a catch in her breath.

He faced her. Damn, he hated it when she cried. He also couldn't stand the desperation in her voice. Even more, he detested being lied to, especially by a woman he'd loved and trusted.

"You've made yourself crystal clear. There's nothing more—"

"Do you have any idea what my life's been like? Since I met Christian I've lost my family, my identity and you."

The guilt returned, if it had ever left. Hunnicutt had put Naomi through hell, but if she'd trusted him enough, he could have helped her. As much as he still cared, as much as he hurt on her behalf, he couldn't do this anymore. He couldn't continue to live with lies or wondering if she was still holding back.

"I'm sorry about your family and what Hunnicutt has done to you. It doesn't change anything. I can't—"

"Crack open your thick stubborn skull and hear me out." She released him and used both hands to wipe her tears away. "I'm exhausted," she said with a weary sigh, and sat at the edge of his desk. "For eight years I've been living a lie. Do you know how tiring that is? To constantly pretend to be someone you're not? To always be ready to run again?" She shook her head. "I've wanted to tell you so many times. When Thomas died, I almost did. But I was so scared you'd act like you are right now."

Conflicted by the guilt and the love he couldn't shake, he crossed his arms when all he wanted to do was hold her. Kiss her. Tell her he'd make everything go away. "Pissed?" he asked instead. Tired of being shit on, he needed to keep reminding himself why they didn't belong together.

She tilted the corner of her mouth with a sad, half smile. "No. Ready to go in guns blazing. If I'd told you the truth, you would have gone after Christian and he would have killed you."

"So you keep reminding me."

"And yet you're not listening." She pushed off the desk and searched his eyes. "I lied to protect you from Christian and from yourself."

"I don't *need* protecting."

"And I don't need to attend another funeral for someone I love. And *that* is the absolute truth."

He looked away. She hadn't said *love* in the past tense, but the present. All he'd ever wanted was her, loving him while he loved her right back. A part of him wanted to let all the lying go and be done with it. That part didn't want to dwell on the past or the lost years, but on the future. The other part told him he'd be a total idiot to even fall for any more of her bullshit.

She touched his cheek and tilted her head to meet his gaze. "You've got nothing to say?"

A rap at the door had him tensing. He didn't want to continue this conversation, but he also didn't want it to end. Once they left this room, their plan would be set in motion and Naomi would be one step closer to a murderer.

"Give us another minute," he called to whoever was at the door, yet kept his eyes on hers. No matter what she'd done to him in the past, a part of him would always love her—even the fabricated version. He couldn't regret the time they'd been together, not when they'd been some of the best in his life.

"I don't know what you want me to say. I loved you, wanted to marry you and you walked." He shrugged. "Now I know why."

Her eyes narrowed, just before she punched him in the arm. "You're such a dick." She hit him again. "A selfish prick."

He grabbed her fists and hauled her against his chest. "I sure as hell don't see it that way. From where I'm standing you're the one who—"

"Quit pointing fingers at me and open your eyes. I love you, Jake. From the moment I met you, I wanted you in my life. I made mistakes, we all have, only mine were monstrous. I can't go back and change the past. I can't go back and right any wrongs, or bring my family back. The only thing I can do is move forward. This past weekend, I believed that could be possible. For the first time in five years, I honestly thought we had a chance. Just remember one thing, Jake. When I was with you, every time we laughed, kissed, touched, made love, that was the *real* me. My name and past didn't matter. All that did was loving you. My feelings were and are real. Like it or not, I love you. Even when you're being a stubborn jerk."

She struggled to break free, but he hung on tight for fear of losing her. Call him pathetic or a glutton for punishment, he didn't care. Deep down, he knew she was right. They'd both allowed her past to hold them down and away from each other. Did any of it truly matter? Two days ago when he'd found out why she'd changed her name, he'd been ready to dive right back in and start over again. She'd lied in order to save him, and right now she was ready to give up her life to save countless others.

Looking at her tear-soaked face, into her blue eyes—eyes he'd been dreaming of for years—humbled him. Selfless and sacrificing, he didn't deserve her love, but he wouldn't reject it. Instead he'd embrace it and, if there were any consequences in the future, he'd deal with them if and when they came.

"I never stopped loving you," he said, bringing her closer to him. "As hard as I tried, I could never get you out of my head. You're right. I am a selfish prick."

She drew in a shaky breath and gave him a small, hopeful smile. "And I'm a liar."

He let go of her fists and cupped her cheeks. "No, you're selfless and generous, and I don't deserve you."

Her warm breath fanned across his lips as she inched closer. "I don't deserve you. Promise me you'll stay in Chicago," she said, her imploring eyes on his.

"I can't."

"Jake, you have to. I—"

He crushed his mouth against hers. Whatever she had to say wouldn't change his mind. His resentment and anger still lingered and it would take time to fully trust her again. But he couldn't deny loving her. Not to her, and not to himself. He'd been calling himself pathetic for wanting a woman who'd lied to him time and again. Holding her in his arms, breathing her in, tasting her—he deepened the kiss. He didn't care what loving her made him. He cared about keeping her alive and them working together to sort out their future.

Someone pounded on the door. He ignored it and, desperate to cling to the moment, feasted hungrily on her mouth.

"Gotta go," Dante called from the other side of the office door. "Now, Jake."

The urgency in Dante's voice had him tearing his mouth from Naomi's. He rested his forehead against hers and sifted his hands through her soft, thick hair. "I don't want to let you go."

"We have no choice." She gave him a quick kiss. "Right now, I think I'm more scared about having my tooth pulled. Will you stay with me while Dante does it?"

He took her hand and led her toward the door. "Of course," he promised, but wasn't sure if he could stomach it or refrain from knocking Dante on his ass. This plan they'd concocted was bad enough. Watching Dante rip a molar from Naomi's head was fucked up.

The former SEAL met them in the hall, his impatience apparent in his narrowed eyes. "We don't have a lot of time." He led them into the evidence and evaluation room, where Ian and Owen were waiting. "And I'm not going to lie, this is going to hurt like a bitch."

"No it's not," Rachel said, breezing through the door. She held up a small brown paper bag. "My contact over at DecaLab came through."

Dante visibly relaxed, Jake did, too. The man might be badass, but Jake had no doubt Dante wanted nothing to do with playing dentist today.

"Thank God." Naomi blew out a breath and sank into a chair. "I have a high tolerance for pain, but I'll be honest. I wasn't sure if I could've handled having a tooth pulled without anesthetic. So what's the alternative?"

"Wait." Owen held up a hand. "I thought DecaLab was who we used for forensic DNA testing."

"It is, but they do a bunch of other stuff, too." Rachel set the bag on the table, then walked to the corner of the room and opened a file cabinet drawer. "Six months ago, Chihiro Kimura, my contact at DecaLab, along with several of their geneticists, began working on a prototype for a private company." She moved back to Naomi's side and touched her shoulder. "I need you to remove your shirt."

Naomi glanced at him just before pulling her long sleeved shirt over her head. Thankfully she'd worn one of those strappy tank tops underneath. They might be under the wire, but he sure as hell didn't want Ian, Dante and Owen seeing Naomi in just her bra.

"And," Dante prompted.

"They've created a small chip, the size of a piece of long grain rice, that can be implanted under the skin," Rachel explained. "This chip will not only be used as a GPS device, but eventually it will be able to monitor the chip-wearer's heart rate and body temperature. DecaLab is going to take it a step further and work on ways to encode the chip with a person's unique genetic sequence." The instrument Rachel pulled from the bag reminded him of a digital thermometer he'd seen one of his sister-in-laws use on her kids. "If they're successful, the chip would perfectly ID the carrier."

"Which would prove helpful in medical or criminal matters," Ian added.

"Sounds a little too Big Brother for my taste," Owen said, watching his wife slip on a pair of latex gloves.

Ian cocked a dark brow. "*I* requested the prototype. But I'm sure the government is working on similar chips. I'm also sure the government's reasons for their version greatly differs from mine."

Ian's pulse on not only the latest innovations used to help prevent crimes or capture criminals, but also his knowledge of high tech gadgets never ceased to amaze Jake. Whatever the case, he agreed with Owen and thought the genetic chips sounded like something out of a shitty, sci-fi cyborg movie. "Do we have a monitor we can use to track Naomi's movements?" he asked, refocusing the attention to the task at hand. "Once we land in Norfolk and Hunnicutt's driver has Naomi, we'll be blind without one."

"Absolutely." Rachel tore open a package of sanitizing wipes. "Along with the prototype, Chihiro gave me the GPS tracking program we can use to locate Naomi. I'll not only have it here on my computer, but I can upload the program onto your cell phone and, in theory, it should work like any app."

"In theory," he echoed. Naomi's life was on the line. He didn't want theories, only hardcore certainties.

"No worries, Jake." Rachel took out a two inch plastic bag. "I'm the one who's been working with DecaLab to design the monitoring program. If we run into a glitch, I should be able to solve it."

"Is that the chip?" Naomi asked.

"Yep, and I'm going to insert it just above your armpit. The mark it will leave is small. If, for some reason, Hunnicutt sees it he could attribute it to a shaving malfunction," she said with a smile.

Naomi would have to be undressed and in a precarious position for Hunnicutt to notice the mark. And that didn't settle well with Jake. At all. Especially when he remembered Naomi telling him about the night Hunnicutt and one of his men had attacked her. He clenched his fist wishing the piece of shit was in the room with them right now. He'd love nothing more than to beat him to death for ever laying a hand on Naomi.

"You'll be monitoring me and can jump in and stop Christian if anything bad starts happening," Naomi said, as if reading his mind.

Her reminder did little to lessen his concerns, but take the emotion away and his logical side knew she was right.

Rachel inserted the chip into the instrument. "Ready?"

Naomi raised her left arm, but quickly grabbed Rachel's wrist with her free hand. "When this is over, I want the chip removed. I'm tired of feeling like I'm being watched."

"Not a problem," Rachel said, her tone soft and understanding.

Naomi let go of Rachel's wrist, closed her eyes and turned her head away. "Do it."

Rachel pressed the tip of the instrument against Naomi's skin and pushed a button. "All done."

Naomi craned her neck to where Rachel had injected the chip. "That's it?"

"Yep. And a heck of a lot less painful than what Dante was going to do to you."

"In my defense, I didn't want to pull your tooth." Dante moved to Naomi's side and inspected the small mark. "Ingenious. If only—" He turned away and headed for the door. "We have to leave. Jake, are you armed?"

"Yeah." He nodded, but didn't meet the other man's eyes. He didn't want to see the pain in them. When he'd first joined CORE, Rachel had told him about Dante and everything he'd lost. If the chip Naomi now carried had been available six years ago, Dante would still have a family.

"Give me five minutes to sync the chip to the GPS monitoring system on my computer." Rachel sat in front of her computer. "I also need to add the program to Jake's phone. For back up, Dante's too."

Dante handed Rachel his cell phone. "I'll be in my car," he said and left the room.

Jake caught a tear trickling down Rachel's cheek as she typed. He couldn't wait for her to have the baby. Since becoming pregnant her emotional highs and lows were unpredictable.

"Don't beat yourself up," Owen said and rested a hand on

her shoulder.

"I know, it's just...chips like this do scream Big Brother, but on the flip side, to be able to find your child?" She rubbed a hand across her cheek, wiping the tear away. "Jake, let me have your phone." She attached a USB cord to his phone and then her computer. In less than a minute, she removed the cord and handed it back to him. "You're good to go."

Jake took his and Dante's phones. "Thanks."

Owen offered his hand. "Kick some ass."

"That's the plan."

"No." Ian stood and leveled Jake with a hard stare. "The plan is to gain the necessary evidence to bring in the FBI. We can't go rogue with this case. Not with it being high profile and the government agencies involved, understood?"

"Understood. But if Hunnicutt so much as lays a hand on Naomi, I don't give a shit how high profile this case is or who's involved. Hunnicutt is a dead man."

Bloomington, Indiana
11:48 a.m. Central Daylight Saving Time

Vince's stomach grumbled as he pulled into the parking lot of a three story office building. He'd have lunch on his way to the next delivery. He wasn't a fan of eating while driving, and it was against company policy, but it would be the only way to stay on schedule and be near the hospital by three.

He checked his tablet, searched for the eight packages he would deliver to four different offices and pulled out the dolly. After the boxes were loaded, he entered the building and headed for the elevator. He delivered the first two packages to an accounting firm, and then headed down the hall to the law office also expecting a delivery. Once finished there, he took the elevator to the third floor, found the dental practice that was next on his list and dropped off another three boxes. With only two packages left, he pushed the dolly down the hall in search of the last company on his list. When he caught the suite number, but no company sign, he rapped on the door.

A young guy, dressed in jeans and a button down shirt answered. He adjusted his black framed glasses and looked from the boxes on the dolly to the BH-Xpress logo on Vince's black jacket. "I'm not accepting those," the guy said and nodded to the packages.

What kind of bullshit was this about? "Come again?" Vince asked and looked at his tablet, then to the suite's number plate next to the door jamb. "Nexus, right?"

The guy scratched his short beard and rested his hand along the door frame. "Right place, wrong time for a delivery." He flipped his wrist and looked at his watch. His eyes widened. "You need to get out of here," he said, then started to close the door.

Vince stopped him. "Look, just sign this and I'll leave the boxes in the hall."

"And get blown to frickin' pieces?" The guy shook his head. "No way, dude. Take them with you. Now, or I'll call the police."

The police? *Serious bullshit.* "Okay, sir," Vince said, when he wanted to tell the guy he was a paranoid fool. This was the second time today he'd been turned away and had packages left undelivered. The first time he'd considered just leaving the packages at the door, but if the customer called into the BH-Xpress offices and demanded they were picked up, he'd have to backtrack and lose valuable time. As it stood, this guy was wasting even more of his time. "You'll be able to pick up your packages at our main—"

"You won't catch me within a mile of your company until the bombings stop."

"Fair enough."

"What's not fair is that this country is contaminated with a disease called terrorism and your company is the carrier doing the infecting."

On that note... "Well, when you're ready for your packages, you can pick them up at our main office."

"You're being brainwashed, man." He checked his watch

again. "The terrorists are coming for us and hitting us where we least expect it. That delivery truck of yours could be a moving bomb. Do yourself a favor. Park it in a field far away from people and run."

Vince grabbed the dolly and backed away toward the elevator. "Have a good day, sir."

"You could be next," the guy called after him and stepped into the hall. "Any one of us could be next. I know the truth. I've been watching reports and I know what's going on out there."

Vince stepped into the elevator and quickly pressed the button that would take him to the ground floor.

"There's a connection," the guy shouted. "The government knows it but isn't telling the public. Another bomb is going to go off in—"

The elevator door slid shut. "Conspiracy freak," Vince mumbled. When the elevator stopped on the ground floor, he wheeled the dolly back to the truck. After stowing the dolly and packages inside, he climbed into the cab and started the truck. He thought back to the concern in his wife's voice when she'd called him after the BH-Xpress plane had exploded, then remembered the lady at the pet shop and how she'd talked about the country being crippled by fear. People had a right to be scared. What was happening was serious and devastating. But paranoia wasn't going to get anyone anywhere.

He pulled out of the parking lot and stopped at a red light. Since he had a ten minute drive to his next delivery, he reached for his lunch box. Still waiting for the light to change, he took a bite of the ham sandwich he'd made that morning and turned on the radio.

"I'm stunned...just stunned," Manny, one of the hosts of his favorite radio show, said.

"Supposedly the President is going to give a press conference about the bombings," the show's co-host announced. "It's about time. How many more bombings will it take before the government steps in and does something?"

The light turned green and Vince stepped on the gas.

"They *are* doing something," Manny countered. "The Feds are involved, along with FEMA, the Department of Defense, the—"

"Yeah, yeah, yeah. We know all of this, but what are they *doing?*" the co-host asked. "I'll tell you what they're doing. Not a damn thing. Airlines are still allowing their planes to fly, schools are still open…hell, the National Guard should be in every major city across the country. In airports, train stations, bus depots, hospitals, universities. People should be sent home and told not to leave until whatever is happening stops."

"Are you crazy?" Manny asked. "If the streets are left empty, imagine all the scum that would take advantage. I'm picturing looting and vandalizing and—"

"What we need is martial law," the co-host said.

"You really *are* crazy," Manny said. "You're talking curfews, suspension of civil law and civil rights. And that's *not* something I'm ready for."

As Vince polished off his sandwich, he couldn't help agreeing. He was no expert when it came to martial law, but didn't like what he was hearing. This kind of talk wouldn't ease people's fears, but intensify them. He, for one, enjoyed his civil rights and didn't want them taken away because the government and their agencies couldn't find who was behind the bombings.

"We need to break for commercial," Manny announced. "Before we go, for those of you just tuning in, there's been another explosion."

"Bombing," the co-host corrected.

"That hasn't been confirmed. What has been is that the riverboat, Delta Rose, was carrying approximately one hundred and thirty passengers when it left the St. Louis dock at twelve-thirty p.m. Central Daylight Saving Time. The Delta Rose exploded thirty minutes later. We have no information on survivors at this time, but will update you as we get the latest news."

A commercial for Sahara Mart replaced Manny's voice. The sandwich Vince had just consumed sat like a brick in his stomach. All he could think about was the guy from the office building.

There's a connection…the government knows it but isn't telling the public. Another bomb is going to go off…

He turned right and pulled into another parking lot to make his next delivery. The guy with the conspiracy theory was right. Now that he thought about it, maybe Manny's co-host wasn't that far off, either. Because bombs were going off every hour on the hour, there *had* to be a connection. Those government agencies the radio hosts were discussing had the people and the means to make that connection. He didn't want martial law and would hate to see the U.S. shut down airports and such, but he, like probably everyone else, wanted answers. Starting with what the government was doing to put an end to the bombings? And who in the hell was behind it?

Norfolk, Virginia
1:07 p.m. Eastern Daylight Saving Time

Harrison stared at the back of Honey Badger's head and pictured what a bullet in the middle of his skull would look like.

Messy. Gory.

Satisfying.

He looked away and glanced down at the open laptop. The codes on the screen…hell, the whole damned system mocked him. He could hack into just about anything he'd tried. Although self-taught, he could probably teach kids coming out of college with a Computer Science degree a thing or two. But he couldn't touch *this* laptop without permission. The irony was just too much. The laptop would give him access to the outside. His fingers itched to stroke the keyboard, to inform the world that the crazy badger behind the bombings was none other than billionaire business owner, Christian Hunnicutt. And no one would believe him. They especially wouldn't believe that Hunnicutt killed innocent people to send a woman a message.

He closed the laptop and caught a smear of dried blood he must have missed when he'd washed his hands earlier. Mickey's blood. His stomach churned with revulsion. No matter how long he lived—and he doubted it wouldn't be until he was old and grey—he'd never forget taking a knife to his twin. Carving into his flesh. The blood. Mickey's cries.

Harrison scrubbed a hand down his face and looked at Hunnicutt's back again. When he'd been in the middle of slicing his brother and Ric's cell phone had rung, the deranged dickhead could have told him to stop. But he hadn't. Even when he knew the woman had received his message, he'd had Santiago keep a gun to Harrison's head and had forced him to continue cutting Mickey.

Fucking bastard.

He'd never met anyone like Hunnicutt and hoped to God it stayed that way. The man didn't care who he hurt. He also didn't give a shit about anyone but himself and his agenda.

Rose Wood.

Harrison didn't know anything about the woman, but if she was smart, she'd stay away. The image of the crudely carved letters on Mickey's stomach ran front and center in his mind. Then again, maybe the woman didn't have a choice. With a gun to his head, he'd sent the signal to each detonator and had caused death and destruction across the country. At this point, he didn't care about his life or even Mickey's. Whether by Hunnicutt's orders or a federal judge's, they were going to die either way. What he cared about was finding a way to make sure Hunnicutt didn't get away with murder. Otherwise, he'd rather have Santiago slit his throat and put him out of his misery. Only now he had someone else to worry about.

Rose Wood had served as Honey Badger's catalyst. He'd used her name to incite every explosion, and she'd connected the dots and received Hunnicutt's messages. Harrison might have pulled the trigger, but *she* was the reason why people were dead and dying. The guilt—he couldn't worry about her guilt, he had enough of his own.

"Ric," Hunnicutt said, turning away from the TV. "Pull out your cell phone and Google Hazel Wood. I'm rather surprised her name wasn't mentioned on the news."

Now that he knew the connection between the bombings, and morbidly curious as to how she fit into the Delta Rose riverboat explosion, Harrison asked, "Who's Hazel Wood?"

Hunnicutt flashed his teeth with a self-assured smile. "She's a banjo player well known for her country and bluegrass music. Decades ago, she and her former band won a Grammy. Best album, I believe."

"Got it," Ric said, scanning the small cell phone screen. "This isn't good. Her performance on the Delta Rose was cancelled yesterday and replaced by a country trio. Apparently Hazel Wood is currently in the hospital recovering from an emergency appendectomy."

Hunnicutt narrowed his eyes and clenched his jaw. Harrison tensed and prepared for the worst. But, as if someone had flipped a switch in the badger's brain, Hunnicutt relaxed and grinned. "I have to admit, this makes me look more ingenious than I already am. The Feds will be spinning their wheels trying to figure out where the Delta Rose ties in and, quite possibly, begin coming up with a new connection."

"Especially with the next explosion," Ric added.

Hunnicutt snapped his fingers. "Exactly." He stepped over to the throne chair and sat at the edge. "This is good. Once Rose arrives, there will be no need to continue with the bombings." He shrugged and leaned back. "We can leave and pretend none of this ever happened."

God, the man had no conscience. How could Hunnicutt pretend he hadn't caused the deaths of hundreds of people? How could he pretend he hadn't shot and stabbed Mickey, and forced Harrison to slice into his own brother's flesh?

"No excitement, Harrison?" Hunnicutt asked. "I'd think you'd be happy about this news."

"I am. I guess I'm just wondering what's going to happen to me and Mickey."

He waved a hand. "You'll be compensated for the job.

And, of course, you'll receive that special bonus I mentioned earlier."

"Thank you," Harrison said when he really wanted to tell Hunnicutt to go fuck himself. He wasn't stupid. There would be no compensation and no bonus. The man was a liar and a manipulator. He and Mickey knew too much, and besides, how in the hell would he explain Mickey's injuries to an ER doctor? He wouldn't, because the man wasn't going to let them walk out of this warehouse alive.

Knowing he and Mickey were running out of time, and not ready to die without killing Hunnicutt first, Harrison ran his hand along the closed laptop. "Does this mean we can leave now?"

"No. You'll stick around until she arrives."

"What if she lied to you and only told you what she thought you needed to hear?" Harrison asked, trying desperately to do the unthinkable. Stay in the warehouse for as long as possible. At this point, he doubted any government agency suspected Christian Hunnicutt was behind the bombings. The laptop was the only link back to Hunnicutt. If the explosion scheduled at four this afternoon went off, the program he'd uploaded back in Bloomington would give those agencies the link they'd need to arrest Hunnicutt. But no more bombings meant no chance of proving the billionaire had been terrorizing the country.

Hunnicutt frowned. "That would be a very bad thing. But considering her concern for the masses, my gut tells me she'll not disappoint. Still, I do think she should be punished, and thanks to you, I've come up with another brilliant idea."

Shit. The last time he'd inadvertently given the man a brilliant idea, Mickey had become a human notepad. "Sir, please. I don't think Mickey can take—"

Hunnicutt chuckled and stroked the lion's head on the throne chair's armrest. "Ric, have I become that predictable?"

Ric sent Hunnicutt a grin that bordered on malevolent. "Not at all. I think Harrison is worried about Mickey."

"As he should be." Hunnicutt nodded. "But never fear, Harrison, your brother deserves time to rest and recoup."

Harrison didn't relax. He might have only met the man today, but Honey Badger had proven time and again that he couldn't be trusted.

"No, my brilliant idea has nothing to do with Mickey, but Rose. If she'd come to me earlier, people wouldn't have had to die. Now I think she needs to understand that I won't be denied what belongs to me."

Against his better judgment, Harrison asked, "And how will you do that?"

Hunnicutt smiled. "I'm going to keep blowing up people."

Harrison leaned into the sofa. He definitely deserved to burn in hell. He'd somehow talked Hunnicutt into continuing to detonate the explosives. He just prayed that when the Bloomington bomb went off, the death toll wouldn't be catastrophic and instead, lead the authorities where they needed to be.

Honey Badger's den.

CHAPTER 12

Flight 9987, Somewhere over Ohio
2:45 p.m. Eastern Daylight Saving Time

JAKE PLACED A blanket over Naomi's sleeping body, brushed a lock of hair off her cheek and released a sigh. Even asleep she looked tense, and he worried how the guilt would affect her down the road. Not the guilt over the lies she'd told him, those he understood—to a degree. But the deaths caused in her name.

Rose Wood.

She didn't look like a "Rose." Although he supposed if they'd met when she'd been Rose Wood, he wouldn't be able to imagine her as Naomi McCall, either. Whatever way he considered it, the name change was kind of a mind fuck. He'd never been in a position where a name actually mattered. If he were to suddenly go from Jake Tyler to…Clyde Whitmore, did the name make him a different man?

No. He'd still be the same person, but he did question how much Naomi had changed since leaving Rose behind. She obviously had trust issues. Sure, her reasons for not telling him about her past made sense to him. Anyone who had been close to Rose Wood was now dead. Still, there had to have been a part of her that had wanted to tell him the truth. If they'd stayed together, married and started a family, all of it would have been based on a lie.

Before she'd become Naomi, had she been trusting and open? Maybe naïve? She must have been to end up associating with a man like Christian Hunnicutt. She had to have been around nineteen or twenty when she'd met Hunnicutt. Maybe her family had money and that's how they'd met. Or maybe she'd grown up in a lower or middle class family and had been impressed by Hunnicutt's wealth. Whatever the case, he couldn't understand why a man in Hunnicutt's position would risk everything for a woman he hadn't seen in eight years.

Then again, he hadn't been able to get Naomi out of his head for the past five years, so maybe he had no room to judge. Only he wasn't killing people to gain her attention.

Careful not to disturb her and needing a change of scenery, he rose from the chair and made his way down the short aisle to where Dante sat. He looked over the other man's shoulder and glanced down at the crossword puzzle Dante held. "Supercalifragilisticexpialidocious," Jake said, and took a seat across the aisle from Dante.

"Are you planning on breaking into song?" Dante asked, keeping his head down and the pen poised over the puzzle.

"Nope. That's the answer to one down."

"No quite, genius. One down is a four letter word."

Jake shrugged. "Maybe it'll fit in one across. But if you need four letter word, I can think of a few. Shit, damn, f—"

Dante held up the puzzle and grinned. "While it's obvious you have strong vocabulary skills, I'll come up with my own answers, thanks."

"Anytime."

Dante looked over his shoulder to where Jake had left Naomi sleeping at the back of the jet. "She gonna be okay?"

He dropped his head against the leather headrest. "She took that last bombing hard."

"Fifty-eight dead, twenty missing…she has every right."

Keeping his head against the seat, he looked to Dante. "I'm worried."

"The GPS—"

"Can be blocked or lose satellite contact." Jake glanced away and toward the ceiling of the cabin. "Hunnicutt is wealthy and unpredictable. That's not a good combination."

"Don't forget obsessed."

"I know, I was just thinking about that."

"Has she told you anything about her history with Hunnicutt?" Dante asked.

He raised his head and swiveled in the seat. After making sure she still slept, he leaned across the aisle. "The only thing she told me was that he used to stalk her, and that the stalking turned violent. What I'm having a hard time wrapping my brain around is why Hunnicutt chose Naomi. With what he's worth, he could have any woman."

"And how many years have you been holding out for Naomi?"

Damn, was Dante a frickin' mind reader? "I was just thinking about that, too. Get out of my head."

Dante's mouth turned in a half smile. "Just stating the obvious. But the difference between you and Hunnicutt—"

"I'd prefer not to be compared with a mass murderer, thanks."

"I'm not about to compare the two of you." Dante set the puzzle and pen on the seat next to the window. "A few years ago, a woman comes to Ian and tells him she's being stalked. The police can't help her because she has no concrete evidence, and the little she did have wasn't anything that would warrant an arrest."

"That sounds a little like what Naomi went through, only he did attack her. He and another guy broke into her apartment and threatened to kill her. Maybe if she'd gone to the police that night, we wouldn't be in a jet heading to Norfolk."

"Well, that would clearly justify an arrest, but I can see why Naomi didn't file a complaint. Hunnicutt's family would have had him out of jail like that." Dante snapped his fingers. "Based on what Hunnicutt's done today, he would have gone after her again. Only he wouldn't have just threatened her." He stretched his legs into the aisle. "That stalking case I was telling you about, I met with a psychologist and got a crash course on the types of people who stalk. You have your psychotic and nonpsychotic."

"The man's psychotic."

Dante half shrugged. "Maybe, but your idea of what's psychotic probably doesn't fit into the clinical term. And by clinical, I'm talking schizophrenia or obsessive compulsive personality disorder, or something along those lines. I'm no psychologist and I've never met the man, but I'm thinking he falls into the nonpsychotic category. Which, in my opinion, makes Hunnicutt more dangerous."

Jake stiffened. "Explain."

"Okay, back to the stalking case. The guy who'd been going after our client was a nonpsychotic stalker. The psychologist I worked with called him a rejected and resentful stalker. He wasn't looking for intimacy, but because the client had broken up with him after just a month of dating, this guy felt the need to not only reverse her decision, but to avenge it."

"So what happened to the girl?"

Dante looked away and rubbed the back of his neck. "She ended up in the hospital with a concussion, shattered jaw, broken ribs and punctured lung. I...ah...my head wasn't on the case and I dropped the ball. She's fine now, and her stalker won't be given a parole hearing for another fifteen years. I still feel shitty about what happened to her."

Recalling what Rachel had told him about Dante, Jake suspected the man's head hadn't been on the case, but on his divorce. "No judgment is coming from my end."

Dante eyed him. "No offense, but I don't care if you judge me or not."

Jake wasn't offended. After spending six months working closely with Dante, he'd learned the former SEAL didn't give a shit about what anyone thought of him. To a degree, he could relate. What he did and how he did it was his business and his choices. Still, he cared what Naomi and his family thought of him, just as he'd cared what the men he'd fought side by side with during his tour in Iraq had thought of him. He wanted them to think he was a good man and a good soldier, and was proud that he'd been both. Only he wasn't proud of how he'd treated Naomi earlier today. Instead of giving her the benefit of the doubt like he'd told himself he would, he'd hit her while she'd been down and was prepared to walk away from her when this was over. She'd spent her adult life running and grieving. She deserved to be safe and happy. And if she'd let him, he'd make sure she had both.

"Anyway," Dante continued, "what worries me about Hunnicutt is that he acts as if he has nothing to lose."

"Agreed. These bombings were calculated. The coordination he'd gone through to execute them so precisely had to take an enormous amount of time. During his press conference a reporter asked Hunnicutt about the possibility of running for Senate and later, for president. Why would he risk his global business and his political affiliations and aspirations over Naomi?"

"And that's what worries me. It's like he thinks he's untouchable."

"In a way, he'd be right. We know he's setting off bombs and that he's after Naomi, yet we can't send in the FBI to stop him." Which frustrated the hell out of him. "I say we go against Ian's orders. I'm not interested in standing down and waiting for evidence or the proper channels to be engaged. I'm only interested in seeing Hunnicutt dead."

Dante's forehead wrinkled as he frowned. "I have no problem with that. Except...if we kill him without having proof he's behind the bombings, even in death he'll have gotten away with murder."

Jake raised a brow. Who knew Dante could throw out a bunch of philosophical bullshit? But, damn. The man was right. "Fine. We'll stick with the plan and get the evidence. After that, he's dead. I don't want Naomi to ever have to look over her shoulder again."

"What are you going—never mind. None of my business."

Jake released a sigh. "I just told you I'm going to kill a man.

There's not a whole lot out there that's more personal than that. Say what's on your mind."

"Fine. Are you planning on getting back together with Naomi?"

Okay, now that was personal. Maybe he cared more about what people thought about him than he'd realized. If his parents and brothers knew the whole story, would they think he was pathetic and desperate? Naomi wasn't the only woman out there and, if he bothered to try, he could probably find someone else and settle down. He'd been calling himself pathetic since he'd first visited her in Woodbine. He'd known she was lying, but had justified her lies to ease his conscience and his way into her bed. Maybe he wasn't any better than Hunnicutt. Maybe what kept driving him back to her was obsession, the need to justify why she'd rejected him and to ease his resentment.

Or maybe he was in love with her.

"I told you it was none of my business," Dante said and reached for his puzzle.

"No. It's okay. I...normally I'd talk to my brothers about this."

"But they're not here."

"And I don't want to get deep or any of that kind of shit."

Dante cracked a smile. "Yeah, that shit's for pussies."

He grinned and relaxed. For a badass Navy SEAL, he'd learned Dante was easy to talk to and had a logical and, yes, philosophical spin on things. "Okay, I love her, but feel like a jackass because I didn't truly know her. What's even worse, I don't care that she lied to me. Pathetic, right?"

"I was watching you in the evidence and evaluation room when Naomi was talking about her brother and how he'd changed her identity for her. You didn't know any of it, did you?"

He shook his head.

"Like I said then, she kept her secrets to protect you. I believe that's what's eating at you. Your woman was protecting you, when we men think that's supposed to be our job." Dante set the puzzle aside again. "Not sure if you're aware, but I was married and had a baby. I'm not going to get into all the details because, no offense, it's none of your business."

"None taken."

Dante's jaw hardened and his eyes narrowed. "I couldn't protect either one of them and I wouldn't let my wife protect me from myself. Sometimes I think that maybe if I'd let her, things would be different. That maybe if I remembered why we'd gotten married, that we were partners who had each other's back in every sense..." He heaved a sigh. "Look past your ego and pride, Jake. I don't know Naomi, but I think I have a pretty good read on you. If you love her, what the hell do you care what other people think? And for whatever it's worth, you're not pathetic."

"Thanks, man. I appreciate it." Dante was an all right kind of guy. Whatever had happened between him and his wife, he didn't know. As for Dante's baby, Jake couldn't imagine going through life wondering if his kid was dead or alive. He didn't know how the man held it together.

Dante picked up the crossword. "Yeah, you're not pathetic. A little fucked up maybe, but not pathetic. Hey, what's a seven letter word for pain?"

Jake chuckled, glad Dante lightened the heavy discussion. "Got any letters to go off?"

"Just a U."

"Torture." Naomi took the seat behind Dante. "Which is exactly what I'm going through after sleeping the way I did in that seat," she said, shifting her head from side to side and rubbing the base of her neck.

Jake's cell phone rang and he quickly checked the caller ID. "It's Rachel."

Naomi stood, climbed over his legs and took the window seat next to him. "Can you put her on speaker?"

"Hey, Rachel," Jake answered. "I have you on speaker. Got any good news?"

"I guess it depends on the news and your idea of good."

Dante dropped the puzzle in his lap and leaned across the

aisle. "Meaning?"

"Let's start with the riverboat explosion. At first I didn't find the entire Rose Wood connection. Our contact at the FBI told me he thinks there's one, but a couple of his counterparts began thinking this might have been a copycat bombing."

"That's ridiculous." Naomi pressed against Jake as she angled her head closer to the phone. "There wasn't another bombing anywhere else, and Ric made it perfectly clear that Christian wouldn't stop until he saw me."

"We're the only ones who know that," Rachel said. "Plus, the parts of the riverboat that are still intact are half submerged in water. The debris from the explosion is either at the bottom of the river or floating on the surface. Finding evidence is going to be tough. I was told divers are in the water searching for survivors. Once they're done, they're going to look for what caused the explosion."

"Good luck with that," Dante said with a shake of his head.

"True, but I actually know what caused the explosion. Before I get to that, I was able to confirm the Wood link to the Delta Rose bombing, which means no one is dismissing it as a copycat."

Then why bring the whole copycat thing up at all? Owen was right about his wife. She was not only a piece of work, she also had a thing for melodrama. "So what's the link?" Jake asked.

"Hazel Wood. She's a banjo playing country singer who was supposed to perform on the Delta Rose. She had an emergency surgery and cancelled last minute. So there's your Wood connection."

Naomi rested her elbow on her knee and her chin in her hand. "I wonder how Christian handled that?"

Jake shifted his gaze to hers. "What do you mean?"

"He doesn't tolerate mistakes." She drummed her fingers along her cheek. "Not that it matters at this point. At least there's one innocent person who survived. So, Rachel," she continued, her tone weary and hopeless, "what caused the explosion?"

"Keep me on speaker and go to your email."

Jake opened his email. "Got it," he said, and studied the photograph of a small piece of circuit board.

"Thanks to our FBI contact, we know how the devices are planted. We also know that Hunnicutt used C-4. It's stable and will only explode when a detonator is inserted into it and it's fired. The picture you're looking at is what's left of the detonator used for the bombing in San Francisco. We also learned that similar pieces have been found at both the Nevada and Wyoming bombing sites. Authorities are still searching the other locations for the exact cause, but are fairly certain the same type of bomb was used."

"If the C-4 needs a detonator," Naomi began, her focus also on the image Rachel had emailed, "how did Christian manage to trigger it?"

"Jake and Dante are familiar with explosives. Either of you want to chime in on this one?"

Dante tapped the pen against his thigh. "I can answer that. A detonator is basically a smaller explosive." He pointed to Jake's cell phone screen. "In this case, he would have used an electrical charge to set off the C-4. A lot of times you'll hear about terrorists using a cell phone or a watch to send a signal to a detonator. The phone or watch works as a shockwave and gives off heat, which is what C-4 requires to explode."

"Exactly," Rachel said. "If you haven't already, scroll down to the next picture I attached in the email."

Jake ran his thumb along the small screen. "Got it."

"It looks like the security key pad I have in my house," Naomi said.

"That's exactly what it is and that's what I believe Hunnicutt used as the detonator."

"How do you know for sure?" Jake asked.

"Because the very helpful FBI agent told Ian they found part of the model number connected to one of Guarinot security systems. A system the San Francisco restaurant does not own. Same goes for the hotel in Nevada and the nursing home in Wyoming. Most security companies now give their customers the option to control their systems from their TVs, tablets, smart phones and computers. You can't use a disposable cell phone to connect wirelessly to any of these systems. Which is good for us. This means that whoever detonated the bomb had to be connected to the Internet. Which also means that they could possibly leave a digital footprint giving us the location of the server they used."

"He obviously didn't do this alone," Jake said. "He could have people planted across the country just waiting for the right time to pull the trigger."

"True," Rachel agreed. "Either way, if Christian Hunnicutt doesn't know about digital footprints, then he wouldn't know that there are ways to eliminate them. Meaning, we could possibly arrest at least one of the guys setting off the devices."

"And if there is no footprint?" Jake asked, not fully understanding how Rachel could even find this digital footprint when the device was no longer intact.

"Then we're out of luck. But, what we do have that the FBI doesn't, is two very useful things."

"And that is?" Dante asked.

"Me, for one, and the fact we know who's behind the bombings."

"No one will deny that you're a genius." Dante looked at Jake and rolled his eyes. "But explain how this is going to help us get the evidence we need to go to the Feds."

"So glad you asked. And, by the by, thanks for calling me a genius."

Dante shook his head and grinned. "You're welcome."

"I told you about the digital footprint. Because the detonators were destroyed in the explosion, there's no way to use them to trace back to where the signal came from. But because we know who sent the signal, I can sic my spiders on Hunnicutt."

"Spiders?" Naomi shook her head. "Pretend none of us has a clue what you're talking about."

"Which we don't," Jake added.

"Sorry," Rachel said. "A Web spider, which can also be

known as a Web crawler, ant or Web scutter, is typically used by Web search engines. It's an Internet bot that searches through the World Wide Web in order to perform Web indexing. For our purposes, I've written code that will have these spiders scurrying through Hunnicutt's company server looking for any signal sent to the locations of the bombings."

"Will you be able to launch this code into Christian's server?" Naomi asked.

"It's already done," she responded. "Considering what Hunnicutt's done today, I thought for sure he'd have a more secure system. Lucky for us, I hacked into it without a problem."

"Any luck?" Dante asked.

"No, not yet. Next to the FBI, you'll be the first to know."

"Oh, my God." Naomi gripped his wrist. "It's five after three. Rachel, was there another bombing and you just didn't tell us?"

"I don't know," Rachel said and Jake could hear her tapping away at her computer keyboard. "I can't believe I didn't pay attention to the time. So far I'm not finding anything."

"Maybe he decided not to send another message," Dante said.

"Or maybe he knows we're watching." Jake rubbed his temple. "Could Hunnicutt's IT personnel detect your spiders?"

She sighed and continued to type. "No way. Not with the code I wrote."

"Could be something went wrong when he tried to detonate the bomb," Dante suggested.

"Could be," Rachel said. "I'll keep looking and let you know if I find anything. Regardless, call me when you land. Naomi's GPS chip is working, but I want to confirm Jake has a lock on her before Hunnicutt's driver heads off with her."

When Rachel ended the call, Naomi stood and climbed over Jake's legs. He snagged her hand when she reached the aisle. "What's up?"

"I'm going to get on my tablet and see if I can find

anything. I don't believe Christian opted not to set off another explosion. Trust me. If he says he'll do something, he will."

After Naomi walked to the back of the plane, Dante glanced across the aisle. "Something else you want to talk about?"

"Nope. I'm good."

"Then why are you still sitting by me and not in the back of the jet with your woman?"

Right. In less than twenty minutes they'd turn her over to Hunnicutt. Although confident she'd be fine considering they had the GPS, using Naomi as bait was still a big risk. There were too many unknown variables. They had no idea where Hunnicutt planned to take her, or how many of his men he'd have with him. In the meantime, he could take advantage of their current situation and spend time with her.

"You're shitty company anyway," Jake said and, crouching to avoid whacking his head on the jet's low ceiling, moved toward where Naomi sat.

Dante's laugh followed him down the aisle. When he sat next to Naomi, she glanced up from the tablet. "What's Dante laughing about? I could use something to lighten my mood."

"I told him he was shitty company."

She grinned and nudged him with her shoulder. "Seriously."

"I am being serious," he said and took the tablet from her hand.

Naomi let him. She'd grown tired of bad news and would, for a few moments, prefer not to look at any more death and destruction. She'd like to pretend they were jetting off to a private, exotic island retreat. That once there, she and Jake could walk along the beach and then later go back to their luxurious room and make love. After their conversation back in his office, and that kiss he'd given her, his demeanor had changed. The concern remained, along with the tension lining his face and shoulders, but at least he didn't look at her as if she were the enemy. Instead, his eyes held warmth and love.

I never stopped loving you…

She'd spent five years waiting to hear him say those words. Now that he had, what came next? Obviously they had to stop Christian, but then what? If they were able to gain enough evidence to put Christian in jail for life or, better yet, send him to Death Row, she'd no longer have to keeping running and looking over her shoulder. She could, if Jake was interested, resume her relationship with him. He knew the truth about her past, about her family and Christian. Now that the truth had been aired, there wasn't anything left to hide. They could settle down together, start fresh and no longer have secrets and lies standing between them.

Only…there was one last thing she hadn't told Jake. If they were to have a future together, she needed tell him. But how to bring it up now when they were supposed to be preparing for her meeting with Christian?

Her stomach flipped and her head tingled with unease. She didn't want to see the bastard. After everything he'd done, the thought of seeing him made her want to vomit. He had a sickness that couldn't be cured. He took what he wanted without a care or any remorse.

She glanced over at Jake. The man she loved was the polar opposite. If Jake wanted something, he went after it, but he did so with good intentions. He was a good man, and she wished she could have told him everything from the start. But she could tell him now. If something went wrong and she didn't survive, she wanted to die without any regret lingering and following her into the afterworld. She wanted to die with a clear conscience and also wanted Jake to have the closure he'd need to move on after she was gone.

Tears burned her eyes. She didn't want to die. She wanted peace and love.

She wanted a future with Jake.

"There's something else I need to tell you," she said before she changed her mind and allowed cowardice to creep in and stop her.

He stopped scrolling through the tablet and set it on his lap. "Another secret?" he asked, keeping his focus on the empty seat in front of him.

"Yeah, but I planned on telling you, only I ended up leaving so I—"

"Wait, leaving from where? Bola?"

She nodded. "The day before I found out my brother was murdered, I'd gotten test results back from my gynecologist." She drew in a deep breath hoping to bolster her confidence. "Jake, I can't have children."

He turned in the seat and took her hand in his. "That's your secret?" His eyes searched hers.

"What, not big enough for you?"

He touched her cheek. "I'm sorry. I didn't mean—I'm an insensitive jackass."

She rested her hand along his. "No, you're not. I guess when you look at everything else I've been hiding, not being able to have kids isn't that big of a deal."

"Liar."

"We've already established that."

He grinned and gave her forehead a quick kiss. "I meant, you're not being honest with me. You used to talk about having a big family. I'm sorry you can't have children, but if you're worried this changes things on my end, don't. All I've ever wanted was to be with you—for you, not the kids you could give me."

His words gave her comfort, but didn't lessen the guilt. "You come from a big family, your brothers now have families and I know you always wanted a big family, too. This is hugely import and something you need to consider if we…"

"If we what?"

"If we got back together," she answered. She'd come this far, she figured she might as well place all the cards on the table. He'd told her that he'd never stopped loving her. Prior to the bombings, they'd tentatively planned on trying out a long distance relationship. After spending too many years living with uncertainty, she wanted to solidify the future.

He caressed her cheek before running his hand through her hair. "If?" He cupped her head and drew her face closer to his. "There are no ifs or doubts allowed in this conversation. I want you. I want to be with you. I'll be honest. I might've lied to you when we were back in Woodbine."

"Good, now I don't feel as guilty."

He half smiled. "You shouldn't feel any guilt. Not anymore. What I lied about was where I saw us heading. I suggested a long distance relationship, but had no intention of doing one. Once I had you in Chicago, I wasn't letting you go."

She grinned at his audacity and confidence, two things she loved about him. With Jake, she always knew where she stood. "And how did you plan to do that?"

"Good question."

"In other words, you had no plan."

"Not exactly. Does sex count as a plan of action?"

She chuckled. "Sex is always a good plan."

"Seriously, though. I want to be with you. I don't want to pick up where we left off, I want us to have a fresh start. I know now isn't the right time to talk about this, but I needed you to know that—"

She cupped his strong jaw and kissed him. "I want a fresh start, too. Jake, I'm so sorry I didn't tell you everything. You're a good man and I trust you more than anyone. You didn't deserve any of this."

"You didn't deserve any of this. Now that I know the truth, I get why you didn't tell me about Hunnicutt." He sent her a rueful smile. "I'm not gonna lie, it was hard for me to accept that my woman was protecting me when it should have been the other way around."

She hadn't thought about how her need to keep him safe might have dented his ego. Her sole focus had been on regaining his trust and starting their lives together all over again. "You're still the toughest guy I know."

"Keep that in mind if you see Dante in action," he said with a quick grin.

"Let's hope Rachel pulls through and that won't be necessary."

The plane started to descend. Her stomach knotted and her

chest tightened.

Jake pulled her into his arms and rubbed a big hand along her back. "You're the bravest woman I've ever known," he murmured against her ear. "We'll get through this."

When the pilot came over the intercom and told them to fasten their seatbelts and prepare for landing, she drew away. "Don't let him take me," she said, as fear seized her by the throat. "I'd rather die than belong to him."

His eyes hardened and turned coal black with murderous rage. "He won't."

Her insides coiled when the jet's landing gear dropped. Minutes from now, she'd be in a car on her way to Hell. She had no idea what lay ahead, or how Christian would react toward her. Based on their past interactions, she had to prepare for the worst. Jake needed to, as well. "You have to listen to Ian. Stand down unless it looks like Christian is going to...kill me."

"Jesus, Naomi."

"Let me finish," she said, then winced when the jet touched the ground. "We need that evidence."

"You are the evidence."

She shook her head. "I'm not enough to have him executed for being a terrorist."

As the jet slowed, he took her hand and raised it to his lips. "Screw the evidence," he said and kissed her knuckles. "Hunnicutt's a mass murderer." He leaned forward and kissed her cheek. "He wiped out your family." He kissed her other cheek. "And he's hurt the woman I love." Pressing his forehead against hers, he ran the tip of his finger along her jaw. "Execution would be too easy on him. He deserves to feel pain for every life he's taken."

Sick satisfaction ran through her. She imagined baring Christian's back and lashing him with a barbed whip. One lash for each life until the flesh fell from him and the pain had become unbearable. Death would be too easy. He needed to suffer.

When the jet came to a stop, her conscience grabbed hold

of her. She blinked several times and tightened her grip around Jake's hand. She wasn't a murderer and neither was Jake. Christian needed to suffer, but she was better than him. She had morals. While revenge sounded sweet, she wasn't sure if she could live with herself knowing she'd killed a man. No matter that he was evil incarnate.

"Whatever you do, don't stoop to his level," she said just as Dante came down the aisle.

"I paid the pilot his bonus. He'll vouch that Naomi is the only passenger if Santiago asks."

"But what if he wants to come on board?" Naomi asked.

"Already asked that question. The pilot said he'd make up some FAA rule and get rid of the guy or threaten to call the police. Hunnicutt is a killer, but he's not stupid." Dante pierced her with his dark eyes. "He's so close to finally having you where he wants, I highly doubt he's going to take any additional risks at this point."

"But what if Santiago threatens the pilot with a gun?" Naomi asked, still unconvinced.

"We shoot him," Jake said as if shooting a man was an everyday occurrence.

"No, we'll hold him at gunpoint and force him to take us to Hunnicutt first." Dante countered. "If you still want to shoot him then—"

"Maybe we should just stick with forcing him to take us all to Christian," Naomi said. With reality setting in, she questioned whether she was brave enough to face the bastard alone.

Jake bent and raised the hem of his jeans where a gun had been strapped around his calf. "Good plan."

"It's not one we're going to attempt. We need a little thing called evidence." Dante reached beneath the seat across the aisle and pulled out a duffle bag. As he unzipped the bag, he glanced to Jake. "Working for CORE is a good gig and not one you want to blow."

Jake shook his head. "I had a good gig until Ian—"

"He saw potential in you." Dante pulled a small gun from

the bag. "There are a number of men and women who would kill to have your job. Follow orders and trust what he says. And trust me on this—you don't want to screw with Ian."

Naomi could tell Jake wanted to say more, but the pilot waved to them and pointed toward the jet's exit. She didn't know what Jake's issues were with his boss and, at this point, it seemed ridiculous to even think about it. When this was over, she'd ask him. She just prayed to God she'd have that chance.

"Stall him," Dante called to the pilot, then shifted his gaze to Jake. "Let's make sure the GPS is still working and call Rachel."

After Jake confirmed he still had a lock on her GPS chip, he contacted Rachel and placed the call on speaker.

"I can tell you landed. How's your signal?" Rachel asked.

"The GPS is working," Jake answered.

"Jake, remember what I told you." Naomi immediately recognized Ian's voice. "Wait until we have the evidence or until I can bring the Feds on board. This has to be done by the book. We can't allow Hunnicutt to get away on a technicality."

Jake and Dante exchanged a look. Dante's was more of an *I told you so*, while Jake's was an *I don't give a shit*. Knowing Ian was right, she touched Jake's arm and mouthed, "Listen to him."

The coldness in his eyes softened. "Yes, sir," he said, keeping his gaze locked on hers.

"My spiders haven't found anything yet, but I do think I found the last explosion," Rachel said. "There's no time for the details, but fortunately only two people were killed. The bombing explosion was obscure and never made the headlines. I'm not sure if Hunnicutt did it to throw everyone off track, or if it was accidental. Either way, I'm hoping this was the last one."

Naomi did too. She didn't want to die, but she would sacrifice her life to stop the bombings. If she survived and the press found out she was the reason hundreds of people had died—

She drew in a ragged breath. She couldn't worry about how

people would think of her once this was over. Her focus had to remain on one thing. Stopping Christian once and for all.

The pilot waved again. "There's a guy approaching the jet."

Carrying the duffle bag, Dante moved toward the bathroom in the back, while Jake took a quick look out the window. "We've gotta go," he said to Rachel and Ian. After ending the call and pocketing his phone, he latched onto her hand and pulled her close. "We'll be right behind you."

She clutched the front of his shirt. "I love you."

He kissed her. She poured her love and fears into the kiss. She didn't want to leave his side. For too many years she'd been on her own, running, hiding, living a lie. The years she'd spent without Jake had been lonely. Always worried about involving others in her life, the few friendships she'd developed while living in Woodbine were superficial. On the surface, she'd become a hollow shell of her former self. Before Christian, she'd been bubbly and fun, daring, yet trusting. She'd loved being surrounded by people, being social—she'd loved life. When she'd been with Jake, she'd begun to go back to her old ways, until the bastard had murdered her brother.

She tore her mouth away. "I want my life back."

"With me in it." His eyes held love, compassion and promise, his voice, strength. "This ends today."

"You need to go," Dante urged her.

She looked at him and nodded, then turned back to Jake. "I'll see you soon."

"Before you know it." He gave her another quick kiss. "Be strong. I love you."

Before the tenderness in his eyes caused her to burst into tears, she rushed down the aisle toward the jet's cockpit. The pilot gave her a somber nod, and said, "I don't want to know what Ian has you doing. But, whatever it is, good luck."

After he opened the door and pressed a lever to drop a handful of stairs to the ground, she looked across the small airstrip. Several small planes sat near a hanger. Unlike a major airport, there was no activity, no shuttles carrying luggage or employees performing maintenance on planes.

She drew in a deep, fortifying breath and took a step. Then quickly jerked back.

"*Hola.*" Terror gripped her as she immediately recognized the man Christian had brought with him the night he'd attacked her in her apartment. The Columbian raked his brown eyes over her body. "Welcome back to Virginia."

Although he offered his hand, she refused to take it. The last time he'd touched her, he'd held knife to her throat. When she reached the bottom step, Santiago grabbed her arm. "Come, *mi querida*, Mr. Hunnicutt is anxious to see you."

CHAPTER 13

Norfolk, Virginia
3:23 p.m. Eastern Daylight Saving Time

CHRISTIAN HUNNICUTT LUNGED from the throne chair, waving Ric's cell phone. "Santiago has her." Excitement, triumph and satisfaction pumped through his body as he handed the phone back to Ric. "It's about fucking time."

"Congratulations," Ric said with a smile, and pocketed the phone. "Your plan worked."

"Of course it did." He looked around the room, ignored the brooding smart brother, then tapped his index finger against his chin. "We won't be able to leave for at least another hour. We'll have to make sure the bitch has suitable accommodations." The throne chair caught his attention. "Yes, she needs to know where she belongs. Vlad," he called.

The Russian exited the back room where Mickey had been kept throughout the day. "Sir?"

"Our guest will be here in about ten minutes. I can't have her roaming the warehouse. What do we have to restrain her?"

"There are handcuffs in the pantry," Ric offered.

Christian studied the leg of the throne chair. Like on the armrests, intricate carvings had been whittled into the mahogany. When he pictured Rose scraping the metal handcuffs along the wood, he shook his head. "No good. She'll damage my chair."

Ric shrugged. "There's plenty of duct tape."

He cracked a smile. "As Mickey certainly knows," he said, and thought about all of the silver tape wrapped around the dumb brother's head and covering what was left of his eye. "But the adhesive might ruin the finish on my chair."

"Does she have to be attached to your throne?" Harrison asked. "You have plenty of furniture in this place. Or why not lock her in one of the other rooms?"

He took a few steps and then sat on the edge of the leather sofa's armrest next to Harrison. "Do you have any idea the amount of planning that had gone in to making today happen? Or how many years I've been searching for her?"

Harrison's bangs fell into his eyes when he shook his head.

"Then maybe you should shut the fuck up."

"Sorry, sir."

He crossed his legs at the ankle. "You should be. But because I'm feeling...generous, I'll share something with you. Rose has been a thorn in my side from the day I'd met her." As Ric chuckled, Christian glanced to Harrison and smiled. "Pun intended."

"I got it," Harrison said, straight faced.

"Not in the joking mood? Understandable. It's not every day that you kill hundreds of innocent people and carve up your brother." He sighed. "You'll get over it. Now, where was I? Yes, the thorn in my side... Rose belongs to me. Now she needs to know her place." He thumbed toward the throne chair. "I want her kneeling at my feet."

"Without damaging your chair."

"You're not making fun of me, are you?"

Harrison's eyes widened. "No, just pointing out a fact."

"That's good. I won't tolerate mockery." He shifted he gaze to Ric. "Isn't that right?"

The sadist nodded. "Mockery could lead to an ugly death."

"Sir," Vlad said as he entered the room carrying a spool of twine. "I found this in utility closet."

He stood and took the spool. "Excellent. This will work for now. Ric, I'd still like those handcuffs. We'll use them on her when we transport her back to the house. The duct tape, too."

Once it had grown dark, he planned to leave the warehouse behind and take her to his plantation. They would use Ric's cottage and take the old tunnel leading to the bitch's new home. "If I recall, she's a screamer, and I don't need the servants hearing her nonsense."

He pushed off the edge of the sofa. The energy buzzing through him made it difficult to stay still. "We should have champagne for our guest. I'm sure after her trip she's probably hungry, too." He looked to the Russian. The man couldn't cook worth shit. "Ric, prepare refreshments for her arrival."

Ric's smile fell and he shifted his gaze to Vlad. "Yes, sir," he said, his tone holding a hint of grievance. The sadist had been with him as long as Santiago had. And while the man had never gone against him and had proven time and again to be a worthy confidant—enough that he'd made him the COO of his company—Ric occasionally needed to be reminded of his place. Like Vlad and Santiago, like all of his servants, Ric was still hired help.

"Looks like your latest bombing finally made the news," Harrison said.

He turned toward the TV and caught the caption running below the President's White House press conference. *Horse trainer Joe Cline and jockey Frank Russell for the prize winning horse, Wild Rose, died in a fire at Woodland Horse Farm, Peoria, Illinois.*

"Shit. Ric, stop what you're doing and Google Wild Rose again. It looks like Harrison's explosion took out everyone but that damned horse." When he caught Harrison looking at him, he added, "That horse was slated to win the Kentucky Derby last year. It cost me five hundred grand."

"You're a billionaire."

"If you haven't figured it out by now, I don't like losing."

"Sorry, sir," Ric said as he left the kitchen and approached. "The horse survived."

"Damn it," he said, staring at the muted TV. Then he chuckled.

Have you come up with another way to destroy the horse?" Ric asked.

He shook his head. "I was just thinking… The President was supposed to give his press conference from the White House Rose Garden."

"It was moved inside due to the threat of rain," Ric said.

"Doubtful. I have a feeling the FBI has definitely made the Rose Wood connection." He laughed and sat in his throne chair. "Too bad the Woodworkers Union wasn't in Washington. Picture it. The President giving a speech from the Rose Garden to the Woodworkers Union. Now that explosion would have made a statement."

Ric laughed, too. "Not that you haven't already."

"True." He nodded, then checked his watch. "She'll be along any minute. Ric, get back to those refreshments. Vlad, make sure Mickey can't make any noise. I want him to be a surprise. Harrison, prepare to pull the trigger one more time. Rose needs to be taught a valuable lesson."

No one runs from him.

Wilshire District, Bloomington, Indiana
2:36 p.m. Central Daylight Saving Time

"Come on and move," Vince bitched and slammed his palm against the steering wheel. He'd finished making deliveries in the Beachmore business district and was trying his best to reach the heart of Wilshire Park. Although Bloomington's Wilshire Park was known for its fancy, upper class neighborhoods, like Rosewood Estates, the area also had a small business district, which was near the hospital he needed to be at in—he checked the clock—less than twenty-five minutes. He didn't know if an accident or construction was what had held up the traffic, all he knew was that he was ten minutes away from the hospital.

As the truck idled, he checked the company tablet. His next delivery was supposed to be in Rosewood Estates, which made logistical sense. The expensive neighborhood was located at the edge of Wilshire Park. Because there was no way he would have time to make all the necessary deliveries in Rosewood, he'd already driven past the turn he'd take into the neighborhood. He scrolled through the tablet and viewed the rest of his route. If the news was good, he could be in and out of the ultrasound in thirty minutes. If it wasn't—

Traffic started to move. He set the tablet in the center console and thought about how he'd handle the rest of his route, rather than the results of the ultrasound. He wanted to remain positive for Anna, even if deep down he was scared shitless. The baby had to be healthy. When they'd found out they were pregnant with Benny, they'd been hoping for a girl. Neither he nor Anna would change how Benny had turned out, but he knew Anna had always wanted a daughter. He had, too. After Anna found out she was pregnant again, he'd secretly hoped for a little girl. When they discovered they were having a girl, he'd instantly pictured taking her to Daddy/Daughter dances and imagined her in a wedding dress as she kissed his cheek and he gave her away to her new husband. Then they'd found out about the cysts.

As the truck inched closer to the center of Wilshire Park, the nervousness that had been coiling through his stomach intensified. *Please, God. Let everything be okay.*

His cell phone rang. He checked the caller ID and quickly answered. "Hi, hon. Are you at the hospital?"

"Yeah, I just parked my car and am heading inside. Where are you?"

"Less than ten minutes away. I'm stuck in traffic."

"I worried about that," she said. "There's construction on Elm Street, along with an accident."

Of course there'd be both construction *and* an accident. "Well, the traffic is moving along now. I'll make it with plenty of time. But you'll definitely be on soccer duty. I had to skip going through your dream neighborhood and will have to do some serious backtracking."

"I don't mind dealing with soccer. I'm just glad you're going to make it on time," she said, and he caught the worry in her voice.

"We're going to be just fine."

"Vin, you don't know that. What if—"

"No what ifs. I love you and besides, we're awesome parents. That's how I know we're going to be fine. Okay?"

"You wouldn't say that if you saw Benny munching on cat food earlier."

He chuckled. "The boy knows what he likes."

"If you say so," she said and it warmed him to hear a smile in her voice. "I'll let you go. I'm heading into the office. Love you."

He ended the call and dropped the phone in his lap. Then swore again when the traffic stopped moving. At this point, he could probably park the truck and sprint the rest of the way to the hospital. Drumming his thumbs along the steering wheel, he looked to the clock on the dash again. Two thirty-eight. Damn it. If the traffic didn't pick up, he'd do just that. Park and run.

The cars in front of his truck began inching forward. With the truck higher than a regular vehicle or SUV, he saw a side street up ahead. Perfect. Fifty or so more feet and he'd turn down the street and avoid the accident and construction. No matter what, he'd make the ultrasound.

Nothing could stop him.

Norfolk, Virginia
3:38 p.m. Eastern Daylight Saving Time

Dante drove the rusted pickup truck they'd bought off the maintenance guy they met at the airstrip. With over three hundred thousand miles, the 1983 Dodge Ram was probably worth seven hundred dollars—if that. Dante had paid fifteen hundred. But renting or having a rental company drop a vehicle at the airstrip hadn't been an option. They weren't supposed to be in Norfolk and hadn't wanted to raise suspicions. He'd suggested they steal something and reimburse the owner later, but then Dante ran into the maintenance guy and now they were the proud owners of a piece of shit.

Jake checked his Colt Delta Elite, then slipped the pistol into its leather holster.

"I thought Ian gave you a Glock," Dante said, as he checked the GPS and made a turn.

Naomi had given him the pistol the Christmas before she'd left him. "He did. But I like my Colt. It has sentimental value." Jake raised his hips and slipped several magazines into the back pocket of his jeans. He glanced at his phone propped on the cracked dashboard. "Looks like they stopped at—shit. I can't tell what the hell street. Is there a map in here?" He flipped open the glove box and found a bunch of empty cans of tobacco.

As Dante turned left, he hit the speed dial on his cell phone and handed it to Jake. "Get Rachel on it."

Jake put the phone on speaker as soon as she answered. "Where are we heading?" he asked.

"I've got her location pulled up on an aerial map. Looks like the driver's pulled into an old warehouse. Hang on, let me check it." As she tapped away, Jake's chest tightened with impatience. The GPS chip indicated Naomi wasn't on the move anymore.

"Got it," Rachel said. "The building belongs to BH-Xpress, but is no longer in use."

"Not according to the GPS."

"Right. What's your location?"

"Forty-third and Lexington," Dante said, slowing the truck.

More tapping came across the line. "Okay, go one block, then hang a right onto Monticello. Take that for a mile until you hit East Fifty-Fifth. Make another right. You'll see a Laundromat on the left. Park in the back. From there you're about one hundred yards from the warehouse. You can use the back of the buildings next to the Laundromat for cover."

Dante made the turn onto Monticello. "Will this GPS chip show which floor of the building Naomi is being held?"

"Unfortunately, no. Remember, this is a prototype. But the main thing we need is the general location, which we have.

Now we just need you inside the warehouse."

What they needed was to storm the place and put a bullet into Hunnicutt's head. "I'll send a text when we're inside." Jake ended the call and handed Dante his phone.

"Reach in the duffle bag," Dante said. "I brought you a knife."

Jake pulled up both legs of his jeans. "Got a knife and a gun. I'm good." He let go of his pant legs, leaned forward and tapped the dash. "There's East Fifty-Fifth." He pointed. "And the Laundromat."

Dante made a quick left, slowed the Ram and pulled into a parking lot filled with gravel and potholes. The backdoor of the Laundromat had been boarded shut. More plywood had been hung from the inside, while broken glass remained in the windows. The worn brick was covered with graffiti. Garbage, broken bottles and beer cans lined the back of the building. Looking to his left, Jake saw much of the same.

After climbing out of the truck, Jake moved to the back of the Laundromat. Dante came alongside him, and they both eased their way down the narrow path between buildings. Jake's boots crunched over more broken glass and trash. The rancid odor of shit and piss hit him from all angles. When they reached the sidewalk, he stopped and peered around the corner of the building. "Rachel's right. The warehouse is about one hundred yards from here."

"He's chosen a good place to do his business," Dante said. "No one would think Hunnicutt is using the warehouse or coming within ten feet of this area. There's also no telling what kind of security he's using."

"We've got the main entrance, which doesn't look worth the effort with the boards and chain lock, and then the dock entrance. But if the gate's wired to a security system, that could be a problem."

Dante opened his coat and pulled out a mini bolt cutter. "It's hard to tell if the fence is electric or not. If it isn't, we'll cut it."

Jake stared at the other weapons and gadgets on Dante's

belt. "Where do I get one of those?"

"Home Depot."

"I meant the Batman utility belt."

"Home Depot."

He rolled his eyes, then said, "Let's go back the way we came. Follow the buildings along the rear until we're diagonal from the warehouse dock. Looked like there were houses next to the last building. We can cross from there."

Nodding, Dante sprinted back down the narrow alley. As Jake ran behind him, he hoped to God they could find a way inside the warehouse without alerting Hunnicutt. He wanted the element of surprise. Even more, he wanted to be able see or at least hear Naomi. Hunnicutt was a sick, crazy bastard. If the man had no qualms about murdering hundreds of innocent people to gain what he wanted, what would he do to Naomi? Then again, because Hunnicutt had spent years looking for her and took the risk of setting off bombs across the country, he might not do anything to her right away. Later, though—

He picked up the pace and ran past Dante. He couldn't think about later. Instead, he had to hope like hell that they gained the necessary evidence in time to haul Naomi out of the warehouse. Stopping where the buildings ended and dilapidated houses began, Jake squatted behind a rusted dumpster. "Are the handles of your bolt cutter plastic?"

Dante checked the tool. "Yeah, why?"

"We'll use that to test if the fence is electric."

"You know this how?"

"And here I thought you SEALs knew all the tricks." Jake kept watch on the warehouse. "My dad taught me when I was a kid. You touch the metal part of the bolt cutter closest to the plastic handle on the fence post. If it's on, we'll see an electric arc. If not, we're good to go."

Dante gave him a curt nod. "Let's do this."

They ran across the street and hid behind a detached garage about forty yards from the warehouse fence. Jake took the bolt cutter from Dante, told him to stay put, crouched and used the overgrown grass for cover. He quickly chose the part of the fence closest to the building and farthest from view of any warehouse window. Naomi had been inside for at least five minutes, and that was five minutes too long for his liking. Needing to be able to see or hear her, he worked fast and tested the fence. No arc.

He turned, gave Dante a thumb's up, then using the bolt cutter, he began snipping the fence. The tool sliced through the metal like a hot knife to butter. By the time Dante reached him, he'd made progress and was pulling part of the fence back. "Ready?" he asked, ducking and stepping through the hole he'd made.

When Dante squeezed through the hole, they avoided the garage and targeted the service door next to it. Dante checked his badass utility belt and pulled out two small tools.

"What are those?" Jake asked in a hushed tone.

"Tension and torque wrenches. Keep watch, I'm going to pick the lock."

Jake slid along the garage and checked the small windows. The white SUV Naomi had driven off in sat along the far wall of the garage. From the angle at which he stood, he couldn't see any other vehicles. He also didn't see any of Hunnicutt's men.

Dante snapped his fingers. Jake rushed to his side, just as Dante turned the knob and opened the door a fraction.

"What'd you see?" Dante asked exchanging the lock pick tools for a gun.

"Just the driver's SUV. Doesn't mean there isn't anyone patrolling the garage."

"Let's go in, sweep the area and check for surveillance cameras."

Jake knew that was the right way to handle the situation, but he didn't want Naomi alone with Hunnicutt any longer than she had to be.

Don't let him take me…I'd rather die than belong to him.

There was no way in hell he'd allow either option to happen. He checked the GPS on his phone, along with the time. "We split up and make this fast. I want to know exactly where she is—now."

Norfolk, Virginia
3:49 p.m. Eastern Daylight Saving Time

Naomi's heart beat fast as the Santiago stopped her at the third floor landing of the old, rundown warehouse. He shoved her against the metal door.

"Remember, *querida*," he said, pressing his mouth against her ear. "Mr. Hunnicutt demands respect." He rapped on the door. "Do yourself a favor and, for once, obey him."

Her legs grew weak, yet the urge to run was strong. The past had finally caught up with her. Christian now had her where he wanted. Desperate. Vulnerable. Alone.

She had no idea if Jake and Dante had made it to the warehouse. The GPS chip had been working when they'd landed, but was it now? Did they know where she was in the building?

The door swung open and she drew back against the Columbian. *Ric Mancini.* She'd watched him during Christian's press conference, had spoken to him on the phone, but seeing him now—up close and way too personal—brought back horrifying memories of pain and terror.

Ric sent her a sadistic smile. "Do you have any idea what a pain in my ass you've been?" He gripped her by the back of the neck and shoved her inside and against the wall. "For eight fucking years he's searched for you. I knew I should have let you bleed to death that night." He took a fistful of her hair and pulled hard until she was bending and at his mercy. "Life would have been so much better without you in it."

"Ric," Santiago said and jerked his head toward another closed door. "Don't mark her. Honey Badger won't like it."

"Not for now anyway." Ric glared at her with disdain, then his lips curved into a cruel grin. "He'll grow tired of the bitch soon, and then she'll be all mine." He leaned in and, pulling her hair until her scalp ached, whispered, "I'm going to enjoy making you suffer."

He let go of her hair and pushed her toward Santiago. She staggered, lost her footing and fell to her knees. Memories from the night Ric had tortured her surfaced and made her head light with fear. She'd put a gun to her head or slit her wrists before ever allowing Ric to touch her again. Christian personified evil, while Ric was a soulless demon.

"I want to kick her so fucking bad." Ric nudged her with his leather shoe. "Get up before I accidentally break your teeth with my foot."

The Columbian laughed and hauled her to her feet. "Poor, *querida*. Not the welcome you were expecting, eh? No worries, Santiago doesn't hate you like Ric does. You're life means nothing to me."

"Christ, Santiago, you're starting to talk like Vlad."

The Columbian frowned and led her toward the closed door. "Quit using the Lord's name in vain."

"Give me a fucking break. If Honey Badger told you to slit the bitch's throat you'd do it in a heartbeat. How is saying *Christ* worse than that?"

While Santiago rattled off something in Spanish, Naomi tried to slow her racing heart. She needed to remain calm and level headed. She had no doubt Ric would make good on his threats. She knew first-hand the man enjoyed inflicting pain. Right now, she'd rather take her chances with Christian. After what he'd gone through to force her to come to him, she doubted he'd kill her right away. He'd likely take pleasure in making her suffer first.

The Columbian turned the knob. Ric shoved him out of the way and latched his hand around her arm. "*I'll* bring the bitch to him."

"*Que te den por culo*," Santiago said through gritted teeth and narrowed his eyes.

"Fuck me?" Ric smiled without humor, while the Columbian's eyes widened. "I've been brushing up on my Spanish, *gilipollas*."

When Santiago sneered, Ric chuckled. "If you don't like

being called an asshole, then don't act like one. Remember who you work for, Columbian. Honey Badger pays you, but I own you. Understand?"

Santiago stepped aside. "Whatever, Rosseta Stone."

Ric ignored the other man and looked down at her. "I suggest you play nice. He's in a good mood right now, but that can change."

Fully aware of Christian's mood swings, she had no intention of provoking him. Doing so would be like poking a stick in a hornets' nest.

Ric wrapped his hand around the door knob. As he turned it, her insides twisted with nervousness and fear. When he pushed the door open, Ric shoved her forward and forced her to walk. As if trudging through quicksand wearing concrete boots, her legs grew stiff and heavy. Dread stilted her steps, worry constricted her lungs and made it difficult to breathe.

Taking shallow breaths, she darted her gaze around the room. Searching for him, preparing for him to pounce.

"Sir," Ric said. "The guest of honor has arrived."

Her heart raced. Her head buzzed. She kept searching the room, saw a young guy on a sofa, a laptop on the table in front of him, but no one else. Then the young guy shifted his eyes toward the large, gaudy chair across from him. She came to an abrupt halt, just as Christian rose from the chair.

With an air of pomp and circumstance, he turned and smiled, revealing the dimples she'd once considered sexy. His midnight blue eyes, heavily fringed by dark lashes, held triumph and pleasure as he assessed her. The tailored suit he wore showed off his toned physique and screamed dollar signs. Chuckling and shaking his head as if he was stunned that she was standing there, he moved his long legs toward her.

When he was only a foot away, he stopped, gently took her hand and raised it to his lips. When he dipped his head, she noticed his perfectly styled, short dark hair hadn't greyed over the years. Concentrating on his hair, rather than the way he held her hand and kissed it, helped to keep her from cringing. Christian was a charming, amicable man. Enraged, he was a monster.

"A rose by any other name would smell as sweet." He pressed his lips against her skin, then met her gaze. "What should I call *my* rose?"

With her mouth dry, her tongue thick and her throat tightening, she swallowed hard. "Naomi."

He frowned and, still holding her hand, led her toward the man on the sofa. "Naomi doesn't suit you. You'll always be Rose to me. Here, let me introduce you to my associate, Harrison."

Harrison didn't look like the type of man Christian would associate with on a regular basis. With his dirty, unkempt hair and stained shirt and jeans, he looked as if he'd been plucked off the streets. Plus, the fear and nervousness in Harrison's eyes matched her own.

"Ma'am," Harrison said, his left leg jerking as he tapped the heel of his sneaker against the area rug.

"Enough of the formalities." Christian offered her a seat next to Harrison. "There's no more time to waste. Harrison, are we ready?"

"Yes." The man opened the laptop and cleared his throat. "On your command."

Whoever detonated the bomb had to be connected to the Internet...

The betrayal smacked her in the face. Not wanting to reveal that she knew he was using a computer to detonate the bombs, she kept her eyes on the laptop. "What are you doing with that?"

"I'm not doing anything with it. You or Harrison will."

"I don't understand."

Christian glanced at his watch. "We only have three minutes until four. There's really no time to waste. As part of your welcome home gift, I'm giving you one of two choices. Shoot Harrison in the head with this." He pulled a gun from behind his back and waved it. "Or you'll detonate the next bomb."

She looked at Harrison's profile. The man clenched his jaw and closed his eyes. When he opened them, he turned to her.

"Kill me. Please."

No way. Her heart pounded hard. She couldn't do it. But she also couldn't trigger the next explosion. Other than Christian, no one else needed to die today. Anger consumed her and ate away at her fear. "You promised. Ric told me you'd stop with the damned messages once I came to you."

"I changed my mind." He shrugged. "I decided you kept me waiting too long and now you deserve to be punished for your insult." He looked at his watch again. "Two and a half minutes. What'll be, Rose? Harrison's life, or detonating the bomb?"

"I can't shoot him."

"I can do it for you. You'd probably miss anyway." Christian raised the gun and aimed it at Harrison's head. "Two minutes, Rose. Make a choice. Harrison or the bomb?"

Bloomington, Indiana
2:58 p.m. Central Daylight Saving Time

Vince slammed the truck into park. The damned thing had been too big to park in the garage and he'd had a hard time finding a spot large enough in the campus parking lot. After circling a couple of times, he'd discovered an opening on the street about a half a block from one of the hospital's entrances. Not the entrance he wanted, and the location would require him to run through half the hospital to the area where the ultrasound would be done, but at least he'd made it in time.

His cell phone rang. He checked the caller ID and quickly answered. "Hey, hon," he said as he made his way inside the back end of the truck. "I'm here. Just locking up."

"Thank God." Anna let out a sigh. "The tech finished her last appointment early and is ready to take me back."

By the time Anna undressed, climbed on the table and the ultrasound tech began placing the goop they used during the testing on Anna's stomach, he could be there. "I'll be less than five minutes. Plenty of time. Let me go so I can make it."

"Okay. See you in a few."

He pocketed the cell phone. As he rushed toward the front of the truck, his boot caught on the dolly and he fell forward. He grabbed the shelf. A package fell to the floor, followed by the telltale sound of shattered glass. He glanced down and swore. Liquid oozed from the cardboard box, along with the strong scent of alcohol.

Just my luck.

Before the booze—that was obviously not packed properly—contaminated the packages on the floor of the truck, he moved to the cab. He searched for the cheap paper towels, a standard BH-Xpress supply. Not his usual truck, he finally found the roll buried under a medical kit near the fire extinguisher. After tearing off a long sheet, he tossed it on the wet spot. "Damn it," he muttered. He didn't need this right now. The towel did jack to soak up the liquid and he had to apply more.

He ripped off another long sheet. He'd make sure the alcohol didn't reach the other packages, then forget about it until after the ultrasound.

But he'd only give the mess another minute.

Time was ticking.

Norfolk, Virginia
3:59:35 p.m. Eastern Daylight Saving Time

Although a chill ran through her, Naomi's underarms grew damp, along with her forehead. She stared at the gun Christian held, then to the laptop on the table, then to Harrison. The choice between Harrison's life and the possible casualties from the detonated bomb weighed heavy on her heart and conscience. In the depths of her soul, she knew the only solution.

"Kill me." She shoved off the sofa and pounded her hand against her chest. "That's my choice. Put me out of my misery and kill *me*, not Harrison and not anyone else."

Christian looked thoughtful for a split second before grinning. "I intend to eventually, but not before we've had a chance to get reacquainted and take a walk down memory lane. Twenty seconds, Rose. Hurry and decide. Or maybe I should just do both. Shoot Harrison *and* detonate the bomb."

Ric laughed softly. She ignored the sick bastard and looked down at the laptop, then slid her gaze to Harrison.

Tears trailed down her cheeks as she stared at Harrison. The acceptance, sadness and pity in his eyes filled her with despair. Their situation was both dire and hopeless.

She'd been raised in a good, loving home. She'd been taught to be empathetic, to show kindness and put others needs before her own.

What had she done to deserve this? Why her? Why couldn't the bastard have left her alone?

Outrage and fury blackened her heart, while misery weakened her convictions. She'd stopped feeling sorry for herself years ago and had accepted her fate. She didn't need Harrison's pity. If anything, she pitied him. With a gun to his head, he obviously wasn't here by choice and, at the moment, his fate looked bleaker than hers.

"Twelve seconds, Rose," Christian taunted. "You better hurry up and decide. I'd hate to have to kill Harrison *and* set off the detonator."

"Don't do this. Please, Christian. I'm here. You have me now."

"Are you begging me?"

God, she hated him. "Yes."

"Get on your knees and beg."

She dropped to her knees. "Please, Christian."

Ric's laugh grew louder.

Harrison's breath grew labored.

"Five seconds. What will you do if I spare his life and not set the explosion?"

"Anything," she said on a sob.

"Promise?" Christian asked and lowered the gun a fraction.

The modicum of relief did nothing to slow her heart rate.

"Yes."

"Liar." He raised the gun and aimed it at Harrison's head. "Time's up."

"I'm not lying. I'll do anything. Please. Don't—"

Harrison lurched forward. "I'm as good as dead," he muttered and hit a key on the laptop.

Panic seized her lungs and stole her breath. She reached for his wrist, but the damage had been done. In a split second, that single key, that simple press of a button changed the lives of many. How many just died? How many lives had she destroyed?

"You insolent, fucking fool," Christian shouted. "You're right. You *are* as good as dead."

She whipped her head toward Christian, just as he pulled the trigger.

And screamed.

PART III

The future depends on what you do today.

— Mahatma Gandhi

CHAPTER 14

GUN RAISED, JAKE spun to the right. Filled with primal fear, he sprinted across the second floor of the warehouse toward the stairs.

His skin pricked with terror. His heart pounded hard.

Naomi.

If he lived to be one hundred, he'd never forget that chilling scream. He had to find her. Now.

Dante caught up with him. "Third floor. Go."

Taking two steps at a time, careful to keep silent, he rushed up the stairs. When he reached the third floor landing, he stopped and pinned himself against the wall near the metal door. Dante did the same on the opposite wall next to the door. "Try the handle," Dante whispered.

Praying the door wasn't bolted shut, Jake wrapped his sweaty palm around the handle and slowly turned it toward him. After a soft click, the door eased open. With one eye, he peered through the small crack he'd made, angled his head and scoped the area. He slipped back and turned to Dante.

"Empty. Long hallway. Three doors, all closed."

Dante gave him a single nod. "I'll text Rachel."

"No." He didn't want to go against Ian's orders, but knew he would. Naomi's life was more important that Ian's precious evidence.

A muscle flexed in Dante's jaw. "You're a Marine. You know the drill. We follow protocol."

"Fuck that and turn it around. Would you sit on your ass

and wait? Or would you go after what's yours?"

Dante let out a short sigh. "Fine. But we don't—"

Jake opened the door and edged into the hallway. He didn't care what Dante had to say. He wasn't a Marine following orders and protocol. This wasn't Iraq and he wasn't fighting insurgents.

He was fighting for Naomi's life.

With his steps muted by the carpet lining the hall, he rushed to the far end and pressed his ear against the door. Nothing. He held his breath and turned the knob. In his peripheral vision, he caught Dante behind him, gun raised and aimed at the door.

Confident Dante would shoot whoever was on the other side should they rush them, he cracked open the door, then released a quiet sigh. Utility closet.

Dante tapped his shoulder and nodded toward the next door.

Jake took a few steps, then pressed his ear against the wood. "I hear something," he whispered. "I'm gonna check."

Dante knocked his hand away from the door knob. "This much," he said, holding his index finger and thumb a half an inch apart.

Keeping his gun raised near the side of his face, Jake slowly turned the knob and cracked open the door.

"You sick bastard," he heard Naomi cry. Grateful she was alive and pissed as hell, he glanced at Dante. The relief on the other man's face matched his own.

A man laughed. *Hunnicutt?* Damn it, he wished he had a visual.

"You should have seen your face when I pulled the trigger," the man said, and Jake recognized Hunnicutt's voice from the earlier press conference. "I wish I had a picture of it. Wait. I just had another brilliant idea. Ric, you'll have to bring the camera out once we're home. I'm sure we can come up with ways to make Rose look just as horrified."

"It would be my greatest pleasure," Ric said with a chuckle.

Damn, he wanted to kill Ric Mancini, too.

"Come, Rose," Hunnicutt said. "Let's make you more comfortable. Sit next to me. Santiago, turn on the TV. I want Rose to see the damage she's caused."

Harrison hadn't crapped his pants since he was four, but he'd come damn near close minutes ago. Honey Badger was a twisted fuck. When he'd pulled the trigger and Rose had screamed, Harrison thought he was a dead man. Until he heard a click, followed by the badger and Ric's laughter. The prick had played Russian roulette and had, unfortunately, let him live.

Holding Rose by the arm, Hunnicutt dragged her to his stupid throne chair. "On your knees," he ordered, then called to Santiago. "Tie her to the chair." As Santiago secured Rose to the leg of the chair, Hunnicutt looked to Harrison. "It's fitting for a beautiful woman to be enslaved to her master, don't you think?"

Harrison locked eyes with Rose, then quickly looked away. He didn't want to see her red, tearstained face or the fear in her eyes. He didn't want to worry about her safety when he had his own and Mickey's on his mind. It was only a matter of time before Honey Badger killed them. Then the woman would be on her own.

Hell, he couldn't let that happen. At least his death would probably be quick. Hers—from the way Hunnicutt had spoken, it sounded as if she wouldn't get off as easily. Just thinking of the inhumane things Hunnicutt and Ric would do to her had bile rising in the back of his throat.

Throughout the day he'd been flip-flopping between wanting to die and wanting to survive in order to see Hunnicutt caught and justice served. With Rose finally here, he had a new mission. Save the girl. But how could he do that when he couldn't figure out a way to save himself and Mickey?

"I think Harrison is mad at me," Hunnicutt said to Rose. "Apparently he has no sense of humor and doesn't care to be the butt of a joke." He shrugged. "Ric, after you find news about the bombing, see to those refreshments."

Ric lifted the TV remote and changed the channel to CNN.

When Rose gasped, Harrison leaned forward and stared at the TV. The incinerated shell of a black BH-Xpress delivery truck blazed outside of a large building. As firefighters turned the hose on the truck, bits of burning debris and ash floated through the air, along with thick, charcoal grey smoke. The sidewalk, where the truck had been parked, as well as the street, had been blackened from the blast. Pedestrians ran and shouted, while police and firefighters struggled to free a driver from an overturned car that must have been driving past the truck when it had exploded.

"I can't hear what the idiot is saying. Turn up the volume," Hunnicutt demanded, his face grim, his mouth turned down in a furious frown.

"As you can see, firefighters are trying to contain the flames," the reporter said, using the chaos on the street as his backdrop. "Again, there's been no word on the BH-Xpress delivery driver, and we're still waiting to discover the extent of injuries the man trapped in the overturned car has suffered." The camera panned out as the reporter extended his hand to the left, revealing the entrance of a hospital. "Other than a few shattered windows, the damage from this latest bombing has been contained and there have been no other injuries reported."

The screen switched to the CNN newsroom. "For those of you catching up, there's been another bombing, this time in the Wilshire District of Bloomington, Indiana, outside of Southwest Hospital. Earlier today in Denver, a BH-Xpress plane exploded during takeoff. With this latest explosion, one wonders if these bombings are as random as they've seemed, or if BH-Xpress is the real target."

"Turn it off," Hunnicutt said, his voice low, seething. "Now."

Since Ric was in the kitchen, Santiago rushed over and shut off the TV.

"Santiago, wasn't I specific?" Hunnicutt asked, steepling his fingertips. "Didn't I say that the explosion was to happen in Rosewood Estates?"

"*Sí*," the Columbian replied. "I personally placed the C-4 on the truck. I also double checked the driver's route. He must've changed—"

"Enough." Hunnicutt slammed a hand on the throne chair's armrest. "I don't want excuses. Damn it, there's no do overs and now the Rose Wood link is lost."

"Maybe that's not such a bad thing," Ric said as be brought a tray into the room.

Hunnicutt glared at the man. "Explain."

"No one will suspect you're behind destroying your own plane and truck, and possibly damaging your company's business."

"I've got the Vice President and several senators and congressmen in my pocket, and the Director of the FBI is a close friend. No one would suspect me anyway, you fool."

Ric dipped his head. "Of course. Regardless, you should probably make a few calls. The press will want a comment and I'm sure the Director—"

"What the hell do I pay *you* for? Take care of—" Honey Badger's cell phone rang. "That's probably him now." He looked at the phone's screen. "Oh, joy. It's Liliana. The bitch can wait. I'm not in the mood to listen to her." He glanced down at Rose and the wickedness in his eyes worried Harrison. He'd witnessed that same gleam several times today, and when he did, each time things ended badly for Mickey.

"Vlad," Honey Badger called. "Bring Mickey into the room."

"Sir," Harrison said, tasting a new kind of fear. Hunnicutt made it clear he would be leaving with Rose soon, and he suspected the time had come to tie up any loose ends. "My brother—"

"Come now, Harrison." He stroked Rose's hair as if she were a dog. "We can't let all of your hard work go to waste. Rose needs to see the masterpiece you've created."

The woman cringed and jerked her head back.

Hunnicutt chuckled and yanked on the twine binding her to the chair, then grabbed her arm. "It's been a while. By the end of the night, my touch will be as familiar as it was eight years ago." He looked over his shoulder when Vlad brought Mickey into the room. "Actually," he began and faced her again, "after I show you the surprise Harrison made for you, we'll go into my bedroom and reacquaint ourselves. It's been too long since I've seen you naked."

Her pretty face contorted with outrage. "I *let* you touch me once. There was never anything familiar between us."

"Your memory is obviously skewed." He dragged his thumb across her mouth, then lower until he held her by the throat. "I'm going to enjoying giving you plenty of reminders. But first, Harrison's gift to you."

Hunnicutt released her when she gasped and her eyes widened with horror. Smiling, the bastard turned toward where Vlad stood, holding up Mickey.

Harrison hadn't seen his brother since he'd been forced to take the knife to his torso. Although it had been several hours since he'd cut Mickey, blood soaked the t-shirt clinging to his brother's skin. Mickey's head hung forward, his injured leg to the side with no pressure on it. If Vlad wasn't half-carrying him, Mickey would probably fall to the hardwood floor.

Filled with hatred and sadness, he fisted his hands and dropped them in his lap. Never in his life had he felt more trapped. Not even in prison, when he'd been caged behind bars and his every movement watched. There, they'd at least been treated humanely and had been able to countdown the days until freedom. Here, there was no compassion, only pain. And absolutely no hint of freedom.

"Harrison," Hunnicutt said. "Go to Mickey and move his shirt so Rose can see what you've done for her."

Impotent, powerless and vulnerable, Harrison stood and approached his brother. When Vlad made eye contact, he saw no sign of the Russian who had given him advice. Instead, the man's ice blue eyes were devoid of any emotion whatsoever. To think he'd trusted Vlad. Thank God he hadn't told him about the program he'd uploaded in the laptop. Then again, both he and Mickey might have been put out of their misery by now, instead of suffering their different tortures.

"Do it," Hunnicutt demanded. "I'm anxious to be alone with Rose."

"Please, don't," Rose sobbed. "Oh, my God. What have you done?"

"*I* didn't do anything," Hunnicutt said. "Harrison did this for you. Now stop your damned crying. Your face becomes ugly when you cry, and I'd prefer to be face to face when we…rekindle our intimacy."

"You mean when you rape me."

Harrison's hands shook with rage. He knew in his gut Rose would suffer worse tortures than he and Mickey combined. He just hoped her death would be swifter than his and Mickey's.

"Rape is such an ugly word," Hunnicutt said, his tone censuring. "I'm not a rapist. I'm a man who gets what he wants."

"You *are* a rapist," she taunted. "A rapist and a mass murderer."

The loud smack that followed made Harrison's face hurt. He turned just as Rose's head tilted back, a red handprint already forming on her cheek. Her free hand flew to her face as more tears filled her eyes.

"Any other names you'd like to call me?" Hunnicutt asked. She didn't say anything and, instead, wept softly. "Good. Harrison, make it quick. Show Rose your brother's stomach."

Harrison's gut seized with a cramp. His throat tightened with the urge to cry alongside Rose. He looked to Mickey's face and gingerly touched his brother's head. Leaning closer, he whispered, "I'm sorry, Mick." He blinked several times to stop the tears from coming. "I promise. Not that much longer." Even though his brother had yet to respond and had showed no sign of consciousness, Harrison hoped he could hear him and forgive him.

He looked over Mickey's head. Vlad kept his eyes forward, but clenched his jaw tight. Maybe the Russian prick felt something after all. Not that it mattered. Vlad had his own agenda and it didn't include him or Mickey.

Not wanting to deal with an angry, impatient Hunnicutt, Harrison reached for the hem of Mickey's t-shirt. Wet blood instantly coated his fingertips. He drew in a deep breath through his nostrils, tried his best to keep his emotions together and slowly tugged the shirt.

The cotton had stuck to Mickey's wounds. As much as he didn't want to hurt his brother, he knew how to make this as swift and painless as possible. "Brace yourself," he said to Mickey, then whipped the t-shirt up his body.

Mickey cried out and shot his head back. His good eye flew open. Wild with pain and accusation, he shifted his gaze around the room until it settled on Harrison. Breathing hard, his face twisting with agony, Mickey stared at him. "Got you into this," he slurred, his eye rolling back before closing. "Never…meant…love you, bro."

"Touching," Hunnicutt said with heavy sarcasm. "You make a better door than a window. Move so Rose can see the note you wrote on my behalf."

No longer fighting the tears, Harrison let them bathe his face. Keeping his focus on Mickey's face, he held the shirt high and took a step to the side.

As Rose cried for his brother, he did, too. And instead of seeing the anguish contorting Mickey's bloodied face or the damned duct tape around his eye, he saw the smiling, chubby kid his brother had once been. Dozens of memories hit him. Making forts out of blankets in the room they'd shared, exploring the woods in the local park, playing football and basketball, shared birthday parties…hiding and holding each other while one of their mom's latest live ins used her as a punching bag.

He cried for the boy who'd never had a chance. For all the plans they'd made and would never accomplish. He cried for his twin—his other half.

"What do you think, Rose?" Hunnicutt asked. "Personally, I'm rather fond of this particular message. It's so much more personal than the others."

"You're sick," she cried, her voice filled with overwhelming grief and disgust. "He needs a hospital. He needs—"

"To die," Hunnicutt finished. "Ric, Santiago, take Mickey into the warehouse and shoot him. Put the body in the back of Santiago's car. He and Vlad can dispose of it when we're finished here."

While Rose protested, Harrison met his brother's gaze. Instead of fear, his eye held relief. Mickey had given up on life. And in that instant, all thoughts of wanting to be put out of his misery alongside his brother, fled. The need to live, to carry on and do something good and right, outweighed the urge to want to curl up and die. Revenge for Mickey, for Rose, for all of the people Hunnicutt had murdered revived him and had become just as important as breathing.

"Stay out of trouble," Mickey said, gasping for air. "You *are* the smart one. Don't be me. Don't do anything stupid."

"I won't." But he would. He'd fight the fucking billionaire and celebrate killing him. "I...I don't know what to say." Tears trailed down his cheeks. This would be the last time he saw his brother alive. The finality of the moment...how could he come up with the right words?

A small, half smile tilted the corner of Mickey's mouth. "Remember Samantha Green?"

Harrison used his shoulder to wipe the tears from the side of his face and gently tugged the stained t-shirt over Mickey's body. "The prettiest girl we've ever seen," he said, completing the lame rhyme they'd come up with in junior high.

"I lied to you," Mickey said, his breath catching when Santiago grabbed his arm. "She did like you best. Everyone did. I've been jealous of you our whole lives. But I loved you more than anyone."

"Enough," Hunnicutt shouted. "You haven't strung together two words all day and now you won't shut the fuck up. Get Mickey out of here. Rose and I want to be alone."

Harrison's heart raced and he quickly took Mickey's hand. "I love you, Mick," he said on a sob. "I...how am I going to do this alone?"

Mickey's strength surprised him when he gripped his hand back. "You never needed me. I was the one who needed you." He hung on tight, even when Santiago was pulling him backward. "Remember that and the good times."

Mickey's hand finally slipped from his. Harrison kept his gaze locked on his brother's as Santiago dragged Mickey from the room and through the kitchen. Ric held the door open for Santiago. After the Columbian hauled Mickey through the door, Ric sent Harrison a ruthless smile and then followed Santiago.

His heart and his head ached. In a matter of minutes, his twin brother would be dead and Rose would be raped. Raw hatred hardened his aching heart. He fisted his hands and glanced at Vlad. The Russian hadn't moved and continued to keep his gaze locked on the wall.

"Harrison, return to the sofa," Hunnicutt said. "Now."

He leaned forward. "Fuck you," he whispered to Vlad.

The Russian blinked, but remained still. Harrison didn't look at Hunnicutt as he moved to the sofa, but he did glance at Rose. The sadness in her eyes gave him no solace. The tears she spent on him and Mickey weren't worth her effort. For what he suspected Hunnicutt would do to her, they were better saved for herself.

"There's another door here," Dante said as he moved across the utility closet.

As soon as Jake had heard Hunnicutt tell Ric and Santiago to execute Mickey in the warehouse, they'd snuck inside the closet. He wasn't sure who Mickey was, or where he fit into Hunnicutt's plans, but he had a brother named Harrison.

Dante cracked the door open and peered outside. "Don't see them."

"Including Hunnicutt, there were six men in the room," Jake whispered.

"Three of them are in the warehouse."

"I say we rush them. You go after Ric and Santiago and I'll go—"

"No. We stand down and follow orders."

"They're going to kill that man." The darkened utility closet made it difficult to see Dante's reaction. But the SEAL had to realize they couldn't, in good conscience, let a man die without doing a thing to try and stop it. "We have to do something."

Dante released a sigh, then swore. "Fine. I'll follow—"

"Wait." Jake's cell phone vibrated in his pocket. He quickly pulled it out and read the text from Rachel. "Yes," he hissed. "Her spider thing worked. She's got a lock on the signal sent to the last detonator. We have our evidence."

Dante took the phone from him, the glow from the screen illuminating his face. "She also said to wait for the Feds. They'll be here in fifteen."

"The guy they plan to execute won't be."

Dante handed the phone over. "I'll go after them." He moved toward the door leading to the unfinished part of the warehouse's third floor. "Promise you won't go in there until we've been given the word."

"You got it," Jake lied. He'd stand down and obey orders, but if Hunnicutt touched Naomi one more time, all bets were off. When he'd heard the smack Hunnicutt had delivered to Naomi's face, Dante practically had to put him in a chokehold to keep him from storming into the room. The threat of rape—Hunnicutt would never have the opportunity to made good on his promises. Even if the FBI wasn't on its way, he'd never allow Hunnicutt the chance to touch her. No amount of evidence was worth letting a man force himself on a woman. Especially his woman.

"You're full of shit," Dante said, opening the door wider. He raised his gun. "Don't do anything stupid. I'll call if Hunnicutt's men come up the stairwell."

Once Dante slipped from the closet, Jake quickly sent Rachel a text, telling her their location. He then opened the opposite door and went back to his earlier post.

"Would you stop your bloody crying," Hunnicutt roared.

"You're an ugly mess. Vlad, bring Rose some tissues."

"And you're a bastard," she shouted back.

"I told you I don't like being called names. Do you need another reminder?"

Jake tightened his grip on the gun and braced himself for the sound of another blow. Which was ridiculous. There was no reason he shouldn't go in there and put an end to Hunnicutt's bullshit. Deciding he'd do just that, he moved the door slightly, ready to enter.

"No," she said. "But I'd like to know why."

"Why Mickey had to die? You have eyes, you saw the man. I did the humane thing."

"You don't know how to be humane," she said, her voice growing stronger. "You've killed hundreds of people, you murdered my family—I want to know why. It's been eight years, why can't you leave me the hell alone?"

"If you'd stayed with me, none of that would have happened. Your parents could be enjoying retirement. Your brother, his career with the FBI." Hunnicutt chuckled. "As for today? The burden is on you. Maybe next time you'll reconsider running from me, not that I'll allow that to happen."

"You still haven't given me a reason. You're married now and have children. You might be ugly on the inside, but you're not on the outside. With your wealth, you could have any woman."

"But I don't want *any* woman. I want you."

"Why?" she screamed, the piercing sound sending a chill through Jake, but he remained still. Naomi needed answers and once the FBI blew into the warehouse, she likely wouldn't have them.

"Before you married your wife, I saw pictures of you in magazines with gorgeous models hanging all over you," Naomi continued. "Compared to them, I'm nothing. I'm not beautiful. I'm not rich or famous. I'm a nobody. Your need to possess me is—"

"Necessary. From the moment I saw you waitressing in that

shitty club, I wanted you in my bed. And when you came to my table and I saw your eyes... You're right, you aren't as beautiful as the others before or after you. But what you possess is what I need to own. I saw it in your eyes, Rose. I saw something that I haven't seen in my own eyes since I was a child. Unabashed innocence. Your childlike optimism and faith in the world made me realize the cynicism I carried weighed me down. You, Rose, were the one thing that could make me stronger."

Jake wasn't buying any of Hunnicutt's bullshit, and when Naomi laughed without humor, he assumed she hadn't either.

"You find that funny?" Hunnicutt asked, a deadly edge to his tone.

"I don't find anything that you've done funny at all," she said. "And I don't believe a word you're saying. You talk as if you loved me, when we both know you aren't capable of loving anyone but yourself. So you wanted to capture my innocence and faith, and do what with it? Bottle it up and on a rainy day drink it in order to reclaim your youth? Ridiculous. Because what you are is a stalker. Plain and simple. I rejected you and your ego couldn't handle it, so you had to prove a point. Christian Hunnicutt always gets what he wants, when he wants it."

Jake had never been more proud of Naomi. While he'd prefer if she didn't stand up to the man and that he could simply waltz in and put a bullet in Hunnicutt's head, he loved that she spoke her mind and refused to allow the bastard to bully her. He also agreed with her and thought back to what Dante had said about the stalking case he'd worked. Dante had used the term, *rejected and resentful stalker*. Add on obsessed, and they had Hunnicutt.

"Stalker." Hunnicutt released a dangerous chuckle. "Really, Rose. Now *that* is ridiculous."

"Is it? You attacked me in my house and told me if I couldn't have you, no one could. Remember that? Remember how Santiago held a knife to my throat?"

Hunnicutt laughed. "I *do* recall that night. But not as much as the one you spent with Ric and I. Remember, Rose?"

Hunnicutt *and* Ric? She'd already endured so much, a part of him didn't want to hear anymore. The other part wanted to know in order to decide how much pain he'd inflict on the men before he killed them.

"Let me refresh your memory," Hunnicutt continued. "I took away your ability to have a child and a future with any other man. I branded you as mine. I sometimes look back on that night and wonder if you grieve for the child that could have been, for the children you'll never have. Do you, Rose? Do you grieve and when you do, do you think of me?"

"When I think of you, I feel sick inside," she said, her voice shaking. "That's what you are. A sickness. I pity your wife and children. At least the child you ripped from my womb will never be tainted by you."

If Jake hadn't been leaning against the doorjamb, he might have staggered back.

The day before I found out my brother was murdered, I'd gotten test results back from my gynecologist...I can't have children.

He hadn't asked why. The jet had been about to land and he'd wanted to make sure she knew he hadn't cared that they'd have a childless future, that all he cared about was being with her. He focused on the hatred and need for revenge coursing through him. He'd grieve for the wonderful mother Naomi could have been later. Right now, he had to fight from storming into the room, unsheathing his knife and giving Hunnicutt his version of a vasectomy.

"Your words crush me, Rose," Hunnicutt said with a mocking laugh. "Despite your attempts to offend me, I find myself...aroused. Vlad, come untie Rose from my chair. We need—"

A phone rang. Jake froze and held his breath.

"Leave Rose tied and duct tape her mouth. I want no interruptions. Tape Harrison's mouth, too."

Footsteps fell across the floor and Jake slunk away from the door. He checked the time. Five minutes had passed since Rachel's text. The Feds should be along soon. But if

Hunnicutt's call was short, and he tried to lay his hands on Naomi, Jake refused to obey orders.

There was no way in hell the bastard would ever touch her again.

"Liliana, this is the second time you've called," Christian said to his pain-in-the-ass wife. "Is there a reason you keep bothering me?" He hadn't wanted to take her call, but would rather deal with her now, than be interrupted later when he was with Rose.

"Christian," Liliana began, her tone quiet, worried. "The FBI is here at the hotel."

Tensing, he moved toward his office and out of earshot of Harrison and Rose. He'd expected her call to be about the latest bombing, or for her to request an extension to her spending limit. He hadn't expected this. "I'm sure they're there because I've not only had a plane targeted, but now one of my trucks. Correct?" They couldn't know about his connection. He'd been too careful.

"I'm sure you're right."

"You haven't spoken to them?"

"No. The front desk just called and said they're on the way up to my suite." She let out a small sigh. "I'm sorry I bothered you. You're probably right. Their visit is likely a formality. I'm sure they've done the same for you."

But they hadn't. Christian hadn't spoken with the Director of the FBI since after he'd bombed his own plane. If the FBI was concerned about the safety of his wife and children, they'd most certainly be concerned about him. After all, he owned the damned company.

"I spoke with Martin earlier today," he said, and glanced out the office door to where Harrison sat on the sofa, his mouth duct taped, his eyes narrowed and filled with disdain. Christian's mind worked quickly. Maybe the smart brother was smarter than he'd thought. Was it possible Harrison had compromised the signals he'd been sending to the detonators?

He shifted his gaze to Rose. Or could the little bitch be working with the Feds?

"They're here," Liliana gasped. "Christian, this is just awful. The kids…I'm worried. We haven't left the suite since the bombing in Denver. I don't want them to know what's happening. They might see these agents and be scared."

He didn't have time for her whining. Since he and Martin were close friends, he'd expect the FBI to contact him before his wife. Because they hadn't, and because he couldn't be sure what this meant, he'd have to move to Plan B.

"Use your head. If you're so worried, have the nannies take the kids either out of the suite or into another room."

"Okay, I will," she said. "I…are you okay? Are you in a safe place?"

"Liliana, are you actually concerned about me?" he asked, amused. His wife hated him, and rightfully so. "Never mind. I don't care. But, if you must know, I'm at my warehouse apartment. Today has been trying and I need privacy."

"Are Ric and your bodyguards with you?"

At that moment, Ric and Santiago entered through the door leading from the part of the warehouse that hadn't been renovated, and into the kitchen.

"Yes, for now." He moved away from the office. "Attend to the agents. I have to go." After ending the call, he smiled. "Well, is it done?"

Santiago grinned. "*Finito.* I wish you'd let me do it instead of Ric. You have no idea how many times I wanted to kill Mickey when we were on the road."

Chuckling, Christian nodded to Ric. "Go into my office. We need to talk."

Ric set down the bottle of water he'd been drinking onto the counter. "Right away," he said and walked past him to the refurbished office that stood between the bedroom and the guest room Mickey had been held in throughout the day.

Once Ric had disappeared, Christian called Santiago to his side. The Columbian rushed over. "*Amigo?* What's wrong?"

"Ric has to go." Which was a damned shame. Good hired

help was difficult to find. "I just found out he's been fucking me over."

Santiago narrowed his eyes. "Never liked that *hijo de puta*. What do you need me to do?"

"Slit his throat. Do you have a problem with that?"

The Columbian grinned. "I've been itching to do it for fifteen years."

Christian didn't doubt Santiago. The Columbian had begun working for him a few months before Christian had met Ric. Because of Ric's background and education, he'd moved into more prominent positions. Where Ric was his yes man, Santiago was his henchman, and there had always been a not so friendly rivalry between them.

"Good. Come with me." As he walked passed Vlad, he said, "Watch Rose and Harrison."

The Russian, whose IQ probably bordered on that of an uneducated fifteen-year-old, nodded. Vlad might not be his brightest employee, but like a well-trained dog, he always obeyed and never bit the hand that fed him.

At the closed office door, Santiago stopped and withdrew the knife hidden in his boot.

"Ready?" Christian asked.

Santiago gave him a single nod.

"Good. Make it quick." While he wasn't sure if the FBI had made a connection to him, in case his suspicions were true, he'd have to act fast. Plan B wasn't his ideal, but it would serve as a brilliant distraction.

Christian turned the doorknob. When he entered the room, Ric moved away from the desk and approached them. "I think we should leave. You still have to make your statement regarding the latest bombing, and the laptop needs to be destroyed."

"Agreed." Christian nodded to Santiago, who took two steps and, with lightning speed, slashed the knife across Ric's throat.

The sadist's eyes bulged with shock and accusation as he clutched his neck. Blood spurted from between his fingertips as he mouthed, "Why?"

Christian moved behind him, careful not to stain his suit with Ric's blood and pulled the gun Ric kept clipped to his belt. "Does it matter? Well, I suppose, after keeping you on as my servant for fifteen years I should give you some sort of an explanation."

Ric, wheezing, gasping and still holding his throat, dropped to his knees.

Crouching low, Christian smiled at the dying man. "I don't like being mocked," he said, wrapping Ric's free hand around the gun and pointing it at Ric's head. "Do you hear that, Columbian?"

"*Si, amigo.*"

"Then you'll understand." Christian quickly turned the gun on Santiago. "I fucking hate being called Honey Badger," he said and pulled the trigger.

CHAPTER 15

JAKE RUSHED INTO the room when he heard the gun shot. Naomi met him halfway. Without saying a word, he latched onto her hand and led her back out the door, down the hall and into the stairwell. Although he wanted to hold her and make sure she was okay, his sole focus was to evacuate before the FBI stormed the warehouse.

"There were two other men," she said, breathing hard while keeping pace with him. "One took the laptop Christian was using to detonate the bombs."

Jake didn't respond. Instead, he reached for his vibrating cell phone. "Yeah," he answered.

"The FBI is there," Ian said. "I've made it clear my men are in the warehouse."

"I have Naomi."

"What? I told you to stand—"

"There was gunfire." He and Naomi reached the garage, just as a dozen agents rushed inside. "Gotta go," he said and, still holding the phone, stepped in front of Naomi.

"We're with CORE," he shouted, raising his hands as armed agents approached them.

While half the agents made their way toward the stairs, the rest either cordoned off the warehouse exits or surrounded them. "Agent Kyle Suts," one of the agents said, reaching into Jake's pockets. Suts pulled out Jake's wallet, looked over his

ID, then handed it back to Jake. "We were told CORE had two men in the building. Where's the other?"

"Jake," Dante called. He had his hands behind his head as a Fed escorted him.

"That's Dante Russo. He's also CORE."

Once Dante reached them, he said, "I just explained to your agent here that two men escaped on foot.

"We're already on it." Suts moved Dante's jacket, eyed the SEAL's utility belt, then found his ID. After he'd cleared Dante, Suts told them to stay put, then he stepped away and made a call.

"What the hell happened?" Dante asked, keeping his eyes on Suts and his voice low. "Before the gunshot, I saw two men running through the warehouse. I tried chasing them down, but they were too far ahead of me. I did get a vague description." He shook his head. "They weren't the same men who killed the guy Hunnicutt called Mickey."

Needing answers, Jake turned to Naomi and raised her arm. The twine that had been wrapped around her wrist, hung loosely. "Who cut you free?"

"One of the men I'm assuming Dante chased after." She rubbed her wrist where the twine had left a chaff mark, and look at Dante. "Big blond guy and another guy with longish brown hair, right?"

"That's them."

"Christian called the blond, Vlad. The little he spoke…I caught a Russian accent. He's also the one who cut me free. The other man was Harrison." She winced and her chin trembled. "Mickey was his brother."

"We're taking you out of here," Suts said, and motioned to a couple of his agents, who immediately began escorting them from the building.

"Wait," Naomi called. "Christian Hunnicutt. Did you find him? He's the one behind the bombings. He also has two—"

"Ma'am, get in the car." Suts opened the door of a dark sedan. "You'll be debriefed when we reach our field office."

Jake nudged her inside the vehicle before she could protest

any further. This was the part of protocol he detested. They'd be detained for questioning, without being given any information, then set free. Because this case dealt with domestic terrorism and had become extremely high profile, chances were they wouldn't know the specifics of what the FBI ultimately found on the third floor of the warehouse.

And that pissed him off. He wanted specifics. Like when, specifically, would Christian Hunnicutt pay for his crimes? Knowing the judicial system, the man could sit in jail for decades before he paid the ultimate price.

He glanced down, caught Naomi rubbing her wrist and thought about everything she'd been through today and the past eight years. Damn it. He should have ignored orders and killed Hunnicutt when he'd had the chance. Prison was too good for the bastard.

"Move, Harry," Vlad ordered and shoved Harrison forward.

"Stop pushing me. I don't want to drop the laptop."

Vlad pointed to a row of older houses that had seen better days. "Should leave behind."

"Easy for you to say," Harrison panted, as he tried to keep up with Vlad. "Your fingerprints aren't all over it."

"No matter. We leave country and hide. Vlad knows people."

A cramp seized Harrison's side, but he pushed himself to keep moving. "I'm not leaving the country and living the rest of my life as a fugitive."

The Russian turned down an ally and led him into a high traffic area of Norfolk. He waved down a taxi and pushed Harrison inside. After giving the driver an address Harrison wasn't familiar with, Vlad rested his head against the cab's torn, leather seat and closed his eyes. Given how much the Russian smoked, Harrison couldn't believe the man wasn't out of breath. His lungs burned from running, while his legs and stomach still cramped. "Listen," he began, "We need—"

"Shh. Vlad need to think."

Harrison hugged the laptop to his chest and stared out the window at the passing cars. Whatever Vlad came up with, Harrison doubted they'd agree on it. The Russian's position was worse than his. Chances were, the FBI would dig into Hunnicutt's employment records and discover Vlad worked for him. Plus Vlad's fingerprints would be all over that warehouse.

His mind raced as he tried to think about the things he'd touched while being held in the warehouse. A water bottle, a pen, the toilet handle, the bathroom faucet. Shit. And once the Feds found Mickey, they'd know about him. A quick check, and they'd see he had a prison record, match the fingerprints and, bam, he was frickin' cooked.

He scrubbed a hand down his face. Throughout the day he'd come to terms with where his future lay. Dead by Hunnicutt's orders, or Death Row for his part in the bombings. When he'd been making peace with whichever way he'd die, he'd envisioned taking Hunnicutt with him in some capacity. While he had no clue what had transpired in the office between Hunnicutt, Ric and Santiago, he doubted Hunnicutt was dead.

You can't kill the boogeyman.

But he sure as hell wanted to try.

The taxi stopped along the curb of a row of two story shops. The signs above several stores were in Russian. Vlad paid the driver, then led Harrison through a door next to one of the stores and up several flights of steps, then down a hall. When they reached the door at the end of the hallway, Vlad pulled keys from his pocket and unlocked it.

"Come, Vlad's apartment."

"I thought you lived with Honey Badger," Harrison said, looking around the small, sparse and dusty studio.

"Vlad like options." He pulled a pack of cigarettes from his pocket. "Honey Badger don't know about apartment." After flicking the lighter, he lit a cigarette. "Ric and Santiago in dark, too."

"Okay, so we're safe here?"

The Russian shrugged. "For now. The woman saw Vlad and Harry's face. Should have done what Vlad says and took her."

Harrison rolled his eyes and set the laptop on the grimy, laminate kitchen countertop. "And be charged with kidnapping, too? The only reason I wanted to free her was to help her get away from Hunnicutt. You know what he was going to do to her."

The Russian released a stream of smoke. "Vlad knows."

"And that doesn't bother you?" He shoved away from the counter and slumped into a ratty chair in need of reupholstering. "You know? Never mind. With how broken up you were over my brother, I know the answer."

Sympathy softened Vlad's eyes as the Russian sat his enormous body on the equally ratty, small floral patterned couch. "Vlad sorry about the mouse."

"Mickey," Harrison said around the lump in his throat. The reality of his loss setting in hard now that they'd escaped from the warehouse.

"Mickey," Vlad echoed. "Vlad made no secret. Mickey not favorite person. But…the mouse Harry's brother."

"Twin," Harrison reminded him.

The Russian shook his head. "Harry want revenge."

"You have no idea." Harrison rested his elbows on his knees and leaned forward. "Not just for my brother, but for what Hunnicutt did to all of those people." He dropped his head. "For what he made me do."

"Harry had no choice."

Harrison looked up and met the Russian's eyes. "I'm starting to question that." When Vlad's brow furrowed with confusion, Harrison admitted, "When Hunnicutt first told me to send the signal and trigger the bomb, I should have told him no. Even then, deep down, I didn't think me and Mickey would walk away from this."

"Ric knew how to signal," Vlad reminded him. "Bombs explode anyway. *And*, Harry did walk away."

"Mickey didn't. Now I have to live with not only being

responsible for hundreds of deaths, but for what I did to my brother."

"With gun to head," Vlad said, his tone harsh. "Vlad see this before. Harry have survivor fault."

"Survivor fault? What the hell are you talking—wait, do you mean survivor's guilt?"

"Fault…guilt." The Russian shrugged. "Same difference. Harry feel guilt for outliving the mouse. Vlad be truthful. Before we go to warehouse, the Columbian told Vlad Harry and Mickey would die."

Show no fear, Harry…Honey Badger loves seeing fear in man's eyes. Keep cool like ice cream. Trust Vlad.

"Vlad like Harry, not Santiago or Honey Badger. I…Harry, this very hard for me. Vlad felt like helpless kitten today."

Harrison half smiled. "You and me both."

"There is difference. Harry had gun to head, Vlad did not."

"You said yourself if you walked, Hunnicutt would kill you and your family."

"True. Vlad also say he would kill Harry if ordered."

"And now?"

The Russian shook his head and lit another cigarette. "No. Vlad hate killing."

"It's not my thing, either. But there's one person I'd like to see dead."

"Honey Badger." Vlad rubbed the blond stubble along his job. "Until he dead—"

"No one is safe. Not me or you. Not your family. Not the woman, Rose." He stood and moved back to the counter where the laptop sat. "There are three explosives remaining. Who's to say Hunnicutt doesn't walk and find a way to detonate them?"

"We disarm them."

"No. We let the Feds do that. But, we can tell them about the bombs. We can tell them everything. If we do, they'd have to believe us and Hunnicutt—"

"Could still walk."

"Vlad, you're not listening. If we—"

"No, Harry not listen." The Russian smashed the cigarette into an ashtray, then stood and folded his arms across his chest. "Vlad not turning to FBI. This not *Law & Order*, this real life. You think FBI will slap wrist? No, Harry." He shook his head. "We help, we get firing squad."

Harrison held up his hands. "Okay, okay. First, that's not how they execute prisoners."

"No matter how. Dead is dead."

Vlad had a valid point. Until he knew they could somehow clear their part in this—which would likely be impossible—they couldn't go to the FBI. Vlad's original idea of leaving the country and living as fugitives started to sound like an excellent option. Before he did any running, he would finish this. If he couldn't kill Hunnicutt, he'd find a way to destroy the man.

"Fine. We don't go to the FBI. But we do need to take care of those three bombs. Remember when we were in Bloomington, Indiana and you left me in the motel to get smokes and coffee?"

"Vlad remember."

"Don't be mad, but when we were planting the devices last week I started suspecting what they were. Because I wasn't one hundred percent sure, I didn't run to the cops. Instead, I messed with the laptop."

"Vlad no understand. What is this mess?"

After Harrison gave Vlad the short version, the Russian grinned. "FBI will arrest Honey Badger."

"I hope so. For now, the laptop is still our leverage. It might not be our get out of jail free card, but it's all the evidence they'll need. Their computer forensics people will be able to link all of the bombings back to Hunnicutt."

"So how do we use laptop as leverage and not go to FBI? How does Harry plan to disarm bombs and not go to FBI?" Vlad released a deep sigh. "We need good plan."

"I know," Harrison said, his mind turning in a million directions and zeroing in on one. "What we need is to know what the Feds are planning to do with Hunnicutt first."

Christian Hunnicutt adjusted the ill-fitting jumpsuit he'd been forced to don upon his arrival to the FBI's Norfolk Division. Never in his life had he worn something so cheaply made and…orange. Not that it mattered. Soon enough he'd be on his way. The FBI had already held him in custody for five hours. Knowing his rights, unless they charged him with something, they'd have to release him. Once that happened, he'd return to his plantation home, take a long hot shower and put on something more respectable.

The door to the interrogation room he'd been led into thirty minutes ago opened. He quickly stood and offered his hand. "Martin, thank God," he said to his longtime friend and the Director of the FBI. "What's happening? Why am *I* being detained?"

"I apologize for the delay," the director said, his expression grim, his eyes filled with sympathy. "Considering our history and the gravity of our investigation, I won't be taking part in your questioning." Two other men entered the room. "These are Agents Suts and Hicks."

"Yes, I remember Agent Suts from the warehouse." He nodded to the agent, who looked as if he'd graduated from Quantico while still sucking on a pacifier. Hicks was older, heavier and balding. "Thank you for your help today. I…" He looked to the stark white wall. "This afternoon was disturbing and terrifying," he said, making sure the sincerity weighed heavy on each of his words. "The woman, Rose. Is she okay?"

Martin headed toward the door. "I'm going to let my agents answer that for you."

"Wait," he said, approaching the director.

The agents moved to stop him, but Martin held up a hand. "It's okay. What is it, Christian?" he asked, weariness in his tone, the strain of today's events etched on his face.

The United States' top cop had definitely had a bad day. Which was a shame. He actually liked Martin.

"Suts and Hicks," he began, keeping his voice low and for Martin's ears only, "I'm sure they're good agents, but I expected you to send in men with more experience." He was Christian Hunnicutt, after all, not some street punk being questioned about a misdemeanor offense.

Martin sent him a tired smile, while his eyes held hints of conflict and apology. "They're good agents. Hicks has been one of the leads during this investigation. Trust me, they have plenty of experience." He reached for the door handle. "I'll speak with you soon," he said, and left the room.

Maybe this was Martin's way of helping him out of the current situation—not that he needed any help. Still, considering his importance and, as Martin had put it, the gravity of the investigation, he would have liked one of the agents to have had *Special* added to their title.

"Please take a seat, Mr. Hunnicutt," Agent Suts said.

He sat across from the two men, a metal table, made to look as if it were wood, separating them. "Can you tell me about Rose? Is she okay?"

"Have you ever met her?" Suts asked instead.

"One night, years ago, Ric Mancini and I had been out with business associates and he picked her up at a club. Honestly, I'd forgotten all about Rose. When I saw the woman in my warehouse, I didn't recognize her until Ric reintroduced us."

"She claims otherwise." Suts looked down at the opened file in front of him. "She says she had a relationship with *you*."

"What? That's preposterous. When Ric was with her, I had just started dating my wife, Liliana, and was busy trying to convince her father that I was good enough for his daughter." It hadn't taken much to convince the old fool of anything. Money was an excellent motivator. "Speaking of which, I really wish you'd let me call my wife. I'm sure she's worried sick."

"Your wife is fine. As you know, our agents met with her in New York."

"But the press. I'm concerned for my wife and kids and how all of this is affecting them." "Your name hasn't been mentioned to the media," Hicks said, then added, "Not yet."

Even though he wanted to wipe the smug look off of Hicks's face with the bottom of the shitty slipper-like shoe they'd forced him to wear, he feigned relief. "Thank God. If my children thought…" He wiped a hand down his face, then pressed his index finger and thumb against his closed eyes. "I don't want them questioning, or thinking I'm capable of being involved with what Ric has done to all of those people."

"Let's go back to that," Suts said. "Starting with why you think Ric had anything to do with the bombings."

Christian dropped his hand in his lap. "He'd been acting…off the past week. If I caught him on the phone, he'd quickly end the call."

"What's suspicious about that?" Hicks asked.

"I didn't think it was suspicious—at first. Then my bodyguard, Santiago Ramirez, disappeared for the entire week. He claimed he had the flu, but then one day I happened to hear Ric on the phone, and after listening to his half of the conversation, I realized he was talking to Santiago."

"It's our understanding that Ric was in charge of your employees," Suts said.

Christian nodded. "True. Only I heard Ric tell Santiago something like, once he leaves Leavenworth, there'd be a plane waiting for him in St. Louis."

The two agents glanced at each other, then Hicks pulled out a large photo from his file and slid it across the table. "Do you know a man named Michael Fairclough? Goes by Mickey?"

When he glanced down at Mickey's prison photo, he furrowed his brows and pretended to think. "No. I have thousands of employees. Does he work for my company?"

"We've checked your employee records and found that he applied. One of our agents interviewed some of your employees who remembered Fairclough. They said he was in a local bar near one of your docks getting drunk and talking about his time in prison. They also said he'd spoken with Ric that night."

"That was ten days ago," Suts added.

"What does this Michael Fairclough have to do with anything?" he asked. "Was he working for Ric?"

"We believe so. Unfortunately, he's dead." Hicks slid

another photo across the table. "Is this jogging your memory?"

He looked to the picture, then quickly turned away and covered his mouth.

"Michael Fairclough had been shot in the leg, stabbed in the eye and had the name Rose Wood carved into his stomach," Suts said.

"He'd been tortured, Mr. Hunnicutt." Hicks took the photo back. "We found him in the back end of the Yukon registered to Santiago Ramirez."

"You mean…the same SUV that Santiago drove into my warehouse garage?" Christian asked, widening his eyes to make sure his shock was apparent. "Oh, my God. Do you think Ric or Santiago killed this man?"

The bald agent nodded. "The bullets we found lodged in Fairclough's leg and head, along with the one removed from Santiago, are an exact ballistic fingerprint to the bullets fired from Ric's gun."

"Oh, my God," he repeated, shaking his head. "I…I just can't believe it."

"Mr. Hunnicutt," Suts said, folding his hands together and resting them on the table. "When agents found you, they said you were on your cell phone and running through the room. They said it appeared as if you were searching for something."

"Your men took my phone. I'm sure they've found that the call I was making was to Martin Fitzgerald." Thanks to Liliana, he'd suspected the FBI might knock on the door of his warehouse apartment, which was why he'd disposed of Ric and Santiago when he had. As for calling Martin, he'd wanted to make sure there'd been a record of his reporting the double murders. After all, *he* was the victim.

"Yes, we know."

"And I was searching for Rose. Ric had her tied to the chair and I—"

"Ms. McCall said *you* tied her to the chair," Hicks said, his tone laced with allegation.

Christian glanced between both men. "McCall?"

"Naomi McCall is Rose Wood," Suts clarified.

"What are you talking about? Are you telling me this woman has two identities?"

Suts nodded. "She claims she changed her name to stop *you* from being able to find her."

"That's ridiculous. Anyone can change their name, but they can't change their social security number without leaving a paper trail. And before you ask me how I know this, I had a paranoid schizophrenic second cousin who tried. My great-uncle was able to find him like that," he said and snapped his fingers. "If her accusations are true, I could have hired someone to track her down. But I didn't because *I* haven't seen or thought about the woman in nearly a decade. And why would I? She was Ric's girlfriend or one-night stand, or whatever she'd meant to him."

"Unfortunately, he's not here to verify that," Hicks said.

"Unfortunately, he's not." Christian honed in on his acting skills and played the part of a grieving friend. "Neither is Santiago. Both men had been with me for fifteen years. They weren't just employees to me." He met Hicks gaze and laid it on thick. "I have very few people that I can trust. Those men were my friends. I trusted Ric with my business and Santiago with my life."

"Mr. Hunnicutt," Suts interjected, "start at the beginning. What happened at the warehouse? How is it that we found blood spattered on your clothes and gunpowder residue on your hand?"

He ignored the accusation in the agent's eyes and thought back to the day he'd discovered there was no treasure in the center of the labyrinth he'd worked so hard to find. He hadn't been lying to Rose when he'd told her he had wanted to possess the unabashed innocence that had first drawn him to her. Eight years ago, cynicism had been weighing him down. He'd just killed his father and had a business to run. The daily pressure had begun to take its toll on his nerves. Meanwhile, he'd been courting Liliana. That, in and of itself, had been hell. With her need to be pampered and doted upon, he'd hated the woman on sight. Couple that with having to deal with her pain-in-the-ass father, he'd been at his wit's end. With the agent staring at him, waiting for him to slip, he went back to the nine-year-old child he'd once been and tapped into those long forgotten emotions, and, *voilà*, his eyes misted with unshed tears.

Damn, he should have been an actor.

He cleared his throat and acted as if he was trying to pull himself together. "I'm sure you know, after the explosion in Denver, I gave a press conference. Ric set it up and was with me."

"We're fully aware," Suts said, looking down at the file on the desk.

"When we finished there and I learned of yet another bombing, I told Ric I didn't want to go back to the corporate offices. Losing those two pilots…did you know that the one pilot, Jerry Rose, not only left behind two young children, but a wife battling breast cancer?" He stared off to the wall behind Hicks. "It's only a matter of time before those kids are orphans."

Suts looked to Hicks. "We didn't know that."

"I didn't either until he was killed. The news hit me hard and I wanted to go to the warehouse and take time to draft the plans I'd spoken about during my press conference. I made it public that I intend to aid those who had been effected by today's bombings." He manufactured one of the looks of grief and sadness he'd practiced in front of the mirror before giving the press conference. "I still intend to do just that." He wiped at his eyes. "When Ric and I arrived at my warehouse apartment, I closeted myself in my office."

"What time was that?" Hicks asked, his pen poised over a notepad.

"About one-thirty, I think." He looked between the men. "Why?"

"We'll get to that." Hicks jotted something down. "What happened next?"

He shook his head. "I don't recall the exact times, but I spoke with my wife, my secretary and my minister." Too bad he'd had to kill Ric. The man had been great at his job and had brilliantly suggested he make those calls, should there ever be a need for an alibi. "I had a headache and tried to sleep it off in my room, but I found myself glued to the TV, anxious to learn about what was happening."

"We found blood evidence in the guest room next to your office." Hicks tapped his pen against the table. "You said you've never heard of or met Michael Fairclough and yet his DNA is all over that room. How is it that you didn't know he was there?"

"*Was* he there when I was in residence?" he asked with exasperation. "Agent Hicks, when I had the third floor of the warehouse converted into a private apartment, I also had the walls soundproofed. I'm not suggesting that I wouldn't hear a man scream— Look, I don't go into that room. It's for guests. Is it possible Ric had him in that room while I was there? Maybe. I don't know. What I *do* know?" He slammed his palm against the metal table. "I. Didn't. See. Him. Here's another thing you should know. I told you Santiago claimed to have the flu. The first time I saw him in over a week was at my warehouse apartment. *After* I arrived from the press conference."

Suts looked to his fellow agent, but Hicks kept his focus on him. "Were you surprised to see Santiago? How was he acting?"

"Of course I was surprised. I thought the man was sick. But he told me he was better and wanted to be by my side because of what happened to the company plane. As for how he was acting." He lifted a shoulder. "I didn't suspect a thing."

"Ms. McCall said Santiago picked her up from the Carlyle airstrip just shortly after three and brought her back to the warehouse." Agent Hicks glanced down at the open file in front of him. "She claims you forced her to decide between detonating another bomb or killing the man you were also forcing to activate the explosions."

Christian rubbed his forehead. Fuck. His Rose was a definite thorn in his side. "I have *no* idea what she's talking about. I have nothing to do with these bombings. As for the man she's referring to…are you talking about this Michael Fairclough?"

"No." Suts shook his head. "His brother, Harrison."

The smart brother. The shithead who took the laptop and ran off with Vlad. God, he couldn't wait to watch them both bleed. "I don't know who Michael is, and I certainly don't know anything about his brother." He slammed his palm against the table again. "Why? Because I had nothing to do with those bombings." He glared at both men, then blew out a breath and ran a hand through his hair. "You're taking the word of a woman who supposedly changed her name to hide from me, a women who I had zero interactions with, other than exchanging a few words before she walked off with Ric—*eight years ago*. Now you're accusing me of threatening a man who I've never seen or met. What else did this *brother* tell you?"

Hicks leaned back in his chair. "He confirmed Ms. McCall's story."

Liar. Harrison wasn't in custody. If he was, they'd likely have the laptop and he would have already been charged with domestic terrorism. During the years he'd been friends with Martin, he'd learned a thing or two about FBI and police interrogation tactics. Martin had, after relaying a closed case that had been made public, explained that his agents had lied about information to lure their informant into cracking.

He wasn't about to crack. Harrison, Vlad…Rose, he had unfinished business to attend to and he couldn't do it behind bars.

"I don't know how that's possible." He tugged at the V-neck of the hideous jumpsuit. "I've never met him and he was never at my apartment."

"Fingerprint analysis says otherwise." Suts pulled out a sheet of paper from his file and examined it. "You can't deny the evidence."

He wanted to tell them to take their bullshit evidence and shove it up their asses. He'd planned for this moment just as methodically as he had planned the bombings. "You're right."

He nodded instead. "I can't. But I'm telling you I never saw or met the man. Is it possible he was at my apartment *before* I arrived?" He shook his head. "Agent Suts, you've been to my warehouse. There are plenty of places a man can hide. Or maybe the man left when I came there. I don't know. What I do know is, again, I *never* saw him."

"Ms. McCall watched Harrison Fairclough detonate the bomb from a laptop," Suts continued. "She said he did it because you had a gun pointed to his head. After the signal had been sent, she also said you pulled the trigger, but there had been no bullets."

"Interesting. You also have the gun I carry—which I have a permit for. I'm sure you've noticed that it's most certainly loaded. But I haven't used the weapon in months. And the last time I did was at a firing range."

"The gunpowder residue on your hand says otherwise."

Christian threw his hands in the air. "It wasn't from *my* gun."

"Right." Agent Hicks continued to tap his damned pen against the table. "It was from Ric's. Why don't you explain how your fingerprints ended up on his gun?"

"Gladly." Oh, how he'd love to shove that pen up the agent's nose and straight to his brain. "About three-thirty—I'm not sure the exact time—I came out of my bedroom. Rose…Naomi, she was there. After Ric reintroduced us, I pulled him aside and asked him what the hell she was doing here. He said she was in town on business and that they'd made plans to get together. I told him to get her the hell out of my warehouse." He tapped his thumb against his chest. "I wanted my privacy. I also told him the apartment was *my* place, not his. That he was not to bring his women back here. So, Ric said he'd get rid of her and put her in a hotel, once he had a room." He shook his head. "I was furious and went back into my bedroom to watch the news. When I saw one of my delivery trucks had been targeted, I rushed out of the bedroom. Rose was tied to the chair and Ric and Santiago were standing by her arguing."

He drew in a deep breath. Now was his time to shine. He stared Hicks directly in the eyes. "I've never been so sickened and scared in my life. I pulled Ric into the office and demanded he tell me what the hell was going on, but before he could explain, Santiago burst through the door."

Rubbing the back of his neck, he relived the scene. Only he added the embellishments, along with the fabricated fear and desperation the moment *should* have called for—if it had been true. "Santiago went after Ric. Ric drew the gun he carried from the clip attached to his back. I tried to restrain Ric and stop him from shooting Santiago. Before I could…" He drew in another deep breath. "It happened so fast. Santiago slit Ric's throat and, at the same time, the gun went off. *That's* how I had the blood on my shirt. And *that's* how I had the gunpowder residue on my hands."

He made his chin tremble and swallowed hard. At the same time, he looked to the desk. "There was so much blood. I…can't believe they're both gone. I *can't* believe that they were behind these bombings. It makes no sense."

Christian kept his eyes cast down, when he really wanted to glare at the agents and tell them to go fuck themselves. Idiots. They had no idea who they were dealing with—at all.

"So," Suts began, "the gun goes off and kills Santiago and…"

"While I called Martin, I ran out of the office to check on Rose." He looked at them and frowned. "When I didn't find her tied to the chair, I started looking for her. I wanted to make sure she was okay and to let her know she was safe. Honestly, I was hoping she could give me answers."

"What kind of answers?" Suts asked.

"Why was she really here? What were Ric and Santiago up to?"

"You didn't suspect they were involved in the bombings?"

"No. Why would I?"

Hicks held up the photo of Mickey and stabbed his index finger at the carvings on the dumb brother's stomach. "Rose Wood."

Christian rubbed his temple and looked away from the picture. "I don't understand what you're talking about."

Suts glanced to his notes. "Do you recall where the first bombing took place?"

"Yes, San Francisco."

"What about the name of the establishment?"

He looked to the ceiling as if thinking. "Redwood Tavern?"

"No. It was Rosewood Bar & Grill. I know you remember the name of the pilots who lost their lives in Denver and—"

"Oh, my God," he gasped. "Jerry Rose and Woody Gilmore. Rose...Wood."

"Every single bombing has a Rose Wood link. The riverboat that exploded in St. Louis was called the Delta Rose. The wood connection there should have been Hazel Wood, but she was fortunate and wasn't on board. Then there's Leavenworth, Kansas, where a bomb went off at the Chapel Woods Presbyterian Church during the funeral for *Rose* Michaels."

"The school in Idaho?" Christian asked, widening his eyes as he looked between both agents.

"Rosewood County," Hicks answered with disgust. "The Sun Valley Hotel and Convention Center in Henderson, Nevada was located on Rosewood Court. Let's not forget Smithfield, Wyoming, where an explosion ripped through Saint Dorothy of the Roses Nursing Home which is located in *Wood* County."

Christian held up a hand. "Please," he said, forcing a word he never used. "I...this is unbelievable. You're telling me that these terrorist acts were all because of a woman?"

"Ms. McCall says you were sending her a message." With a smug tilt of his mouth, Hicks leaned back and folded his arms across his chest. "She says she's been hiding from you for years and that this was your way of forcing her to come to you."

He allowed a bit of his anger to surface for effect. "She's *lying*. I'm happily married. I have children. And if I wanted to have an affair—which I don't—I'm sure I could go about it in a much more discreet manner." He let out frustrated breath. "I plan to run for the Senate this fall. I'm friends with your director, with senators and congressmen, with the Vice President of the United States. Why would I jeopardize my marriage and potential political career? Let's not forget that I not only lost valuable employees, but an eighty-six million dollar plane. My company is going to take a huge hit. I'm terrified customers will associate BH-Xpress with violence." He shook his head. "More than all of that, I'm a devout Protestant and follow Christ's teachings. Mass murder is not part of my DNA or my moral fiber."

"What about abortion?" Suts asked.

"Agent Suts, I just told you my religious beliefs. I'm also a Republican. Abortion is *not* something I believe in—at all," he said with indignation. "I'm sure that's not why you brought it up, though."

"No. Ms. McCall alleges that you got her pregnant and then had Ric, and a man claiming to be a doctor, abort the baby." Hicks face twisted in disgust. "Without proper medical care or equipment. Because of this, she can no longer have children."

Christian slammed his palm against the table. "Again, I did not have sex with that woman. If I did and I impregnated her as she claims, the child would be alive and well. I don't believe in abortion. I couldn't even imagine looking into my son and daughter's eyes knowing that I had taken part in destroying a child that belonged to me." He gripped the edge of the table. "What evidence do you have for this ridiculous allegation? Where is the doctor? Where did this supposedly take place? Instead of questioning and accusing me of things I had nothing to do with, maybe you should look more into not only Ric and Santiago's background, but Ms. McCall's. I'm sorry she'd been put through what she had today, and these…terrorist messages." He rested his forearms on the table. "I'm not saying I don't believe her, but have you looked into her mental health? Or her financial situation? I'm worth billions. She wouldn't be the first person looking for a bit of my wealth."

Instead of acknowledging his gripping rebuttal, Hicks moved forward and sifted through his file. "At twelve twenty-six p.m., Central Daylight Saving Time Monday afternoon, Ms. McCall called Ric's cell phone. We have a recording of the exchange between them. Where were you at that time?"

"I told you," he said with a tired sigh, when what he really wanted to do was punch the wall. The bitch had been working with someone after all. He'd find out who and make sure they were taken care of, as well. He would not allow any of this to taint his company or political career. "At my warehouse apartment and in my office."

"You didn't hear or witness this exchange?"

"No. Is my voice on this recording?"

Suts shook his head.

"So, again, why are you questioning me? What Ms. McCall is accusing me of is a ridiculous travesty. From where I'm sitting, and from what you've told me, it's clear Ric was behind everything. Honestly, if I hadn't seen Ms. McCall tied to a chair and witnessed what Ric and Santiago did to each other...I wouldn't believe Ric capable of such horrors."

Hicks lifted a piece of paper and looked it over. "At any point today did you witness Ric on his phone?"

"Of course. He set up my press conference and fielded several calls. Plus he—"

"Not just phone calls," Hicks said while still looking at the paper.

Considering his current position, he'd let the arrogant agent's rude interruption slide. "Meaning?"

"Did you see Ric using his smart phone for research?"

"I...maybe, I'm not sure. We were busy discussing business in the morning, then when the plane went down, our focus was on that."

"Records show that Ric had Googled Rose Wood several times throughout the day. Each time he'd done it had been shortly after one of the bombings. You know nothing about this?"

Of course he did. From the start, he'd refused to allow any evidence to be tied back to him. Having Ric look for information from his phone had been a calculated stroke of genius, along with the perfect way to keep the evidence on Ric and off of him.

"No. I don't."

Hicks set the paper on the table and took out another photograph. "Do you know this woman?" he asked and slid the picture across the table.

Christian stared at the driver's license photo of Allison Hobar and instantly remembered how the maid had serviced him. "Yes. She works as a kitchen maid at my house. Why?"

"When was the last time you saw her?"

He pretended to think. "I'm not sure. My wife is better at that sort of thing. She would know. Better yet, check with my head of housekeeping."

"We have. Miss Hobar's family reported her missing three days ago. They said she never came home from *your* house."

"Are you now accusing me of doing something to my maid?"

Instead of replying to his question, Suts asked, "Why did you give Ric the cottage on your property?"

"I didn't *give* him anything. He pays rent. He's also single and I admit to being a demanding CEO. I liked having him within arm's reach."

"You grew up on your property." Hicks pulled out more photos and began laying them across the table. "Tell me about the underground tunnel leading between the cottage and the main residence."

They'd searched his property. He hid his panic and looked at the photographs of the tunnel, the private chambers Ric had created for Rose, and the basement of the cottage. "According to family history, the tunnel was used to hide Confederate soldiers during the Civil War. Later, during the prohibition era, it was used to smuggle alcohol." He continued to study the pictures, his earlier panic abating when he focused on the photo of the cottage's basement. "What are these?" he asked, playing ignorant and pointing to the evidence markers throughout the picture.

"Each marker indicates blood evidence," Suts replied.

"DNA testing proves Allison Hobar had been in the cottage basement."

Christian looked up from the picture and widened his eyes. "And she's still missing? Do you think Ric?" He shook his head and pushed the photo away. "I'm stunned. I thought I knew him. My God, do you know how many times he's been in my house? Around my wife and children? Whatever way I can assist you in finding—"

"We already found her," Hicks said. "She was buried in the flowerbed behind the cottage."

Christian rubbed his forehead. "I feel responsible. I let that monster into my life. I trusted him and he...oh my God. I—"

The door to the room opened. He looked up just as Martin entered.

About fucking time.

"Agents," the director said with a curt nod. "We have everything we need."

CHAPTER 16

Two days later…

NAOMI TOOK THE last piece of clothing from the bag she'd taken with her to Chicago, and stowed it in her dresser drawer. As she put her toiletries away, she glanced at her reflection in the mirror. For the first time in eight long years, she stared at a free woman. Unfortunately, that freedom had come with a huge cost.

As of this morning, two hundred and seventeen people had died from the bombings. The number of those injured remained at one hundred and eight, with a third of those people suffering from lost limbs, third degree burns, disfiguration and broken bones. Yes, freedom didn't taste as good as she'd dreamed it would. Instead, all she tasted was regret and guilt.

Tossing her make-up bag beneath the cabinet under the bathroom sink, she let the tears fall. Considering how much she'd cried these past two day, she'd thought the well would eventually run dry. With so much sadness and grief remaining, there would be no drought. The psychologist Ian had suggested she speak with over the phone last night had told her to look for symptoms of survivor's guilt. That she might experience anxiety and depression, insomnia, nightmares and uncontrollable crying jags.

She finished putting away her toothbrush and toothpaste, then looked at her reflection again. What the psychologist didn't realize was that she'd been experiencing all of those symptoms since the death of her parents. Anxiety and depression had been commonplace. Since leaving Jake, insomnia and nightmares had been a constant in her life. She reached for a tissue and blew her nose. If only the crying could cleanse her of the guilt. Of course the psychologist had said that once she came to the realization that the consequences of the bombings and the deaths of the innocent were the result of misfortune and not her actions, she could move forward and look at herself as the victim, not the cause.

After tossing the tissue into the trash can, she moved into the bedroom and slumped on the bed. Yes, she was a victim, but the psychologist was wrong. She *was* the cause. She hadn't detonated the bombs, she hadn't asked for Christian's unwanted messages, but she'd been the reason behind them. Although she wanted to live, a large part of her didn't think she deserved to be alive. How could she celebrate life when her name had now become synonymous with death?

Christian had scarred her in more ways than one. The night he'd had her restrained so Ric and that quack of a gynecologist could abort the child she carried—Christian's child—had been one of the worst nights of her life.

Or so she'd thought.

Monday afternoon, after she, Jake and Dante had been brought to the FBI's Norfolk Division, the agents had separated them, sticking her in a room for over two hours before finally debriefing her. Their line of questioning hadn't been what she'd expected, and after an hour's worth, she was glad Jake hadn't been in the room. While she'd never had the impression that the agents thought she'd been involved in Christian's terrorist attacks, they kept twisting and turning her words against her. Knowing Jake, he would have raised hell and told the agents to screw themselves—just not that eloquently.

As the exhausting and stressful debriefing had gone on, she'd given them a graphic and detailed version of the forced abortion, hoping to shed light on the type of man Christian truly was. The agents had, in turn, grilled her about a date, time, location and the name of the gynecologist involved. But she hadn't been able to answer any of their questions. She'd been drugged and when she'd woken, she had found herself bound and at the mercy of Ric and the doctor. Reliving that night had been hell. What had made it worse was seeing the doubt in the agents' eyes. In a small way, she couldn't blame them. She had no proof. Not about the abortion, about her parents' or brother's murders, about the stalking or the night Christian had ordered the Columbian to hold a knife against her throat.

In the end, along with the senseless deaths of hundreds of innocent people, what they had was a case of he said, she said. Yes, they had the Rose Wood connection, and evidence that a signal had been sent from Christian's company server to the last device detonated, but would it be enough?

She shivered and rubbed her arms. Her stomach turned when she pictured Mickey's abused body. He was dead, along with Ric and Santiago—the man she'd known as the Columbian. Harrison and the tall blond, Vlad, might have severed the twine binding her to Christian's chair, but they'd immediately disappeared with the laptop. Of the seven people that had been in Christian's warehouse, only two were available for questioning.

Her and Christian.

"Hey," Jake said with a soft rap on her opened door. "Want me to fix you something to eat?"

The thought of food made her stomach sour. "I'm good, thanks. But you go ahead if you're hungry. I'm not sure what's in the fridge and pantry, though."

He walked to the bed and sat next to her. "I see you unpacked," he said, nodding to the empty bag.

"You were on the phone and I needed something to do."

He draped an arm around her shoulder and pulled her

close. Monday, after she and Jake had been debriefed, she'd gone to the hotel room Rachel had secured for her. Jake had an adjoining room, and while she would have loved for him to stay with her, wrap his strong arms around her and make her feel whole again, she'd needed time alone. The agents' line of questioning, the accusation and disbelief in their eyes—living through the abortion, her parents' and brother's death, along with the fears she'd harbored for eight years, had been like ripping open a wound that had just started to mend.

She'd needed time to decompress and digest everything that had happened throughout the day. She'd needed to dress that wound and pray that this time around, it would heal. With the many wasted years looming over her, and freedom from Christian no longer a fantasy, but a reality, she hadn't wanted to screw anything up with Jake. In the thick of the moment, he'd promised love and a bright future. Now that they were no longer up against the clock and lives weren't on the line, to secure that future she needed to come to terms with the guilt and bitterness weighing heavy on her heart and shoulders.

He kissed the top of her head. "Do you plan to put the bag away, or are you going to use it again?"

Yesterday, she'd kept to her hotel room and slept most of the day. The agents she'd met with the night before had paid her another visit, asking her a few follow-up questions before telling her she could go home. Jake had also come to her room several times, bringing her food and something to drink. During their last conversation, he'd made it clear he wanted her to come back to Chicago with him. Vulnerable, she'd agreed.

This morning she'd changed her mind. She'd been living in Woodbine, Georgia, for nearly five years. Right now, she needed her familiar surroundings and the quiet, easy pace of a small town. Instead of taking the private jet back to Chicago, Jake had decided to join her in Woodbine, saying he wasn't ready to go their separate ways.

"Eventually," she finally answered. "I'm sorry. I know I said I'd go home with you, but I need to figure out what direction I need to take."

"Can you dumb it down for me? Or am I completely forgetting a conversation."

She smiled against his chest. "What I mean is that I need to decide what to do now that I no longer have to hide."

"Your job and house here? Or me?"

Drawing back, she took his hand. "The media doesn't know about me yet, but I think it'll only be a matter of time before Rose Wood is resurrected. If my face is attached to that name, I'm worried I'll have to hide again."

"None of this was your fault," he said with vehemence.

"You keep telling me that, but that's not the impression I got from the FBI." They'd made her sound as if she was suffering from psychosis. That she might have brought this onto herself for associating with Ric. That she'd lost contact with reality and had, because of the severity of the situation, projected her fears and disillusionments onto Christian rather than Ric.

"Those agents have no idea what they're talking about." He gave her hand a gentle squeeze. "Hunnicutt's an asshole. A pathological narcissist."

She cocked a brow. "Did you talk to the psychologist after me?"

The corner of his mouth tilted in a sheepish grin. "No. Rachel. She loves looking up things and after we had a conference call, she researched narcissism. Everything she found fits Hunnicutt. The man has no boundaries and no shame. There's no limit to his arrogance, and he carries a strong sense of entitlement and considers himself superior." His grin grew. "End of quote."

She touched his strong jaw. Monday night, she knew then, just as she knew now, she shouldn't care what those agents had thought of her. She knew the truth and so did Jake. And *he* believed her.

But what would the rest of the world believe?

"When people find out—"

"If they find out," he corrected her.

She stood and hugged herself. "I'll carry the stigma of being the reason for hundreds of deaths for a long time. It was bad enough knowing I was the reason Christian wiped out my family, but this…" Her chin trembled and her eyes burned with tears. "I don't know how to carry on from here."

He came next to her, sifted his hands through her hair and cupped her head. "Let's worry about it together. Come back to Chicago with me. You have nothing to hide, and nothing to feel guilty for. You're just as much of a victim as the people Hunnicutt killed."

"Are you sure you didn't talk to that psychologist?" she asked, and wiped a tear from her cheek.

"I don't need a degree in psychology to understand the truth. Don't let him win. Not now. Not after everything you've been through. You've finally stopped him and he can't hurt anyone else."

"I know. Honestly, although I'm scared about testifying against him, I want him to be given the death penalty. What's even scarier, I want to witness his execution and make sure he's confirmed dead." She sighed. "God, I'm a horrible person."

"I've wanted to kill him, at the least, a dozen different ways and I don't think I'm a horrible person."

She gave him a quick kiss. "You're definitely not horrible. Death is too easy for a man like Christian." She kissed him again. "I have to say though, I had no idea you were so vindictive."

"I'm normally not." Still cupping the back of her head, he drew her closer. His warm breath fanned across her lips, his scent embraced her and brought a rush of familiar memories. "But he went after the wrong woman."

The heat in his eyes, along with what his words implied, warmed her cheeks. He'd made it clear he wanted them to be together again, yet she still worried about the repercussions once her involvement went public. "I'm worried about you. I think I should hold off on coming to Chicago."

His eyes darkened and became possessive as he ran a hand

along her side. "Still trying to protect me?" he asked and gripped her hip.

Always. She loved Jake so much, she'd never forgive herself if her association to the bombings and Christian's trial affected him negatively. They lived in a world where information technology and social media left little in the way of privacy. The bombings, the billionaire behind them and the woman he did it for would be too huge of a story to ignore. Once leaked, her picture would go viral and Jake's likely would, too. There would probably be people who sympathized with her, while others would make her the target for their blame. People liked having answers, especially if the question was so unfathomable.

"I'm not going to apologize for wanting you to remain detached from anything having to do with me and Christian."

"Do you really think I could remain detached from you? If you told me you didn't want me in your life, I wouldn't like it. But I'd respect your wishes and leave you alone." He moved his hand from her hip to her rear. "Did I mention I wouldn't like it?" he asked, pressing her against his pelvis.

"Twice now," she said, breathless. With his hard, muscular body, firm kissable lips and skilled hands, Jake always had a way of making her come alive no matter the circumstances.

"Actually, I'd *hate* it if you asked me to walk away. I'd hate myself even more if I didn't fight for what we have. With the way you're talking, it sounds like I'm going to have to do just that."

Now cupping her bottom with both hands, he moved her backward until they reached her bed. He eased her onto the mattress. After sliding one leg between her thighs and resting his knee on the edge of the bed, he braced his arms on either side of her shoulders.

"It's time we talk this out and settle everything between us," he said, inching closer.

With his lean body hovering over hers and anticipation coiling through her belly, she had a hard time remembering what they needed to talk about.

"When I first saw you sitting near the beach wearing that

pretty white dress, your long hair moving with the breeze coming off the Gulf, I needed to know you. I'm not going to lie. I was very interested in what was under that dress. But when you smiled at me…" He shook his head and grinned. "I knew you were it for me."

She touched his cheek. "I felt the same way."

He inched up until his thigh nestled against her sex. "When you left, it was the worse day of my life. I'd rather be in full battle rattle in the thick of fighting Iraqi insurgents than go through that again." He brushed a tear sliding down the side of her face and kissed her forehead. "I couldn't eat or sleep. I drank too much and was a bastard to anyone who made the mistake of trying to talk to me."

Keeping his thigh pressed against her heat, he sat back and slipped his warm, rough hand beneath her shirt. Goose bumps rose along her skin. Not only from his touch, but from his words. She knew she'd hurt him, but not to this extent. For him to compare wearing fifty pounds worth of gear and risking his life in battle to her leaving? She looked away. When will there be a day she would no longer carry an ounce of guilt?

He touched her chin. When she met his gaze, he moved his hand over her breast and to her stomach, where he continued to caress her. "I was bitter and pissed. Not with you, but me. I'd accepted that our relationship was over without fight."

"That's not true. You asked me, but I—"

"Lied?" He shrugged. "Your lie was weak. I knew it then, but I let my pride get in the way. I'll be honest, if Ian hadn't forced me out of my job as sheriff, I would've probably run for another term and would still be stuck in Michigan, kicking myself in the ass for not demanding more from you and myself." Starting from the bottom and slowly working his way up, he began unbuttoning her shirt. "You told me you couldn't handle living in a small town, but didn't want a long distance relationship. You know what I heard?" He let either side of her blouse fall to the side and exposed her bra and stomach. "*I don't love you anymore.* That's what I took away from your excuse and I kept telling myself that had to be the reason. And I kept telling myself that over and over, hoping to drill it into my thick skull. Hoping like hell I'd get over it and you."

Her eyes stung with more tears, with regret and a sudden rise of anger. Why was he telling her this *now*? Every stroke of his hands belied every word that he spoke and she couldn't take anymore. "You came to me. Uninvited. Apparently your skull is still thick," she said, and shoved his hand away.

He gripped her wrists and held them above her head with one hand. "Because I couldn't let go of the past, I did come to you." With the pad of his thumb he wiped away more of her tears. "No more of these. I didn't mean to make you cry."

"Then why are you telling me this?"

"Because I'm an idiot."

"There's something we can agree on."

A strange mixture of amusement and sadness filled his eyes. "I should have fought for you. Instead of accepting your excuses, which I knew in my gut were just that, I should have demanded answers and fought for what we had. Right now, you're giving me more excuses. I get them, but I don't like them. Knowing the real reason why you left—it bugged the hell out of me that you felt like *I* needed protection."

Past tense. "Are you saying it doesn't bother you anymore?"

"No." He wrapped her leg around his back and brought his face inches from hers. "I'm a guy. It's been ingrained in my head that I'm the one who should be doing the protecting. But I like knowing you have my back. Now I need for you to realize I have yours. I love you. You. Rose…Naomi, I don't care if you start calling yourself Brunhilde. None of that matters to me, but losing you a second time around because you're worried about me, does. I don't want to walk away again. I want to be by your side and get through this together." He let go of her wrists and kissed her cheek where a warm tear began to trickle. "I thought I said no more of these."

Cupping his face, she twined both legs around his back. She had no regrets walking away from him the first time around— his life was too important to her. Based on what Christian had done to draw her to him, not to mention what he'd done to her family, she honestly believed Jake wouldn't be on top of her right now if Christian had known about him. He'd be dead. But Christian couldn't physically hurt him now. After spending so many years on her own, she'd love to have Jake by her side while she dealt with the media and trial. She loved him and wanted to move past this phase in their lives and start again. "You're sure about this? I'm so worried about the way people will treat you when they know you're with me."

"Have you ever known me to care what people think?"

God, she loved this man. "No. That's one thing I've always admired about you." She arched up and gave him a lingering kiss. "I love you, Jake. I'm sorry I hurt you. But I'm glad you didn't fight for me then, because I might not be with you right now."

His jaw hardened beneath her palms. "He would have had a hell of a time killing me. Now he won't be able to do anything but count down the days until his life ends." He smoothed her hair away from her face, then lifted up, drew his t-shirt over his head and tossed it aside. "I don't want to talk about him anymore. Too many years have already been wasted because of him."

"You're absolutely right," she said, reaching for his belt buckle. As she unfastened his belt, then jeans, he slid her yoga pants over her hips.

"No underwear," he said staring at her exposed sex.

"No panty lines." She shoved his jeans down and reached for his arousal. "Brunhilde, huh?" she asked, grinning. "Not the sexiest name."

"You can make anything sexy." He twined his hand through her hair and sucked in a breath when she stroked him. "For the record, I honestly didn't come into your room for this," he said, holding her head steady and stopping her from taking his length into her mouth.

She continued to stroke him and massaged his testicles. "So climbing on top of me and unbuttoning my shirt was an accident?"

"Something like that."

"And you want me to stop what I'm doing?"

"God, no."

She ran her fingers along his hard abs. "Then why are we doing all of this talking?"

He touched her chin and tilted her head. "Because I don't want to come off like I'm insensitive to what you need. You've been through a lot. Sex might always be on my mind but maybe you need—"

"You. That's all I need and all I've ever wanted." She went back to stroking and massaging him. "And right now, I need to taste you."

His eyes grew impossibly dark and hungry. The moment he loosened his hold on her head, she bent and took him in her mouth. He dragged in a ragged breath and ran his hand along her back. With his other hand still wrapped in her hair, he coaxed her, gently easing her and gliding her over his length.

He was holding back. Sex between them had never been gentle, but rough and hot. Rather than treating her as if she were fragile, she wanted rough and hot. Today started a new beginning and she wanted celebrate by losing herself in his body. Now it was time for her to let him know.

She grazed her nails along his sac. His knees buckled slightly and he let out a low moan. Encouraged, she sucked and licked him as if she was starved. As she slid her mouth along him, he began to thrust. Slow at first, then he held her head with both hands and moved harder, faster. She looked up at him. Loving the passion in his eyes, she hummed her approval, then tore her mouth away. Still stroking him, and anxious to have him inside her, she scooted back a few inches and spread her legs.

Instead of letting her guide him between her outstretched thighs, he took her wrists and pinned them above her head again. "I told you I was trying not to be insensitive," he said, and flicked his tongue against her nipple. "I'm also trying to make this about you."

She arched her back hoping to encourage him to give her

other breast attention. "Stop worrying and let's make this about us." She met his gaze. "I know what you like, and you know I like it, too."

The heat in his eyes had her sex aching for him—his mouth, his fingers, his stiff length. Keeping her arms above her head with one hand, he moved the other to her breast. Her nipples grew painfully hard when he brushed his lips along one rigid peak. "Damn, I love you," he said against her breast, while skimming his hand along her torso. When he reached her sex, he rubbed her clit with the tips of his fingers. "I want to make love to you, not fuck."

"If we love each other, does it matter what we call it?" She struggled against the grip he had at her wrists. She wanted to free herself so she could take his hand and show him exactly what she wanted. "Besides, with all the talking, we're not doing much of anything."

A sexy smile curved his mouth. "Let's rectify that." He drove his fingers deep inside her and pumped them in and out. Never losing contact, he let go of her wrists and moved to the edge of the bed. "I do know what you like," he said right before grazing his tongue along her clit.

She groaned, ran both hands through his hair and held his head steady. With each flick of his tongue, and each press of his fingers, her core coiled tighter and tighter. She looked down the length of her body. When she met his heated gaze, caught the love and lust in his eyes, then glanced to where he pleasured her with his mouth, something inside her snapped. Her breath caught on a moan as her orgasm swiftly rushed from within her sex and tore through her body. Tensing, still holding his head in place, she embraced the ecstasy, the pure sensual and emotional bliss. She loved Jake so much. Loved every level of their relationship and didn't want the moment to end.

When he stood, gripped the back of her thighs and glided his straining erection inside her, she couldn't imagine ever letting him go again. She couldn't picture not being with him. Not sharing their passionate desires. Not being held by him late into the night. The hot kisses. The playful teasing. More than that, the deep conversations, the comfort of knowing what they had together was unbreakable. A bond like no other and one she'd fight for until the day she died.

Breathing hard, his eyes intense and fierce with love and desire, he leaned forward. Caging her with his arms, he moved his hips harder, faster. When she wrapped her legs around his back, he grasped her hip, dipped his head and captured her mouth. His demanding, rough open-mouthed kiss sent a cascade of goose bumps along her skin. She met each stroke of his tongue, each thrust of his hips. Ran one hand over his muscled ass and the other along his chiseled bicep.

On a groan, he tore his mouth away and rested his forehead against hers. His warm breath puffed along her mouth. "I love you," he murmured and kissed her temple. "Stay with me."

"Always."

He lifted his head and kept his eyes on hers as he continued to drive himself deep. "Come with me."

Her inner walls gripped his length. Her body burned with unadulterated pleasure.

He moved faster, each rock of his hips stronger. Her orgasm suddenly ripped through her. As her legs went limp and fell to the side, she clung to his rear and bicep, closed her eyes and arched her back. His muscles tensed beneath her hands. Wanting to share in the pleasure of his release, she forced her eyes open and stared at his handsome face. Only his gaze was on her and held so much love and dark longing, tears stung her eyes.

She cupped his face and brought their lips together. Poured her own love and longing into a kiss that would forever remain in her memory. This moment marked a new beginning between them. Her past or his—no longer mattered. And she couldn't wait for their future to begin.

After a long, lingering kiss, he moved their bodies until they lay on the center of the bed. He pulled the sheet and comforter over them, then cocooned her against his chest. His heart beat along her cheek, while his breathing began to return to normal.

Loving the hard contours, she feathered her fingers through the dark dusting of hair, then rested her palm on his solid chest.

"So, Brunhilde," he began, squeezing her closer and kissing the top of her head. "I know we were multitasking a few minutes ago, but if I recall correctly, you said always when I asked you to stay with me."

She grinned against his pectoral muscle and gave his chest hair a slight tug. "I would've said anything at that moment."

He let out a chuckle and she shifted her head to look at him. Grinning, he ran his fingertips along her cheek. "I want to be with you," he said, his grin fading, his eyes filled with a mixture of determination and uncertainty.

She never wanted him to ever be uncertain about anything when it came to them. She loved him. Trusted him. Wanted to be with him.

Always.

"I want to be with you, too," she said, caressing his chest. He knew everything about her past, had endured and accepted why she'd lied to him, and he still loved her. If they were going to begin anew, there was still one last thing she needed to tell him. While she doubted her secret would change how he felt about her, if they were going to make a fresh start, they'd do it the right way. No more secrets.

"Then you'll come to Chicago?" he asked, hopeful.

She nodded. "For a while. I'll have to tell my principal what's happened. I'm not sure if the school will want me to stay on, but I'm not comfortable leaving them high and dry without a nurse."

"And from there?" he asked, drawing circles along her upper arms with his fingers.

"I've always loved Chicago."

"That's good, because I happen to live there."

She forced a smile, while her stomach knotted with nervousness. "There's still something else."

"If you're worried about finding a job, take your time. Ian pays me well, so you don't have to rush into anything."

"It's not that."

His face hardened. "I told you I don't want to talk about him."

She had no choice, not if she were going to do this right the second time around. "I have to tell you this," she said, shifting her body until they were chest to breast. "I...on the jet to Norfolk, I told you I couldn't have children."

"And I told you what matters to me is being with you, not the kids you could give me. That's not why I fell in love with you."

Damn, could he make this any harder? "I remember. And you have no idea how much that meant to me. When we were together and used to talk about having a family, I would picture a houseful of kids, little dark haired, dark eyed boys that were the spitting image of you."

"And beautiful little bossy girls that were the spitting image of their mother," he said with a sad smile.

"Yeah," she said, blinking back tears. God, how she'd wanted that life. Only *he* had taken it away. "When I got the result from my doctor and found out that wasn't a possibility, I was devastated. I worried how you'd react—"

"Hey." He rubbed her shoulder. "I told you it's okay."

"It's not okay. If I couldn't have children because my body wasn't made right, that would have been one thing." She kissed his chest, looking for the strength to admit the truth. When she lifted her head and met his eyes, she found it.

"I told you I met Christian when I was working as a cocktail waitress. I was nineteen, going to school, working my butt off. He was, believe it or not, very charming and I was very attracted to him. Before Christian, the guys I dated were from high school. They were young and immature. Christian was older and sophisticated. He'd take me to nice restaurants, buy me flowers...he made me feel special. I was really into him, but kept telling myself this wouldn't last. Between his wealth and family connections, I couldn't imagine our relationship going anywhere. I also told myself to enjoy the moment and made the mistake of having sex with him. Only once, because that was enough. I'm not going to get into the details. Let's just say I didn't enjoy it and never wanted him touching me again."

Which was an understatement. She loved it when Jake was a little rough and domineering during sex. She also trusted him and knew he'd never hurt her. The night she'd had sex with Christian, he'd taken dominance to a violent level. She might have gone to him as a willing partner, but when he'd begun to hurt her, she'd begged him to stop. He wouldn't. Instead, he'd become even more sadistic. As if her cries and pleas only fueled his desire to control her.

Jake gave her shoulder a gentle squeeze. "You don't have to tell me this."

"Actually, I do. You know everything else, and this is something that affects both of us." She drew in a fortifying breath. "After that horrible night with Christian, I refused to see him again. He didn't like it. He called constantly, would show up at my apartment, at the club where I worked or catch me on campus when I was rushing to get to class. I saw the callous man lurking beneath the good looks, charm and money and didn't believe his apologies or his excuses. Then a couple of months later I found out I was pregnant."

She searched Jake's eyes looking for disappointment or disgust. Instead she found a combination of sympathy and anger. "At the time, I didn't realize he had the Columbian following me. Christian found out I was pregnant, and without asking me what I planned to do, he took it upon himself to decide for me."

Jake's jaw tightened and his body tensed. Beneath her palms, his heart rate accelerated.

"I came home from school in the afternoon and the next thing I remember was waking up in a cold cellar, strapped to a table."

Leaning his head against the pillow, Jake ran a hand over his face. After a moment, he looked at her, the rage and horror in his eyes contradicting the way he continued to gently massage her shoulder. "He's the reason you can't have children," he said, his voice low and filled with loathing.

She nodded. "Christian brought in a man he claimed was a retired doctor, then stood and watched as the doctor and Ric gave me an abortion. Afterward, Christian took me back to my apartment. He told me to not bother going to the police, because it would be my word against his. And he was right. I had no proof that I was carrying his baby."

"You were obviously drugged. The police—"

"I know where you're going with this. The night it happened...I was bleeding badly. My main concern was to get to the hospital. I explained to the ER doctor what had happened. After he stopped the bleeding and made sure I'd be okay, he ran a tox screen and later found chloroform in my system. The doctor and nurses encouraged me to call the police. Once I was moved to a hospital room and had time to think, I decided they were right. When I was about to call for a nurse to help me contact the police, a man wearing scrubs and pushing a cart filled with flowers, came in the room. When he stepped from behind the flowers and I saw Ric's face, I knew going to the police wasn't an option."

"What did Ric do to you?" he asked, his tone deadly.

"Threatened and taunted me. He made it clear that Christian's team of attorneys would destroy me and my family. They'd make me out to be a money grubbing slut, say that the baby could have been any man's and that I was crazy enough to do this to myself. After all, I was going to nursing school and knew my way around the human body."

"Bullshit."

"Of course it was, but I was scared and knew Ric was right. Rather than drag my family into my problems with Christian, and drag my name through the press by making accusations, I let it go. I had my regular doctor check me and while she said I had scar tissue, she thought I'd be okay. Unfortunately, she was wrong."

When Jake didn't say anything, she blew out a stream of breath. "Now you know everything. I'd rather you find out now, from me, than during the trial."

"You told the Feds?"

"I told them everything."

"Virginia gives Death Row inmates the option of lethal injection or the electric chair," he said, his eyes narrowing as he looked away from her. "Either one would be too easy for the bastard." Barely glancing at her, he kissed the top of her head. "Thanks for telling me. I know that had to have been hard for you."

After giving her shoulder a soft pat, he separated their bodies and swung his legs over the side of the bed. As he stretched, she stared at his back, at the scars from where the shrapnel had been removed after he'd been caught in an explosion while in Iraq. "Why don't you take a nap?" He turned and rested a hand on her hip. "I'll see if I can find something to make for lunch."

She pulled the comforter to her chin. "Sure, sounds good," she said, hurt, confused and disappointed. "Give me an hour."

He leaned over and kissed her cheek. "Love you," he whispered against her ear, then he pushed off the bed. Once he'd gathered his clothes and left the room, she flipped onto her back and wiped the tears from her face.

Thanks for telling me. I know that had to have been hard for you.

Hell, yeah, it had been hard. She hadn't expected him to spout out a bunch of philosophical or emotional crap to try and make her feel better, but she sure as hell had expected more than a *thanks for telling me.* That's something she'd say to a server after they told her about the soup of the day.

Thanks for telling me.

How about a couple words of comfort? How about letting her know this didn't change anything between them? With the way he'd acted, she had the impression that knowing she'd not only willingly had sex with Christian, but that he'd forced her to have an abortion obviously didn't settle well with Jake. Although she understood, he didn't have to be so damned blasé about it. Upset or not, he could have given her an encouraging word or two.

Unable to close her eyes without reliving their conversation, she slid off the bed and headed into the bathroom to shower. She loved Jake, and once she spoke with her principal about her job, she still planned to go to Chicago. She'd keep her house in Woodbine, though. At least for a little while. If *thanks for telling me* was Jake's idea of being supportive, especially during the trial when all of her secrets were aired, she might have to take a break from him.

Jake might love her and want them to have each other's back, but she needed him to show it. After so many years of running and worrying, of dealing with her past on her own, she needed to be sure she could rely on him in every sense.

Otherwise there would be no future for them.

CHAPTER 17

CHRISTIAN EXITED OFF Georgia's US 17 and pulled into a one pump gas station. He looked at the paint peeling off the small storefront, the weathered billboard advertising bait and Coca-Cola, then to the gas pump. What a shithole. He slid out of the Ford Focus and stretched. Because he wasn't supposed to leave Norfolk, he hadn't been able to rent a car. And because all of his vehicles were extremely expensive and noteworthy, he hadn't wanted to take one of them, either. Fortunately, Vlad had left his car behind when he'd gone with Santiago and the twins last week. Unfortunately, the car was small and compact. How the hell Vlad had fit inside, he didn't know.

"Afternoon," a man called.

Christian glanced over and refrained from rolling his eyes. Typical redneck. Wearing faded, stained coveralls, and a cheap mesh ball cap that made his head look at least four inches taller, the old man approached, a slight limp in his step.

"Does this thing work?" Christian asked, pointing to the rusty gas pump that looked as if it had been there since the 1970s.

"Sure does," the old man said, then spit onto the cracked asphalt. Using the back of his hand, he wiped at his long, white beard. "Cash only."

He pulled out his wallet and handed the man a fifty dollar bill. "Obviously."

After shoving the fifty into his pocket, the man limped to the pump. "Want me to wash your windows?" he asked and unscrewed the Ford's gas cap.

"No."

"Only take a minute or two. Your windshield's a daggone bug cemetery."

"How far to Woodbine?" Christian asked, not interested in being at this filthy excuse for a gas station one minute longer than necessary.

"About forty-five minutes," the old man replied, removing the nozzle from the pump. "Heading there to do some fishing?"

Christian watched the numbers on the pump slowly turn. One number at a fucking time. "Hunting. I also heard Woodbine has a beautiful garden and offers tours."

"Don't know." The man turned his head and spat. "Not much into flowers."

He smiled. "And I'm rather partial to roses."

"Mmm, thorny suckers." He kicked the pump and the numbers flipped a bit faster. "If you stick around, you can catch the crawfish festival later this month. Good eatin', good music, but I recommend taking a flask. Beer ain't cheap."

Christ, why the hell hadn't he stopped for gas earlier? He stared at the numbers on the pump, wishing they'd roll by faster. It had taken him seven hours to reach this point. Add on another forty-five minutes, plus the time it would take to kill Rose, he figured he could be back on the road by late afternoon. Since he shouldn't have left Norfolk, he would need to drive the almost eight hours back to his estate tonight.

During the early hours of Tuesday morning, after he'd finally finished speaking with those idiot FBI agents, and Martin had subsequently released him due to lack of evidence, Agent Suts had dropped him off at his plantation estate. Christian had then spent the remainder of the day locked in his bedroom suite. Other than having the small kitchenette fully stocked, he'd ordered his servants not to disturb him. As he'd sat in his room, a room he'd planned to share with Rose while his bitch wife and kids were in New York, he planned his next move.

Martin had assured him his name would not be leaked to the press. Years of friendship, told him he could trust the Director of the FBI. As added insurance, he'd still made a few calls. The Vice President had plans to run for president in the next election, and was rather fond of Christian's campaign donations. Christian had also been in contact with his secretary and PR people. They were to handle BH-Xpress's stance on the bombings, and were to make sure that the financial aid he'd promised to the bombing victims started immediately.

He continued to watch the slow rolling numbers on the rusty gas pump. Rose had cost him a lot of money. When he considered how much he'd spent on investigators over the years, the C-4 Ric had purchased for the bombings, his eighty-six million dollar plane and now the fucking financial aid—she owed him. Plus, he'd lost a COO and his two best bodyguards.

He leaned against the silver Focus and considered Vlad and Harrison. As much as he'd love to find and kill them, they would have to wait. Martin might not leak his name to the press, but that didn't mean the director wouldn't have his people watching him. Thanks to his state of the art security system, he knew they weren't—yet. Still, it would behoove him to maintain caution. In time though, Vlad and Harrison would pay.

The pump finally dinged. "That'll do it." The man moved the nozzle away from the car. "You sure you don't want me to—whoa," he shouted, and pulled a small hatchet from his back pocket.

Christian stepped back and raised his hands.

"Don't move unless you want to get hurt."

What the hell? If he was going to die, his executioner wouldn't be a hatchet wielding redneck. Lowering his hands, he prepared to use the gun he kept clipped to the back of his belt.

"She's a beaut," the man said, scratching his beard and staring at the ground.

Christian followed the man's gaze, then jumped to the side when he saw the snake. "Is that thing poisonous?"

"Yep," he said, holding the hatchet steady. "Won't kill ya or anything, but it'll hurt like a son of a bitch. Been finding a bunch of them lately. I gotta get into those woods next to the station and find their nests. One of these little bastards killed my cat and that pisses me—" He whacked the blade against the asphalt. "Gotcha."

Christian watched in fascination as the decapitated snake's body squirmed and its mouth still moved.

The man wiped the blade along his coveralls, then spat. "When I was in Nam, I had a platoon leader, Cap'n Dumbass we called him." Still watching the snake, the old man chuckled. "Cap'n Dumbass used to tell us how we gotta cut off the head of the snake. Once done, the bodies, meaning Viet Cong, would flounder around and eventually die. That dipshit never cut off a snake's head. See how its mouth is still snappin'?"

"How long before it stops?" Christian asked, thinking how ironic this conversation truly was. He'd anticipated killing Rose, cutting off the snake's head, so to speak. Once she was gone, there wouldn't be anyone left to accuse him of anything.

"I've seen some take a few hours."

Christian shook his head and pulled the keys from his pocket. "So what's the best way to kill a snake?"

"You pretty much just saw it," the man said, tucking his hatchet back in place. Then he laughed. "Unless you got yourself a honey badger. Ever see that YouTube video. Funny stuff, right there. That damned badger took down a cobra and the venom didn't even stop him."

Fucking honey badger.

Christian let out a bark of laughter. Talk about true irony. Yes, he'd seen the stupid video. The moment he'd overheard his men calling him Honey Badger, he'd looked up the creature. While he thought the video mildly amusing, what he'd read about the animal had intrigued him. Although he considered himself more of a lion than a small, vicious weasel, even a lion couldn't necessarily stand up to the honey badger.

And right now his lion, or rather his cobra consisted of Rose and some small time, private dick agency.

"You sure about that windshield?"

"I'm good," he said, opening the car door. He glanced down at the still moving decapitated snake. "I need to be back on the road."

"Happy hunting." The old man chuckled. "And flower watchin'."

Christian smiled. "I do love roses."

Harrison's eyes burned and watered as he stared at the closed laptop. Thanks to Vlad's damned chain smoking, a hazy fog hung in the Rainbow Lodge's small, shitty room, reminding him of the week they'd spent planting the bombs. Only now they were in Woodbine, Georgia, trying to figure out a way to disarm the bombs without being caught. "Why do I feel like we've come full circle?"

"What is this circle Harry says?" Vlad asked and blew smoke rings.

"We started this in a crappy motel and are now planning to end it in another one."

"Harry plan to end it. Vlad is…on rail. We should never have come and go straight to Florida, like Harry say."

Four years ago, the Norfolk PD had arrested him and Mickey for robbing a bank, and while they'd recovered most of the stolen money, the police hadn't realized Harrison had set up an account in Titusville, Florida. Neither had Mickey. If his twin had had a clue, the money would have been carelessly squandered. Prior to their arrest, Harrison had created fake IDs for him and Mickey. They had social security numbers, Florida driver's licenses, along with a bank account.

After collecting interest for the past four years, he had over one hundred grand waiting for him, along with his and Mickey's bogus IDs in a safe deposit box at the same bank. Vlad could easily assume Mickey's fake ID. The driver's license photo would be a problem, but at least Vlad would have a new name and they'd both have an opportunity to hide in plain sight.

"Rail?" Harrison asked, trying to keep up with the Russian's use of the English language.

"Vlad not interested in Harry's plan with woman. Big mistake. But," he said with a sigh and snuffed the cigarette in an ashtray. "Three last bombs must be found." He shrugged. "So, Vlad on rail."

Vlad needed to learn his idioms. "You mean on the *fence*."

"Fence, rail, no point in making mincemeat out of Vlad's words. I grow tired of being corrected. Beside, Harry understood."

Mincemeat? Man, did Vlad need some serious schooling. Based on how the Russian kept teetering on him, he'd let this one slide. He didn't necessarily need Vlad on his side, but at this point, Vlad was all he had. He'd lost his brother, his twin, his best and only true friend. He couldn't count on his mom. Hell, anymore, he didn't even know where she lived. He'd never met his dad and had no clue if the man was dead or alive. With no family to speak of, no friends to count on, he was left with the one person who actually acted as if he gave a shit about him.

A six foot six, two hundred and forty pound, former heavy weight boxer who referred to himself in third person, smoked like a frickin' chimney and couldn't quite master the English language. What a pair they made.

"Look," Harrison began, "you need to get off your *rail* and trust me on this. We go to the woman, give her the laptop, tell her what we know and then leave for Florida. Simple and easy."

"No." Vlad took out a fresh pack of cigarettes and smacked it against his palm. "Not easy as fucking pie. What if she calls FBI?"

"We'll be long gone."

"Bullshit. We might go, but Feds will know the state we are in and put APP on our asses."

"APB," Harrison said under his breath.

"What? Speak loud." The Russian pushed off the wall. "Do you correct Vlad again?"

"You know what? I did." Harrison stood. Between bonding over stories about their past and a heart-to-heart over their time at the warehouse, all of which involved too much vodka, he knew in his gut the Russian wouldn't do anything to him. "It's APB, which stands for All Points Bulletin."

"That what Vlad said."

"No, you said, APP. Depending on the right situation, if you threw that out there people might think you have to *take* a pee-pee."

"You know what Vlad think? Vlad think we should part way."

Harrison's stomach seized. The only time he'd been on his own and without someone he could trust was during his two years in prison. And he did trust Vlad. The Russian could have left him behind, but he hadn't. And when it came to Mickey, Vlad had showed extreme remorse. "Remember yesterday and what I told you about Mickey?"

Nodding, Vlad took a drag off his cigarette. "I told you the mouse reminded me of my brother, Erik." Grief filled his eyes and he released sigh. "It why Vlad didn't like Mickey. Like Erik he could have done more with life."

Monday night, while doing shots and arguing about what to do with the laptop, they'd discussed Mickey at great length. Because they were on the run and Harrison knew he wouldn't have the opportunity to bury his twin without being apprehended by the FBI, with the help of a fifth of vodka he'd done his own version of a eulogy. After he'd finished highlighting all of Mickey's highs and lows, Vlad had told him about his brother, Erik. Erik had been born ten months after Vlad and they'd been tight—as tight as twins—from the stories Vlad had told. Only Erik had gone in a different direction and was now buried in the family cemetery.

"I'm sorry if I keep correcting you, but that's a shitty excuse to walk away from doing the *right* thing." He drew in a deep breath. "I get why you stayed with Hunnicutt. You had no choice." Harrison honestly believed this. Vlad was more of an indentured servant than hired help. Hunnicutt had used the Russian and had threatened him and his family. "If you'd rather we go our separate ways, then fine. As for me? I'm going to see this through. If I end up caught, then at least I did the right thing." He looked away. "It might not keep me from burning in hell, but at least it'll be off my conscience."

"Right thing put Harry on row of death." Harrison looked at Vlad, who chuckled. "Kidding. Vlad know it Death Row. Vlad also know it where Harry heads. But..." He took a long drag off the cigarette. "We do this. Vlad and Harry, we do this. Then go look at pretty women in bikinis."

Relieved, Harrison grinned. "Awesome. Okay, the sooner we do this, the sooner we can leave. I'll wipe the computer clean of my prints and put it in that plastic grocery bag I saved. Then we'll stakeout Rose's house again." They'd gone there last night, but she hadn't arrived yet. When they'd tried again today, they saw her walking inside with a man. "I don't know anything about that guy she's with—"

"Vlad been thinking."

"About?" he asked, using the motel's thin bath towel to clean the laptop.

"He not FBI like Harry first thought."

"Then who the hell is he?"

The Russian shrugged. "Vlad think he and other man, one who chased us from warehouse, are together. Think, Harry. That guy chase Vlad and Harry *before* FBI shows."

"*They* caught the signal sent from the BH-Xpress's server, not the Feds." He scratched at the three day old beard stubble along his jaw. "Could be another government agency."

"CIA?"

"The bombings were domestic, but maybe ATF? I guess it doesn't matter. What does is making sure we get to Rose when he's not around. I'm not interested in finding out who he works for, I just want to make the drop and get the hell out of here."

Harrison looked at Vlad's white-blond hair. "Before we go,

I'm wondering what you'd look like if we changed your hair color."

"Vlad wonder what Harry look like with missing front tooth."

Harrison shook his head and smiled. "No need to threaten me. All you had to do was say no."

"No."

"Well, if we're not already, I guarantee we'll be on the FBI's most wanted list soon. It's not like you blend in."

"No dark hair." Vlad ran a hand over his cropped hair. "Unless Harry shave head bald."

"Fine. We'll keep our hair. But when we get to Florida, we're going to have to get rid of the car."

"No."

"It's too conspicuous." Yesterday morning, while Harrison nursed his hangover, Vlad took the ten grand he'd stashed at the apartment and went in search of a car. Two hours later, and thirty-three hundred dollars poorer, he'd driven up in an olive green 1966 Oldsmobile Toronado. "Unfortunately you probably won't make your money back, but—"

"No. Vlad love car. Much better than teeny-tiny Focus."

Satisfied he'd wiped off all of his prints, Harrison placed the laptop in the plastic bag. "The interior and exterior are the same color as boogers. At least consider having it painted. Black would work."

Vlad drew out another cigarette. "Maybe."

"Please don't light that."

The Russian rolled his eyes. "Ah, yes. Harry worry over laptop."

"No. I worry about your health. Besides, we need to wipe down the room and get rid of our fingerprints. It's less than a forty minute drive to the Florida border. If Rose is alone, we can be drinking daiquiris at a beach bar by Happy Hour."

Vlad put the cigarette back in the pack and retrieved a bath towel. "Vlad like the sound of that. But, what if man there all night?"

Harrison stopped wiping the table he'd been sitting at and

rubbed the tension at the base of his neck.

He did *not* want to hurt the man. There had been enough killing already this week, and it was only Wednesday. They needed to make sure they gave Rose the laptop, and they also had to do it in person. Not interested in leaving any additional evidence behind, he wanted to tell her where the last three bombs were located rather than write a note or leave a message. With the way the laptop program worked, the locations weren't listed. The codes were, but they'd been encrypted. Sure, the FBI or whoever had found his original signal could likely break those codes, but he didn't want to run the risk of them taking too long and one of those explosives accidentally going off or, God forbid, a kid finding one.

Harrison thought about where Santiago and Mickey had planted the last device. About how many kids in the Norfolk area were on spring break and how warm the weather had been this week. Damn. About how the Virginia Zoo had picked this week to celebrate their long awaited elephant exhibit.

News clips from the Coolidge Middle School bombing ran through his head. Unease settled in the pit of his stomach as he reached for the duffle bag Vlad had brought with them.

"We've got guns," he said, the weight of the weapons in the bag bringing him some semblance of security.

Vlad moved his jacket slightly. "And knife."

Harrison swallowed hard as he stared at the sheathed dagger clipped to Vlad's belt. "No matter what, he'll cooperate."

Jake slumped onto the patio chair and wondered what the hell he'd done wrong. It had been about forty-five minutes since he'd left Naomi's bed, forty-five long minutes since she'd admitted to not only having consensual sex with Hunnicutt, but the gruesome details behind the forced abortion. When he'd first learned about the abortion while at the warehouse, he'd wanted to remove Hunnicutt's balls with a piece of jagged glass. Instead, he'd followed orders and remained on the other side of the door, waiting for the moment he could strike. That moment never came. Now that Hunnicutt was in custody, the justice he'd planned to serve would forever remain a sick fantasy. Although he had vengeance on the brain, going vigilante and killing the bastard wasn't worth going to prison. He and Naomi had already spent too many years apart because of Hunnicutt.

Now, for some reason, she was hardly speaking to him. Maybe dredging up the past had taken its toll on her. What she'd been through had been beyond traumatic and something no woman should ever have to experience. If she needed space, he'd give it to her. If she wanted to talk, he'd listen.

He reached for the iced tea on the table and tried to ignore his grumbling stomach. His search for something to make for lunch had resulted in a couple of frozen burgers, wilted lettuce and stale bread. Monday morning, they'd left in such a hurry, neither of them had bothered to put away the breakfast stuff Naomi had setting on the kitchen counter. When they'd been rushing to leave and catch the jet to Chicago, neither had noticed the refrigerator door hadn't been completely shut. The best he could probably do for lunch would be to make a can of cream of chicken soup and pop a bag of popcorn.

After setting the glass of tea on the table, he looked out at her spacious backyard. The woman he loves had just told him how a mass murder had violated her, and here he sat contemplating what to make her for lunch.

Fucking pathetic.

He rubbed his temple and watched two squirrels chase each other up a tree. Instead of worry about feeding her, maybe he should get off his ass and go talk to her. What he'd say, he didn't know. Now that he thought about it, listening to the exchange between Naomi and Hunnicutt had almost been easier than holding Naomi in his arms and not only hearing the anguish in her voice, but seeing the fear in her eyes as she relived that horrible night. Lying in bed with her, picturing everything that had happened to her had been utter hell.

He hadn't known what to say, so he'd kept his emotions

and reactions in check—for her. He'd wanted to be strong, to let her know that anything she told him wouldn't change how he felt about her. She'd been trying to protect him for too many years, and he'd been hell bent on proving he didn't need that protection. That he could handle the truth and move forward—with her. Which *was* the absolute truth. Was he disappointed they couldn't have kids? Yeah. Would he sacrifice spending the rest of his days with Naomi over it? Hell, no.

To finally have her in his life again was all he'd wanted. He'd thought he made that clear when they'd flown into Norfolk, and had thought he'd made his stance equally clear before they'd made love. He had her back. He loved her. He wanted to be with her no matter the circumstances.

The patio door slid open. He turned just as Naomi stepped outside. Her long hair, still damp from her shower, was pulled over one shoulder. Her eyes were puffy, as if she'd been crying. Damn it, had he been the reason for the tears?

He quickly stood and reached for her. She let him hold her, but gave him a limp hug and a pat on the back.

She fucking patted him on the damned back.

He held her at arm's length. "What's going on?"

"Nothing. I'm just tired."

Knowing she was a good liar, he wanted to call *bullshit*, but refrained. If he was the reason for the way she was acting, now wasn't the time to start an argument. "I told you to take a nap."

She stiffened and stepped away. "And I told you I couldn't sleep."

Right. Shit, she was pissed and he didn't need an anvil to the head to figure out it was because of something he had or hadn't said. "So, did you get in touch with your school's principal?"

He caught her eye roll before she moved toward the faucet just off the brick patio. "Yes," she said, picking up the hose and turning on the nozzle. "I told him I had a family emergency that might require me to take an extended leave of absence." She sprayed the pink and white azalea bushes in the flowerbed. "He didn't think it'd be a problem to find a replacement, which I don't doubt. I got lucky with my job. This is a good school system, and I have a decent salary and great benefits."

Although eager to bring Naomi to Chicago and finally make his condo feel more like a home once she was living in it, her lack of enthusiasm dampened his excitement. "That's great. Not to push you, but when do you think you'll be ready to leave?"

"When does Ian want you back?"

Yesterday. "I'll need to be at work Monday morning."

She shifted the hose from the azaleas to the tulips and daffodils. "Well, if you need to go, I can fly in on my own later next week."

"Did I do something wrong?" he asked, before that anvil came dangerously close to whacking his thick head. What the hell was he missing? Should he have said more after she'd told him about what Hunnicutt had done to her? He'd wanted to. Actually he'd wanted to stop her, save her from having to relive the terrifying experience, and confess what he'd already known. He also believed that sometimes a confession could cleanse the soul.

Because the abortion had left her unable to have children, and was a huge deal for her and their future, he hadn't wanted to take that admission away from her. In his mind, it would have been like letting her start a joke, but interrupting her with the punch line. Only this was no joke. Her mental and emotional health ranked top on his list of priorities. Making sure she made it through a trial that would likely be long and drawn out, was of utmost importance to him. Giving her the comforts of a new home, starting a new life together...he wanted to make sure he did everything right by her, but he wasn't a mind reader. With the way she continued to ignore his question and drown her flowers, he wished he were.

He walked over to her. After taking the hose from her, he shut off the nozzle. "Talk to me."

"I'm sorry. Everything is catching up with me," she said,

her tone flat, her gaze on the muddy flowerbed.

"Naomi, if I did something—"

"You're fine." She finally looked at him and gave him a smile that didn't reach her eyes. "It's me. I have a lot to think about. Too much. I love my house and my job…the kids at school. Don't get me wrong, I'm looking forward to staying with you in Chicago, I guess I just need time to adjust."

Staying with him in Chicago. Not *moving in* with him. His chest tightened with unease. What the hell happened to *always*? "Take whatever time you need. When you're ready, I'll help you pack and hire movers. I like your furniture better than mine. We can sell my stuff and—"

"Let's not do anything drastic yet. I think I'd like to keep my house until after the trial is over."

He dropped the hose on the grass and wiped his hands on his jeans. "It could be a year, maybe longer before there's even a trial, and who knows how long that'll drag out." He placed his hands on her upper arms. "I told you, I won't walk away without a fight."

"Hopefully it won't come to that," she said softly, her eyes holding hints of both relief and sadness.

What the hell did that mean? Was she already predicting they'd have issues? Less than an hour ago they'd been making love, making confessions and renewing their commitment to each other. Now she acted as if none of those things had happened.

"It won't," he said, giving her arms a gentle squeeze, before pulling her in for a hug.

He didn't understand what had happened, but assumed her current mood and the way she'd suddenly guarded herself had to do with the abortion. Maybe between dredging up those memories while still dealing with the aftermath of the bombings had been too much for her. From where he stood, their future looked bright. If he were to put himself in her position, he could understand her lack of commitment and her air of hopelessness. He could also understand why she might hesitate to leave Georgia. Moving to Chicago with him would take her away from her safety net. If only she realized *he* could be her safety net.

After pulling back, he tucked a lock of her hair behind her ear. "You need to eat something."

"I'm fine."

"You haven't had anything since yesterday evening and I noticed you'd picked at your dinner. Come on, I'll drive you to the grocery store. If we're staying until Monday, we'll need to stock your fridge."

Her eyes widened as if she were panicked by the thought of leaving. "I...I'm tired. Do you mind if I stay here and take a nap?"

Sensing she might want some time alone, he nodded. "Make me a list?"

"Sure," she said, crossing her arms and heading into the house.

While he put the hose away, he wondered if maybe he'd pushed her too hard and expected too much. Or maybe he was blowing her reaction out of proportion. Damn, he didn't know. Whatever the case, he didn't like the way she'd distanced herself from him. Not when they finally had the chance to be together again.

"Here's the list," she said, handing him a piece of paper when he walked back inside the house. "Thanks for going. Let me get my purse and give you some cash."

He shoved the list in his back pocket. "I've got it covered." He leaned forward and gave her a kiss. When she puckered up and kissed him back, some of his unease disappeared and he realized he needed to get out of his head and quit overanalyzing everything she said or did. With everything that had happened to her, Naomi was bound to have both good and bad days. He'd just have to make sure she knew he'd be there for her no matter what kind of day she was having.

After saying good-bye, he climbed into the SUV he'd rented that morning, then headed into town. As he drove through her quiet development and then through the quaint town, he had to admit to loving Woodbine. He loved Chicago, too. After spending years as a sheriff in a backwater town, city life appealed to him. He liked not knowing everyone he passed on the street, liked having variety when it came to restaurants and nightlife. He even liked his job.

He parked the rental outside the grocery store and shook his head. He'd been so damned angry with Ian for forcing him into working at CORE. But seeing how Ian and the other agents had worked quickly to resolve and help apprehend Hunnicutt, he realized he, once again, needed to set his pride and ego aside. CORE gave him opportunities he'd never have if he'd remained in Michigan. He loved solving cases, just not ones that involved his woman. The agency also gave him a sense of belonging. The last time he'd experienced that had been with the Marines.

As he headed into the grocery store, he decided it was time to stop butting heads with Ian. The man had set everything aside to go to bat for Naomi. For that alone he would be forever indebted to Ian.

Pulling out Naomi's shopping list, he grabbed a cart and began navigating the aisles. When he was halfway through the list, his cell phone rang. Assuming Naomi had forgotten to add something, he quickly retrieved the phone.

"I see you're at Naomi's house," Ian said.

Jake placed a loaf of bread in the cart. "How did you—Naomi's right. We'll need to remove her GPS chip." He sure as hell wouldn't like people knowing his every move. "Any word on Hunnicutt?"

The FBI still hadn't made it public that they'd arrested the bastard. Ian had contacted his Bureau connections and had been hounding them for information. Even though CORE had helped the Feds apprehend Hunnicutt and had stopped him from detonating any more bombs, they'd stonewalled Ian. When he'd spoken with Ian last night, his boss had been in a foul mood. Ian, like Jake and Naomi, and everyone else involved with the case, wanted answers.

"You need to bring Naomi back to Chicago. Rachel already has a jet waiting for you at Kingsland Airport."

The urgency and concern in Ian's voice had him stopping the cart in the middle of the aisle. "What's happened?"

"Jake, Hunnicutt was released yesterday morning."

I'm anxious to be alone with Rose... Maybe next time you'll reconsider running from me, not that I'll allow that to happen.

What Hunnicutt had said to Naomi in the warehouse apartment came back to him in a rush. With fear crawling under his skin, Jake left the shopping cart in the aisle and sprinted for the door. *The bastard had been free for over twenty-four hours.* "He knows Naomi's new ID, which would make it easy for him to-"

"Don't go there," Ian said. "Hunnicutt's not stupid. Going after Naomi now would be a huge risk for him. I still want you two here. If Hunnicutt does try anything, CORE will make sure she's protected."

After telling Ian they'd be at the airport in an hour, Jake climbed into the SUV and shoved the key in the ignition. Ian was right. Hunnicutt wasn't stupid, but he was arrogant. At this point, Naomi was the only one who had witnessed what the bastard had done. Considering the man had everything to lose—his billions, his company, his political career, he could also be desperate.

Maybe next time you'll reconsider running from me...

Hunnicutt was also obsessed.

Jake gripped the steering wheel tight as he sped out of the parking lot. His gut told him Hunnicutt wasn't finished with Naomi and that he'd eventually strike again. Until Hunnicutt was either convicted of his crimes or dead, she'd never be truly free. But this time around, she wouldn't be running and she wouldn't be alone.

Whether she liked it or not, she was coming home with him, where *he* could protect her.

CHAPTER 18

HARRISON'S SWEATY PALMS stuck to the plastic bag as he clutched the laptop to his chest. A few minutes ago they'd pulled alongside the curb, five doors down from Rose's house, and had been debating whether or not to make a move.

"There's no car in the driveway," Harrison said and stared at the house. "I'm telling you, she's alone."

"Garage closed." Vlad tapped the steering wheel. "Maybe he park there."

"Her car is in the garage. Remember?" When they went to her house yesterday, he'd gone to the service door on the side of the garage and had looked through the window. Rose had a two car garage, but her lawnmower, gardening equipment and a bike took up half the space, only her car would fit inside.

"Vlad remember."

He reached for the car door. "Then let's do this."

The Russian grabbed his arm. "Maybe she go with him?"

"We won't know unless we go to the house."

"And knock on front door?"

"I'm not going to break a window and scare the shit out of her. She'll call the cops and then we're cooked."

"Vlad don't like this."

"There's something new. You've been saying that since Monday." Still staring at Rose's house, he released a frustrated sigh. "Look. All we have to do is hand over the laptop, then it's off to Florida. I see a beach bar in your—holy shit, duck."

As Rose's front door opened, Harrison slid down the passenger seat. He glanced next to him and saw that Vlad had done the same. "She's getting her mail," Harrison said, peering out the window. "Now we know for sure she's home *and* alone."

"Fine. Harry go do good deed. Vlad honk horn if man return."

Harrison's stomach knotted with a mixture of eagerness and apprehension. What he was about to do could go one of two ways. Smooth or complicated. Based on the way Rose had acted at the warehouse, he was leaning toward smooth. She'd made it obvious she hated Hunnicutt just as much as he did. She'd also been very concerned over the bombings. The laptop was his insurance. If she so much as screamed or made their encounter complicated, it would remain with him.

"She back in house now. Well? Harry go or not?"

Harrison used the back of his hand to wipe the perspiration from his upper lip. Between the warm weather and his nerves, he couldn't stop sweating. "You'll honk?"

The Russian nodded. "Vlad honk, Harry run from back of house, get in car from street behind."

"Do you remember which house is behind hers?"

"Harry stalling. Go. Get done and over."

Harrison rolled up the window, then curved his fingers around the door handle.

"Remember to keep bag," Vlad reminded him.

Right. His prints were all over the plastic bag and could be easily lifted. "I will." He took a deep breath. "See you in five."

Vlad jerked him back and shoved his head down. "What the hell, Vlad?" he asked, trying to push the heavy Russian off of him.

"Honey Badger."

"What?" That couldn't be. The FBI couldn't have let him go.

"Look," Vlad said, easing up his hold. "Careful. See, behind bush near side window."

"He's going in through the back gate." Frustrated and angry at the bullshit turn of events, Harrison smacked the back of his head against the seat several times. "Shit, shit, shit."

"We go now," Vlad said, shifting the car into drive and hitting the gas.

"No," Harrison shouted and opened the car door.

Vlad slammed on the brakes. Harrison's body lurched forward and he smacked his hand on the dash, stopping his head from making impact.

"What the fuck," Vlad roared. "Harry stupid ass. Vlad don't want to deal with Honey—"

"Screw the goddamn Badger. Come on, Vlad. You were in the warehouse. You *know* what he'll do to her."

The Russian smashed his hand on the steering wheel. "She not Vlad's problem."

"Well, she's mine. How can I *not* do anything?"

"Fine. We drive, then stop and Harry call police."

"Brilliant. Fucking brilliant. And what do you think the cops will find when they get to her house? I'll tell you what, either a dead body or a missing woman. He set off all of those bombs and forced me to carve her name into my brother's stomach." He pounded his fist on the dashboard. "I had a gun pointed to my head and cut my twin, my flesh and blood's stomach. Hunnicutt can't get away with this. And those stupid, asshole Feds…damn it." He hit the dash again, then wiped a hand down his face. "Give me a gun."

"No."

"Fuck you, Vlad. Give me a damn gun."

The Russian glanced at him, then out the windshield. "Мать ублюдок," Vlad yelled and drove his fist into the roof of the car. Breathing hard and mumbling Russian, he reached into the back. "Here. Harry want gun to get revenge, Harry get what he want."

Harrison had no idea what Vlad placed in his hand, only that it was big, heavy and made him feel like Dirty Harry. "Is it loaded?"

"Yes."

His stomach seized. "Do I just aim and shoot?"

"Yes."

Harrison blew out a breath and looked to the house. Hunnicutt was likely inside by now doing God knows what to Rose.

"Harry want revenge and be hero. Now chance."

Gripping the gun in one hand and still clutching the laptop with the other, he leaned toward Vlad. "I'm no hero. Saving Rose won't make me one, not after what Hunnicutt made me do. Maybe you might be able to, but I can't just drive off and let him have her." Harrison set the gun in his lap, then reached for the handle and opened the car door. "If you want to go, then go. If I get caught helping Rose, then I'll probably get what I deserve."

"No."

"No, what?" he asked, hoping to God Vlad would help him. He had no problem killing Hunnicutt, but he'd love to have Vlad at his back. The Badger was unpredictable.

The Russian shifted the gear into PARK. "Vlad and Harry friends, yes?"

Nodding, Harrison glanced back to the house. Where the hell was the guy who was staying with Rose? "Yes. Probably the weirdest friendship I've ever had," he said and picked the gun up from his lap. "Vlad, I've got to go. I'm not going to argue with you while Hunnicutt's inside there." He pointed to the house. "How long does it take to slit someone's throat? Or strangle them?" After pushing the door open with his arm, he dropped his foot on the curb. "I couldn't save the bombing victims or Mickey. But I *can* help Rose."

Vlad reached into the back seat and pulled out another gun. "And Vlad can help Harry," he said, checking the weapon.

Thank God. "Good. How do you want to do this?"

"We go in the way of Honey Badger."

"Okay, then what? Do I just shoot him? Won't that be noisy?"

Vlad lifted a shoulder. "Harry rather use Vlad's knife?"

Harrison's heart pounded hard. He was going to kill a man of his own free will. His moral radar should be dinging right now, but he kept seeing the images from the bombings, kept picturing Rose crying and tied to the chair as she looked at Mickey's stomach.

"I wouldn't have a problem cutting him."

"Good. Here." Vlad unsheathed the knife at his belt and handed it to him. "Give Vlad gun before Harry shoot off foot."

As he reached across and exchanged weapons with Vlad, he glanced out the car's back window. "It's the guy. Holy shit, it's him," he said as a black SUV raced toward them.

Vlad yelled something in Russian while Harrison set the laptop on the passenger seat. "What Harry doing?"

"The right thing," he responded and slammed the door shut, then quickly stepped onto the curb, waving his arms.

The man they'd seen walking into Rose's house earlier slowed to a stop behind the Toronado, then jumped out of the vehicle and aimed a gun at Harrison. "Drop it and tell the other guy to exit the car. Slow. Hands raised."

Stepping onto the tree lawn, Harrison realized too late he still clutched Vlad's knife. With his heart racing fast, he slowly bent and set the knife on the grass. Vlad climbed out of the car and closed the door. With his hands raised, he narrowed his eyes at Harrison.

"Vlad tired of being right."

Harrison ignored the Russian. "Hunnicutt's inside with Rose," he called to the man. "We saw him on the side of her house and watched him go inside the gate. We think he went in through the back patio."

The man clenched his jaw, shifted his gaze toward Rose's house, then back to Harrison. "Get over by him," he said to Vlad. "Move. Quick."

The Russian rushed around the back of the car and met Harrison on the grass.

"We're telling the truth. If he went inside when we think he did, he's been with her for almost five minutes."

The man looked between them. "Harrison Fairclough and Vlad Aristov?"

Harrison nodded. "We came here to give Rose the computer I took from Hunnicutt's warehouse. Are you FBI?"

"No. Where's the computer?"

"In the car," Harrison nodded to the Toronado.

"How do I know you're not working for Hunnicutt?" the man asked, reaching in his pocket and pulling out his phone.

"Because he killed my brother. Look, the codes for the bombs are on the laptop. We also came to give Rose the locations of the three bombs Hunnicutt hasn't detonated. Yet." Why the hell was this guy wasting time? "Hunnicutt is dangerous. We need to get inside before he does something really bad to Rose."

"Did you detonate the bombs?"

"With a gun to my head or my brother's. Why the hell do you think we ran from the warehouse?"

"Hunnicutt's alone?"

"We think," Vlad said. "Hard to tell."

He slipped the phone back into his pocket. "Give me the knife."

Anxious to run into Rose's house and kill Hunnicutt, Harrison picked the knife and handed it over to the man.

After he tossed the knife into the SUV, the man slammed the car door. He looked to Vlad. "Do you have a weapon?"

"Yes."

"Where?"

"In car."

"Throw me the keys."

Vlad flashed Harrison another dirty look before tossing the keys.

The man pocketed them, and said, "I'll go through the patio door, Harrison, watch the front and, Vlad, you stay by the door leading into the garage from the side of the house. Those are the only exits. Holler if he tries to leave. If Hunnicutt's in there, he's not coming out. Let's go."

"Wait," Harrison said. "Aren't you going to call the police?"

"I used to be a sheriff, so we're good."

"But don't you want back up?"

Jake looked between Harrison and Vlad. "You two are my back up," he said and started to move.

"Aren't you worried we're going to run and leave you high and dry?"

"Do what you have to do," Jake said to Harrison, then he took off at a sprint between houses. He could give a shit if they disappeared on him. Naomi had told him all about the two men and he had no quarrel with them. His sole focuses were making sure no harm came to Naomi and killing Hunnicutt. The fucking FBI let him walk once and Jake refused to allow that to happen again.

He ran across a backyard, hopped a short, picket fence, then quickly moved through the next backyard, and then the next. One more home and he'd reach Naomi's. As he rushed across her neighbor's yard, a part of him hoped Harrison and Vlad would stick around just in case Hunnicutt left through the front or garage door. Especially if he had Rose.

Maybe next time you'll reconsider running from me…

Jake ran through the neighbor's flowerbed, then through the tall hedges at the exit of the backyard. When he reached Naomi's gate, he checked his surroundings and caught a glimpse of Harrison and Vlad running through the neighboring front yard and toward Naomi's.

With adrenaline pumping through him, he slid the lock and opened the gate. The yard was quiet. The glass of tea he'd drank earlier sat on the patio table. The sliding door was closed and he hoped to God it hadn't been locked. He didn't have a key to her house, and didn't want to break any windows and alert Hunnicutt.

Keeping his back against the vinyl siding, he crept along the bricks. When he reached the glass door, he peeked inside. The sheer drapes allowed him a view of the kitchen. Empty. He reached for the door handle. Gun raised and angled toward the kitchen table, he slid the door open, then crouched and moved inside behind the kitchen island.

Staying low to the floor, he eased his way through the room, then quickly rushed down the short hall off the kitchen toward Naomi's laundry room and office. After checking both rooms, he reentered the kitchen, scanned the living room and caught Harrison's silhouette through the frosted glass near the front door.

With the house eerily silent, his stomach and chest clenched with anxiety. There were only three more rooms to check, the guest bedroom and bathroom, and Naomi's room. He stopped at the guest room first, and after finding it empty, he looked inside the bathroom. When he reached the end of the hallway, he placed his ear on Naomi's closed bedroom door. Running water? Not from the sink or shower, but from the bathtub.

Had Harrison and Vlad lied to him or maybe been mistaken about Hunnicutt? Would the bastard really come to Woodbine right after the FBI released him?

Drawing in a deep breath, he reached for the door knob and turned. Keeping his gun raised, he eased the door open and peered inside the darkened room. A stream of light came from a partially broken blind hanging haphazardly from the window furthest from the bathroom. The nightstand near the window lay on its side. Glass, from the lamp that had once rested there, littered the hardwood floor. He glanced to the left. The bathroom door stood ajar, the sound of running water growing louder as he crept into the room.

Careful not to make a sound, he kept his steps light and moved to the wall adjacent to the bathroom door. Heart racing, he crept closer, and adjusted his grip on the gun. Scared of what he'd find once he opened the door and now kicking himself in the ass for not calling for back up, he drew in a deep breath. Fuck it. Hunnicutt wasn't leaving alive. The bastard would never hurt Naomi or anyone else again.

Jake took a step back, raised the gun and kicked open the door.

Naomi.

His throat tightened and his legs grew weak. His arms shook, while terror and rage tore through him and settled deep in his gut. He aimed the gun at Hunnicutt's head. The man sat on the marbled edge of the bathtub, his gun also on the ledge and within arm's reach. Instead of going for the gun, Hunnicutt gave him a smug smile and smoothed the damp hair away from Naomi's pale face.

The bath water, reminding him of the color of pink roses, came up to her collarbone. Blood trickled from her nose to the duct tape covering her mouth. She whimpered and groaned. Her tear-soaked eyes were on Jake and filled with a mixture of agony and horror.

Hunnicutt turned off the faucet. "I am so tired of being interrupted." He looked to Naomi and reached into the tub.

"Don't touch her."

"I already have…with a butcher's knife," he said, moving her left leg until her knees and hands jutted from the water. Duct tape bound her calves together. The tape had also been wrapped around her opened palms and circled her lower thighs, just above the knee, making her arms immobile. Blood oozed from the horizontal slices running from the inside of her wrists and flowed into the bath.

Jake kept his aim steady. "You're fucking dead," he said, curving his finger around the trigger, then froze. He slid his gaze to the mirror above the counter. Vlad stood behind him, the gun in his hand pressed against the back of Jake's skull.

Hunnicutt chuckled and pressed Naomi's bound legs back into the water. "Vlad. I knew I could count on you," he said, shaking water from his hand. "Kill him." He looked at Naomi with disgust. "She should be dead shortly and then we can leave. Rose was always a bleeder." He ripped the duct tape from her mouth. "Isn't that right?"

An overwhelming sense of helplessness filled Jake with anguish. The woman he loved lay in a tub of her own blood, dying. He could still put a bullet in Hunnicutt's head. But if Vlad also fired, who would know to come for Naomi? With the way Hunnicutt had slashed her wrists, the bastard was right. She wouldn't make it for very long. Damn it, why hadn't he called for backup? He'd been hell bent on making sure

Hunnicutt didn't leave alive, had stupidly assumed Vlad and Harrison were on his and Naomi's side. Harrison might have been, he'd acted sincere. Considering Vlad had a gun to his head, he figured Harrison was already dead, betrayed by the man who'd helped him escape.

"Don't," Naomi gasped and let out another cry. "Vlad, please help us."

"My men are loyal. He won't help you," Hunnicutt said. "If I recall, you begged Ric, too. Just before he helped removed my child from your womb."

When Jake fingered the trigger, ready to take the risk and shoot a bullet in the center of Hunnicutt's forehead, the bastard smiled at him. "Vlad, keep the gun on our would-be hero, but don't kill him yet. I'm guessing we have another twenty to thirty minutes before Rose bleeds to death—and I want to make sure she's dead before we leave. Besides, thanks to the way the FBI stormed into my warehouse, Rose and I haven't had a chance to catch up yet. Eight years is a long time to be apart. Tell me, Rose…is this man your lover?" When Naomi remained silent, Hunnicutt's smile grew. "By the bloodlust in his eyes I'm going to make a solid assumption and take that as a yes. Interesting. Well, lover, did you know Rose used to be my whore?" He reached back into the tub and grabbed Naomi's breast through her t-shirt.

Her faced twisted in pain and outrage. She thrashed her body and raised her bound legs. The gashes along her forearms bled profusely, as if the movement increased the blood flow. Jake didn't know much about the human body, and had no idea if remaining still would slow the bleeding. "Naomi, stop," he said, worried she was causing more damage to herself.

Crying, she drew her knees toward her chest, then stilled. Blood continued to ooze from her wounds and trickle into the tub and onto Hunnicutt's hand at her breast.

"That's disgusting," the bastard said, using the towel on his lap to clean his hand. "By the way, lover, do you even know her real name?"

When he met Naomi's gaze, his stomach tightened with

dread. The fear and apology in her eyes was killing him. Their situation was fucked, but he didn't want her giving up on him. Based on the crash course Rachel had given him on narcissism, along with what Naomi had told him about Hunnicutt, Jake doubted he could talk their way out of this. But Hunnicutt acted as if he was in the mood to talk. Good, let him. Jake could use this time to figure out a way to save Naomi.

"Yes, I know her real name."

"Don't answer any of his questions," Naomi said on a sob.

"Oh, Rose. Does it really matter?" Hunnicutt shook his head and looked Jake directly in the eyes. "I'm going to kill him anyway. Before I do, I think you both deserve to suffer."

"I've suffered enough," Naomi shouted. "You've taken everything away from me."

"Everything but your current lover, which I'll rectify momentarily. Before I have Vlad splatter his brains all over the bathroom, I'd like your lover to know a few interesting details about you."

"He knows all about you and what you did to me and my family."

Hunnicutt kept his eyes on Jake. "So she told you how she used to love to get down on her knees and suck my dick?"

Jake had been holding the gun steady for several minutes. The urge to lower his arm was there, but he fought it and the need to pull the trigger.

"Or how she used to love to bend over and let me fuck her?"

Clenching his jaw, he did his damnedest to keep his temper in check. Earlier, Naomi had admitted to having sex with Hunnicutt. From the way she'd talked, he'd suspected the encounter had been bad and had refused to push her for answers as to *how* bad. His imagination had already given him enough answers, and part of him had feared knowing the reality would have been much worse.

"Yes," Hunnicutt continued with a smile. "She was a lovely whore. But then she ended up pregnant. Does it bother you to know she carried my child?"

Jake looked to Naomi. Her face had grown paler, her breathing shallower. He had no idea how much blood she'd lost or how long before the bleeding would result in complications or death. "No. Her past means nothing to me," he said, wondering if giving Vlad a solid throat punch would do the trick. Without looking at it, he remembered the gun on the ledge and played out the scene. Him hitting Vlad, Hunnicutt picking up the gun and shooting.

"Interesting. Chivalrous, really. Personally, I couldn't tolerate such a thing. Why, just the other day when my wife threatened to have an affair with the pool boy, I told her I'd have his dick cut off and stuffed down her throat." He chuckled. "And that threat was only over an affair. If she'd become pregnant by my pool boy?" He shook his head and let out a low whistle. "It wouldn't be pretty." He stroked Naomi's hair, then grabbed a fistful. "Rose knows all about that. Tell him. Tell your lover how I had you bound to a table in the cellar of my home. How Ric and the good doctor spread your legs, reached into your vagina and destroyed the life you carried."

Naomi shivered and arched her neck. Although her hands and arms had started to grow numb, and breathing had started to become an effort, the sharp pain to her scalp served as a reminder that Christian hadn't won yet.

"Give your lover the gory details. Explain to him how you could never have his children. That *I* wouldn't allow him or any man to have you."

Thanks for telling me.

To think she'd let Jake's words bother her. Looking at him now, seeing the misery and distress etched on his handsome face, along with the love and fear in his eyes, she'd let those four words affect her judgment. Instead, she should have focused on his actions and on the three words that mattered the most.

I love you.

"He knows," she said, her tongue thick, her mouth dry.

"He knows what?" Christian taunted her. "Say it Rose. Say

he knows I branded you as mine."

Tears welled in her eyes and slid down her cheeks. Her stomach grew nauseous and she tasted bile. Lightheaded, she closed her eyes. "He knows the only man I've ever loved was him."

"And Naomi knows I love her, no matter what you did to her."

Jake's strong, confident and soothing voice gave her a sudden dose of clarity. She forced her heavy lids open and met his eyes.

"You didn't brand her, you violated her. And because you're a cowardly pussy, you had to pay people to do it for you."

Christian stood. "How dare you—"

"Yep, a pathetic pussy who couldn't handle being rejected by a woman."

"You're dead," Christian said, his tone seething with rage. "Vlad, kill him. This conversation is over."

"Not quite," a man called, his voice breathless.

Naomi looked to the door, just as Harrison stepped into the bathroom wielding one of her steak knives.

"What took so long?" Vlad asked, keeping the gun to Jake's head.

"You said we weren't sticking around after we killed Honey Badger, so I had to break into the car to get the laptop."

Vlad rolled his eyes. "Fucking cowboy."

"Boy scout," Harrison said, then looked to her. His eyes widened. "Holy shit, Rose needs to get to a hospital."

Yes, she definitely needed medical care. She knew the symptoms for blood loss and had quite a few. She also knew with proper treatment she could survive this, but not if everyone kept standing around bullshitting as if they were at a bar and not in her bloody bathroom.

"Tell Vlad to take his damned gun off my head," Jake demanded, his eyes trained on Christian.

"Seriously, Vlad." Harrison asked. "This wasn't part of the plan."

Vlad shrugged. "Honey Badger Harry's kill."

She shivered again. Between the cold water, her dropping body temperature and bound arms and legs, her limbs were growing as numb as her forearms. At this point she didn't care who killed Christian, so long as the deed was done. He proved today he would never let her rest in peace until she was—

Christian's arm shot toward the gun he'd left on the ledge of the tub. Jake lunged and knocked the gun away.

Vlad quickly aimed the weapon he'd held to Jake's head at Christian. "Don't move."

While Christian held his hands in the air, Jake slid his gun into the clip attached to his belt. He grabbed a towel off the rack and pulled her from the tub. "Oh, my God," he said, concern cracking his voice. He knelt to the floor and began drying her, careful to avoid the gashes along her wrists. "I'm calling 911."

"No," she said, her teeth chattering. "Not until he's dead."

Christian let out a bark of laughter. "You people are the pathetic pussies."

Jake cradled her to his chest with one arm and turned to face him. "I don't think so," he said, reaching for his gun. In a split second, he had it trained on Christian.

"Really? How are you four going to explain this? All of you want me dead. Lover boy could have called the police before barging into the bathroom. Vlad also had ample time, but my Russian friend wouldn't take the risk, would you? Don't bother answering. The question was rhetorical—not that you have a clue what that means. The only reason I kept you in my employment was because you looked scary and could throw a mean punch. Too bad you aren't mute. Because when you open your mouth you sound like a fucking idiot with your Vlad this and Vlad that. But here's the thing, *Vlad*. I pay you very well. You redirect your gun elsewhere and I could pretend none of this happened. You'll be able to continue to send money to your family. I'll keep you in the country without you having to worry about being sent back home. I *know* you don't want that." Christian cocked his head to the side. "Yes, if I recall the Russian mafia still has money on your head." He lowered one arm and looked at his fingers as if studying his cuticles. "I guess you shouldn't have slept with the mob boss's wife."

Vlad's stony expression never wavered.

"I can make sure you don't go back there. Get me out of here and you have my word."

"He's...lying." Naomi's stomach cramped and she let out a groan. "Jake, wrap my wrists."

Jake produced a knife and cut the duct tape. "Harrison, get some towels from the linen closet."

"Are you people serious?" Hunnicutt asked with a sarcastic chuckle. "Rose is bleeding to death and you're too worried about me to save her?" He scratched his chin. "In a way, that doesn't surprise me. I usually am the most important person in the room."

"You're a fucking asshole is what you are," Harrison said, handing the towels to Jake. He raised the steak knife. "The only one who finds you of any importance is yourself. Do you not even see that?"

"Why Harry waste time?" Vlad asked. "Harry want to be hero. Now is chance. The woman, she needs saving. Honey Badger needs killing."

Jake wrapped an arm around her, grabbed the gun he'd set on the floor and aimed it at Christian. "Gladly."

"No," Vlad roared. "Harry, you want this. For Mickey, no?"

Harrison's chest rose and fell. He used his shoulder to wipe his mouth, then blinked several times. Raising the steak knife, he nodded. "Yes. For Mickey." His chin quivered, but he clenched his jaw. "You made me press a button and kill all of those people." His body shook and tears ran down his face. "You made me cut my twin brother. Now I'm going to cut you."

When Harrison didn't move, Christian laughed. "Now I'm going to cut you," he mocked. "Again. Who's pathetic? All of you want me dead and no one has the balls to—"

The deafening gunshot blast reverberated through the bathroom. Naomi tensed and jerked. Out of instinct, she reached for Jake, who quickly covered her with his body. Pain resonated from the wounds along her arms and shot straight to her head. Blinking away the wave of dizziness, she shook her head and looked over Jake's shoulder. Vlad remained as he'd been, gun raised and pointing at Christian. Harrison stood a few feet from him, the small knife wrapped in a fist, his mouth gaping, his eyes also on Christian. She followed his gaze and stared at the blood trickling from the bullet hole in the center of the bastard's head.

She turned away and pressed her forehead to Jake's chest. His heart beat fast as he kissed the top of her head. "It's over," he murmured.

"Is it?" She looked up at him. "I'm not sorry Christian's dead. Honestly, I wish his death wouldn't have been so quick and easy. But he was right. How are we going to explain this?"

Vlad lowered his weapon. "Honey Badger need to shut the fuck up. Vlad grow tired of Talky Tina."

"Chatty Cathy," Harrison said, running a hand through his hair. "Damn it, Vlad. *I* was supposed to—"

Vlad grabbed Harrison's arm and raised it. "With kiddy knife?"

"Enough," Jake shouted. After he shoved his gun back into the belt holster, he lifted her in his strong arms. "Vlad, give me the gun."

The enormous Russian turned and shook his head. "No."

"I need to get Naomi to a hospital and don't have time for this. Vlad, I don't give a shit about your past or who you worked for. You cut Naomi's ropes back at the warehouse and gave her the freedom to run. But you also just murdered an unarmed man."

"Who slit Rose's wrists," Harrison said. "That's got to count for something."

"In my mind it certainly does, but Naomi's right. We need to be able to explain this."

"No we. Vlad and Harry leave now."

"I've got your keys."

Vlad shrugged. "We take woman's car."

"Then I'll have to tell the FBI, because you *know* they'll be all over this, that you two came in here with the intent to kill Hunnicutt. And they'll believe me. That bullet in Hunnicutt's head won't match one coming from my gun. No matter what Hunnicutt's done, you'll both be wanted for murder."

"We were trying to help you," Harrison said with exasperation. "Now you're going to turn us over—"

"Would you all just stop," Naomi shouted. Her head hurt and the nausea had become worse. Her wounds weren't life threatening yet, but they hurt like a hell. "Listen to Jake. Vlad, give him the damned gun. And Jake, give Vlad his keys."

Jake shifted her in his arms, then reached in his pocket and tossed the keys to Vlad. In return, Vlad handed him the gun.

"Good. Now will someone please call—"

"Cover your ears," Jake said, raised the gun and fired. The marble tile above Christian's head shattered. Vlad and Harrison both ducked, then looked to Jake. "Sorry, but it'd be hard to explain how I shot Hunnicutt, with the unregistered gun I carry, without having gun residue on my hand."

Oh, my God. He was taking the blame. "Jake," she gasped. "I don't want the FBI coming after you for this."

"The only thing they could get me for is owning an unregistered weapon."

"So does this mean you're letting us go?" Harrison asked, taking a step toward the door.

"Only Vlad." Jake glanced to her and she caught the regret in his eyes before he turned his attention back to the men. "Sounds like he's been running for a long time. I'd rather see him keep running than sent back to Russia."

Vlad nodded and released a deep sigh. "Vlad would die."

"And I won't?" Harrison threw his hands in the air. "They'll give me the death penalty. Once it's made public, my name will become a synonym for terrorism."

Jake set Vlad's gun on the ledge of the tub and, still holding her, reached into his pocket. "Naomi told me Hunnicutt forced you to detonate the bombs," he said, sitting them next to the gun.

"But I helped set up the signals to the detonators. At the time, I thought we were setting up security devices. If I'd known they were bombs, I wouldn't have taken the job with Mickey."

Jake dialed 911 but didn't hit send. "And you were the one who made sure someone would figure out where the signals were coming from."

"Yeah." Harrison stood straighter. "I had to find a way to stop Hunnicutt."

"You were a victim in this, too," Naomi said. "Why did you come here?"

"To bring you the laptop and tell you where the last three bombs were located."

"You did the right thing." Jake thankfully sent the call through. After he spoke with the police dispatcher, he pocketed the phone. "Give yourself up and I'll do everything I can to help you."

"Vlad agree. Harry not fugitive."

Harrison's face contorted in confusion and fear. "I don't want to go back to prison."

"Harry rather spend life running? Not good. Vlad know this well."

"I do, too," Naomi said. "Do right by yourself, Harrison. Trust us."

"I…" Harrison dropped the knife, shoved both hands through his hair and held them at the back of his head. He looked to Vlad. "So this is it."

"This it." Vlad moved for the door. "Police on way. Vlad must go. Now."

"Wait."

Vlad stopped.

"Why did you kill him?"

Turning, Vlad gave Harry a sympathetic smile. "Harry think he a murderer because Honey Badger make him blow up bombs. Vlad has killed many before. Harry no murderer and no killer." He took a step and placed a hand on Harrison's shoulder.

Harrison's eyes filled with tears as he nodded. "Thanks, man. You better go before the cops come."

Vlad shook Harrison's hand, then pulled him in for a quick bear hug. "до свидания друг." He stepped back and waved. "Good-bye, friend," Vlad said, then disappeared around the corner.

Naomi used the towel around her wrist to wipe her eyes and nose. Jake held her tight and kissed the top of her head. "Police and ambulance will be here any minute. Let's get our story straight."

PART IV

For last year's words belong to last year's language
And next year's words await another voice.
And to make an end is to make a beginning.

—T.S. Eliot

CHAPTER 19

Marymount Hospital, Brunswick, Georgia
7:38 p.m. Eastern Daylight Saving Time

JAKE PULLED A chair next to Naomi's hospital bed and stared at her beautiful, sleeping face. She'd been out of surgery for several hours, and had awoken briefly about fifty minutes ago, then had promptly fallen back to sleep. Between the anesthetic and everything that had happened this week, he hoped she'd sleep for the next twelve hours. Her body and mind needed to heal.

His heart aching for her, he smoothed the hair away from her face. Knowing Naomi, she'd never overcome the guilt, but, with time, he hoped she'd be able to move forward and learn to love life now that she was finally free of Hunnicutt.

A soft rap at the door had him turning. "Ian," he said quietly and rose from the chair. "What are you doing here?"

His boss stepped into the room and looked over Naomi's sleeping form. "How is she?"

"Two hours of surgery and eighty plus stitches later, her radial artery and her median and superficial radial nerves are repaired. The doctor says she'll be able to resume most of her regular activities in about four months. In the meantime, she'll need physical therapy."

"I know people and will help her find the best therapist."

Ian glanced at him. "She *is* moving to Chicago, correct?"

"That's still up in the air." Not wanting to disturb Naomi, he motioned Ian toward the door and into the hall. "I'm sure you didn't fly to Georgia to check on Naomi."

Ian let out a deep breath and crossed his arms over his chest. After glancing around the empty hallway, he said, "One of my agents killed a man today—with an unregistered gun."

"Yeah, about that. I got the gun off a guy when I was living in Michigan. I never got around to registering it."

"You were sheriff. Part of your office's job was to approve permits for firearms."

"Right. Like I said, I meant to take care of it."

Ian pinned him with a hard stare. "Who'd you get the gun from?"

"A trucker passing through my county. I can't remember who he drove for, but his name was Bob Smith."

Ian arched a brow. "I spoke with the Director of the FBI. He wondered why you not only had that particular gun with you, but chose to use it as opposed to the one on your belt. I admit, I wondered that myself."

Since Ian hadn't exactly asked him a question, he chose to ignore it and keep his lies to a minimum. "Did the director say what would happen to Harrison Fairclough?"

Ian cracked a smile. "Thanks to Fairclough, the last three bombs have been found. Had he come forward with the computer and given his statement Monday, I don't believe the FBI would have ever released Hunnicutt. Regardless, Fairclough filled in the blanks and it's clear anyone who was involved is either dead or in custody."

"Will Harrison be charged for his part in the bombings?"

"His attorney said he thinks Fairclough is going to take the deal the Attorney General offered him. Two years for conspiracy, minimum security federal prison. He'll be out in nine months."

Club Fed. Not a bad deal. "What, did you speak with his attorney?"

"Of course. I hired him."

While it was on the tip of his tongue to ask Ian why, he refrained. From what he had heard and experienced, Ian never did anything without an agenda. Whatever, his plans for Harrison wouldn't happen for several months anyway. Right now, his focus was on Naomi's health and making sure he stayed clear of a criminal conspiracy charge in Hunnicutt's murder.

"As for Christian Hunnicutt," Ian continued. "Based on his attempt to murder Naomi, and between what she told the FBI, along with Fairclough's statement, it's clear Hunnicutt was the mastermind behind the bombings. According to the director, the FBI is going to further investigate Hunnicutt's actions during the months prior to the bombings. I'm not sure how much will be made public though. Hunnicutt had many acquaintances in very high places. I highly doubt the Vice President wants to have his name associated with a domestic terrorist." Ian checked his watch. "The director and I go way back. He's the type of man you don't want to cross. Hunnicutt might be dead, but I believe Fitzgerald will do everything in his power to destroy what's left of Hunnicutt's name."

"I'm sure that will give the victims' families some sense of closure," Jake said, with little credence in his own words. He never believed in closure. Knowing who had murdered their loved one and the reasons behind the senseless killing wouldn't bring the victim back.

"Let's hope," Ian said. "I need to be at the airport."

"Heading back to Chicago?"

"Florida, for a long weekend."

Jake eyed his boss. Ian claimed he'd made the pit stop in Georgia over an unregistered weapon, and he wasn't buying it. "Why did you really come here?"

"Again, one of my agents was involved in killing a perpetrator." He held up a finger. "One more thing about that, how is it that the police found your vehicle parked in the street more than five house away from Naomi's."

Shit. Ian was trying to blow holes in their story. As his heart sped up, he kept his demeanor calm. "It's like I told the FBI and the local PD… After I talked with you, I was upset and worried. I've only been to Naomi's twice and most of the homes on her street are a ranch-style like hers." He shrugged. "When I pulled up, all I kept thinking about was how I was going to explain to her that the man who had been stalking her and killing innocent people—in her name—was now free. It wasn't until I heard her scream that I realized I was at the wrong house."

"Well, it's a good thing you happened to hear her five houses away. It's also a good thing Harrison Fairclough happened to be there ready to hand over the computer and himself."

"I don't believe that was Harrison's intent," he said, sticking to their story. "When I got to the house, I went in through the opened gate. Harrison was there in a panic, telling me he heard Naomi scream, too. Together we went inside through the kitchen. I guess that's when he picked up the steak knife—I don't know, I was ahead of him and rushing into Naomi's room. When I saw Hunnicutt with her…" He glanced away, the memory of Naomi bound in a tub with her wrists slit brought back the fear and agony. "As soon as Hunnicutt reached for his weapon, I shot him." He looked at Ian. "I'm sure anyone in my situation would have reacted the same way."

"Because it was self-defense. You or him, and if you die, so does Naomi."

"Exactly."

Ian checked his watch again. "I'm glad we have that straightened out. Your unregistered gun will not be returned to you. You will have to pay a fine—out of your pocket, not CORE's. If you have any other unregistered weapons, I suggest you take care of them properly."

"Yes, of course," Jake said, relieved. He'd been worried the evidence would leave a trail of doubt and the Feds would investigate further. He hadn't expected to worry about Ian, though. Then again, his boss was so damned by the book.

"Then I'll see you at the office on Monday. I still have that cold case I want you to work on."

"Can we make it Tuesday?" he asked, hoping he wasn't pushing his luck. "The doctor said Naomi would be discharged Friday. I'd like to give her a couple of days before travelling."

"Tuesday it is." Ian took a step forward and offered his hand. "I'm grateful Naomi is alive and Hunnicutt is no longer a threat. Good job."

Jake shook his hand. "Thank you, sir."

Ian's grip tightened as he pulled Jake closer. "But," he began, his voice low and intense, "don't ever break protocol and go rogue on me again. The FBI and Woodbine PD might buy your bullshit story, but I don't. I find it fascinating that a trucker named Bob Smith just so happened to sell you a Russian handgun and Hunnicutt's Russian bodyguard is still missing."

"I don't know anything about that," Jake said, looking Ian directly in the eyes.

"Of course you don't." Ian smiled and released his hand. "Give Naomi my best," he said and, with a nod, he headed down the hallway.

After Ian turned down a corner and disappeared from sight, Jake puffed his cheeks and let out a deep breath. Shit, Ian knows. Based on his parting words, he wasn't going to do anything about it. That assurance slowed his pounding heart, but didn't stop his mind from racing. Were there any other tracks they hadn't covered? Could the FBI discover evidence they hadn't thought about and find a way to bring him up on murder charges?

"Jake?" Naomi called.

He rushed into her hospital room. "Hey," he said with a smile and approached her bed. "How you feeling?"

"Like someone shoved white hot pokers into my wrists."

He moved toward the door. "I'll get the nurse to bring you pain medication."

"No, wait."

After pulling the chair closer to her bed, he took a seat. "What do you need?"

"Was that Ian I heard in the hall?"

"Yeah. He stopped by to see how you're doing." Worry lines creased her forehead. He reached over and smoothed them away. "He also had a few questions." Since the two of them had had enough lies between them, he refused to hide the truth and told her about their conversation and his concerns.

"I don't think you should worry," she said, the relief clear on her face. "He *is* expecting you to be back at work on Tuesday. I'm glad he's giving you an extra day. Considering I can't move my wrists and hands, you'll be on your own with the packing."

"I'm sure I can manage a couple of suitcases," he said, not wanting to be presumptuous and assume she was ready to move in with him permanently.

She gave him a tired smile. "My kitchen dishes aren't going to fit in a suitcase."

Hope had his heart pounding again. "Remember I have a thick skull. Does this mean you're coming to Chicago, for good?"

"For the best reason." When she tried to raise her arm, she winced and squeezed her eyes shut. "Damn it. I want to touch you."

He moved to the edge of the bed and stroked her cheek. "There'll be plenty of time for that," he said, wishing he could hold her and show her how much he loved her. "In the meantime, you need your rest and pain meds." He gave her a lingering kiss, then pressed his forehead against hers.

"I love you so much," she whispered. "Thank you for not giving up on me."

"I couldn't give up on us." His hands shook as he gently cupped her cheeks. "I love you, Naomi. You're all I've ever wanted."

"Good." Her smile filled his palms. "Because I was thinking about doing one last name change."

"Brunhilde?" he asked, grinning.

She chuckled. "Not quite. How about Mrs. Naomi Tyler?"

"That has a nice ring to it. But isn't the man supposed to be the one who proposes?"

"Then what are you waiting for?"

He looked into her beautiful blue eyes and peace settled in his soul. He'd spent so many wasted years trying to forget her, to hate her for leaving him, when all he'd ever wanted was to have her back in his arms. Now he would have her as his wife. His heart soared with the prospect of their future. There might not be any kids, but there would be the two of them. And that was enough.

"I love you more than anything," he said, before giving her quick kiss.

"Even when I'm bossy?"

"Especially when you're bossy. Naomi, will you be my wife?"

Tears filled her eyes and she gave him a watery smile. "Yes," she said with a catch to her breath. "I love you, too. Forever and always."

Two month later...
Bloomington, Indiana
2:30 p.m. Central Daylight Saving Time

Vincent D'Matto handed his wife a package decorated with Noah's Ark wrapping paper and a giant pink bow. "Last one," he said, just as Benny toddled over and wiped his frosting covered fingers on Vince's khaki pants.

Anna looked at the stain and shook her head. "At least he stopped eating crayons."

While the women in the room chuckled, Anna rested the box on her pregnant belly and opened the card. "This is from Aunt Faye," she said, tearing off the wrapping paper. After she lifted the box's lid, she pushed the tissue paper aside and let out a dreamy sigh. "It's darling." She held up a pretty pink dress. "I love it."

With two boys, they'd been living with a masculine color palette. Now Vince was in pink overload. Not that he minded.

They needed a little pink in their lives.

"Thank you for throwing us this shower," Anna said to her sister, and then she thanked the rest of their twenty plus guests. "How about some cake before Benny eats it all?"

As the women made their way into the kitchen for cake, Vince leaned over and kissed his wife on the cheek. "Today was nice," he said, placing his hand on her stomach. Beneath his palm, the baby kicked. "Holy cow, did you feel that?"

Anna winced. "Uh, yeah. From the inside. With the way she's been moving, I think our girl will be kicking a soccer ball before she even starts walking."

"I can't wait to meet her," he said, gently pressing Anna's belly hoping for another kick. "I know she'll be beautiful, like her mother. I just can't wait to see how beautiful."

"And healthy," Anna added.

Yes, and healthy. The cysts the doctor had found on their baby's brain had, as Anna's obstetrician assured them initially, gone away on their own. In less than six weeks, they would have a perfectly healthy little girl to complete their family.

Vince had always considered himself fortunate, but now he knew what it felt like to be blessed.

Anna's cousin, Gina, who had flown in from Albany, walked over carrying two plates of cake. "Here you go," she said, handing them each a plate.

Anna grabbed Gina's hand. "I'm so thrilled you were able to come today. I've missed seeing you."

Gina patted his wife's hand, then knelt in front of their chairs. "I wish I could have come two months ago."

"Your house was under construction, Mario was travelling and you have four kids," Anna said. "Your life is so busy, it makes my head spin just thinking about how you deal with it."

"Vodka." Gina chuckled, then sobered. "Seriously, though. I was so worried about you guys. When I saw that delivery truck on the news..." She blew out a breath. "What happened that day?" she asked and looked directly at him.

A miracle. "Well, I obviously didn't blow up," he said with a grin. When neither Anna nor Gina smiled, he shrugged.

"Sorry, bad joke."

Anna elbowed him. "Extremely bad."

He kissed her cheek. "Anyway, I was in a hurry to get into the hospital and make Anna's ultrasound. But nothing was going right. Traffic was bad, I couldn't find a parking spot, and then when I was getting ready to lock the truck, I accidently knocked a box off the shelf. I think there was white wine in the box. Whatever it was, it was getting all over the place. So, there I am, already running late and on my hands and knees trying to clean the mess up before it ruined the other packages."

His chest and stomach tightened. Whenever he thought back to those final seconds, he was overwhelmed with a combination of anxiety and gratefulness. "Then I had this moment. I don't know what to call it or if maybe I just imagined it, but something inside me said, what are you doing? You need to go. Now."

Gina nodded. "Mario doesn't believe me, but I have psychic moments like that."

Vince was with Gina's husband. He didn't believe she or anyone else was psychic, but he did believe in gut intuition. And that afternoon when he'd been panicking about being late for the ultrasound, then panicking even more over spilled wine, his stomach had knotted so bad, he'd thought maybe he was having an ulcer attack. In that moment, he realized he had to go, leave the truck and go to his wife. She needed him. Anna and the baby she carried were more important than spilled wine or even his job.

"So," he continued, "I dropped a wad of paper towels on the spill, climbed out of the truck and locked the door. I ran up the steps, and just after I entered through the hospital's revolving door, my truck exploded."

"Oh. My. God," Gina gasped. "If you would have stayed in your truck even ten seconds longer…" She shook her head. "I had no idea it was that close."

"I didn't either until after we left the ultrasound room," Anna said and elbowed him again.

"Wait." Gina held up a hand. "Vince, you actually made it

to the ultrasound?"

Hell, yeah, he did. He'd made a promise to his wife that he'd be there, that whatever the results they'd work through them together.

"When he walked into the room, he was a sweaty mess," Anna answered for him. "His clothes were dusty and I remember thinking, geez, he must've run to make it on time."

"Yeah, the explosion knocked the glass out of the hospital entrance and knocked me on my butt. For a second, I sat there shocked. I mean I was *just* inside the truck."

Gina made the sign of the cross. "Thank God you weren't."

"That was my first thought. My second, was that I needed to get to Anna. With all the explosions that day, I didn't know if there'd be another one, maybe in the main hospital. Figuring they might evacuate the building, I wanted to be there for her."

His wife set the untouched plate of cake on the end table next to her and took his hand. "After he walked into the room, a nurse rushed in and said what happened. I looked at Vince and…" Tears misted in her eyes.

He propped the plate on his stained khakis and held her hand with both of his. "It's in the past."

"I know, but when I think of how close I came to losing you."

"I'm sorry I brought this up," Gina said, her tone laced with regret. "I didn't mean to dredge up bad memories."

"It's okay." Anna sniffed and sent her cousin a small smile. "Every time we talk about the explosion, it makes me more grateful for everything we have and less worried about what we don't."

That was the truth. Vince gave Anna's hand a squeeze. For months before the explosion, he'd been so caught up in worrying about money, bills, work, his college courses and giving his family a bigger house, he'd forgotten what was truly important. He'd forgotten to appreciate the gifts God had given him—his beautiful wife, his sons and a healthy new baby on the way.

An hour later, after everyone had left and his sons were

watching TV, Vince asked Anna to come to their bedroom.

"What's going on?" she asked.

"I have one last gift for you and it wasn't something I wanted everyone else to see."

She laughed. "Good Lord, Vince, the kids are still up and I'm as big as a house. You can't possibly want to fool around right now."

He hadn't thought about bringing her upstairs for sex, but now that she mentioned it... He shook his head. *Later.* "I don't care how big you get, I'll always want you. For now, open this. And if you play your cards right, after the boys go to bed I'll show you exactly how much I want you."

Chuckling, she took the envelope he'd opened earlier that morning, and slid out the contents. His smile grew as her eyes widened. "Is this real?" she asked.

He moved behind Anna. As he wrapped his arms around her, he looked over her shoulder. "Very real," he said, staring at the five hundred thousand dollar check signed by Ms. Liliana Hunnicutt.

CORE Offices, Chicago, Illinois
3:47 p.m. Central Daylight Saving Time

Dante Russo sat in the corner of CORE's evidence and evaluation room eating the cake Ian's daughter had made for Rachel's surprise baby shower. Normally he loved anything sweet and anything Celeste baked. Unfortunately, being surrounded by baby stuff had the rich chocolate and banana cream cake souring in his mouth. While he was thrilled for Owen and Rachel, he couldn't help the stab of jealousy or the unwanted memories of the baby shower his ex-wife's family had given them six years ago.

Ian entered the room wearing a scowl. He locked eyes with Dante and headed in his direction, waving off Celeste's offer of cake. Dante cracked a smile when she stuck her tongue out at her father's back, then watched as she took her four-month-old daughter from her husband, and his coworker, John Kain.

"Now that everyone has cake, let's start opening presents," Celeste's sister, Eden, said, propping her six-month-old daughter onto her hip.

As Owen handed a very pregnant Rachel the first gift, Ian stopped in front of Dante. "I'd like to know who authorized turning my evidence and evaluation room into a showroom for Babies 'R' Us."

"That would be your daughter and Eden."

"I see." Ian scowled and glanced around the room. "What the hell is that thing sitting on top of my twenty thousand dollar printer?"

"That would be a diaper pail."

Ian let out an exasperated sigh. "If a client walked into the office they'd think we're running a daycare as opposed to a criminal investigation agency. Now I know why Hudson was so eager to take on his last assignment."

"I highly doubt Hud chose to go to Cleveland to avoid a baby shower." Since Hudson had married Eden, he'd done everything he could to fight for cases within driving distance from Chicago. The former CIA agent doted on his wife and six-month-old daughter and hated being away from them. Dante knew for a fact the only reason Hudson took this particular case was to help out an old friend.

"Regardless, they could have done this elsewhere." Ian looked toward the door. "Here come the newlyweds," he said as Jake and Naomi entered the room.

Jake carried a gift over to Owen, while Naomi took a seat next to Celeste. Although Naomi hadn't lost the wrist splints, he noticed the way she curled her finger around Celeste's daughter's chubby little hand. Which was great. There had been concern that she might lose some dexterity in her fingers after the way her wrists had been slit.

"You keep referring to them as newlyweds," Dante said. "Sounds like you're bitter they eloped and didn't invite you."

Ian shifted his gaze to him. "I have better things to be bitter about. But, in my opinion, eloping is a cheat. The couple might have a marriage license and an Elvis impersonator as a witness, but for the family and friends, it's as if it never happened."

"If a tree falls in a forest and no one is around to hear it, does it make a sound?" Dante set his plate on a nearby table under Rachel's beloved white board. "I can assure you that, one, they were married at an island resort with, according to Naomi and Jake, about fifty sunbathers as witnesses—not an Elvis impersonator. And, two, they are legally married. Considering they'd been separated for five years, I thought what they'd done suited them. Why drag out a long engagement?"

Ian glanced to the door. "When I need philosophical advice, I'll let you know," he said, then nodded to Jake as he approached them. "It's good to see Naomi. How's her therapy going?"

Jake smiled when he looked at his wife of two weeks. "Great. She has a couple of more months before she can go back to regular activities."

"How's she dealing with everything else?" Dante asked, knowing the guilt from the bombings had been hard for her.

"Touch and go. Thank God her name was never released."

When Dante glanced to Ian, his boss quickly looked away.

"Yes," Ian began, "I was very pleased the FBI left Naomi as an anonymous informant. Harrison Fairclough, too. Neither deserved to have their names linked to Christian Hunnicutt."

"No, they didn't," Jake said, looking across the room at Naomi. "I still can't believe what Hunnicutt's wife did for the victims from the bombings. I know she could afford it, but still. Five hundred thousand dollars?"

Once Liliana Hunnicutt had found out what her husband had done, she gave a check for five hundred thousand dollars to each family affected by the bombings. The grand total— over two hundred million dollars. She also paid for the millions of dollars' worth of damage the explosions had caused.

"I spoke with Martin Fitzgerald last week," Ian said. "Liliana Hunnicutt will legally change her name back to Liliana

Stewart, once the sale of BH-Xpress is complete. She's doing the same for her children."

Jake leaned against the corkboard and watched Rachel unwrap her next gift. "That doesn't surprise me. She had him cremated and his ashes dumped in a landfill. There's no headstone in the family cemetery, either."

Dante hid a smile. Very fitting for a man like Hunnicutt. The megalomaniac narcissist had cared about no one but himself. No one mourned him or celebrated his life. Actually, he'd heard his widow had hosted a party to celebrate his death.

"Fitzgerald also told me the FBI finally finished excavating the property surrounding Hunnicutt's Virginia plantation home. In the labyrinth at the back of the estate, they uncovered the skeletal remains of twenty-six victims. Based on the clothing found, they believe some of the victims were buried there as far back as the 1920s."

Jake crossed his arms and shook his head. "Sounds like Hunnicutt inherited more than money. Speaking of which, Liliana came to see Naomi and offered her one of her checks. Naomi never wanted anything from Hunnicutt and didn't want the blood money Liliana offered. She turned it down and asked that it be placed in a fund for women who are victims of stalking. Liliana not only did, but doubled the fund."

"An excellent solution." Ian glanced toward the door again. "I'll be right back."

When Ian walked away, Dante asked, "How's Naomi adjusting to Chicago?"

"She's doing great," he answered and shoved his hands in his pockets. "In a few months she should be able to start working again. In the meantime, she's been busy either entertaining my family or decorating our condo. Thank God for my mom. That first month, Naomi couldn't use her hands at all and I couldn't always be at home. I think Naomi loves having my mom around. As much as I love having her around, too, now that Naomi can use her hands, I'm looking forward to having the place to ourselves."

Dante grinned. "I'm sure. Starting off a marriage living with your parents can't be a lot of fun."

Jake chuckled. "Don't go there because— Who's the woman with Ian?"

Dante looked to the door, just as Ian walked in with a petite woman with long, dark straight hair. With the slight tilt of her almond shaped eyes he detected a hint of Asian descent. "I have no idea."

"Oh, look," Rachel said from across the room. "A gift from Uncle Ian." She held up a breast pump. "How thoughtful."

Ian stopped. His eyes widened a fraction, while his face flushed. The young woman at his side whispered something to him and he nodded. "It was on the baby registry and I prefer practical gifts," he said, then led the woman toward Jake and him.

"Lola Tam," Ian began, "this is Jake Tyler and Dante Russo. Dante is the agent I told you about."

After Lola shook Jake's hand, she offered Dante hers. "It's a pleasure to meet you," she said, eagerness brightening her unique, hazel eyes. "Ian told me all about your background. A former Navy SEAL. How exciting. I'm really looking forward to training with you."

Training? Great, he was stuck with another new recruit. While he didn't necessarily mind, up until a few months ago he'd had Jake tied to his side, which had made it difficult to pursue his *personal* investigation.

"Yes," Ian began, "Dante will show you everything you need to know about CORE. Hopefully you'll be ready to work in the field on your own within about a year."

A year? Hell, no. "With my training, hopefully sooner," Dante said, and caught the appreciation in the young girl's eyes.

"Come, Lola," Ian said. "Let me introduce you to everyone else. I can assure you our evidence and evaluation room doesn't usually look like this. We're a top-notch criminal investigation agency."

The rest of Ian's words faded as he and Lola moved toward the others. When Dante met Jake's gaze, he said, "Don't go there."

"What?" Jake asked. "Sorry, but you're single and she's not ugly."

He was also still in love with his ex-wife. "I'm old enough to be her father." At forty, he preferred a woman closer to his age. Thirty-five worked. He also preferred a particular blonde with dark brown eyes and a smile that made his heart pound. Picturing his ex-wife, Jessica, and remembering how things had used to be with them, filled him with a sense of loss. Or maybe being surrounded by baby stuff was what had him down.

"I've done my duty for today," Dante said, tossing the plate of cake in the trash. His cell phone vibrated. He pulled the phone from his pocket and quickly read the text.

I know who took our daughter.

His hand shook and his gut twisted with both unease and excitement. He and Jessica had been down this road more times than he'd care to remember. He couldn't allow himself to hope, because when those hopes were stomped on by reality, the grief was unbearable and it was like losing his wife and daughter all over again.

He glanced at Rachel, who held up a tiny pink dress. Remembering seeing his little girl in something similar, he looked back at the text.

I know who took our daughter.

Dante rushed from the room and to the elevator. He didn't know if Jessica was on another wild-goose chase, but if there was a chance, even a small sliver of hope his ex was right, he'd do everything in his power to find their child.

And then he'd make whoever took her pay.

THE END

LOOK FOR DANTE'S STORY AUGUST 2014...

ULTIMATE FEAR

BOOK TWO OF THE ULTIMATE CORE TRILOGY

OTHER CORE TITLES AVAILABLE BY KRISTINE MASON

SHADOW OF DANGER
BOOK ONE OF THE CORE "SHADOW" TRILOGY

Four women have been found dead in the outskirts of a small Wisconsin town. The only witness, clairvoyant Celeste Risinski, observes these brutal murders through violent nightmares and hellish visions. The local sheriff, who believes in Celeste's abilities and wants to rid their peaceful community of a killer, enlists the help of an old friend, Ian Scott, owner of a private criminal investigation agency, CORE. Because of Ian's dark history with Celeste's family, a history she knows nothing about, he sends his top criminalist, former FBI agent John Kain to investigate.

John doesn't believe in Celeste's mystic hocus-pocus, or in her visions of the murders. But just when he's certain they've solved the crimes, with the use of science and evidence, more dead bodies are discovered. Could this somehow be the work of the same killer or were they dealing with a copycat? To catch a vicious murderer, the skeptical criminalist reluctantly turns to the sensual psychic for help. Yet with each step closer to finding the killer, John finds himself one step closer to losing his heart.

SHADOW OF PERCEPTION
BOOK TWO OF THE
CORE "SHADOW" TRILOGY

What happens when negligent plastic surgeons receive a taste of their own medicine...?

Chicago investigative reporter, Eden Risk, receives an unmarked envelope containing a postcard ordering her to watch the enclosed DVD...or someone else dies. No Police. After Eden watches the DVD, a gruesome, horrifying surgery, she turns to the private criminal investigation agency, CORE, for help. Only she hadn't expected that help to come with a catch. Her former lover, Hudson Patterson, has been assigned to the case.

Hudson would rather have another CORE agent handle the investigation. Two years ago, he'd screwed things up with Eden...bad. And as more DVDs arrive, Eden and Hudson find themselves not only knee-deep in a twisted investigation, but forced to deal with their past, and the love they'd tried to deny.

SHADOW OF VENGEANCE
BOOK THREE OF THE
CORE "SHADOW" TRILOGY

Welcome to Hell Week. You have seven days to find him...

At Wexman University, male students will do anything to get into a top fraternity. They'll prove their worth during Hell Week by participating in various physical, psychological and even juvenile pranks. But those shenanigans aren't so funny when pledges start disappearing. What kind of evil has stalked this small Michigan university for the past two decades? Theories range from obscene scientific experiments to grotesque satanic killings...but they're all wrong. The murdered boys serve a single purpose...the ultimate revenge.

Rachel Davis, forensic computer analyst for the private investigation agency CORE, has been itching to leave her desk behind and work in the field. When her brother Sean, a student at Wexman, is found beaten and his roommate kidnapped during Hell Week, she gets her chance. Only her boss insists former U.S. Secret Service Agent, Owen Malcolm, helps her with the investigation. Owen is the last person she wants on this assignment. She'd been secretly half in love with him for over four years, until the night he'd crushed her ego and destroyed her hopes for any kind of future with him.

For his own reasons, Owen refuses to risk becoming involved with a coworker. Now that he and Rachel are stuck working side-by-side to solve this perverse investigation, he's having a hard time fighting his attraction to her...an attraction he's tried to deny from the moment they met. But time is ticking. They have seven days to find the missing pledge and catch a killer. Seven days before the body count rises and the pledge ends up another victim of Hell Week.

CONTEMPORARY ROMANCES BY KRISTINE MASON

KISS ME

When is a kiss...

After a series of bad relationships, Jenna Cooper wants a sex buddy—no-strings, no emotional involvement, and absolutely no expectations of commitment. She sets her sights on Luke Sinclair. A player and commitment-phobe, he'd make the perfect boy toy. Only Luke's tired of playing the scene and wants a serious relationship with Jenna, not a series of one-night stands.

...More than a kiss?

When Luke makes Jenna an offer she can't refuse, the sexual tension between them combusts and their emotional chemistry becomes too hard for Jenna to ignore. They both end up with more than either bargained for, especially when Jenna's wild past is exposed and threatens to tear their relationship apart. Now Luke will do anything to make things right between them, but knows it's going to take more than a kiss...

PICK ME
BOOK ONE OF THE
REALITY TV ROMANCE SERIES

For the chance of a lifetime...

To help save the TV reality show, *Pick Me,* from cancellation, Valentina Bonasera swaps her position as the show's Production Assistant, to play the role of Bachelorette, only to discover Bachelor Number One, rancher and sports agent, Colt Walker, happens to be her one and only one-night stand she'd snuck away from six months ago.

...Pick me.

Colt had never forgotten the hot, sensual night he'd shared with Valentina, or how she'd left him without so much as a note or her contact information. He'd spent months searching for the woman who'd given him a night he couldn't forget and thought he'd never see again. Now that she's in Dallas, he's determined to make her his...

LOVE ME OR LEAVE ME
BOOK TWO OF THE
REALITY TV ROMANCE SERIES

Love me...

Carter James, real estate agent for the hit reality show, *Renovate or Relocate*, has been crazy about the show's designer, Brynn Dawson, for years. He's been aching to take their friendship to a new level and when he gets his chance to spend a hot, sensual night with her and fulfill his wildest fantasies, he falls hard for Brynn. When the director of the show reveals that Brynn could possibly be fired, Carter knows he has to act fast before she's booted from the show. He'll not only jeopardize his reputation, but he'll go behind her back to help her keep her job. Knowing Brynn's pride is also at stake, he hopes his deception doesn't come back to haunt him in the end. He can't imagine life without the woman he loves.

...or leave me.

Brynn has been aware of Carter for years. How good he smells, his sexy smile, his lean, muscular body, his big, rough hands and what she'd like him to do with them. When she takes a chance by going from friends to lovers, she risks both her heart and their friendship, but discovers it's the best decision she could have ever made. Despite having her job on the line, she also knows that as long as she has Carter by her side, she can get through anything. Until she finds out what Carter's been up to. Hurt and betrayed, her emotions raw and her love for him tested, she'll have to decide whether she can move past the deceit and love him or if his lack of faith in her will force her to leave him.

ABOUT KRISTINE MASON

I didn't pick up my first romance novel until I was in my late twenties. Immediately hooked, I read a bazillion books before deciding to write one of my own. After the birth of my first son I needed something to keep my mind from turning to mush, and Sesame Street wasn't cutting it. While that first book will never see the light of day, something good came from writing it. I realized my passion and found a career I love.

When I'm not writing contemporary romances and dark, romantic suspense novels (or reading them!) I'm chasing after my four kids and two neurotic dogs.

You can email me at authorkristinemason@gmail.com, visit my website at www.kristinemason.net or find me on Facebook https://www.facebook.com/kristinemasonauthor and https://twitter.com/KristineMason7 to connect with me on Twitter!